The House Next Door

The House Next Door

Maine Justice Series, Book 5

By Susan Page Davis

Chapter 1
Tuesday, April 4

April came in slowly, and Jennifer Larson was impatient. Impatient for spring, which was always late in Maine, but more anxious for the arrival of her baby. She and Harvey had waited nine long months, and emotionally she was past ready to deliver. Her due date was April 24.

Harvey was terrific. He never told her how huge she was. He would come home from work and rub her back and tell her what a great job she was doing, that it was only X number of days until they would have their precious son. He had enjoyed the pregnancy, and Jennifer had, too, but she'd had enough. She'd reached the point where she wanted to quit being the expectant mother and start being the mother.

"Hey, gorgeous," Harvey said, walking through the door one Tuesday evening. It was his standard greeting, and it always made Jennifer smile.

He kissed her, which was also standard, but somehow he managed to make it special every day.

"How'd it go?" she asked. He and his four men were wrapping up a difficult murder case. As captain of the Portland Police Department's Priority Unit, Harvey carried all the headaches of administration, but also got in on the field work. Without that, he'd never have tolerated the job. He was not made for a desk job.

"Not too bad. Court tomorrow. Probable cause hearing for Fletcher. Shouldn't be any surprises."

"You ready to eat?" She had the table set for two and supper in the oven.

"Sure." He put his hand on her tummy. "How's Connor today?"

Connor was the name they had ninety-percent settled on for the baby. It was Harvey's mother's maiden name.

"Kicking like crazy." She took chicken and biscuits out of the oven, and they sat down at the table together. Having just the two of them at the table was nice. That wouldn't last long, but Jennifer still wanted Connor to be born soon.

Jennifer's sister Abby lived with them, but she had gone to work, for her three-to-eleven shift at Maine Medical Center. A registered nurse, Abby had come to help Jennifer out in the difficult early stages of her pregnancy, which meant that Harvey and Jennifer hadn't actually spent much time alone. They'd been married the previous July and decided to start a family right away. Harvey was forty-one when they got married, and he'd wanted kids for a long time. It was a great satisfaction to her to discover she was able to grant him that wish almost immediately.

Jennifer filled their plates and carried them to the table. "The house next door is for sale."

"Really? Mr. Fuller's house?" Harvey said.

"Yes, I saw the sign this morning. Casco Realty."

"Maybe I'll give them a call tomorrow." Harvey sat down with her at the small kitchen table.

"Are we interested?" Jennifer was no longer surprised when Harvey decided to make a deal. They weren't rich, but he had fantastic financial instincts. He was a whiz at stocks and was the kind of man who paid cash for houses. She figured if he had been a stock broker, they'd be millionaires. But he liked police work and dabbled at investing as a profitable hobby.

"Well, Jeff might be," he said.

"It would be great to have Beth and Jeff next door," Jennifer said.

Harvey nodded as he loaded his plate. "Let's look into it. If they don't want it, we'll ask Eddie, all right?"

"Sure." Eddie was one of Harvey's detectives, and he was dear to both of them. "Is Eddie into house buying?"

"He's got a nest egg," Harvey said. "He's probably got enough for a down payment."

That was music to Jennifer's ears. Eddie loved her younger sister, Leeanne, who had landed an internship at the *Portland Press Herald* and would stay with them while she worked there over the summer.

The next morning before Harvey went to work, he and Jennifer walked across the lawn. Most of the snow had melted, and the dead grass was soggy. As Harvey copied down the phone number from the For Sale sign, a car pulled into Mr. Fuller's driveway, and two women got out.

"Hi there," said Harvey.

"Hello," said the older woman. She had auburn hair and wore a smart suede jacket, a skirt too short for a fiftyish woman, and high heels. Her companion was younger, heavily made up, with shoulder-length blonde hair out of a bottle.

"I'm Harvey Larson. I live next door." He gestured toward his house.

"I'm Myrtle Holt, and this is Terri Bachelder," said the older woman. "We're with the real estate company. Mr. Fuller's executor hired our firm to supervise the sale of the house and its contents."

Harvey gave them his most charming smile. "It happens I'm interested in the house. I was just getting the phone number so I could call you later."

"That's great," Myrtle said. "Today we're having an appraiser come in and help us price the furnishings. We plan to hold a big sale on Saturday."

"A yard sale?" Jennifer asked. They both loved yard sales. Harvey's motto was, "Never buy anything new."

"Well, an estate sale," Myrtle said, as though trying to add more dignity.

"What's the house valued at?" Harvey asked.

Myrtle named the asking price. Terri just stood by, and Jennifer wondered if she was apprenticing under Myrtle.

Harvey nodded without batting an eyelash. It was a little more than he had paid for their house, even though Mr. Fuller's was smaller. But then, the former owner of the Larsons' home had given Harvey a good deal.

Myrtle said, "If you'd like to come over and tour the house later, I can show you around."

Harvey looked at his watch. "I have to leave for work now. Will you still be here at noon?"

"Oh, I doubt it." Myrtle probably never stayed on her feet that long. Jennifer's feet hurt, just looking at her heels. "Maybe your wife could come over …"

"No, I don't look at houses without Harvey," Jennifer said quickly.

He looked at his watch again, and she could tell he didn't want to lose first option on Mr. Fuller's house. "Could you just run me through quickly right now?"

"Well … the appraiser's due here any minute …" Myrtle looked down the street, then back at them.

"My brother-in-law is looking for a house, and we'd really love to have them next door to us," Harvey said.

"Okay." Myrtle took a briefcase from the back seat of her car. "Come on, but when the appraiser gets here, the tour is over."

"You got it." Harvey pulled his cell phone from his jacket pocket and speed-dialed Eddie as they walked to the front door. Terri unlocked it.

"Hey, Ed, I may be a few minutes late. You get over to the courthouse by eight, and I'll meet you there. No, I won't be too long. Okay, thanks."

The stone bungalow's front entrance had a tiny roofed porch, with vines that would green up soon. In summer, when the flower beds were in bloom, it was a perfect little English cottage. Each window was divided into twelve small panes and had chocolate brown shutters, and the chimney was of fieldstone.

"Have you been inside before?" Myrtle asked.

"No," Harvey said.

"It's a story and a half." Myrtle led them into the living room, which had a cathedral ceiling with a loft above, and rooms closed in over the kitchen and dining room. "There's one bedroom down here, and two more upstairs, but they're pretty small."

"How many bathrooms?" Jennifer asked.

"One down here, one upstairs."

Myrtle took them through the house. The rugs and drapes were in great condition, and Jennifer saw some furniture she wouldn't mind grabbing first at an estate sale. Mr. Fuller had lived in the house alone for some time. A few months after the Larsons moved in, he had been taken to the hospital by ambulance. A few weeks later, they'd heard he was in a nursing home, and at the end of March, his obituary had appeared in the *Press Herald.*

"Full basement?" Harvey asked as Jennifer examined the walnut cabinets and wall oven in the kitchen.

"Yes, with a dirt floor."

He raised his eyebrows. "This house is older than I thought."

"Yes it was built in the thirties," Myrtle said. "The neighborhood was developed in the fifties, but a few of the houses are older."

"How's the wiring?" Harvey asked.

"It was redone before Mr. Fuller bought it, about twelve years ago," she said. "The foundation is sound. The furnace, however, will probably have to be replaced. While Mr. Fuller was in the nursing home this winter, the pipes froze and the basement flooded."

"So, the plumbing needs work, too?"

"Well, the immediate problem was fixed, but we're going to have the entire plumbing system checked just to make sure. The furnace is almost certainly unrepairable."

"Hmm," said Harvey. "Are the owners taking that into consideration?"

"I believe the asking price includes the new furnace," Myrtle said.

"I'll make an offer today, as is," Harvey said and tossed out a figure fifty thousand dollars less than the asking price. Jennifer pretended she was fascinated by the pantry so she wouldn't reveal her anxiety.

"Oh, I doubt…"

"It would save you the headache of doing the plumbing and the furnace," he pointed out.

"Yes, but that's a large reduction," Myrtle said.

"Yes, it is." Harvey didn't say any more, just opened the electric box and studied the breakers.

He poked around for a few more minutes, and Jennifer checked out the bathroom. Not bad, but it could use fresh paint and a larger vanity.

The doorbell rang.

"That must be the appraiser," Terri said. "I'll let him in." She strode toward the front door.

"All right, thanks," Harvey said to Myrtle. "You can take my offer to your boss. If you want it in writing, I'll fax it to your office this afternoon."

"If you're serious, I have some forms here." Myrtle opened her briefcase on the kitchen island. "But I doubt the executor will accept such a drastic reduction."

"In cash?" said Harvey. "You might be surprised."

"Cash?" Myrtle stared at him.

"In your hand within forty-eight hours." Harvey took out a business card, turned it over and wrote on it, then handed it to her. "This is my work number. My cell's on the back. You know where we live."

He took Jennifer's hand, and they headed for the door. She looked back as they passed Terri and the appraiser. Myrtle was still staring.

"Have a nice day, Myrtle, Terri," Harvey said, and they went out.

In their own kitchen, he picked up his briefcase and gave Jennifer a lingering kiss.

"That was fun," she said. "Think they'll call?"

"If I don't hear from them by tomorrow morning, I'll up the offer," he said. "I'd hate to lose out on it by playing games. That little house has a backyard twice as big as ours." He patted her stomach. "Be a good boy, Connor."

She smiled. "You be a good boy, too."

"I'll call you."

*****

Harvey had meant to get home for lunch that day, and Jennifer hadn't packed one for him, but he and Eddie were held up longer than expected and had to return to the courthouse in an hour, so he phoned home.

"Sorry, gorgeous," was his opening. "Eddie and I got stuck at the courthouse."

"Just eat something." He caught the resignation in her voice. Harvey tended toward low blood sugar, and Jennifer had enlisted Eddie to watchdog him when he didn't get home for lunch. Harvey hated to be nagged, so he made an effort to remember to eat.

"Ed's putting our order in right now," he assured her. "We're at the Blue Bobcat."

He had taken Jennifer to lunch there once. It was usually filled with lawyers and their clients at noon.

"Did you tell Eddie about the house?" she asked.

"Yeah. He thinks it's a great idea. I told him if it comes through we'll give Jeff first refusal, but he's next in line."

"He's interested?"

"That's an affirmative, contingent on Leeanne's approval." Unless he was mistaken, Eddie would soon be his brother-in-law.

"I wish we had another house on the other side," Jennifer said.

It was tempting to imagine a whole block of Wainthrop siblings and their families, with all the cousins growing up together.

"Let's not mention it to Jeff and Beth until we hear from the real estate agent," he said. "I'd hate to disappoint them."

"What if they can't make the down payment?" Jennifer asked.

"I'll buy it anyway, and I'll work out the terms with Jeff. They could even rent it from us for a while if they wanted to."

"Sure, rent with option to buy."

"That would be great, wouldn't it?"

"I've been praying about it all morning," Jennifer said.

"Did you tell Abby?"

"No, I wasn't sure you wanted me to."

"I don't mind. Why don't you just give old Myrtle a call this afternoon and see if she's submitted my offer?"

Their orders had arrived, and Eddie was checking under the lid of his club sandwich. Harvey said, "Gotta go, sweetheart. Talk to you later."

Chapter 2

Myrtle was not in the office when Jennifer called Casco Realty at two-thirty. Abby had just left for work at the hospital, and Jennifer called from the phone in the bedroom, thinking she would take a nap afterward. Harvey was a real electronics lover, and he also liked landlines for dependable service. He and Jennifer had smart phones, but he'd had traditional phones installed in the kitchen and master bedroom downstairs, and in Abby's room upstairs. He was planning to put an extension in Leeanne's room, too, when she moved in.

"Could I speak with Myrtle's supervisor?" Jennifer asked. She knew Harvey would be disappointed if she didn't get some word on his offer.

"This is Mr. Foote."

"Mr. Foote?" She wasn't sure she'd heard correctly.

"Yes, Milton Foote. May I help you?"

"Mr. Foote, this is Jennifer Larson. My husband put in a bid on a house with Myrtle Holt this morning, and I just wanted to check and make sure the offer was being considered."

"Hmm, let me see..." She heard paper shuffling, then far-away voices, another phone ringing, and what sounded like a file cabinet drawer slamming.

"Yes, I have it," Milton Foote said at last. He read off Harvey's offer. "In cash. Hmm. For 135 Van Cleeve Lane. Asking price is ... Hmm."

"Well, sir, what is the procedure on this?" Jennifer asked.

"We'll take your offer to the owner."

"But the owner is dead," she said. "His estate is selling the property."

"Then, we'll take the offer to the executor."

"When will the offer be considered? We're very anxious about it."

"I'm not sure, Mrs. ... Larson. Perhaps Myrtle could give you a call when she returns to the office."

"And when will that be?"

"Let's see … she is showing a house to a client."

Jennifer sat up straighter. "Not 135 Van Cleeve Lane?"

"Hmm…well…ah, here it is. One-three-five—well, what do you know? She's out there right now."

"Thank you, Mr. Foote." Jennifer hung up. She pulled on her sneakers, grabbed her blue fleece jacket, and waddled as fast as she could out through the sunroom and kitchen to the entry.

Sure enough, Myrtle Holt's car was parked in the driveway next door.

Jennifer walked across the squishy lawns. Water oozed up, soaking the uppers of her sneakers. She got onto the walkway, squelched her way onto the little porch, and knocked. Myrtle opened the door with a look of surprise.

"Hello." She looked pointedly at Jennifer's stomach. "Mrs. Larson, isn't it?"

"Yes, Myrtle. I was just speaking with Mr. Foote."

"Oh?" Her eyebrows shot up, and she frowned.

"Yes, he was going to have you call me later, but then I saw your car and thought I'd check with you in person."

"I'm with clients, Mrs. Larson. Perhaps I could step over to your house when I'm finished here."

Peering past her, Jennifer saw a man in a leather trench coat and a woman with perfect hair and nails gazing up at the cathedral ceiling with awe.

"My husband will raise his offer," she said quickly. "Please come see me as soon as you can."

"I will." Myrtle closed the door in her face.

Jennifer hopped back over the soggy turf and kicked off her wet sneakers in the entry. She wasn't sure whether or not Harvey was still at the courthouse, and she didn't dare call his cell phone. Instead, she dialed his desk phone at the police station.

"Captain Larson."

"Harvey, Myrtle's showing the house to a rich couple," Jennifer blurted. "I told her you'd raise your offer, and she says she'll come see me when she's done with them. What do I do?"

"Not much you can do, I guess. She won't tell you what they offer, assuming they do make an offer."

Jennifer sighed. "There goes Jeff and Beth's house."

"Honey, let's pray about this. If God doesn't want us to get it…"

"I know," Jennifer said. "God is in control, and he knows better than we do who our new neighbors should be."

"No question about it."

"But this couple…They don't look like *our* kind of neighbors, Harvey."

"What do they look like?"

"A couple of DINKs."

He laughed. "Double Income, No Kids?"

"Bingo."

"Well, maybe the Lord wants to put a mission field next to us. If we get Jeff and Beth in there, we might be so comfortable we'd never reach out in the neighborhood."

"Do you think so?" She didn't want that to happen. "We reach out to Bud and Janice." The Parkers lived across the street, and they were now good friends with Harvey and Jennifer.

"Just pray about it," he said. "When Myrtle comes over, if you think it's appropriate, up the ante."

"How much?"

"Well, I'd go the asking price if I had to."

"What if someone else offers five percent more? Do we let them have it and lose Beth and Jeff's house for lack of a few thousand dollars?"

"Jenny, you're taking this too personally. Remember, it's not up to us to house everyone in your family." *He* was telling Jennifer this, when he'd spent long hours and a lot of money on upgrading rooms for her sisters. When Leeanne moved in, she'd be getting a brand new computer system and a canopy bed with her free rent. "If God wants Jeff and Beth in there, we'll get the house. Period. Don't panic over it."

"Okay." Jennifer sighed.

"I did think it would be nice to take down the fence and throw the two back yards together," he said. "We could put up one of those big wooden gym sets."

"Or a flagstone path to a secret little gate between the yards," Jennifer suggested.

"That would be neat. Make a hedge tunnel or a maze or something. Only our kids would know how to get through the gate."

"How much would a new furnace cost us?" Jennifer asked.

"A lot. Let's hang up, and I'll get some quotes."

*****

At 3:15, Myrtle rang the doorbell. Jennifer let her in, trying not to seem too eager.

"So, Mrs. Larson, your husband wishes to alter his offer on the Fuller house?"

"Well, he's open to that. We would really like to see my brother and his wife have the house, but if it doesn't work out…"

Myrtle looked a little disappointed.

"Is the couple who just saw the house interested?" Jennifer asked.

"Quite. They're not thrilled about the furnace situation."

"My husband is getting quotes on a new furnace as we speak." Jennifer tried not to sound snooty.

"So he's not increasing the offer?"

Jennifer hesitated, feeling a little lightheaded. She'd never made a purchase larger than her ten-year-old car.

"He said he would if necessary." She held her breath. Maybe she could offer Myrtle a "bonus." Horrified at her own thoughts, she decided to tell all. "Look, Myrtle, we really want the house. Of course, we'd like to get it for as low a price as possible, because it seems like we'll have to put quite a bit of money into it. But we believe God is in control of everything, including the sale of this house."

Myrtle eyed her skeptically.

Jennifer went on, "We'd like you to present the offer Harvey made, but if anyone else makes a higher offer, I think it's safe to say my husband will meet their price—within reason—and he will pay cash. You won't have the financing headaches. I don't know if that affects your commission, but we'd like to settle this as quickly as possible."

Myrtle's eyes narrowed. "Perhaps I should speak to your husband."

"By all means," Jennifer said. "Would you like to use our phone?"

"No, I need to get back to the office. I'll call him from there."

When she was gone, Jennifer went into the bedroom and prayed. She realized how badly she personally wanted that house for Jeff and Beth. She had been like Jacob in Genesis for a few seconds there, wanting to do things her way instead of waiting for God to act.

"Lord, forgive me for coveting a house and neighbors I love. Please help me to follow your way." At least for that moment, she felt she could wait on the Lord as long as it took.

She lay down on the bed and closed her eyes, but she couldn't sleep. Connor kicked and did a series of somersaults. She practiced her Lamaze breathing, but she was getting tired of that, too. She and Harvey had been so eager, they'd taken the Lamaze classes too early. If they'd waited, it would have given her something fresh and stimulating to think about during those last tedious weeks of pregnancy. She got up and went into the study. Connor's gymnastics wouldn't keep her from working on a new software program she was constructing.

Harvey walked into the house at 5:15, unable to hold back a huge smile.

Jennifer pounced on him. "Did Myrtle call you?"

"She did. She said she would take our offer to the executor immediately."

"You don't think Myrtle would skim the cash, do you?" Jennifer asked, her eyebrows morphing in a frown.

"I'll make sure we get it in writing, notarized," he said.

"I thought about bribing her," Jennifer confessed.

He laughed and wrapped his arms around her.

13

"It's not funny," she protested. "I really did."

"Oh, Jenny, there's never a dull moment with you." He hugged her tight. "How did I ever convince this woman to marry me?"

"Careful," she said. "Connor's being sadistic today. He'll pound the stuffing out of you if you stand this close to me."

Harvey held her closer.

*****

Harvey called home from work the next morning at ten. "Hello, gorgeous. Mr. Fuller's executor turned down our first offer."

"So, what now?" Jennifer asked.

"So, I told Myrtle to go back with an offer ten grand higher."

"Okay. And what if they get a higher offer in the meantime?"

"Then we lose out."

Myrtle's response that afternoon was that the executor wanted to think about it. As Harvey had expected, Jennifer wasn't happy with that response, but he advised her to stay calm.

"If we don't get this house, we'll look for another one."

"But *next door*, Harvey."

He smiled. "I know, gorgeous."

When they went to prayer meeting at their church that evening, Harvey was still confident that God would arrange things for the best, but Jennifer's tension wore off on him a little. He didn't like the uneasy feeling that the situation was hanging fire. When the pastor asked for prayer requests, he asked for prayer for a financial matter. After the service was over, Peter Hobart approached him.

"Harvey, are things okay with you folks?"

"Sure, Peter, what do you mean?" Harvey asked.

"If you need some cash…" Peter was Abby's current love interest. She'd held him off for quite some time, but he and his two little boys had taken first place in her heart. From where Harvey stood, it looked as though Abby would soon agree to become Mrs. Hobart. He and Jennifer both liked Peter, and he had the mature stability that Abby needed to balance her impulsiveness.

Harvey smiled. "No, but thank you, Peter. It's not a cash flow problem. It's more of an investment that we're not sure the Lord wants us to make."

"I see. Anything I want to get in on?" Peter asked. Abby had probably told him about Harvey's forays in the stock market.

"Actually, it's—" Harvey stopped. "Well, I probably shouldn't say anything yet. There are some family members we haven't told about it, so I guess I shouldn't open my mouth. Sorry, Peter."

"That's okay." He eyed Harvey closely. Peter owned a Chevy dealership, and he did all right. Harvey wondered if he had some extra cash lying around and was looking for a tax shelter.

"Say, Peter, I never get to talk to you anymore," Harvey said. "Abby's always monopolizing you. Why don't you come over to the house for a while?"

"The boys have school in the morning," Peter said. "I'd better not. Maybe I'll see you Friday night, though."

Abby's nights off were Friday and Saturday, and lately she and Peter had a standing date on Friday night and often spent Saturdays together with his two boys, Gary and Andy.

"Big night for us this Friday." Peter winked.

Harvey wondered what the cryptic air was about. Maybe Peter was planning to pop the question, but he'd proposed at least a dozen times in the last six months, so that wouldn't be unusual.

"What's up?" Harvey asked.

Peter reached into his jacket pocket and pulled out a small box. He opened it and held it out to Harvey. "What do you think?"

Harvey stared for a few seconds. "We are talking major crystallized carbon here." Jennifer had come over beside him, and he turned the box so she could see the ring. The diamond was huge. Not exactly garish, but about three times the size of the diamond Harvey had given Jennifer as an engagement ring.

"Wow," she said.

"Think she'll like it?" Peter asked anxiously.

"Absolutely," Harvey said. Abby liked flamboyant jewelry. "Think she'll wear it?"

Peter said, "Well, I figure if I've actually got the ring in hand, she has to give me an answer."

"You may have something there," Harvey said. "I wish you success."

"Thanks."

"Need a baby sitter?" Jennifer asked.

"No, my mother's all lined up for that, thanks."

Eddie had been talking with Rick Bradley, Beth's brother, but he came and joined them then.

"What are we talking about?" he asked.

Peter glanced around and then showed him the ring.

Eddie gave a low whistle. "That's some rock."

Peter nodded in satisfaction. "I hope the next time you see it, it's on Abigail's left hand. So, when are you and Leeanne going to make it official?"

Eddie looked thoughtful. "Soon, I hope."

The whole family knew Eddie had hoped to settle things with Leeanne on her twenty-first birthday, in the middle of March. Her father would prefer that Leeanne finish the school year at least, before she became engaged, but Eddie felt they'd waited long enough. He didn't want to displease her parents, but he'd told Harvey he was ready for marriage, and he was pretty sure Leeanne was too.

Harvey remembered the first time he'd met George Wainthrop and the heavy weight of responsibility he'd felt because he was dating the man's daughter. Why did they go through it in this day and age? A woman could make up her own mind. But if your girl was old-fashioned and said she wanted her parents' approval, you asked her dad. So far, Leeanne was still ringless.

Jennifer had threatened to call her father and berate him for interfering in the romance of the century, but Harvey had advised patience. If they waited a couple of months, it wouldn't hurt Leeanne. She still had a summer internship and one semester's

16

worth of college credits to take next fall, before she would qualify for graduation. But Harvey was optimistic. He'd gone through years of depression, and he was over that. Why should he borrow trouble when he'd found happiness he'd missed out on for years?

"I called Leeanne last night. She'll be down this weekend," Jennifer said, and Peter nodded with approval.

"Fantastic." Eddie's killer smile was back.

"Call her when you get home," Harvey said.

"I will. I really miss her."

Eddie, with his French roots, was a natural romantic, with dark hair, big, brown puppy-dog eyes, and a firm jaw. Add a detective's badge, and he was a pretty impressive package. Harvey and Jennifer hadn't been at all surprised when Leeanne fell for him.

The two had met ten months earlier. Eddie had seen Leeanne again at Harvey and Jennifer's wedding in July, then a couple of times in the fall. By late October, Eddie's affections were settled. Leeanne hung back, a little in awe of him, and with becoming shyness, but by Christmas, it was obvious they were madly in love.

"Things will work out for you kids," Harvey said with confidence.

"Thanks," Eddie said. "I hope you're right."

*****

Myrtle called at 7:30 Thursday morning. Jennifer was loading the dishwasher, and Abby had just staggered into the kitchen in her robe and was pouring herself a cup of coffee. Harvey actually had his briefcase in his hand, about to walk out the door, but he took the call.

"Are you supposed to tell me this?" he asked.

Jennifer frowned and went to stand beside him.

"Okay, well, thanks. I'd go five higher, but that new furnace is going to cost me a lot."

When he hung up, Jennifer said, "They turned down our second offer?"

17

"Yes, and that DINK couple is submitting one a little bit higher. Technically, she should just take their offer to the executor without telling us."

"But they want the furnace replaced and the plumbing fixed, don't they?"

"I'm not sure."

"So why did she tell us?"

"She knows we want the house. Also, the more it sells for, the bigger her commission. I'm sure that enters into it."

"What if she's telling the other couple what we offered to see if they'll go higher?" Jennifer asked.

"I don't know. It would be unethical on her part, but it wouldn't surprise me."

He kissed her and left for work.

Chapter 3

"Gorgeous, the house is ours," was the word when Harvey called at noon. "I'm about to liquidate some stock, and we'll meet with Myrtle Holt at two o'clock tomorrow. See if we can get together with Beth and Jeff tonight."

Jennifer called Beth immediately. "Harvey and I have something really important to tell you guys. Is Jeff home?"

When he was on duty, Jeff stayed at the fire station on Congress Street for three days at a time. Jennifer's brother was an EMT with the Portland Fire Department. He had married Jennifer's former roommate, Beth Bradley, the previous Christmas. The newlyweds rented the tiny house Beth and Jennifer had lived in when they were single.

"He came in at six this morning," Beth said. "He's asleep."

"Well, can you guys eat supper with us tonight?"

"Sure. What's it about?"

"Something good. Tell you later."

"You didn't have the baby yet," Beth said, clearly fishing for more information.

"Unfortunately, no," Jennifer replied.

"Okay, what time should we come?"

"Fivish? Harvey will be here around 5:15."

Jennifer spent the afternoon getting ready at a leisurely pace. She and Abby talked about the house, and Abby was excited at the prospect of having Jeff and Beth for neighbors. She promised not to spill the secret if she saw either of them. After she helped Jennifer with some spot cleaning and planned the menu, Abby ran to the store for a couple of items and then went to work.

Jeff and Beth arrived just before five. At six feet, two inches, Jeff towered over Jennifer, but everyone said he looked like her. Or she looked like him.

Jeff, Abby, Travis, and Jennifer all had their mom's blonde hair and their dad's blue-gray eyes. Leeanne and Randy had dark

19

hair, but Leeanne had the blue eyes. Randy, the youngest, was the only one who ended up with their mother's brown eyes.

"You gonna have that baby soon?" Jeff leaned down and gave Jennifer a gentle squeeze.

"I hope so."

Beth kissed her and handed her a small pot of daffodils. "Just so you'll know spring is really coming."

"Sweet." Jennifer set them on the table.

"What's the big mystery?" Jeff asked.

"Can't tell you 'til Harvey gets here." Harvey loved surprising people and giving gifts, and she wasn't going to rob him of the pleasure.

"Okay," said Beth. "Tell me what to do to help you, and we'll try not to think about it."

She and Jennifer put the food on the table, and Jeff sat down and gave them a blow-by-blow description of his last seventy-two hours on duty with the ambulance crew. A heart attack, two automobile accidents, a choking toddler, a stroke, standing by during a structure fire, and to round things out, a woman battered in a domestic quarrel.

When Harvey came in, they sat right down, and he asked the blessing. They passed the meatloaf, potatoes, salad, and rolls.

"All right, brother-in-law." Beth fixed Harvey with a stern look that said she wasn't putting up with this nonsense any longer. "What's the big news?"

Harvey smiled. Jennifer could tell he was getting a lot of enjoyment out of this.

"You guys have been saving up for a down payment for a house, right?"

"Right," Jeff said. "I hope we can find something in our price range this summer. If not, we'll have to wait, but I don't want Beth to keep on working."

"Well, Jenny and I have found a house that we think would be perfect for you," said Harvey.

"Wow." Beth stared at him. "Where is it?"

"How much?" Jeff asked.

"Close to here, and not too much," said Harvey.

"Really?" Beth's eyes lit with anticipation. "We'd love to live near you guys. How close?"

"Wait a sec," said Jeff. "How much is not too much? I don't think we can afford anything over a hundred and fifty grand, and this is a pretty snazzy neighborhood. I was thinking more of something outside the city limits."

"I think you could swing this," Harvey said. "Your payments wouldn't be any more than you're paying in rent now."

"You sure?" Jeff's eyebrows lowered. "What's the down payment?"

"Nothing."

"Oh, come on, you're pulling my leg."

"Nope." Harvey's smile grew.

"Oh, I get it," Beth nodded sagely.

"What?" asked Jeff, still in the dark.

"Harvey's going to buy the house, and we buy it from him with no down payment."

"We can't do that," said Jeff.

"Why not?" Harvey's face fell.

"You'd lose money. I know you, Harvey. You'd give us such a good deal you'd go bankrupt."

"No, I wouldn't," he said. "Look, if you guys don't want the house, there's somebody else I'll offer it to, but Jenny and I were really hoping you'd be our new next-door neighbors."

"Next door?" Beth cried. "Right next door? Which house? I can't believe this!" She put her arms around Jeff's neck. "Honey, next door to Harvey and Jennifer. How can we not look into this?"

Jeff spread his hands. "Number one, we can't afford this neighborhood. Number two, I don't want to take advantage of Harvey's good nature. Number three, living next to Jennifer might just drive me nuts. Especially now that they've got Abby living here, and Leeanne is coming down next month."

"It would make it easy for Mom and Dad to visit us all," Jennifer said.

Jeff scowled at her. "How much is the house?"

"Not too much," Harvey said.

21

"Don't give me that." Jeff sounded a little argumentative. "If it's over a hundred and fifty thousand, forget it. It would take us the rest of our lives to pay for it. I'm a fireman, not a doctor, and you know we can't get much of a house for that in Portland."

"He's right," Beth said.

Harvey sighed. "How about if Beth babysits once in a while and you mow our lawn?"

Jeff turned to Jennifer and drilled her with his eyes. "How much, Jennifer?"

She started to open her mouth, then grabbed Harvey's hand. "Not too much."

Jeff spluttered.

Beth laughed.

"Look, here's the deal," Harvey said. "The old man who owned the house went into a nursing home last fall. Over the winter the pipes froze, the basement flooded, and the furnace got ruined. Then the man died. His estate is selling the property. I got them to knock the price down because of the furnace. Jennifer and I will buy it. That's a done deal, whether you want to live there or not. I'll have the furnace replaced and fix anything else that needs it. If you want it, we'll work out a payment you can afford. Period."

"So, how much will *your* monthly payment be?" Jeff asked cautiously.

"No monthly payment. I'm paying cash."

Jeff sat back and whistled. "You're just out my league financially, Harvey."

"Ah, don't worry about the payment," Harvey said. "We want you guys to live there. It's number one-thirty-five."

"The stone cottage?" Beth asked eagerly.

"Yeah. It's got three bedrooms," Jennifer said.

Beth turned to Jeff. "Let's at least look at it."

He sighed. "I don't want to get into something over our heads, Beth. We agreed you'll quit working and we'll have babies, remember?"

"I know," she said tenderly. When she turned back to Harvey, her eyes hardened. "Okay, Captain, just the facts. Give us some numbers. Now."

"Well, uh, what's your rent again?" Harvey asked, not meeting her gaze.

"Nine-fifty a month," Jennifer said. She and Beth had split the rent before she married Harvey.

"They put it up to ten-seventy-five," said Beth.

"On that little tiny house?" Harvey pulled a calculator out of his pocket. Jennifer knew he'd been crunching numbers all day. "Well, let's see, if you pay a thousand a month, the house will be all yours in...twenty-four years."

"Ouch," said Jeff.

Beth pursed her lips. "That's not so bad."

Jennifer did some fast mental calculations. She didn't think Harvey was including the price of the furnace.

"Or," said Harvey, "If you'd like a smaller payment, say eight hundred a month —"

"Forget it," said Jeff. "I don't want to be paying for the house when I'm eighty."

"But you need to be able to put something away for the kids' college," Harvey said.

"I want to hear it," said Beth. "How long would it take us to pay it off?"

"Uh..." Harvey punched some keys. "Thirty-four years."

"Huh," said Beth.

Jeff rolled his eyes. "It's just too much house. We can get a nice little ranch outside the city limits for half that and pay it off in fifteen years."

"But, honey, next door to your sister," Beth wheedled.

"And how much are the property taxes?" Jeff asked.

Harvey frowned. "You've saved up for a down payment, right?"

"Right. We think we'll have about eighteen thousand by the time Beth's done working in June."

"That's respectable." Harvey pushed more buttons. "Okay, here's the bottom line. You make an eighteen-thousand-dollar down payment, which I hate to see you do, and pay us five hundred seventy-five a month, and the house is yours in thirty-five years. Or, with an eight-hundred-a-month payment ... just over twenty-five years."

"We could do that," said Beth.

"He's not including interest," Jeff said. "And what if we have six kids and outgrew it in the meantime?"

Beth's jaw dropped. "Six? I hope you're not serious."

"You sell it," Harvey said. "We'll keep our eyes peeled for a bigger house for you later on."

"Aw, come on, Harvey." Jeff shook his head and took a bite of meatloaf.

Jennifer put her hand on Harvey's sleeve. "Maybe Jeff wants to find his own house."

Harvey paused, then nodded. "Okay, sure. It was just an idea." He put the calculator away.

"But you're buying the house anyway?" Beth asked.

"Yes, I'm committed. We're fixing the terms tomorrow, and the closing is next Tuesday, if all goes well. If you wanted to, we could put it in your names..."

"No, Harvey, we can't do that," Jeff said. "What if we defaulted on the payments?"

"You wouldn't."

"Yeah? Well, what if I lost my job?"

"I could work for another year or two," Beth said, but Jeff's expression darkened.

Harvey sighed. "Here's another scenario, Jeff. While you guys are looking for an affordable house outside the city limits, you rent this three-bedroom house from us. It would give you a little more space than you have now, and we'd have some fun together. If you decided later on you wanted to buy it, we'd put the rent toward the purchase price."

"I dunno, Harv..."

"Eight hundred a month," Harvey said.

Jeff's jaw shifted. "You can't do that."

"Sure, I can. I can set the rent at whatever I want."

Beth looked at Jeff with huge brown eyes.

"We'll talk about it," Jeff said.

"That's all I ask." Harvey reached for his coffee cup. "If you honestly don't want to live there, fine. Jenny and I will be disappointed, but, like I said, there is another party that's interested, so we know we'll have good neighbors, no matter what."

They moved the conversation on to less controversial territory, but later, when they were cleaning up the kitchen, Beth let Jennifer know she was still thinking about it.

"Anybody else would charge fifteen hundred a month or more to rent that house, and you know it."

"No, I don't know it," Jennifer said. "It's not that great. I mean, it's attractive, but the basement is a mess, and we'll probably have to replace some of the plumbing. And the two upstairs bedrooms are really small."

Beth eyed her cautiously. "Jeff won't want to feel like we owe you guys."

Jennifer shrugged. "Harvey wants to do this."

"Give us a good deal, you mean?"

"Yeah. Family has always been important to me, and he loves having a big family now. He was talking last night about our kids and yours growing up together. He's planning to put a gate in the backyard fence so we can go back and forth out there. He'll probably have a swing set out there by the end of the summer."

Beth's face softened. "This is such a great neighborhood for kids. It has a real small-town feeling. Guess I'd better quit thinking about it, or I'll be in the covetous mode."

"They're having an estate sale Saturday, to get rid of the furniture. Come over early, and we'll go together. You'll get to see it with some furniture in it."

The patio door opened and closed in the next room. Through the kitchen window, they could see Harvey and Jeff walking in the back yard. After a while, they went over to the fence on the side next to Mr. Fuller's house and looked over. Jeff leaned on the fence and talked to Harvey.

The three sisters did a lot of giggling and hugging when Leeanne arrived at four on Friday afternoon. Harvey claimed they were outrageous when they were together. He called it the Wainthrop Sister Pajama Party and usually managed to be out of the house for the first hour or two, until they calmed down.

After she put her things away in her room upstairs, Leeanne pumped Abby for the status of her relationship with Peter.

"Well," Abby said, lacing her words with import, "We're going out to dinner tonight, and afterward we're heading for a surprise destination."

"Ooh," Leeanne said. "Did he give you any hints?"

"No, and I tried wheedling and bribing. I don't know what he's planning, but I got the impression it's a big deal."

Jennifer kept her own counsel, although it was difficult.

Then Abby pumped Leeanne about Eddie. Leeanne blushed a little and beat around the bush, but admitted she'd missed her guy and couldn't wait to see him again. The latest separation had lasted three weeks. Jennifer was surprised Eddie hadn't driven to Skowhegan to see her, but the Priority Unit had been very busy lately.

Jennifer heard the garage door go up. "Harvey's home." She stood up carefully. She liked to meet him at the door, but lately she was moving slowly. Leeanne ran ahead of her to the entry door, paused, then opened it and tore outside, and Jennifer knew Eddie had followed Harvey home.

She got to the garage as Harvey climbed out of his Explorer and got a huge hug. Eddie's truck had pulled to a stop in the driveway. He jumped out and had Leeanne in his arms in record time.

"They're so sweet," Jennifer said.

Harvey shook his head. "I hope they get married soon."

"I know." Jennifer watched them through the garage door. "That's a little affectionate for the driveway, don't you think?" Leeanne was quite timid, and it surprised Jennifer that she was letting Eddie kiss her so passionately in front of them, let alone all of Van Cleeve Lane.

"They're in love," Harvey said. "Do you think they'll stick with your dad's wishes and wait until she graduates?"

"I don't know," Jennifer said. "She won't finish school until December. That's a long time when you're that invested."

"Yeah." Harvey kissed her, then turned back toward the garage door. Eddie was still kissing Leeanne. Harvey gave a sharp whistle, and Eddie looked up.

"Take it inside, Ed."

Eddie was used to following Harvey's orders and didn't take offense. He walked into the garage with his arm around Leeanne's waist. She blushed a little, but grinned from ear to ear.

Harvey kissed her on the cheek. "Welcome back. Good trip down?"

"Yeah, it was okay," Leeanne said. "Traffic wasn't bad."

They all went in, and Abby was talking on the phone but hung up as they entered.

"That was Peter. He'll be here in half an hour. I've got to get ready. Hi, Eddie."

Abby was through the sunroom and heading for the stairs in the living room before Eddie could say hello, but he was absorbed by the thrill of being with Leeanne again, anyway.

Jennifer put supper on the table, and Harvey helped. Eddie and Leeanne drifted into the sunroom, and they let them go.

"Think they can wait until Christmas?" Harvey asked, pulling the chicken out of the oven.

"Well ... you never favored long engagements yourself."

"True," Harvey admitted. "They're committed to each other. They ought to make it official soon, in my opinion."

"Well, I'm glad they respect Daddy's wishes," Jennifer countered. "But they're both of age now. They can get married whenever they want."

"Leeanne really wants to make your folks happy."

"Well, if they make a big issue of it, they'll make her miserable."

Harvey shrugged. "Eddie's trying to take the high road. He's matured a lot this year. If your father knew him better, he wouldn't have any doubts."

27

"I don't think Dad mistrusts him exactly." Jennifer set down the dish of carrots. "Supper's ready. Do you want to go pull the mature lovers down from Cloud Nine?"

"Not really, but I will." Harvey strolled toward the sunroom.

Chapter 4

Jennifer had told Leeanne about the house next door, and she was enthusiastic.

"I hope Jeff will do it," she said. "It's a cool house, and they'd love it. You know they would."

"That's what I thought," Harvey said, "but Jeff has a real mental block against being indebted to us. It's okay to owe the bank, but not your sister and her husband."

"Well, sometimes when relatives make deals like that, things go sour," Eddie said. "My sister Monique asked my pop to co-sign a car loan for her and Wyatt a few years ago, then they decided the payments were too high. They couldn't get their money out of it, and my pop ended up with a mess on his hands. I don't think he ever got over that, and he said he wouldn't ever lend them money or sign anything for them again. Or for Elise or me, either."

Eddie's father had died in January, and they all nodded soberly.

"Jeff wouldn't back out of a deal," Jennifer insisted.

"I know," Eddie said, "but you just never know what's going to happen."

A car drove in, and Harvey got up to look out and see who it was.

"Peter?" Jennifer asked.

"Jeff and Beth."

Leeanne got up and ran to the door for hugs, and when the greetings were over, they found chairs and sat down.

"Did you guys eat?" Jennifer asked.

"No, but that's okay," Beth said.

"We have plenty." Jennifer got two extra plates and silverware.

"Seems like we eat at this restaurant a lot." Beth passed Jeff a tumbler.

"The food is great," said Jeff.

Eddie grinned. "The price is right, too."

"And it's so convenient if you live in the neighborhood," said Harvey.

Jennifer was afraid he was pushing it too far, but Jeff got a sober look on his face. "Are you serious about this rent with option to buy, Harvey?"

"Absolutely. Pick your own rent level."

Jeff looked at Beth, and she looked back, not saying anything.

At last Jeff said, "When can we move?"

Harvey smiled his irresistible smile. "Brother!" He held out his hand to Jeff.

"Thanks, Neighbor," Jeff replied.

They started talking details. Harvey thought he could take possession of the house on Tuesday and had lined up a heating service man and a plumber to come on Wednesday. He would go in to work late so he could talk to them about the furnace and any necessary plumbing repairs.

"As soon as the work is done, you can move in," he said. "We'll help you."

"I suppose it might take a few weeks," Jeff said.

"Maybe. I've been thinking we might run a concrete floor in the basement. Then if you wanted to finish off a room down there later, you could. I haven't looked at it yet, but it might be a good idea, since we're having a new furnace put in anyway."

He and Jeff got technical, and Jennifer got Beth to help her get out ice cream and cookies. Eddie and Leeanne were lost in each other's eyes.

"Were we that mushy?" Beth sneaked a glance at them. Eddie looked as if he could just slurp Leeanne up.

"You and Jeff?" Jennifer asked. "No. Well, yes."

Beth laughed.

"It's not funny," Jennifer said. "When she moves down here, they'll be together practically every day. Do you think that level of tension can be sustained for another eight months?"

"That long?" Beth frowned.

"Dad and Mom want her to finish school before she gets married. That means next Christmas. She'll be done December twentieth."

"Wow." Beth frowned. She and Jeff had been engaged two and a half months. Harvey and Jennifer had limited their engagement to six weeks.

"Some people are engaged for years," Jennifer mused.

"I don't know how they do it," Beth replied.

"Well, frankly, I don't see them waiting that long." Another car drove in, and Jennifer looked out the window. Peter. She sent Leeanne to call Abby downstairs.

Peter was flushed and looked more nervous than Jennifer had ever seen him, except the first time he asked Abby out. Harvey drew him into the house rental conversation, explaining to him that it was the investment he'd mentioned on Wednesday night.

"Oh, that's a great problem to have," Peter said. "Congratulations, Harvey. Glad it went in your—."

Abby came in through the sunroom, and Peter stopped talking in the middle of the sentence, his eyes lighting up. She looked awesome, very sophisticated in a soft blue dress that made her eyes look bluer. Peter was dressed up, too, in a gray suit that made him look like an executive. A love-struck executive.

"You look fantastic." Peter approached her eagerly. Abby had better say yes, finally, or Jennifer would clobber her. Peter was the kind of man who would cherish her forever.

"Wear your warm coat," he told her.

"Where are we going?"

"You want to know now?"

Abby considered, then shook her head. "I like surprises."

"All right, we'll see you all later," Peter said, taking her hand. The others called goodnight as they went out the door.

"She'd better say yes," Harvey said grimly.

"Yeah," said Eddie.

Jeff looked at them. "Tonight's the night?"

Harvey shrugged. "Peter says it is."

Leeanne shook her head. "He's asked her a gazillion times."

31

"Tonight's different." Harvey stood and walked to the counter with his coffee mug.

"I hope we're not going through another disaster with Abby," Leeanne wailed. Jennifer knew she was thinking of Abby's break-up with Greg, who had given her an ultimatum several months earlier.

"I don't think so." Jennifer studied the diamond between two small sapphires on the ring Harvey had given her the year before. "I think Peter will hang in there if she does put him off again, but ... I think she's ready."

The six of them settled down in the living room with dessert, and Jeff and Harvey hammered out a lease.

"I'm glad you're doing it this way," Harvey said.

"Seriously?"

"Yes. Rent for a while, see if you really love the house, and if you think you can handle being a homeowner. Meanwhile, your down payment nest egg is growing. If you decide you want to buy, you'll have more to start out with."

Jeff nodded. "What do you think about our investments? Most of it's in mutual funds."

"You could be a little more aggressive, since you won't be using the principal right away." Harvey told Jeff about some promising stocks he was following.

Jennifer turned to Beth. "So, should we try to get in on that boring conversation, or get out a game?"

Beth looked over at the sofa, where Eddie was whispering adoringly to Leeanne. "I don't know. Do you get the feeling nobody would notice if we left the room and had a gab fest in the kitchen?"

*****

Beth came at seven on Saturday morning, ready for the estate sale. Jennifer had woken Harvey early, though she hated to do it, but he wanted to be one of the first at the sale, too. Leeanne and Abby slept in. Harvey had finally kicked Eddie out at midnight, and they'd heard Abby come in an hour later.

They were on the cottage's doorstep when Myrtle and two other Casco Realty employees arrived, but she told them they'd have to wait. No early birds. They went in and closed the door.

Beth gazed at vine-draped entry. The little stone house with mullioned windows would have been right at home as the setting for a Snow White movie.

"Jeff could have a dog," she said.

Jennifer smiled, remembering how her brother had loved the sheltie they'd had on the family farm years ago.

By the time the agent opened the door, at least thirty people were lined up behind them. Harvey went quickly through the rooms where items for sale were displayed, looking at everything without lingering. Beth and Jennifer went slower, Beth looking at the house and Jennifer looking for a bargain. The stairs were roped off, so Beth didn't get to see the upper bedrooms.

The furniture was priced high. Jennifer decided there was nothing she couldn't live without. Harvey rejoined them in the living room after a few minutes.

"See anything you want, gorgeous?" he asked.

"Not at these prices." Jennifer lifted the lid of a walnut lap desk that rested on a Sheraton side table. Inside was a small silver key on a loop of string. The desk had a drawer under the paper compartment, and two smaller compartments at the back.

"How about that?" Harvey asked.

"We don't need it."

"We don't need a thing," he said. "Do you want it?"

She turned over the tag that hung from it. "Yikes. No, thanks."

"How much?"

"Seventy-five."

"Seventy-five dollars? That's not bad." Harvey picked up the lap desk and examined it closely. "This is old. It would make you a nice Mother's Day gift."

In the end, she let him buy it for her. Beth bought an old coffee tin for the collection of antique tea and coffee containers she was slowly building, and that was it. They went back across the lawns. The sun was out, and Jennifer hoped the spongy turf would dry out soon.

Eddie's truck was in their driveway.

"Hey, Ed, what are you doing here so early?" Harvey asked when the three shoppers went inside.

"I came to see Leeanne," Eddie said, as if that should be self-explanatory. Both were sitting at the kitchen table drinking coffee. Leeanne looked maybe half awake, but her hair was brushed, and she had on black sweat pants and a UMF T-shirt.

Harvey looked at his watch. "How long were you home? Six, seven hours?"

Eddie looked a little confused. "I'm sorry, Harv. Do you want me to leave?"

Harvey sighed and shook his head. "No make yourself at home. I told you this place is always open to you, and I meant it. I just don't know how you kids go without sleep like that. Personally, I'm exhausted."

"Eat some breakfast, then take a nap," Jennifer said.

"Maybe I'll just get the nap first."

"No, you need some carbs." Jennifer put an English muffin in the toaster and poured him a glass of orange juice.

"All right, gorgeous." Harvey took the glass. "Too bad you married an old man."

"Don't start that," she warned.

Beth eyed Harvey critically. "Still, you'd better get all the sleep you can now. In a couple of weeks, the baby's going to be keeping you up all night."

"I can hardly wait." He looked at Jennifer. "Don't know why I let you wait on me. Sit down, Jenny." He brought the juice carton to the table and poured her a glass. "Want some, Beth?"

"No, thanks."

"So how did you like the house?" Leeanne asked.

"I love it," Beth said. "I don't know as our pitiful furniture will go with the décor."

"Early Matrimonial," Jennifer told her. "That's what my mom calls it. She thinks I missed some character building because I didn't have to go through that stage with Harvey."

34

"It's a pretty ritzy house, compared to what we've been living in," Beth said. "Especially with those antiques in it."

"They'll be gone in a few hours," Harvey said. "At least four dealers were dickering over the furniture."

Jennifer knew well the little cracker box rental Beth and Jeff shared, with plywood cupboards and sagging steps. "You'll love living over there, Beth. It's going to be so great. We can run back and forth for tea. When Jeff's on duty, you can come over and rock the baby for us."

"What did you buy at the sale?" Eddie asked.

Harvey brought the lap desk over and showed it to him. Eddie took out the key and tried to put it in the key hole on the front.

"This isn't the right key."

"Let me see." Harvey took it and tried the key. "Sure enough. It won't even go in the keyhole. Oh, well."

"I wonder what it goes to," said Leeanne.

Harvey held up the key and frowned at it. "I'd say the key is newer than the desk."

"Well, whatever it went to was probably sold this morning, and we'll never know," said Beth.

"Hey, guys." Abby stood in the sunroom doorway, yawning. She had on jeans and a sweatshirt.

"Where did Peter take you last night?" Eddie asked.

Sunlight glinted off the ring on Abby's left hand. Jennifer launched out of her chair and to her side.

"You're wearing it!" Jennifer couldn't hold back tears as she hugged her sister. A huge wave of love and relief threatened to drown her.

Abby threw her arms around Jennifer's neck and hugged her close. She cried, too, when Jennifer pulled away and dove for the tissue box on the counter.

"Hey, Abby!" Harvey was right there to kiss her and look at the ring. "Congratulations, sister. You made the right decision."

"Finally, you mean." Abby smiled tremulously.

"No, this is the right time," Harvey said.

35

Jennifer's love for him surged when she heard that, and she put her arm around him. He always said the right thing. She had loved him to distraction for nearly a year now, but he always came out with something that made her appreciate him more.

The love he consistently demonstrated to her family was one of the things that continued to amaze her. He thought in-laws were wonderful and went out of his way to make them happy. He'd never had a huge extended family like Jennifer had, and he reveled in it.

Beth, Leeanne, and Eddie got in line for hugs from Abby, and they all sat down with decaf or high-test coffee to hear the details. Dinner in a very posh restaurant, Abby told them, then a cruise on the last ferry of the evening to Chebeague Island and back, just for the ride. There weren't many folks on the return trip, and Peter had found a secluded spot on the moonlit deck to pour out his heart to Abby and give her the ring.

"What made you say yes?" Leeanne asked.

"I love him," Abby said simply.

They all knew he had asked her over and over, but something had changed. It didn't sound silly. She was sure.

"Abs, I'm so happy for you," Jennifer said.

"Thanks. He and the boys are coming for me at ten, and we're taking them to the Children's Museum."

"Again?" Harvey asked.

"Yes, they love it. Then we're going to Grandma Hobart's and tell her."

Eddie reached for Leeanne's hand with a wistful, almost mournful look on his face. Jennifer knew he'd stay at the house all day, or else take Leeanne out somewhere. But he would spend every minute of the day with her, because she was leaving the next day, and part of his soul would go with her.

She felt a sharp tug in her abdomen and let go of Harvey, putting her hand on her tummy, up high where she thought Connor's feet were.

Harvey was right there, concerned, his arm around her.

"You okay, Jenny?"

"Yes, just one of these silly Braxton-Hicks contractions. I wish they did some good."

*****

They managed to get into the Fuller house again that afternoon, and Harvey took a flashlight. Myrtle let him go down cellar, and he made a minute examination of the foundation and the dirt floor.

"I think you'll want a concrete floor," he said to Beth when he came up. A few stragglers were looking over the remnants of the sale. "It's dry down there. I think we can have it done fairly soon."

"You're the landlord," Beth said.

Myrtle reluctantly let them go upstairs after Harvey reminded her that his offer had been accepted.

"I thought you said these bedrooms were small," Beth said as they stood in the one with a dormer overlooking the backyard.

"Well, they are," Jennifer replied.

"Compared to yours and Harvey's, maybe. This one's bigger than ours."

Jennifer remembered the room she'd slept in for two years in the little house and was suddenly embarrassed. She'd gotten used to living in a roomy home, luxurious by comparison to the old rental, and forgotten what it was like to exist from paycheck to paycheck.

"So, you think this house will be livable once the repairs are made?" Harvey asked.

Beth's eyes shone. "For us, it will be like living in a castle!"

"Speaking of castles, I was thinking Jeff and I could build a fort or something in the back yard for the kids, you know, a playhouse. A tower, maybe, and ladders and swings."

"Don't you think our children need to be born first?" Jennifer asked.

Beth chuckled and said, "Go ahead and draw up the plans, Harvey."

*****

37

Eddie had taken Leeanne to the mall on Harvey's suggestion, just to keep everyone from tripping over them all afternoon. They ate supper out and came back around seven-thirty. Abby wasn't back yet from her expedition with Peter and the boys.

Jennifer and Harvey were watching an old movie, Nelson Eddie in *New Moon*. Harvey held Jennifer on his lap in his favorite armchair and kept one hand on her stomach so he wouldn't miss Connor's back flips.

She got up when Eddie and Leeanne came in, not sure if she was self-conscious about being caught in the intimate pose, or if she was afraid they would be embarrassed.

Eddie and Leeanne sat down on the couch. Jennifer pulled a footstool over near Harvey and sat on it, leaning against the side of his chair and his arm. They talked a little, then resumed watching the movie.

When it was over, they talked for another hour, about everything from Abby's engagement and Leeanne's classes to the house next door and Harvey and Eddie's current caseload at work. Jennifer started to droop. Every once in a while she felt the ineffectual contractions and wished they were the real thing.

Harvey yawned. "I'm sorry, but Jenny and I are both pretty tired."

"Okay," Eddie said.

They stood up. Just then they heard Abby coming in the entry, and Harvey and Jennifer went around to speak to Peter. He was kissing Abby sweetly in the doorway, but greeted them without embarrassment.

"Peter!" Harvey shook his hand warmly. "Congratulations! We're very happy for you both."

Peter smiled with a contentment Jennifer had never seen in his eyes.

"We've set the date," he said.

Abby smiled at them. "June third."

Harvey looked at Jennifer. "Wow, that's soon."

Jennifer laughed. "When it was us, it couldn't be too soon to suit you."

"Well, Abigail says she knows what she wants, and it won't take long to pull it together," Peter said.

"My mom's been through it recently," Jennifer agreed.

Abby reached for her hand. "Be my matron of honor?"

"If I'm thin again," Jennifer said. "Sometimes I feel like I'm going to be pregnant forever."

Abby chuckled. "You'll be skinny as a rail again by then, and we'll get you a dress that will show everybody how great you look, even with a six-week-old baby."

When Peter left, Harvey and Jennifer headed for the bedroom. Abby went to the living room doorway and said loudly, "Well, hi, Eddie. Fancy meeting you here."

"Oh, boy," said Harvey and headed for the living room. Jennifer followed as far as the doorway.

"Did you have a nice day, Abby?" Leeanne asked.

"A wonderful day." Abby gave her a radiant smile. "Be my bridesmaid on June third?"

"Of course. Thank you."

Harvey saw Eddie out, and Leeanne and Abby went upstairs.

Jennifer waited for Harvey. "Eddie's a pretty passionate guy," she said tentatively.

"Tell me something I don't know."

She hated for Harvey to be even a little bit upset with his friend. "I don't think he'd cross the line, but … well, he's just … He's from a different background."

"Certainly his upbringing has a part in it," Harvey said. "He's physical. Always has been."

Jennifer frowned as they walked into the bedroom. "When I worked at the police station last summer, I would see the girls watching him. Clerks, dispatchers, female cops, it didn't matter. When Eddie walked through the room, they all watched him."

Harvey nodded. "Don't remind me of all the heartbroken women. Eddie's attractive, and he had a lot of girlfriends before he was saved."

"But he's been really good since he met the Lord. You've seen him change," Jennifer said. "He's serious now."

39

"Yeah, the only trouble is, he's serious about one woman, and she happens to be your little sister."

"She loves him. We have to trust Eddie."

"I know. And I do. This is a lifetime thing for both of them, and I'm happy for them. Really."

"What do you think they should do, elope?"

Harvey unbuttoned his shirt. "No, not really."

"Good, because I want to be there when they get married."

"Remember Leeanne will be your folks' fourth child in a year announcing her engagement."

She nodded. "Dad and Mom will be glad, but I suppose they might be a little overwhelmed. And it can be hard for men Dad's age to suddenly have no control whatsoever over his children."

"Aw, George isn't that out of touch with reality," Harvey said.

"Well, we'll see how he and Mom react when Abby calls with her news."

Harvey shrugged and continued undressing. "I know what love is, but December's a long time away."

"If Abby's getting married in June, Leeanne and Eddie just have to wait a while."

"At least your folks should have a break before Travis and Randy are ready to get married.

Jennifer chuckled and shook her head. "Did you set the alarm?"

"Yeah. We're all set." They'd been using an alarm system at night and when they went away since they'd been burglarized the fall before.

Another contraction hit Jennifer, one hard enough that she started using Lamaze breathing.

"You okay?" Harvey sat down beside her on the bed and smoothed her hair back from her forehead.

"I think so. Maybe I'll get a shower. When I do something different, they go away."

Chapter 5
Sunday, April 9

The next day at church, word spread quickly of Abby and Peter's engagement. They sat holding hands through the adult Sunday school class, something Jennifer had never seen the conservative Peter do before. Eddie and Leeanne had gone to the singles class, and she imagined they were holding hands, too, but with Peter and Abby it was something of an event.

Abby was surrounded by women between Sunday school and church. Everyone wanted to see the ring, hear about the proposal, and know when the wedding would take place. Peter stood by and beamed. Gary and Andy were wound up and told anyone who would listen that their daddy was getting married.

Mike Browning, the police chief, and his wife, Sharon, came over to talk to the Larsons.

"Another wedding in the family," Mike said to Harvey.

"Yes, we're really happy about it."

"How about Eddie?" Mike asked. "He and Leeanne going to tie the knot?"

"Eventually."

Sharon grinned at Jennifer. "I love this church. Weddings and babies everywhere you look."

Jennifer squeezed her hand. "We love having you here. Keep praying for me, Sharon."

"Are you uncomfortable?" Sharon's concern showed in her tender expression.

"Who isn't, the last few weeks? But I hope it's soon. I'm seeing my doctor tomorrow."

They took Peter and his boys home for lunch, and, of course, Eddie. Harvey also invited Mike and Sharon, along with Jack and Rachel Stewart. Jack was the deputy police chief and had been with the department only four months. He was the man Mike had needed to eradicate some of the pressure of his work

41

load. The Stewarts were also fine additions to Victory Baptist Church.

After lunch, Harvey took everybody out to look at the house next door. He didn't have a key yet, but they walked around into the back yard and looked in the windows.

"So, you'll have your brother next door," Sharon said. "You're a tight family."

Jennifer smiled. "Yes. We'll lose Abby in June, but she'll be just a few miles away." Peter had a house on the north end of town.

"She certainly seems to love those little boys," Rachel Stewart said.

Jennifer nodded. "I think she loved them first. She was hesitant to commit to Peter, partly wondering if she was attracted to him because of the boys."

Abby had Gary and Andy with her in the chair swing in the Larsons' backyard. Peter sat across from her, watching them and smiling, pushing the swing with a lazy rhythm.

When they got back to the house, Mike, Jack, and Harvey began discussing an involved case Harvey's unit was working on, and they drew Eddie into it. Jennifer took the women upstairs to show them the newly-decorated guest room and nursery. Now that Abby and Leeanne had their own rooms at the house, all of the rooms had a designated purpose.

"I thought this house was so huge when we bought it, and now it's hardly big enough," Jennifer said ruefully. "Harvey was going to hire me a maid. Then we got Abby instead."

Abby smiled at her. "This house is a lot easier to keep clean than Mom and Dad's, with the wood furnace and the driveway that turns to mud every spring."

After all the company except Eddie had left, Abby called her folks and told them about her engagement. Jennifer could hear her mom shrieking, and she was six feet away from the phone.

She got on the extension in the bedroom. "You need to come down and help Abby make plans, Mom."

"Can't she come up here?"

"Well, Leeanne promised Eddie she'd be back next weekend," Jennifer said. "If you and Daddy come down, we'll all be together, and we can plan Abby's wedding."

"I wish you'd wait a little longer, Abby," Marilyn said. "It's such short notice."

"It will be great," Jennifer insisted. "We can get the social committee to do the food again, and my rose garden will be blooming, I think. That will save you a bundle in flowers."

"Oh, do you think so? We spent so much for flowers for your wedding!"

"Not to mention the two cakes." Jennifer made a mental note to take Abby around to see the baker after her doctor appointment the next day.

"Have you picked your bridesmaids?" Marilyn asked.

Abby said on the kitchen phone, "I've asked Jennifer and Leeanne. I might have one more."

"Well, you'll need to look for dresses right off, and order the invitations right away."

"See, Mom?" Jennifer said. "You need to come down. Beth will help us, too. She had some great ideas for her wedding, and they're still pretty fresh in her mind."

"I'll see if I can persuade your father," their mother agreed at last.

"Great! If he can't get away, come by yourself. Either way, you can stay in our guest room."

"No, that would definitely be too much for you, so close to your due date. We'll stay with Jeff and Beth."

"Let the boys stay with them," Abby said. "You come to us."

"Well, I think Randy and Travis are going on a youth outing Saturday," her mother said. "I'd better check things out and get back to you."

*****

Eddie and his partner, Tony Winfield, interviewed a couple of witnesses for their current case on Monday morning. When they were finished, Tony escorted the visitors down in the elevator, and Eddie called the patrol sergeant to arrange for some uniformed officers to back them up that afternoon.

A few minutes later, Sarah Benoit came in from the stairway. She came straight to Eddie's desk.

"Hey. You pulled me and Debbie. That okay with you?"

"Sure," Eddie said. Sarah was an ex-girlfriend of his, but he was pretty sure they were over the awkwardness of that. "Where's Debbie?"

"She's checking out the car. She'll be up in a minute."

"Okay. Well, have a seat," Eddie said.

Sarah pulled a chair over, and Eddie did a quick scan of his messages.

"So, how are you doing?" he asked, watching the computer screen.

"Not so great."

He looked over at her. "What? Something going on?"

Sarah shrugged. "My sister."

"What's going on with her?" Eddie asked.

"You don't want to know."

Eddie raised his eyebrows but didn't ask any more questions. He knew that Nicole had gone to live with their father when their parents split, and Sarah continued to live with her mother. Last he'd heard, the two halves of the family weren't talking to each other. He suspected that Mr. Benoit had abused his wife and otmaybe even his two daughters, but Sarah had always avoided talking about that. Eddie had never understood why Nicole would want to live with him instead of her mom.

He did one more check for updates. The stairway door and the elevator opened at the same time

b, and Tony and Debbie both came into the room.

Eddie glanced at Sarah as he stood. "Well, if you need to talk sometime, I'm here for you."

"Thanks."

He briefed the two women on what he and Tony had planned, and the four of them headed down to the garage. Sarah was very aware of his relationship with Leeanne, and Eddie doubted she would call on him for a sounding board.

Harvey met Jennifer at Margaret Turner's office for her checkup. He had taken his lunch hour late so he could be there, but was late anyway for her one o'clock appointment with the obstetrician. A nurse took him to the exam room just as Margaret finished the basics. Jennifer lay on the examining table, covered by purple drapes.

"Hi, Margaret." Harvey bent over to kiss Jennifer. "How's things?"

"Looking good." Margaret peeled off her latex gloves and tossed them in the trash. "I'd say we'll probably be meeting in the delivery room within the next week."

"Really? Fantastic!" Harvey squeezed Jennifer's shoulder. "Almost there, gorgeous!"

She smiled at him. "It's been a great nine months, but I won't be sorry when it's over."

"Okay, make an appointment for next Monday, but I doubt you'll need it," Margaret said.

A knock sounded on the door, and she opened it to her husband, Carl, who was the Larsons' general practitioner.

"Did I see Harvey come in here?" he asked.

"Yes, but Jennifer's not dressed," Margaret told him. "You have to stay out."

"Well, tell him to come down to my office before he leaves," Carl said.

Jennifer appreciated that he didn't just walk into the exam room, even if he was her doctor. Carl had a rather cavalier way with his patients, and she'd had to tell him what she thought about it once.

Margaret consulted her laptop. "Anything else we need to talk about?"

"I think we're all set," Harvey said.

"Beyond all set," Jennifer told her.

"Great. Just call the hospital and tell them when you're going in, and they'll call me."

Jennifer smiled. "I'll try not to make it in the middle of the night."

"Don't worry about that. I'm used to it."

Margaret left them, and Harvey went on down the hall to Carl's office while Jennifer got dressed.

When she walked down there a few minutes later, she peeked in the open doorway. They were sitting on either side of Carl's desk, drinking coffee.

"You are just having a ball with this pregnancy, aren't you?" Carl asked Harvey.

"I've loved every minute of it," he said.

"Yeah, I remember how it was when Margaret was expecting." Carl smiled. Their only child, Julia, was nearly nine.

"How come you guys quit with one?" Having an only child was unthinkable to Harvey.

Carl shrugged. "Margaret said it wasn't nearly as much fun for her as it was for me. And she felt she lost a lot of ground in her career. Took six months off, but she really wanted to practice medicine. I don't know. Sometimes I wonder if we did the right thing for Julia, getting a nanny and all."

"She a terrific kid," said Harvey.

"Yes, but I have the feeling your kids are going to spend a lot more time with their parents than Julia ever did."

"Well, Jenny's planning to stay home," Harvey conceded.

Carl looked up and saw her standing in the doorway and got to his feet. "Here's the beautiful mother-to-be now. Getting anxious, Jennifer?"

"A little." She went in, and Carl kissed her on the cheek.

"Well, I've got to say, Harvey is the luckiest man I know."

She smiled. "How do you mean?"

"He found a gorgeous woman who loves him unconditionally, and now he's going to have a son."

"We don't believe in luck," she reminded him gently.

"That's right. God has favored you." Carl shook his head a little. "Maybe there's something to that."

Harvey stood up. "There's everything to that, Carl. I didn't believe in God when he brought Jennifer into my life, but now—well, now I wonder how I could ever have doubted he exists."

"And he just keeps giving you good things," Carl said.

"We've been blessed," Harvey agreed, "but we've had some difficult times, too. Knowing God is there and that he'll bring us through even the worst of it is very comforting."

Carl was quiet, looking at his shelves full of medical books. "Sometimes I think you're right, and sometimes—well, sometimes I think you just went off the deep end, Harvey. You used to be so sane."

"No, I wasn't. I was fatalistic and neurotic. I was really messed up."

"Well, you sort of made sense to me, I guess, because I feel that way a lot."

"Come over to our house some evening," Harvey said quietly. "We can talk about it."

"Margaret wouldn't come."

"Ask her."

Carl's smile was not happy. "I love her. I know she loves me, too, but … if it's my idea, it doesn't sit right somehow."

Jennifer hadn't thought Margaret was that way, but she didn't know her as well as Harvey knew her and Carl.

"If you tell her it's important to you," Harvey suggested.

Carl laughed a tight little laugh. "It doesn't work that way. You think I didn't tell her it was important to me to have another child? A son?"

Harvey stepped nearer to his friend and put his hand on his shoulder. Jennifer felt as though she was intruding.

"Carl," Harvey said softly, "I'm sorry. I didn't know it went that deep. Is there something …"

Jennifer slipped out into the hallway and walked slowly back toward the exam rooms.

"Jennifer," Margaret called from the corner of the hall. "I thought you guys had left."

"No, Carl and Harvey are talking."

"You guys are a real inspiration," Margaret said.

Jennifer walked closer to her. "How do you mean?"

Margaret smiled. "I see pregnant women all day, every day. About one in ten has her husband with her for the first appointment. About one man in a hundred comes to more than one of her appointments. I think Harvey's been here for every single one of yours."

"He missed one."

"Right. One. That's real dedication." Margaret slipped her stethoscope from around her neck and held it, tapping her hand softly with it. "He's going to be a great father."

"I know. He can hardly wait."

"Seeing you two almost—*almost* makes me want to have another baby."

Startled, Jennifer said shakily, "So, why don't you?"

Margaret shook her head. "I'd have to give up my practice."

"Couldn't someone else handle it for you for a while?"

"I don't think so. I tried that last time. Carl has this really chauvinistic view that if we had another child I should quit practicing and be a full-time mother." She looked at Jennifer contritely. "Oops. Sorry."

Jennifer shrugged. "You haven't offended me. It's a choice. Harvey and I both want it that way. We think we'll all be happier if I'm home with the children."

"So does Carl. He made me feel so guilty for leaving Julia with a sitter. Well, I just don't want to go through that again."

"Is being a doctor so much more important to you?" Jennifer found it hard to relate to Margaret's feelings on that topic. She had been a software designer, not in the same category as medicine, it was true, but she couldn't imagine leaving her precious little son with someone else so she could go back to work. And she could keep working at home and set her own hours. Margaret couldn't do that.

Margaret hooked the stethoscope around her neck. "I think I'd stifle if I had to give it up."

"There must be some middle ground. Maybe you could bring the baby to the office while he's small."

She shook her head. "Carl and I have fought more about that than any other issue."

"I'm sorry, Margaret." Jennifer couldn't remember fighting with Harvey seriously over anything, unless she counted his obstinacy the previous fall about wanting to track down a man who had assaulted her several years earlier. But that wasn't really a fight, to her way of thinking.

Of course, there had been little disagreements, but when it really mattered, she was willing to give Harvey the final word. She wanted it that way in their house, and she felt secure knowing she'd never tried to undermine him. But she understood that not all women would agree with her.

Margaret shrugged. "If it weren't for that one subject, I think we'd have been a whole lot happier. Not that we're not happy together," she said hastily. "It's just ... hard to be married to another doctor. I feel as if I have to keep proving my professionality to Carl. Otherwise, I'm just a woman."

"Just a woman? Margaret!" Jennifer put her hand on the sleeve of her white jacket. "Being a woman is a wonderful gift. And to give your husband your love and respect is another."

Margaret's jaw tightened. "But he should respect me, too."

"You don't think he'll respect you if you're not practicing any longer?" Jennifer was baffled by that one.

"I'm not sure I want to find out," Margaret said.

"Do you think Harvey doesn't respect me?" Jennifer looked into her troubled brown eyes.

Margaret considered for a moment. "No, I honestly have to say that he shows you more respect than I've ever seen a man show a woman. It perplexes me."

"I want what he wants, and he knows that." Jennifer was beginning to realize the caliber of man God had given her. "Come over to our house, Margaret. We can have supper some night and talk. Bring Julia, too." She hesitated. "Or, maybe you'd go to the Bible study at our church."

"Bible study." Margaret shook her head. "What does that have to do with whether or not a man respects his wife?"

"Do you think Harvey has changed in the past year?" Jennifer asked.

"Yes, I do. He was always a gentleman, but since he met you, he seems so contented, so settled. Before, he was sort of drifting. After Carrie left him, I mean. And he drank—" She looked anxiously at Jennifer.

"I know all about that."

"Well, I never saw him drunk," Margaret said.

"But he *has* changed. And it's not because of me."

"It's not? Carl said you'd completely reformed him."

Jennifer laughed. "Carl overestimates me. Harvey's faith in God has done this. Look, why don't you and Carl come have dinner with us some evening. Friday, maybe? We can talk about some of these things."

"Carl wouldn't," she said. "He doesn't believe in God. Very cynical man."

"Do you?"

Margaret sighed. "I suppose not, or I'd be scared, wouldn't I?" She looked at her watch. "Heavens, I'm keeping ten patients waiting. I hope to see you soon at the hospital." She kissed Jennifer on the cheek.

"Come see us," Jennifer said again, as she walked away.

Harvey came up behind her. "Ready to go, gorgeous?"

"Yes."

"Why so glum?"

"I asked Margaret to have dinner with us and she kind of brushed me off."

"I'm sorry. She's a busy woman."

"Yeah."

Jennifer made another appointment at the receptionist's desk and waited until they were in the parking lot before she said, "Margaret and I talked some."

"What about?" Harvey asked.

"The same things you and Carl were talking about. Babies, marriage, God."

"Really?"

"Yes. I heard what Carl said about coming over to talk about it—that Margaret wouldn't if it was his idea. Well, I invited her to the Bible study, and like I said, to our house. She basically said Carl wouldn't want to talk about their marriage. But he *was* talking about it with you."

"Guess we've got something to pray about."

"I'll say. If they did come over, I'd probably be all nervous."

"Why? We've been to their house."

"I know." Jennifer shrugged.

Harvey walked her to her car and put his arms around her. "I didn't get to see much of you today."

"Just come on home with me," she said, knowing he couldn't.

Harvey smiled. "Ah, to be independently wealthy. My office is calling to me. Go home and take a nap, sweetheart." He kissed her tenderly.

"Margaret says you hold the record for dads at prenatal visits."

"Do I get a medal?"

"No, you get a happy wife and a contented mother for your baby."

He kissed her again. It was something to smile about that afternoon.

Abby was getting ready for work when Jennifer got home, and they had to postpone the trip to the bakery. Jennifer spent a little time on the computer. Her former coworker, John, had started a new software company, and he'd asked her to make a new recordkeeping program for educators. There were quite a few on the market already, but he wanted something with a lot of extras for the teachers. Jennifer had started setting up the parameters, and she worked on it for an hour, then clicked to another project she had started on her own—a learning game for preschoolers.

After half an hour of that, she caught herself yawning and realized she was tired. She lay down in the bedroom and dozed off. She woke up to Harvey's kisses.

"You're home early." She sat up.

"No, I'm not."

"It's after five? Wow, I was really out of it! I don't have supper ready."

"That's okay, let's eat out," he said.

Jennifer smiled. In her book, Harvey held the record at a lot of things, not just doctor visits.

*****

Harvey went to the bank on his lunch hour Tuesday for a certified check for the closing on the house, and Jennifer met him afterward at Casco Realty. Myrtle and Mr. Foote went through the paperwork with them and Mr. Fuller's executor, who turned out to be their neighbor on the other side of the house they'd just bought, Ralph Penninger.

He told them Mr. Fuller had asked him to be his executor three years earlier, when he'd written his will. "He didn't have any relatives in the area, and he didn't want to have a lawyer do it."

"Doesn't he have children?" Harvey asked.

"No, he was never married," Ralph said. "There was a nephew, but I don't know where he is. He's not mentioned in the will, anyway, so it doesn't matter as far as the estate distribution goes."

"Who benefited?" Harvey asked, curious as to where his money was going.

"The cancer unit at Maine Medical, and the Portland Historical Society," said Mr. Penninger.

"Could have been a lot worse," Jennifer whispered to Harvey.

When they left with the deed, closing agreement, and house keys in hand, Harvey said, "If I'd known the executor was Ralph Penninger, I'd have gone over there and talked turkey with him about the price of the house."

Jennifer shrugged. "Maybe he didn't want to talk turkey with the police captain. Otherwise he might have told us, after we submitted our first offer."

Harvey eyed her with chagrin. "Yeah, you're probably right. Smart woman."

Chapter 6

While Harvey went back to work, Abby met Jennifer at Patricia Lundquist's bakery on Market Street.

"Peter said to pick out whatever I want," Abby said.

Jennifer just smiled, remembering the day she and Harvey tasted Patricia's cake samples. Abby ended up choosing a four-tiered square cake with white-on-white decorations and a floral topper.

They went to a couple of bridal shops in South Portland, and Jennifer found a dress she really liked for herself, provided she regained her figure in time.

"We can bring Leanne in to try it on this weekend," she said.

Abby was agreeable to that, but she hadn't found what she wanted for her own gown. "I think there's another shop on Congress Street." She looked at her watch. "I don't think there's time to find it before I have to go to work, though."

Jennifer had about reached her limit of being on her feet.

"Why don't you just wear mine? We're almost the same height and have pretty much the same proportions when I'm not nine months along. Unless you don't like it."

"I love your gown," Abby said.

"Well, why didn't you say so, instead of dragging me all over South Portland?" Jennifer asked irritably. Her back hurt and her feet were swelling.

"Sorry. I didn't think of it," Abby said contritely. "If you really don't mind, I'll try it on tomorrow." She kissed Jennifer on the cheek. "Go take a nap before Harvey comes home, honey."

By the time Jennifer got home, the contractions had kicked up again, and Connor was kicking hard. She dragged into the bedroom, pulled her shoes off, and flopped on the bed.

Half an hour later, she woke to a hard contraction. She rolled onto her other side and went back to sleep.

Another half hour. Another hard contraction. She did the first stage Lamaze breathing and wondered if it was the real thing. She couldn't go back to sleep, so she pulled out the prayer list she and Harvey kept in a notebook and started at the back.

Carl and Margaret. She prayed for their salvation and for their attitudes toward each other. The purchase of the house next door. Angela Williams at church, who'd had pneumonia. Abby and Peter were next, and Eddie and Leeanne's relationship. Leeanne's schoolwork, and her internship for the summer. Rick Bradley, Beth's brother, whose job situation looked precarious. Her parents' salvation. Travis, her eighteen-year-old brother.

Another contraction hit, and she looked at her watch. Twenty minutes. She got up and went to the bathroom and then checked her Lamaze bag and her hospital suitcase.

When the next one came, she timed it. It lasted nearly half a minute and was twenty minutes after the previous one. She allowed herself to start getting excited.

Three contractions later, Harvey came home. She called to him from the bedroom, and he came in there.

"How you doing, gorgeous? Did you and Abby do too much shopping today?"

"I think I'm in labor." It was a relief to say it to someone at last.

"Really?" He looked doubtful at first, then excited. "*Really?*"

She nodded. "My feet are all puffy, though."

He sat down on the bed and started rubbing her feet.

She felt the next one coming on. "Time this one." She took a deep breath.

"Thirty seconds," he told her when it was over. "Did it feel like it's doing any work?"

"I think maybe."

"Should I call the hospital?"

"Not yet."

He sat with her and rubbed her feet and talked softly about the case he and Nate and Jimmy had worked on that afternoon. The next contraction, twenty minutes later, didn't seem as strong.

"Do you want to eat?" she asked him.

"Maybe I should. How about you?"

"I don't think so."

They went to the kitchen, and Jennifer fixed him a plate and microwaved it. She sat down at the table with him, a bottle of spring water in her hand.

After he'd asked the blessing, Harvey looked at his pocket notebook, open on the table beside his plate, then looked warily at her.

"Twenty minutes," he said.

Jennifer scowled. "Nothing."

He ate, and they talked. She told him about her shopping expedition with Abby.

"Twenty-five minutes," he said.

She felt a little twinge, but nothing like what she'd felt earlier.

"I think they're going away," she said drearily.

He pulled her over onto his lap. "It's going to happen, Jenny. It really is."

*****

Harvey left early the next morning so he could meet Jeff and Eddie at six o'clock to run. They did that three times a week when they could. Jennifer took her time getting up and made a pot of coffee for them. The men all had a cup when they returned. Then Eddie went home to change for work and Jeff got in his truck and drove away. Harvey took a shower and changed and then sat down to breakfast with Jennifer and Abby.

"Really good pancakes," he said after eating two.

"I didn't make them," Jennifer said. "Abby did."

"Oh, well, please accept my compliments, Abby."

"Thanks. A truck just pulled in next door." Abby rose so she could see better through the entry window.

Harvey got up and looked out. "It's the furnace guy. I told Eddie I'll be late this morning. I'll go over there now and show him the old furnace."

He walked across to the stone cottage. Jennifer tried to quit thinking of it as Mr. Fuller's house and was beginning mentally to call it Jeff and Beth's house.

55

The wind had blown in off the bay for a couple of days, and the mud was drying up. She hoped the lawns were firmer, and Harvey could walk across the grass without getting his shoes wet. A little green had appeared in the turf.

After Abby left for work, Jennifer cleaned up the breakfast things. When she looked across at the cottage again, a black pickup was parked behind the heating service truck.

Harvey came back twenty minutes later.

"How's it going?" she asked.

"Great. The concrete man came in to give me an estimate."

"The black truck?"

"Yup. The furnace man was still there, so that was good. They're going to come tomorrow and start getting the floor ready. He thinks they can pour concrete on Friday."

"Terrific," Jennifer said.

"Yeah, I didn't expect to get it done so fast. And they'll take the old furnace out this afternoon. The new one will go in after the concrete's had a chance to cure."

"How long will that take?"

"A week, maybe."

A week. "Wow! Jeff and Beth can move in after that?"

"As soon as the new furnace is working," Harvey agreed. "Ten days to two weeks from now, I guess."

"Can I tell Beth?"

"Sure. Maybe they want to give their landlord notice."

That afternoon, Jennifer's mother phoned.

"Dad and I will be down Friday evening," she said.

"What about the boys?"

"Staying at the pastor's house until we get back Sunday."

"That's great, Mom. Abby will be off all day Saturday, and we can get a lot done. You're going to stay with us, right?"

"I guess so. Jeff has to work Saturday. I talked to him last night. He said Beth will come over and show us their new house, next door to you. That is so exciting!"

"I can't wait until they move in," Jennifer said. "We just need to get the new furnace up and running. There is a fireplace, but it's still too cold nights."

"Well, they need time to pack, anyway. Beth says she's started sorting things and cleaning cupboards, but she's got two more months of teaching left, so she only has evenings and Saturdays free."

"I'm sure she can get a lot done this weekend if we all help." Jennifer secretly hoped Jeff and Beth could settle into the new house before the baby was born. Not that she wanted to delay the birth—she didn't. But it would be so nice to have all that done before the really big upheaval in their lives.

*****

Jennifer felt disgustingly normal on Thursday. No contractions, no nausea, nothing. Connor did his calisthenics as usual, and she decided to take a walk down Van Cleeve Lane and see if spring was progressing.

Janice Parker called to her from her yard across the street, where she was cleaning out a perennial bed. "Where you headed, Jennifer?"

"Just out for a stroll. Come with me?"

Janice threw down her gardening gloves and joined her on the sidewalk.

"How are you feeling?" she asked.

"Fine. My doctor told me Monday I'd probably go within a week, but nothing so far."

"It's early yet," Janice said.

"Yeah, eleven days to my due date."

"So you've bought Mr. Fuller's house." Janice gazed at Mr. Fuller's old home as they strolled past it.

"Yes, and my brother Jeff and his wife are renting it from us."

"Fantastic." Janice had met Jeff and Beth. "They'll be great neighbors."

"If you see any other For Sale signs in the neighborhood, tell me," Jennifer said. "Eddie and my little sister, Leeanne, will be in the market soon."

"Really? They make a cute couple."

"You knew Abby and Peter got engaged last weekend?"

"No. My goodness, your mother must be beside herself."

They strolled down Van Cleeve Lane, catching up on the news and looking at everyone's front yard, searching for daffodil shoots and crocuses.

"The Hensons' lawn is definitely turning green," Jennifer said.

"How are the rose bushes?" Janice asked.

"Harvey says we should have the Baileys' old gardener come in, at least a few times, to make sure they get off to a healthy start this spring. Unless you and Bud want to advise me."

"It would probably be a good idea to have Mr. Fournier take a look," Janice said. "He worked for the Baileys for several years and took care of the roses after Mrs. Bailey got so sick."

When they came around the block, the black pickup was parked in front of Beth and Jeff's new house.

"What's going on?" Janice asked. Two men were carrying spades and rakes around the corner of the house.

"They're preparing the basement floor for concrete," Jennifer said.

"I saw the old furnace go out yesterday."

"Yes, it was hopeless. We're having a cement floor poured, and they'll bring the new furnace next week. Then Beth and Jeff can move in."

"They're not using the front entrance," Janice observed.

"No, Harvey gave them a key to the bulkhead door. It's in the backyard." Jennifer turned toward Janice. "Come have a cup of tea with me. I need company today."

"Where's Abby?"

"She met Peter for lunch, and they were going to the formalwear shop after to pick out the tuxedoes for the wedding. She's going right to work from there."

Janice kept stride with her up their walkway. They went inside, and Jennifer made tea in a china teapot and set out a plate of fancy cookies Abby had made. Half of them had gone to the Hobarts' house, but Abby had left Harvey and Jennifer a supply as well. They talked about Abby's upcoming wedding, and Bud and Janice's plans for a vacation in Bermuda in July.

58

The doorbell rang. Jennifer got up and waddled to the entry.

"Mrs. Larson?" The workman had on blue twill pants and a matching shirt that said "Rudy" on the breast pocket.

"Yes."

"Your husband's got me and a couple of boys, uh, leveling the dirt floor in the basement next door."

"Yes?" Jennifer glanced out and saw that there were now two pickups in front of 135 Van Cleeve Lane.

"Yes, ma'am, and—is your husband home?"

"No, he's at work. Is there a problem?"

Rudy's face looked a trifle strained. "Well, ma'am, it's just that there's something I'd, uh, like him to take a look at before we, uh, proceed any further."

"Something to do with the plumbing?" Jennifer asked.

"No ma'am. It's—" He broke off, and she thought he was sweating, although he had no jacket on and it was cool outside. "Didn't Mr. Larson tell me he's a police officer?" Rudy asked.

The back of her neck felt prickly. "Yes. He's the captain of the Priority Unit."

"Could you call him, ma'am? Would that be all right?"

She started to ask him again what was wrong, but thought better of it.

"Come in." She opened the door wide. "What was your name?"

"Rudy Thomas."

"Right this way." Jennifer walked into the kitchen. Janice sat sipping her tea and watching curiously. Jennifer took down the receiver from the wall phone, punched in Harvey's desk phone number, and waited.

Paula, the Priority Unit secretary, answered.

"Paula, this is Jennifer Larson. Is the captain in?"

"No, he went out with Cook and Miller about half an hour ago."

"Thank you." Jennifer hung up and called his cell phone.

"Well, hello, gorgeous," he said.

"Do you have a minute?"

"For you, any time."

Jennifer looked at the workman. "Rudy Thomas, the concrete man, is here. He says there's a problem in the basement. He'd like to speak to you."

"Sure, put him on." Harvey almost never sounded worried or annoyed. He was able to take most things in stride. For all she knew, he was looking at a murder victim while he talked to her in that pleasant tone.

Jennifer handed the receiver to Rudy and stood back, leaning against the counter, frankly listening to his end of the conversation. She glanced at Janice. She was listening, too.

"Uh, Captain? This is Rudy. Uh, we've, uh, found something in the basement that, uh, I think you should, uh, take a look at, sir."

There was a pause, and Rudy shot a worried glance at Jennifer. "Uh, no, sir, nothing like that. It's, uh, something, you know, that we, uh, found when we were digging."

Another pause. Janice's eyes went wide. Jennifer shrugged.

Rudy said, "Well, sir, over in the, uh, corner, where there was some wood piled, we, uh, took that all out, and it was kind of bumpy, so we, uh, were smoothing it out, you know, for the concrete, and, uh, Billy raked up something that looked like a, well, a ... a bone, sir."

Jennifer and Janice stared at each other.

"Uh-huh. A bone. No, sir. It's too big for that. Well, it could be a deer bone. Like maybe a deer leg or something, but, uh, we started, you know, digging around a little more in that spot, and, uh, well, we found some more, sir. I really think you ought to see it."

He paused, listening. "Yes, sir."

He handed Jennifer the receiver. She wasn't sure whether or not Harvey had hung up, so she put the receiver to her ear and said, "Hello?"

"Jenny, make sure he understands I don't want them digging around anymore until I, uh, get there, uh, you, uh, know what I mean?"

She smiled. "Ten-four."

"Good. I'll be there in fifteen minutes. I love you." He hung up.

Jennifer turned to Rudy, who waited patiently.

"The captain says he'll be here in fifteen minutes. You and your men are to wait until he gets here. Don't do any more digging, don't disturb the dirt any more. Do you understand?"

"Yes, ma'am."

"If you'd like to take a coffee break, I'll make a pot of coffee for you and your men."

"Thank you, ma'am, I think we all could do with some coffee," Rudy said.

He went out the door, and Jennifer measured coffee into the machine's basket.

"What do you suppose they found?" Janice asked.

"Sounds like a bunch of bones."

"Yeah, but—human bones?"

"I don't know. Harvey seemed inclined to think it was animal bones." But Rudy had looked spooked.

When the coffee was ready, Jennifer put the pot and three mugs and a plastic bag of cookies on a tray. Janice carried the tray, and Jennifer walked beside her to the next lawn. They went through the gate into the back yard. Rudy and two other men were standing near the open bulkhead talking.

"Thank you, ma'am," Rudy said, coming to meet them.

The other two men smiled. One, a dark-haired young man with a mustache, wore the same blue work clothes Rudy wore, but with a plaid wool jacket over his shirt. The other man was older, forty-five or so, with a broken tooth in front and Texan eyebrows that met over his nose.

"You're welcome. Just bring the tray back when you're done," Jennifer said and turned back toward her house.

"Don't you want to know what they found?" Janice asked.

"Harvey will tell me."

Chapter 7

Harvey pulled into the driveway at the Fuller house, took a powerful flashlight from the glove box, and got out. He looked toward his own house. Jennifer waved, and he waved back and walked toward the gate to the backyard.

Rudy set a coffee mug on the tray that rested on the ground. "Cap'n, sorry to bother you."

"That's okay," Harvey said. "What have you got?"

"Come see for yourself."

Rudy led him down the stairs into the basement, and the other two men followed. The room was poorly lit with one bare bulb overhead and a droplight that probably belonged to Rudy.

"It's, uh, right over here." Rudy walked toward one corner and stood about six feet from the wall, looking down.

Harvey recalled seeing some firewood stacked there earlier. It had been removed, and the earthen floor was torn open in an area about four feet square. Several bones lay in a pile at the edge of the excavation. He turned on his flashlight and crouched to examine them.

Ten minutes later, he entered his house with his cell phone at his ear.

"Yeah, send a forensics team over here ASAP," he said to Jack Stewart. "Get Thibodeau and Winfield out here, too. No, I put Miller and Cook on that homicide in Deering today. Well, Eddie was in court this morning, but he should be available now. Got it. Thanks, Jack." He shoved the phone into his pocket.

Bud and Janice Parker both sat at the kitchen table with Jennifer.

"Hi," he said. "Got any coffee?" He bent toward Jennifer to kiss her.

"I left the pot with the concrete men," she said.

"I'll go get it," Bud offered.

"Thanks, Bud," said Harvey. "Just stay out of the basement over there, okay? I don't want anybody else in there until forensics goes over it."

"Sure, Harvey."

Bud went quickly out the door. Harvey took off his jacket and went to the sink to wash his hands.

"What is it over there?" Jennifer asked, handing him a clean towel.

Janice leaned forward. "Did somebody bury their dog in the cellar?"

"No, it looks like human remains to me." Harvey sank into a chair.

"Cookie?" Jennifer nudged the plate toward him.

"Love one." He supposed he shouldn't be surprised that Jennifer showed no alarm at his pronouncement. She was used to it by now.

Janice, however, looked somewhat unsettled and even a bit excited. "And we've been staring across at that house all these years." She shook her head. "Who do you suppose it is?"

"I have no idea at this point," Harvey said.

Bud was soon back with the tray, and Jennifer started a fresh pot of coffee.

"I sent the concrete crew home," Harvey told her. "I told Rudy I'll call him tonight and let him know what's going on. It may be weeks before they can pour that concrete."

"So Jeff and Beth will have to wait," Jennifer said.

He hated to think that was going to happen. "If it gets warm enough, they could move into the house, I suppose, as long as they stay out of the basement."

"What exactly did they find?" Bud asked eagerly.

Harvey said, "First they found some long bones, then a couple of teeth, then when they got their spades going, they turned up a hand. They kept at it 'til they found the skull. Made a royal mess, is what they did. We could have uncovered that skeleton nearly intact if they'd left it alone when they started finding bones."

Jennifer scowled. "I told Rudy what you said."

64

"He claims the other two had kept digging while he came over here to call me."

"But they didn't know they were human bones at first," Janice said.

"No, you're right. I would have kept looking myself," he admitted, "but I'd have done it a whole lot more carefully."

*****

Eddie and Tony arrived in Tony's Mustang, blue light flashing. Harvey went out and talked to them in the driveway next door, and Tony took a roll of yellow crime scene tape from his car and headed for the backyard. The forensics team rolled up in a van. Eddie went around the house, and Harvey stood talking to the forensics men for a minute, then they all followed Eddie.

"Not much to see from here," Jennifer told Bud, who was watching out the kitchen window. You could see only a corner of the backyard next door from there.

"Can I go out in your backyard and look over the fence?" he asked, just like a kid, except a kid wouldn't have asked. He would have just gone.

"Sure, but you can't see into the cellar from there."

She took him into the sunroom and let him out through the patio door.

When the coffee was ready, Jennifer put the pot and some clean mugs on the tray and called to Bud. He came in and got it and went happily next door with the tray for her. He came back all excited.

"They're trying to determine exactly where the skeleton was, and how deep it was buried," he said. "Harvey tells me they'll be able to tell what gender and how old the deceased was, and approximately how long ago it happened. And guess what? They found a button."

"You should have been a cop," Janice said. Bud was in insurance, and was within sight of retirement.

"I know it." He sighed. "I really missed my calling."

"He reads mysteries all the time," Janice said.

Half an hour later, Bud and Janice went back across the street, and half an hour after that several men left the house next door with a body bag. The forensics van left soon after, and Harvey and his two detectives came out the gate. Tony festooned it with crime scene tape, and the three of them walked toward the Larson house. Eddie carried Jennifer's tray, laden with used cups and the coffeepot.

"Got any more coffee, Jenny?" Harvey asked.

She made another pot. As it dripped into the carafe, she sat down on a stool and rubbed her tummy. She'd been on her feet quite a bit, and she was tired. Harvey and his men sat down at the table and talked about what they had found.

Jennifer got up slowly and went to the cupboard for more cookies. There were a few left, and she put them on a clean plate. Then she rummaged in the freezer for something else to feed them. She knew Tony and Eddie had appetites.

"As soon as we get the lab report, I want you to start on the ID," Harvey told the two detectives.

Jennifer came up with a box of squash doughnuts from the back of the freezer and took them and the cookies to the table.

"Do you guys like frozen doughnuts?"

Tony grinned. "My favorite." He was twenty-four, but looked sixteen with short, light hair and freckles and a little-boy smile. His main claim to fame was being the governor's nephew, but he was making his mark in the Priority Unit, and Harvey and Eddie were working hard to mold him into an excellent detective. He was intuitive and had already helped solve several high-profile cases.

"It's nearly five," Harvey said. "You guys don't have to go back to the office unless you want to, but first thing in the morning I want you ready to move on this."

"Right," said Eddie.

Tony nodded. "Will do."

"What about that case Nate and Jimmy are on?" Eddie asked.

"Pretty straightforward," Harvey told him. "I went out there this afternoon. In fact, I was there when Jenny called me about this. They've got things under control. Nate's in charge, and he's got three good witnesses. I expect it to be a textbook case. Good practice for him and Jimmy to see it all the way through. I'll meet with them again in the morning, but I think that one's all set."

"Good," said Eddie. "We just don't know what we're up against with this one. How long did the old guy own the house?"

"About twelve years, I think," Harvey said, "but that's one thing we can check right now. Jennifer and I got a copy of the deed search Tuesday, when we closed the deal. Hang on." He got up and went into the study.

Jennifer poured coffee for the three men, got herself a glass of milk, and sat down.

"Here it is." Harvey emerged from the study with a file folder in his hand. "Carleton Fuller bought the house twelve years ago. Before that, it was owned by a Robert Chapel for nearly thirty years." He laid the paper on the table between Eddie and Tony, and they bent their heads over it.

"Eddie, you can do some research on those buttons first thing," Harvey said. "They look like military issue, but it could be a fashion statement." He turned and looked at Jennifer for a few seconds, then a smile came out slowly. "How's my beautiful bride doing?"

"A little tired," she admitted.

"Why don't you lie down for a bit?"

"No, I've got taco fixings ready. I intend to feed you a decent supper." She looked at Eddie and Tony. "Would you guys like to stay?"

"Thanks, but I promised my dad I'd help him with something tonight," Tony said.

"I'll stay, if you're not too tired." Eddie sounded almost apologetic.

"No, I'll feed you, and then you and Harvey can load the dishwasher."

"Deal," Eddie said, flashing the smile everyone loved.

She stood. "We used up all of Abby's cookies, but I think there's a cheesecake in the freezer downstairs."

"We don't need cheesecake," Harvey said.

"No, but someone else could drop by. I'd better at least have it thawing. We've had a lot of people in and out of here lately."

"Okay, I'll get it." Harvey headed for the cellar door in the entry.

"You don't have to give me dessert all the time, you know," Eddie said.

"It's okay." Jennifer sat down in her chair with a sigh. "At least we already have a concrete floor in this basement."

Chapter 8

Eddie and Harvey brainstormed about the skeleton during the meal. Eddie jotted notes on possible avenues of investigation. Harvey was putting Eddie in charge, but Jennifer knew her husband would be right in the middle of this one himself, since the remains were found on their property.

About the time they opened the cheesecake, Beth arrived at their door. Harvey let her in, telling Jennifer to sit still.

"Hi," Beth said. "Jennifer called and said there's some holdup on the house?"

"Sit down, Beth," Harvey said. "Cheesecake?"

"Mmm, thanks. Just a little piece."

Harvey brought another plate, and Jennifer cut her a slice. As she handed it to Beth, she felt an ineffectual twinge and wished the pregnancy was over.

"Jennifer, you haven't gained much weight with this baby," Beth observed.

"She's gained exactly sixteen pounds," Harvey said. "Her doctor would like to see her gain a little more, but she says Jennifer and the baby are healthy."

"I feel enormous," Jennifer said.

Eddie looked up from his notebook at Harvey. "So, about the corpse next door. . ."

"What corpse?" Beth stared at him as if she might either laugh or scream, depending on what he said.

"Uh. . ." Eddie winced. "Sorry."

"There was a skeleton in your basement." Harvey said.

"Not really." Beth's face turned pale.

"Unfortunately, it's true. I had intended to break the news a little less abruptly, but there it is. The concrete crew found some human remains over there this afternoon."

"What does this do to our moving into the house?" Beth asked, shaky but practical.

"Well, it will delay things for sure," Harvey said. "We can't pour the concrete until the investigation is complete. We don't want to obliterate any evidence."

"Of course not," Beth said. "Was it a murder victim?"

"We don't know yet. Eddie and Tony Winfield will be looking into it. We hope to get a preliminary lab report tomorrow."

"Jeff will love this," Beth said.

"Well, we won't be able to get the new furnace in as soon as planned." Harvey spread his hands. "We'll want to examine the entire floor now, to make sure there's nothing else that needs attention. If it warms up a little, you and Jeff could move in and rely on the fireplace for a little heat. I don't think you should just yet, though. It's still freezing nights."

"We told our landlord we'd move out the end of April," Beth said, a question in her voice.

"Today's what, the thirteenth? That should be fine," said Harvey.

They talked about it some more, and after a while Beth seemed to have accepted the turn of events.

"Do you want me to tell Jeff, or tell him yourself?" Harvey asked her.

"Maybe it's better if you tell him. He'll have questions."

Harvey nodded. "If he comes to run with me and Eddie in the morning, I'll talk to him then. Otherwise, just ask him to call me when he has a minute."

*****

Harvey went to Eddie's to run Friday morning, then came home to change. Jennifer was feeling contractions again.

"Don't you try to do too much today," he warned, tying his tie.

"I won't."

"I know you. Your family's coming tonight, and you'll be wanting to make beds and bake and clean. Don't do it." He put on his shoulder holster and sports jacket and started loading his pockets with his gear: notebook, handkerchief, evidence bags, tape measure, cell phone, ammo clips, pocketknife.

"Did you talk to Jeff?" she asked.

"Yeah. He's not happy, but I expected that."

"You're doing everything you can."

"Yeah, but you know Jeff." Harvey glanced at her in the mirror. "He was cautious about the whole idea of the house from the beginning."

"He won't back out, will he?"

"No, but he probably needs to think about it awhile and then talk some more."

"And think some more," Jennifer said.

"Yeah."

"Coming home for lunch?"

"I'll try. Eddie and Tony may be over here again today. The forensics team will tell us if any bones were missing, and if they were, we'll be sifting some more dirt."

"I thought that cellar floor was pretty hard packed."

"Most of it is, but under the wood pile it was softer."

"Like it had been dug up?" Jennifer asked.

"Precisely."

"And you have to dig up the rest now?"

"I hope not. Rudy said the area where they found the bones looked disturbed. We haven't found anything like that in the rest of the basement. But we have some other resources."

"Cadaver dogs?"

"Probably not, unless we suspect there's something there. But there are electro-magnometers and other tools that can be helpful."

"Really?"

She stood and walked with him to the door. He glanced at the thermometer in the kitchen window on the way and got his jacket from the coat closet.

"I'm serious about you taking it easy," he said. "Let Abby help you." He put his arms around her, and she clung to him. "It's going to happen soon, gorgeous." He kissed her hair, and she lifted her face so he could kiss her lips. He held her another ten seconds and then said, "Yeah, I'll come home for lunch."

Abby did help her, and she took Harvey's side, making Jennifer sit and supervise her work. She wouldn't even let Jennifer go upstairs to check the guest room and Leeanne's room, but did it all herself, assuring her sister they were spotless and that she had cleaned the bathroom upstairs as well.

Abby's next project was baking. She made muffins and brownies. Jennifer sat at the kitchen table and chopped nuts for her, then peeled potatoes, plopping them into a kettle of water. Every twenty minutes or so she had a twenty-second, ho-hum contraction.

"You've done enough," Abby declared about eleven o'clock. "Your nurse orders you to lie down until the invincible captain arrives for lunch."

"I was going to make spaghetti," Jennifer said.

"I'll do it. Besides, we're having a big meal tonight when Mom and Dad are here. Do you really want spaghetti at noon?"

"I don't. I don't feel like eating anything."

"Well then, I think Harvey and I will have sandwiches," Abby said.

She followed Jennifer to the bedroom and insisted on untying her shoes for her. Jennifer lay down, and Abby pulled Grandma Lewis's pinwheel quilt up over her.

"Close your eyes."

She tiptoed out, and Jennifer did shut her eyes. After a few minutes she rolled over, trying to find a comfortable position. Connor kicked. Her abdominal muscles tightened, then relaxed. She drifted off to sleep.

She woke up, and Harvey was sitting on the edge of the bed, taking his shoes off. His jacket lay over the back of a chair.

Jennifer edged over, and he lay down beside her, putting his arm under her head.

"How you doing?"

"Okay."

He kissed her.

"You'd better eat lunch," she said.

"Abby fed me."

"How long have you been here?"

"Fifteen minutes. You were pretty zonked, so I let you sleep."

She put her arms around his neck. "Don't go back to work."

He laughed. "If you really want me to stay, you'll have to start labor. I get three days of family leave for that."

"Did you find out any more about Mr. Bones in the basement next door?"

"A little. Ryan Toothaker got wind of it somehow. He's after me to give him an exclusive for the *Press Herald*."

"Too bad Leeanne's not down here yet to do the story," Jennifer said, but Leeanne's internship wouldn't start for several weeks.

"Well, the lab report told us the bones were from a male, approximately sixty years old, a little arthritic. The skull had a fracture. Probably that was the cause of death."

"Could it have happened after he died?" she asked. "I mean, like when they dug up the skull?"

"No. I asked that, too."

"Were all the bones there?"

"Well, we're missing a few teeth and some phalanges."

"Fingers?"

"And toes."

"So now what?"

"Eddie and Tony and the forensics team will be back over there after lunch, looking for the missing bones."

"What if this guy just happened to be missing a few teeth and fingers?"

"Then we won't find them."

Jennifer sighed. "How long has he been there, in the basement?"

"Eight to twelve years, best estimate so far."

"Since Mr. Fuller moved in," she said uneasily.

"Probably."

Harvey held her close.

"Stay here," she said.

"I will until Eddie and Tony show up next door. I told Abby to let me know when they get there."

Another contraction started, and she took a deep breath. She breathed slowly, rhythmically, and Harvey put his hand on her tummy.

When she took a cleansing breath at the end of the contraction, he said, "Man, that really is doing *something*. How long are these things lasting?"

"I don't know."

"Half a minute at least, that time," he said.

"Think so?"

"Yeah. Tell me when you're getting another one, and I'll time it." He took his notebook and pen out of his shirt pocket and wrote down the time.

Jennifer frowned. "I can't go today."

"Why not? You've been wanting to go so badly."

"Mom and Dad are coming tonight."

"So, they'd be here for the birth. That's okay."

With Harvey saying it, Jennifer could almost believe it was the ideal timing. He took off his holster, and she lay with her head on his shoulder for twenty minutes, talking with him about the baby. They agreed his name was Connor, then agreed not to change their minds. Then another contraction came.

Harvey timed it, and she breathed. She was an expert by now, so bored with the breathing patterns she didn't care if she never used them. She picked a focal point at random, looking at the picture of her and Harvey on his dresser, focusing on his face. They were sitting on the rocks at Portland Head Lighthouse, and he was smiling at her. Maybe she should just forget about the Lamaze breathing, she thought, but she kept on.

"Forty seconds," he said when it was over. "That's pretty long for a Braxton-Hicks, isn't it?"

"Who knows?" she moaned. "I refuse to get my hopes up again."

Abby knocked softly on the bedroom door. "Eddie's next door."

"Okay, I'll be right there," Harvey called.

He kissed Jennifer again, thoroughly. "I love you, gorgeous. Write the times down. If they get closer, send Abby over to get me. Otherwise, I'll check in on you in a little while."

"Okay," she whispered.

He sat up and put on his shoes and squeezed her one more time before standing up.

She kept the log in the little notebook he'd left behind and wondered if he needed it at the investigation. It was so odd to have the crime scene next door, with the police line beginning at the edge of the driveway.

The contractions kept on, about every twenty minutes, and she finally decided to get up and see if they would quit. She put her sneakers and sweater on and wandered out to the kitchen. Abby was still at it, taking two apple pies from the oven.

"You'd better get a nap now," Jennifer said. "It's your turn."

"No, I'm fine. I don't have to work tonight."

"Are you and Peter going out?"

"No, he's coming here. I asked him to come and spend the evening with Mom and Dad. You don't mind, do you?"

"No, that's great. They need to get to know him better, and we can talk about the wedding details. Have you guys talked to Pastor Rowland?"

"Yes, we're starting our premarital counseling tomorrow afternoon."

The doorbell rang, and the door opened. Leeanne marched in, smiling.

"My sisters," she cried, and they hugged all around. "I got out of classes early and decided to come right down."

"Are you hungry?" Abby asked.

"Starved."

Abby began pulling leftovers from the refrigerator. Leeanne selected a few items, and Abby fixed her a plate while Leeanne dragged her suitcase upstairs and Jennifer breathed through another contraction.

"What's going on at Jeff and Beth's house?" Leeanne asked when she came downstairs.

"Uh, nothing much," Jennifer said. "Just a murder."

75

"You're kidding, right?"

"No, they found a body in the basement."

"Ha, ha."

Abby said, "They really did, Leeanne. The men that came to pour the concrete floor dug up a skeleton." She took Leeanne's plate from the microwave and put it in her hands.

"Ooh, gross!" Leeanne set the plate down quickly on the counter. "I'm not hungry anymore."

"Well, there's one good thing about it," Jennifer said.

"What?"

"Eddie's over there."

"Really? Can I go over and say hi?"

"No, we're not allowed," said Abby.

"It's a crime scene," Jennifer told her. "You can't cross the yellow tape."

Abby leaned precariously over the sink so she could see more from the kitchen window. "Ryan Toothaker's out there."

"That reporter from the *Press Herald*?" asked Leeanne. "No fair!"

"I know," Jennifer said. "Seems like you ought to get this story. Right next door. It'll never happen again."

Abby made a face. "We hope."

Jennifer went to the telephone and started pushing buttons.

"Who are you calling?" Abby asked.

Jennifer just smiled. "Detective Thibodeau? When you have a moment, you might want to check out a package that just arrived at the Larson house. That's affirmative." She hung up and smiled at Leeanne.

Leeanne hugged her. "Thanks, Jennifer."

"Oh!" The contraction started with a stab, instead of the gradual buildup Jennifer usually got. She sat down quickly on the stool by the phone.

"Are you okay?" Leeanne asked.

Abby hurried over. Jennifer started her breathing, focusing on the hot pies. She had a vague impression of Abby watching the clock and her at the same time, and Leeanne holding her hand.

As she took her final cleansing breath, Abby said, "That was pretty strong, wasn't it?"

Jennifer nodded.

"It lasted almost a minute."

"Do you think it's the real thing?" Jennifer asked.

"I don't know." Abby worked in obstetrics at Maine Medical Center and wanted to be there when the baby was born.

"Where's the notebook?" Jennifer looked around, feeling a little disoriented.

"What notebook?" Leeanne asked.

"Harvey's little notebook. I've been keeping a log in it. I guess I left it on the bed."

Leeanne went through the door to the sunroom, and Abby started rubbing Jennifer's shoulders.

"How you doing now?"

"Fine," Jennifer said.

Leeanne came back with the notebook, and Jennifer wrote down her estimated time for the last contraction. "Still twenty minutes apart."

"All right, you tell us when the next one comes, and Leeanne will time it," said Abby.

The front door opened, and Harvey and Eddie came in. Eddie went quickly to Leeanne and threw his arms around her.

"*Ma chérie.*"

He kissed her, and after about five seconds, Leeanne pushed him away, blushing and glancing around at the others.

"Welcome back, kiddo," Harvey said and kissed her on the cheek.

"Thanks," Leeanne said.

Abby caught Harvey's gaze. "Jennifer just had a very convincing contraction."

"All right!" Harvey grinned at her. "Way to go, gorgeous." He came closer and put his arm across her shoulders. "When are the folks getting here?"

"Around five, I think," Leeanne said.

"You guys want coffee?" Abby turned and picked up the carafe.

77

"Sure," Harvey said.

"We've been going through the coffee really fast," Abby observed when she took the lid off the can. She started a fresh pot and wrote "coffee" on the shopping list.

They all sat down together. Eddie kept his place at Leeanne's side and his arm around her, but refrained from kissing her at the table.

Harvey didn't linger long over his coffee. Within ten minutes, he told Jennifer, "We need to get over to the police station—unless you need me. How are you feeling?"

She frowned. "No contractions since you walked in."

"I'll check in next door first. When we left, Tony had found a couple of finger bones. He and the forensics team will probably stay over there for a while. But Eddie and I had better go do some work, unless you tell me otherwise. And I mean, call me if you think things are happening." He looked at Abby.

"I'll keep an eye on things," Abby said.

"Thanks." Harvey leaned over to kiss Jennifer and then got up. "Ready, Ed?"

"Yeah." Eddie kissed Leeanne's cheek and winked at her. He followed Harvey out the door.

"So, how's it going with you two?" Abby cut herself a paper-thin sliver of cheesecake and flopped it onto her plate.

"Good," Leeanne said. "We talked a lot on the phone this week."

"Get any homework done?" Jennifer asked.

"Yeah, but. . ." Leeanne darted a glance at her then lowered her eyelashes. "We set a few rules. Limits."

Abby smiled. "Eddie's not used to boundaries."

"He realizes that. I . . . I told him things were moving kind of fast, and he said I was probably right. He apologized."

"Good," Jennifer said.

"But anyway, we really do want to wait and to keep our relationship . . ."

"Pure?" Jennifer said.

Leeanne nodded, flushing bright pink.

"I don't know," Abby said, readying a bit of cheesecake on her fork. "Nobody ever taught that boy to bide his time."

"That doesn't mean he can't learn," Jennifer said. "He's actually done pretty well for the best part of a year now."

Abby sighed. "You're right, he has. I'm actually proud of him."

"And I'm going to help him more than I have been," Leeanne said. "But he really doesn't want to wait until Christmas."

"So, he proposed?" Abby said.

"Not officially, but we talk about it. We have to."

"Sure." Jennifer smiled at her.

"You know what?" Abby said.

"What?" Jennifer asked.

Abby laid down her fork and pushed the plate away. "I shouldn't be eating this. I've got to fit into *your* wedding gown."

"You're wearing Jenn's gown?" Leeanne's voice rose almost to the point of giddiness.

"Yup, if I can fit into it. I was going to try it on today, but I decided to wait until Mom gets here."

"Can I wear it for my wedding?" Leeanne asked.

Jennifer burst out laughing. "All three of us, married in the same dress?"

"Wouldn't that be a hoot?" Abby said. "It's a great dress."

"And so economical," Jennifer added. "I'm sure Dad would like the idea."

"Yeah, but you got married in July, and Abby's is in June," Leeanne said. "If Dad has his way, mine will be a winter wedding."

"You might want something else," Jennifer said. "Let's wait and see, okay? But if it works out, I'm happy to let you use it."

"Thanks."

Jennifer smiled at her sisters. "It's exciting, knowing you're both getting married. And I love both your fiancés, although they're about as different as they could possibly be."

"Do you still pray for us?" Leeanne asked.

"Of course. Every day." Jennifer looked at Abby. "We pray for you and Peter, too. But for different things."

Abby laughed. "Oh, yeah. Our issues are somewhat different from Leeanne and Edouard's."

The doorbell rang, and Abby went to open it. A moment later, she called, "Jennifer?"

"Coming." Jennifer rose and walked out to the entry. Abby had the door open, and a heavyset woman of about fifty, with short, light brown hair, stood in the breezeway peering in.

"Hello," Jennifer said. "May I help you?"

"Thank you. I heard the police crime team was over here yesterday and today, and I had to come over. This young woman says you actually own that house over there?" The visitor pointed to the stone cottage.

"Yes," Jennifer said. "My husband and I just bought it."

"I see. Well, I wondered if the police—" Her mouth worked for a moment, and then she said, "I heard they found a body. Is that true?"

Chapter 9

"How may I help you, Mrs. Leonard?" Harvey asked, scanning the woman's face.

Jennifer had sent Leeanne dashing to the house at 135 to fetch one of the officers. She had caught Harvey having a last word with Tony before he went to the office, and he had come immediately to meet the woman.

"I heard there was a body in that house, and, well, my son. . .I thought it could be my son." Her voice broke.

"Your son?" Startled, Harvey looked her over again. "I'm sorry, ma'am, but I don't think that's possible. May I ask how old you are?"

"Forty-nine."

"Then it's definitely not possible."

Tears filled her eyes. "Are you sure?"

Something about her stirred Harvey. "Would you like to come in and sit down for a minute, Mrs. Leonard?" He glanced at Jennifer, who stood in the doorway to their home. "Jenny, I'd like to bring Mrs. Leonard into the study for a few minutes."

"Of course," Jennifer said, stepping back. "Could I fix you a cup of tea, ma'am? Or coffee?"

The woman sighed. "You don't need to, but a cup of tea would be nice."

Jennifer nodded and hurried away to the kitchen. Harvey ushered his guest in and took her into the study and closed both doors.

"Please sit down, Mrs. Leonard." He pulled out Jennifer's desk chair for her, then sat down in his own. "This investigation is just beginning, and we haven't released much to the public yet, but I assure you, any remains found on that property could not be those of a boy or a young man."

81

"I see." She sniffed.

Harvey glanced around, spotted a box of tissues on top of Jennifer's bookcase full of reference volumes, and set it on the desk beside Mrs. Leonard.

"How old was your son?"

"He was seventeen."

Harvey nodded as she dabbed at her eyes. "When you're ready, would you please tell me what made you think his remains might possibly be found in this area?"

She drew in a shaky breath and met his gaze. "Jacob disappeared nine years ago. The police said he ran away, but I've never been able to—" She shook her head vigorously. "Mr. Larson, we've never heard one word from him, and he was close with his brother. He wouldn't just up and take off like that."

"What do you think happened?" Harvey asked gently.

"I don't know. But he came over here after school that day see if Mr. Fuller was ready to have him start mowing the lawn. It was early—end of May—but it was warm that year. The grass was coming on."

Harvey's brain started clicking. "He had mowed Mr. Fuller's lawn before?"

"Yes, for two summers."

After a soft tap, Jennifer opened the door and came in with a tray. She set a mug of tea and a napkin before the visitor.

"Would you like cream or sugar?"

"No, thank you," Mrs. Leonard said.

Jennifer smiled at her, handed Harvey a mug of coffee, and went quietly back to the kitchen.

Harvey sat back in his chair, thinking. Mrs. Leonard took a cautious sip of the hot tea, then set down the mug.

"I'm sorry I bothered you, Mr. Larson. I just hoped. Whenever they find a body, I hope."

"I'm so sorry about your son," he said. "Can you tell me about Jacob?"

"He was a good boy. Oh, he had his moments, like all teenagers, but he never took drugs or anything like that. He played on the school's baseball team, and he was dating a girl. He'd been accepted at Bowdoin College for the fall."

"He was graduating that year?"

"Yes. He only had about two weeks of school left. He planned to go into engineering." She shook her head. "My husband and I kept hoping we'd hear from him, but there was no word."

"Your husband didn't come with you today."

"No. He passed away last year."

"I'm sorry. You reported Jacob missing nine years ago?"

"Yes."

"Tell me about that."

"He left to ask about the lawn and never came home."

Harvey frowned. "What did he say before he left?"

"I don't know. I was at work. But he'd told me he would go check on it after school. Usually he got a call from Mr. Fuller, but he hadn't heard from him, so Jacob said he'd come ask him if he should mow. And ... that's all I know. At suppertime he wasn't home. His brother hadn't seen him. We called his friends, but nobody knew where he was. This was the only place we knew of that he'd planned to go."

"Did you call Mr. Fuller?" Harvey asked.

"Yes, and my husband came over to see him in person. Mr. Fuller told him Jacob hadn't been there that day."

"He never showed up at the house."

"That's what he said." Mrs. Leonard took a sip of her tea. "We called the police around midnight. We were scared."

"Did an officer come to your house?"

"Yes. And we went in the next day and talked to a detective."

"Do you remember the detective's name?"

"Fowler, I think."

Harvey nodded. Arnie Fowler had retired in December, but he could get hold of him. Harvey had been in the regular detective squad at that time, but he didn't remember the case.

Mrs. Leonard took another drink and set down the mug. "Well, I guess I'm wasting your time. Thank you for listening."

"It's all right," Harvey said. "I'll read the report on your son's disappearance, but I can tell you for certain, the remains you'll read about in the paper tomorrow are not his."

She shot him a keen glance. "Is it a woman that was found?"

He hesitated. "This person was older than your Jacob."

She nodded and got slowly to her feet. He walked with her out to the driveway, where she'd left her car.

"Well, thanks. And please thank your wife for fixing me the tea."

"I will." Harvey gave her his business card. "If you have more questions, Mrs. Leonard, this is my number at the police station."

Her eyes flooded with tears again. "God bless you."

*****

Marilyn and George drove in just ahead of Harvey and Eddie that evening. The sisters had supper ready, and Harvey and Eddie helped bring in the Wainthrops' luggage and stow it in the guest room. They squeezed everybody into the kitchen and enjoyed a noisy meal together. Jennifer didn't eat much, but she sat with them, enjoying her family.

Jennifer felt Harvey's gaze on her often. Twice during the meal, she focused on something other than the conversation while she breathed slowly through a contraction. He noticed and checked his watch each time she took her final cleansing breath.

Peter and the boys came about six-thirty, and Abby took them and her parents into the living room, where she had laid out some books and games for Andy and Gary. Eddie and Leeanne helped Harvey clean up the kitchen, and Eddie mostly kept his hands off Leeanne.

Jennifer reached for a dirty plate and started to get up.

"No, no, gorgeous," Harvey said. "You sit still. Tonight, you do absolutely nothing."

"Oh, who made me queen?"

"I did." He stooped and kissed the top of her head. "You're having contractions, aren't you, Your Majesty?"

She smiled. "I'm trying to ignore them."

"I can tell. Let me know when the next one starts."

He was loading the silverware when she felt the strong tugging sensation again. "Got one."

Harvey shoved a handful of spoons at Leeanne and hurried across the kitchen. "Breathe, beautiful."

She nodded and let out her cleansing breath then started the rhythmic routine. When it was over, Harvey said. "What do you think?"

"About the same," Jennifer said.

"Okay." Harvey wrote "40 sec., 18 min." in his notebook.

When the dishes were done, Eddie said, "I'd like to take Leeanne out for a while. Is that okay, Harv?"

"Sure, if Leeanne wants to go."

"Where are we going?" she asked.

Eddie shrugged. "I don't know."

"Let's look in the paper," Leeanne said. "Maybe there's a good movie or something."

Eddie said, "Yeah, okay. You got a paper?"

"In the study," Harvey said.

Leeanne took Eddie into the next room to find the newspaper.

"Come on, Jenny, let's go see what Mom and Dad and Abby and Peter are cooking up for the wedding." Harvey put out his hand, and Jennifer grabbed it. He started to pull her up, but she sat back down and took a big breath.

"This is a big one, I think," she said.

"Really? Great!"

"Don't look so happy. It makes me want to slap you."

Harvey blinked at her. Jennifer had never spoken so sharply to him, even when he'd done a background check on her before they started dating.

He said nothing but started timing, and she used his eyes for a focal point.

"You're not supposed to look at me," he said softly.

"Tough." She kept staring at him and breathing. When it was done, she said, "Maybe I'll use the second stage breathing next time."

"Hey, great, maybe we're getting somewhere." He consulted the notebook. "Only fifteen minutes since the last one, and it lasted forty-five seconds."

Jennifer drew him to her. "I'm sorry."

"What for?"

"I barked at you."

He laughed. "One of those books of yours said women get that way sometimes during labor, but I didn't believe it. Not you, Jenny. But sure enough, you let loose on me. Still feel like slapping me?"

She hung her head, but couldn't keep from smiling. "Not really. I'll try to remember how nice you are to me next time."

She put out her hand and he tugged on it, giving her leverage to rise. They walked slowly through the sunroom to the living room. Gary and Andy had the Stratego game out, and Peter was telling George about his business.

"My father started it, but he had a heart attack ten years ago," Peter said. "I'd been working with him, but I didn't really have a lot of experience. My mother was doing the bookkeeping at the time. When my father died, we just muddled along and learned together."

"I'd say you've done very well," George said.

"Yes, God was gracious," Peter told him. "The business has grown. I have twelve full time employees now—salesmen, mechanics, the parts and shop staff. My mother retired herself last year, and I have a new bookkeeper."

Abby was leafing through a dress catalog, and she held it out to her mother.

"Jennifer would look fabulous in that."

"I thought you said she found something."

Abby shrugged. "She did find one that looks nice. Leeanne hasn't seen it yet."

Harvey and Jennifer sat down and joined the conversations by gender.

Abby showed Jennifer the bridesmaid's dress in the catalog. "Those would look good on you, Leeanne, and Peter's sister."

"Janelle is going to be a bridesmaid?" Jennifer asked.

"Yes, I thought I would ask her," said Abby. "I really like her, although I don't know her very well. She and Peter were the only children in their family, and they were very close when they were young."

"That's sweet," Jennifer said.

"Peter's asking Janelle's husband, Tom, to be his best man."

The talk went on, and the boys were getting tired of Stratego. After a few minutes Harvey got up. "Gary, we've got some other games in the study. Let me get you something else." He walked toward the doorway, and Jennifer heard him say, "I thought you two went someplace."

She felt another contraction coming and thrust the notebook into Abby's hands. "Time me."

Abby immediately went into coach mode. "Forty-five seconds," she said when it was done. "I wrote down the time. Sixteen minutes."

"You're not going to the hospital tonight, are you?" her mother asked.

"I don't know," Jennifer said. "I wish I was, but I don't want to get my hopes up."

Harvey came back into the room, handed Gary a box of dominoes and a Clue game, and said, "George, could I talk to you for a minute?"

"Where are Eddie and Leeanne going?" Jennifer asked.

"There's a concert downtown. They're going to go over for a while."

George and Harvey went into the sunroom, and Jennifer said, "Know what? I think I'll lie down for a while."

"Good idea," said her mother. "You holler if you need anything." She smiled and kissed Jennifer before she went.

Harvey and George were sitting in wicker chairs near the patio door, half turned away from her, when she walked through the sunroom.

"Well, George, I understand that," Harvey said, "but you've got to realize how these kids feel. They are, for all practical purposes, engaged now."

"They've discussed it?" George asked.

87

"Well, of course," Harvey said. "How could they not talk about a future together? They're in love."

Jennifer didn't mean to eavesdrop, but she stopped involuntarily when she realized he was talking to her father about Leeanne and Eddie's situation. That surprised her, since he had told her that it wouldn't hurt them to wait a while. Harvey glanced toward her and reached out with one hand, so she walked over to him.

"Well, yes, but is Eddie ready for marriage?" George asked. "Do you think he'll take care of Leeanne?"

"Yes, I do," Harvey said. "I really do."

"Leeanne is so young," George said. "She just turned twenty-one. Some people think that's mature, but I'll tell you, a lot of people would do better to wait a while."

Harvey said, "Well, yes, and they're willing to wait, but it's killing them. And it's driving Jenny and me nuts to watch them."

Jennifer ruffled his hair, and he looked up at her and smiled.

"Well, you told me you'd keep an eye on the situation," George began.

"Yes, sir. But they're adults. And Eddie's responsible. He's been saving his money, and he's shown leadership and dependability on the job. He's ready to commit, and I think Leeanne is, too. This is a lifetime thing for them, and it's not going to cool off." He put his arm around Jennifer's waist and held her there.

Her father sighed. "Abby just got engaged, and we've got to pay for that wedding in June . . . you think they can't wait until Christmas?"

Harvey considered. "Well, yes, sir, I think they could. Leeanne truly wants to please you in this. She's talked to us about it, and she knows it's God's way, to respect her parents' wishes. And Eddie will toe the line, too. They both want to please God in that. But it's hard when you're that age and you're in love. And it's not the way most people do things today."

George grunted. So far as Jennifer knew, the argument about pleasing God wouldn't cut any ice with her father, unless he'd changed his beliefs recently. Her mom seemed receptive, but her dad usually clammed up when the conversation turned spiritual.

Harvey put his hand up to Jennifer's hair. "From my own experience, I'd say your daughters are very loving women, and once they make up their mind about a man, that's it for life. I can't see much point in dragging the courtship out any longer than necessary."

This was the kind of thing that made Harvey Jennifer's hero. It wasn't easy to take on a father-in-law over a sensitive issue and swing him around to your viewpoint. Harvey knew that, but he kept at it. If her dad had really made a fuss, Harvey would let it go, rather than create bad feelings in the family, but he seemed to be making progress.

"All right, I'll talk it over with Marilyn."

Harvey smiled. "That's all I'm asking."

He and George stood up.

"I'm going to lie—" Jennifer grabbed Harvey's arm. "Where's the notebook?" She sucked in a deep breath.

"Sit down, Jenny. Breathe."

She sank onto the chair he'd vacated and started the slow breathing, then switched to the faster pattern.

"You're doing good," Harvey said. "Thirty seconds." When it was over, he said, "Where *is* the notebook?"

"I think Abby's got it."

He went to the living room and came back with it. "Only twelve minutes between that one and the last one. You want to lie down?"

"I don't know. Do you think it's real?"

"I never saw anything so realistic."

"Stay with me," she begged.

"You got it." He went with her into the bedroom and sat down on the edge of the bed when she lay down. She couldn't blot her father's expression from her mind—somewhere between pride and terror. She started laughing.

"What's so funny?" Harvey asked.

"If I have the baby tonight, my dad will have fits."

"He's got six kids," said Harvey. "It shouldn't bother him."

"Oh yeah? I remember when Randy was born. Dad was a basket case."

"Did he go in the delivery room?"

"Are you kidding? He was a waiting room pacer."

"He missed out on a lot." Harvey stroked her hair back from her forehead.

"Maybe I should braid my hair," Jennifer said.

Harvey got up and retrieved her brush from the dressing table.

"Feel like sitting up?" he asked.

She rolled over and sat up slowly, and he started brushing her hair for her. The slow, gentle strokes soothed her. When he'd brushed it all smooth, she quickly made her Rapunzel braid, and he brought her a covered elastic. As she twisted it around the end of her plait, the next contraction started.

He coached her through it, then said, "Lie down for a bit, baby. That was ten minutes. If the next one's that close, I'm calling Margaret."

"We're supposed to call the hospital, and they call Margaret."

"Tough. I'm calling Margaret."

Jennifer smiled. Margaret would probably give him a gold star.

*****

An hour later, they decided they were going to the hospital. Marilyn and Abby had been fussing around the house. Marilyn had inspected the nursery upstairs and the gifts from the baby shower the church ladies had thrown Jennifer a few weeks before. She and George had bought a cradle Connor would use for the first few weeks, and that was in Jennifer and Harvey's bedroom. Harvey had assembled a new crib in the nursery upstairs. Everything was ready.

Abby put Jennifer's Lamaze bag and suitcase in the Explorer. Jennifer hadn't eaten much at supper, and Abby asked if she wanted any water or ice, but Jennifer turned her down. Realizing the family took her seriously brought on a wave of excitement. The contractions steadily grew more powerful.

90

"I really think tonight's the night, Abs."

Abby squeezed her shoulders. "Harvey's so happy he can't sit still. He's telling Peter. I think Peter's going to take the boys home, so I can go to the hospital with you. Do you mind if I ride along?"

"Not at all. They'll let you in the delivery room, even if you're not working tonight, won't they?"

"They'll let in anyone you say to let in."

That was a little disconcerting. "I just want you and Harvey and Margaret."

"Then that's who'll be in there," Abby said. "And there'll probably be one or two more nurses. There's always at least one nurse for the mother and one for the baby."

"You'll be my nurse, won't you?"

"I sure will."

Abby called Harvey in eight minutes after the previous contraction, and he was ready when the next one hit. After that one, he called Margaret and told her they'd be heading out soon.

"You ready to go, gorgeous?" he asked when he'd finished the call.

"Let's wait 'til after one more."

"Eddie and Leeanne are back. Abby called and told them what's going on." Harvey put his arms around her and managed to sit still for a few more minutes. The next contraction was more than a minute long, just eight minutes since the last one.

"Let's go," he said.

Jennifer stood up, and he helped her put on her sweater, then put his arm around her. They walked slowly out to the sunroom. George stood in the corner by the patio door with Eddie.

Eddie was saying quietly, "Yes, sir, I think it would. You have my word, sir."

"Well, I want things to go smoothly for you kids. It's not that I don't think you can handle it. It's just, well, Leeanne's very young, you know."

"Yes, sir. Thank you for your trust. I'll do everything I can to make sure you're not sorry."

91

It was painful just to listen to him. They went on into the kitchen. Leeanne was sitting at the table, chewing her knuckles. She looked anxiously from Jennifer to Harvey, then toward the sunroom door.

"Are you going to the hospital?"

"Yup," said Harvey.

"What does Daddy want with Eddie?" Leeanne eyes were wide.

"I think they are discussing your future," Harvey said.

"But they already did that."

"Sometimes you have to regroup," Jennifer said gently.

Leeanne looked as if she would cry. "He's not—I mean, he said the end of the school year. He's not going to change that is he? Eddie was willing to do what he wanted. Is he mad at Eddie? What did you guys tell him, anyway?"

Jennifer went to her and put her arms around her. "It's okay. Nobody's mad at anybody. And if you're truly invested in this, maybe you should be in there telling that to Dad, instead of letting Eddie take the heat alone."

Leeanne stared at her.

"We'd better get going, gorgeous," said Harvey.

"Hang on." Jennifer sat down in a chair.

"Hey, it's not time yet," Harvey protested, looking at his watch.

She breathed with it anyway.

Eddie came slowly into the kitchen and glanced quickly at Harvey, then at Leeanne and Jennifer.

"So?" Harvey asked.

"I can't believe it," Eddie said. "Whatever you said to him, thanks, Harv."

"No problem. Just keep your end of the bargain."

"I will." He looked at Leeanne. "Your dad's cool with it. He just said to give them a little time to recover after Abby's wedding."

Leeanne launched out of her chair, into his arms.

Jennifer took her final cleansing breath, and Harvey pulled her up out of the chair. "Let's go. Now."

Abby came bustling into the kitchen. "Are we ready to go?"

"Past ready, I think," said Harvey. "Five minutes between the last two."

"Okay, I'll drive and you can coach." Abby strode past them toward the garage.

Harvey walked with Jennifer in slow motion. Her parents, Leeanne, and Eddie came and called goodbye. Jennifer was already breathing with the next pain.

"So Dad gave his blessing for an immediate engagement?" she asked when she could think straight again.

"Apparently so." Harvey found the end of her seat belt and buckled it around her.

"Fantastic." Jennifer leaned against him. "Case closed, Captain."

"All done but the paperwork," he agreed.

*****

"He's absolutely beautiful," Margaret declared as Harvey cuddled Connor against his chest.

Harvey felt he was truly in his element. He had done his best to be Jennifer's mainstay all the way through, had not fainted or even gotten dizzy, had said what she seemed to consider were all the right things at the right times, and had remembered to coach aggressively when she started to lose it.

His reward was a euphoria beyond anything he had expected. After he cut the cord and Jennifer held the baby for a few minutes, Harvey laughed and cried at the same time, cradling his son tenderly. Abby snapped pictures of Harvey and Connor, Jennifer and Connor, Harvey and Jennifer and Connor, Harvey and Margaret and Connor. . .

"Can I come in?" Carl Turner called from the doorway.

"Do you want him in here?" Margaret asked, throwing Jennifer an anxious glance.

Jennifer hesitated. They were nearly finished in the delivery room. She had nursed Connor for the prescribed two minutes on each side, and the placenta was history.

"Just cover me up," she said.

Harvey couldn't have been prouder of her. He smiled at her and leaned over to tuck the sheet in securely around her. Carl was feeling left out, and she didn't want to deprive him of sharing their joy during the first few minutes of their son's life. Harvey knew Carl, wearing green scrubs, had not been on Jennifer's delivery room guest list. But he was Harvey's friend, and he'd been feeling rejected lately.

"Come on in," Harvey called while Abby and Margaret adjusted the drapes over Jennifer's legs.

"Hey, he's a beaut," Carl said, approaching Harvey.

Harvey held the baby out so Carl could see him better. Carl touched Connor's fuzzy hair with his fingertips. Connor's tiny hands and feet flailed, the wrist and ankle identification bands sliding up and down.

"He's got your eyes, Harv," Carl said.

"How can you tell?" Harvey asked. "Jenny and I both have blue eyes."

"No, his are big like yours and brighter blue than Jennifer's."

"You wanna hold him?" Harvey asked.

"Sure."

Jennifer watched apprehensively as Carl took Connor and smiled at him. "Hey, fella." He turned toward his wife. "Margaret, look. Isn't that precious?"

Margaret went over to stand beside him and leaned her head against Carl's arm.

"You're so handsome," she said in baby talk to Connor.

Carl said quietly, "We really gotta get one of these, honey."

Connor started a little rattle that became a wail.

"Guess you'd better take him, Daddy." Carl handed him back to Harvey.

Harvey held Connor's head up to his cheek, then cuddled him against his shoulder, and Connor's cry settled to a whimper, then stopped. Joy shot through Harvey. He'd never felt so competent. He sat down on the stool next to Jennifer and leaned over to kiss her, for the thousandth time that night.

"He's perfect," he whispered. "So are you."

Chapter 10

Abby took Jennifer to her hospital room while Connor's nurses bathed and weighed him and put a tiny T-shirt and a disposable diaper on him. Harvey stood in the hallway smiling, watching them through the nursery windows. They wrapped Connor in a blanket and put a soft little cap on his head, then put him in the small, clear plastic crib on wheels and brought him out to his father. Harvey wheeled him to Jennifer's room and very proudly lifted him out of the crib and carried him to her.

"You take him," he said, his voice cracking. "I'm going to call the folks."

Jennifer lay looking at their beautiful little son while Harvey called the house to inform her parents, Leeanne, and Eddie, who had stayed there waiting for news.

It was nearly midnight, so they decided to wait and tell the extended family and their friends the next morning. Harvey pulled out his notebook and made a list: his two sisters, Randy and Travis at the pastor's in Skowhegan, Grandpa Wainthrop, Beth and Jeff, the Rowlands, Bud and Janice, Mike and Sharon, Nate, Tony, Jimmy. There was a longer list in Jennifer's suitcase of people they would send printed announcements.

Harvey put the phone away and sat down next to her.

"Can we pray?" Jennifer asked. "I've been thanking God, but ..."

"Yeah, let's do that together." Harvey put his arms around them and offered thanks for his family.

"Do you want to sleep now?" he asked, stroking her forehead and looking at Connor.

"I couldn't sleep now," she said.

"You worked awfully hard."

"I know, but I'm so wound up. It was fun, wasn't it?"

"Fun?" He stared at her skeptically.

"Carl's right. Connor's eyes are like yours."

"You call what you just went through fun?"

"Well, exciting," Jennifer said. "To know a new life was beginning. I know he's been alive for nine months, but it's just…almost overwhelming." Tears rolled down her cheeks.

Harvey nodded and reached out to touch Connor's cheek. "He's so soft."

He stayed until 2 a.m., holding the baby most of the time, and then she sent him to return Connor to the nursery and go home, with orders to sleep. He hated to leave the hospital, but sleep actually sounded pretty good.

*****

Jennifer lay awake a long time, then slept a little. The nurse brought Connor back, screaming, and she fed him and talked to God in the quiet early hours.

Harvey returned at nine in the morning. He looked as though he'd had barely enough sleep, but he couldn't stop smiling. Jennifer was feeding Connor when he arrived, and he just beamed.

"I'm so proud of you, Jenny." He pulled his chair up close beside them and kissed her, then kissed the top of Connor's head. "You'll have lots of company after lunch. I hope you're not too tired."

"I'll nap a little if I can," she said. The adrenaline had dissipated, and the long night was beginning to catch up with her.

Margaret knocked softly and stuck her head around the doorjamb. She broke into a huge smile when she saw them.

"May I come in?"

"Of course," Jennifer said.

Margaret walked to the foot of the bed. "Do you have your camera?" she asked Harvey. "This is really a picture of the ideal family."

Harvey gave her his phone. She snapped the photo, then Jennifer handed the baby to Harvey, and Margaret got down to business.

"You look pretty good," she said. "Take it easy today, and we'll send you home tomorrow."

"I don't want to spend the whole weekend here," Jennifer said. "My parents are down from Skowhegan, and Leeanne is here. We were going to show them Jeff and Beth's house today and plan Abby's wedding. And I want to take Connor to church tomorrow."

"Slow down, Jenny," said Harvey. "You can't do all that right now. I left the key with Abby, and she and Beth will show off the house. I told them they can go over this morning, as long as they don't go in the back yard or the basement."

"I want to keep you here at least twenty-four hours," Margaret said.

Jennifer gazed up at her. "Some women go home the same day."

"Some women have their babies at home, too," Margaret countered. "You had a hard time early in the pregnancy, and I want to make sure you're on track before I release you."

"Listen to Margaret," Harvey said. "I'll come for you tomorrow. If you feel up to it, we'll take him to church tomorrow night."

Margaret met his gaze. "Come after lunch."

"I want to go home today," Jennifer said feebly, knowing it was no use.

While Harvey cuddled the baby in between feedings that morning, she napped. He stayed all day and gave everyone who came in the grand tour. They had to send Connor back to the nursery when there was company in the room, and Harvey walked down the hall with each visitor and pointed out the finest specimen of boyhood in the nursery.

Her parents came first, with Leeanne and Eddie, and before they left Mike and Sharon walked in. Leeanne brought them that morning's *Press Herald* and pointed out Ryan's article on page three of the local section: *Skeleton discovered in cellar.*

"If I'd done the story, I'd have written a front-page job," she said.

Pastor and Mary Rowland were next, and they had a nice visit, but Harvey fidgeted. Then Beth came in. Jeff escaped the fire station on his supper hour, and after he left, Jennifer managed to have the baby in the room for an hour and feed him again. When Nate and Jackie Miller showed up, teddy bear in hand, Harvey was almost, but not quite, irritated because Connor had to go back to the nursery. He went into the Proud Papa mode again and gave them the nursery tour. Jack and Rachel Stewart were next, and Peter and Abby came in afterward, bringing a tough little overalls outfit for the tough little guy. Tony Winfield came with a stuffed penguin, and Jimmy and Shelly Cook brought a baby book.

They could hear Connor screaming all the way down the hallway as the nurse rolled his crib toward Jennifer's room.

"Sorry, but Master Larson is hungry," she said. "The visitors will have to clear out."

Jennifer was glad, as she was more than ready to hold her baby again, and Harvey looked relieved, but was gracious in saying goodbye to the stragglers.

Jennifer settled down with Connor in her arms, and Harvey came and sat on the bed with his arm around her.

Fifteen minutes later, there was a soft knock on the door. Harvey opened it and found retired detective Arnie Fowler in the hallway carrying a bouquet of flowers. He explained to Arnie that Jennifer had the baby in the room and stepped out into the hall with him for a few minutes. A passing nurse offered to find a vase for the flowers.

Mayor Jill Weymouth arrived, and Harvey asked Jennifer if he could just take Connor to the door for a second so Jill and Arnie could see him. As she handed him over, she almost said, "Don't let anyone breathe on him," but restrained herself.

Jill stepped to the doorway and waved. "Hi, Jennifer! The captain's son is so beautiful! You did a great job." She handed Harvey a package. "'Bye, now. Congratulations!"

Arnie peeked in for a second and waved.

"Thanks," Jennifer called. She opened the package after the mayor and Arnie were gone, while Harvey sat contentedly patting Connor's back for a burp. In the box was a silver-plated piggy bank.

Jennifer looked the pig over and smiled. "Very appropriate for *your* son."

"Aw, Jill likes you, too," Harvey said.

"Only because I married you." Jennifer laughed and set the piggy bank aside. "Not every new baby gets a visit from the mayor."

"That's right. We'll tell him about this years from now."

At ten o'clock, Jennifer caressed Connor one last time before sending him to the nursery.

"I'll come back in the morning," Harvey said.

"Go to church and come after." Jennifer had accepted Margaret's verdict, and she could see the wisdom of a few more hours of rest before she went home into the maelstrom.

"I could come before, too."

"No, sleep late and go to church with the family. Connor and I will be ready when you get here."

"You might have gotten more rest at home." Harvey bent down and kissed her, then sat down on the bed and kissed her again. "Jenny, I'm so happy."

"I know." She leaned against him, with the baby cuddled between them. "This has been a really fantastic day."

They prayed together, and he took Connor and gently laid him in the crib, picked up his jacket and went down the hall. She could hear the wheels rolling all the way down to the nursery, but she was asleep before the elevator opened for Harvey.

*****

Jeff and Beth were at the house when they arrived home with the baby on Sunday afternoon. Abby, Peter, Gary, Andy, Marilyn, and George were also on hand, eagerly awaiting their arrival. Leeanne and Eddie had gone to the hospital with Harvey, and Leeanne proudly carried Connor inside.

"The sweetest nephew in the world," she declared.

Harvey installed Jennifer in their bed.

"I don't need to be in bed," she said.

"Humor me," said the father of her child.

So she let herself be pampered. Connor made the rounds of the aunts, grandparents, uncle, and cousins- and uncles-to-be. When he began to whimper, Beth brought him to Jennifer for his feeding.

"Stay here and talk to me," Jennifer said, and Beth pulled up a chair. "What did I miss? Any word on the skeleton?"

"They expect a complete forensics report on Mr. Bones tomorrow," Beth said.

"Harvey said they found a button," Jennifer recalled.

"Several buttons, actually, and some shreds of fabric."

"Fabric? It didn't all rot?"

"Apparently not." Beth seemed to have gotten over her squeamishness where the skeleton was concerned. "There were some small pieces underneath the bones, with the buttons, and a wedding ring."

"A wedding ring!"

"Yes, so Harvey's thinking he wasn't a robbery victim."

"Well, maybe they just couldn't get his ring off," Jennifer said.

"What's that?" Harvey came into the bedroom.

"I was just telling Jennifer about the fabric shreds and the ring they found next door."

"Yes, very interesting," Harvey said. "Tony Winfield put in some time yesterday. He called me this morning. Seems there was a uniform buried with the corpse."

"Buried with it?" Jennifer asked. "Not on it?"

"That's what we're thinking at the moment. The fabric and buttons were below the bones."

"The buttons might have fallen down through," she mused.

"Yes, but there weren't any fibers of the fabric found above the bones."

"It rotted away," Beth said.

"And those concrete men disturbed the site," Jennifer reminded them.

"Yes," said Harvey. "I've got to go over it all again, but I don't think Mr. Bones was wearing the uniform. For one thing, the biggest piece of fabric was on top of a button. And the ring.

102

That's a funny thing. It was underneath everything, as if it had been tossed in the hole, then the uniform was put in, and the body was heaved in on top."

"Heaved in?" Beth looked a little queasy.

"Well, as near as I can tell from what Rudy Thomas told me and forensics found, the body was in the grave face down."

"Yuck," Beth said.

"So the buttons would be on the bottom," Jennifer persisted.

"Good thinking, gorgeous, but the ones they dug out last, that hadn't been disturbed yet, were face up. If the corpse was wearing the uniform, they'd have been face down. I think the uniform jacket was folded and laid in the hole first."

It didn't add up. "Throw a ring in the hole, fold a coat carefully and lay it in, then heave in a body?" Jennifer asked skeptically.

Harvey shrugged.

"What was the ring like?" she asked.

"A plain gold wedding ring. A man's, size ten. Eighteen carat gold, five millimeters wide."

"That's it?" she asked, disappointed.

Harvey smiled. "No. That's not it."

"Something inside?" she asked hopefully.

He smiled broader. "I wish I had you in my unit, gorgeous."

"No, you don't," she said. "I'm right where you want me."

"As usual, you got that right." He'd said many times that one of his greatest blessings was coming home to find Jennifer waiting for him. He went around the bed and climbed onto it, moving over beside her. "There were initials engraved inside."

"Which were?"

"DS-ML," he replied.

Jennifer frowned. "Any date?"

"We should be so lucky." He edged closer and put his arm around her.

"Uh-uh," she said.

"Right. No such thing as luck. Well, God didn't see fit to give us that little clue. Too bad. If we had a wedding date, it would be easy, wouldn't it?"

She leaned back against his shoulder. "So where do you go from here?"

"Tomorrow Eddie and Tony will do a lot of legwork. Trying to trace the ring, of course, and trying to have the uniform identified."

"You're sure it was a uniform, not just a military-type jacket or something?" asked Beth.

"That part we're sure of. It was a Navy-issue uniform jacket. The fabric isn't used anymore, so we might get an approximate date from that. Also, the buttons were manufactured by a particular company for the U.S. Navy for a fourteen-year period. They're large ones, three fourths of an inch diameter, used on coats. A Navy representative has promised us a more complete report tomorrow."

"Someone could have bought the coat at a surplus store," Jennifer said. "If it had been a complete uniform, you'd have found more buttons, and a zipper at least."

"Maybe not, on a sailor's uniform," Harvey said. "Some of their blouses didn't have buttons. Dress uniforms would."

"That's pretty interesting," said Beth.

Jennifer cocked her head to one side. "Still, shouldn't Mr. Bones have been wearing something? Most men's bodies would come complete with a zipper and shoes and maybe some more buttons, even if all the cloth disintegrated."

"I have no explanation for that," Harvey said. "Now, if you really want to go to church tonight, I prescribe a nap."

*****

George and Marilyn left late in the afternoon, after Marilyn had a chance to hold her first grandchild for a while. George put a hundred dollars in Connor's silver piggy bank.

"You open a savings account for him this week."

"Daddy, you don't have to do so much," Jennifer said. "You've got Abby's wedding—"

"Hush, daughter."

She hushed.

Her mother promised to come back soon. She would have liked to stay, but George definitely wanted her to go home with him. Abby had gone to work, and Peter and his boys had gone home. Leeanne decided to stay the night and go back to campus in the morning. That made Eddie happy.

"So tell me about you guys," Jennifer demanded when her parents were gone. The four of them sat in the living room, and Harvey had built a fire in the fireplace.

Leeanne smiled radiantly and looked at Eddie.

Eddie got very sober. "Well, we're getting married."

"I *know* that," Jennifer said. "When?"

He smiled then and reached for Leeanne's hand. "Middle of August. I'm taking my vacation then, okay, Harv?"

"Of course," Harvey said. "Will you be done with your internship, Leeanne?"

"Yes. We'll take two weeks off before I start classes again."

Harvey nodded. "Sounds like a plan."

"Thanks for talking to Daddy," Leeanne said.

"My pleasure. Or at least, I'm pleased now. It was awkward, but hey."

"You don't have your ring yet," Jennifer observed.

"It happened so fast," Eddie said. "My Mémé asked Leeanne if she would like to wear her diamond."

"And I would." Leeanne snuggled against Eddie's side. "But her setting was really old-fashioned, and the band had worn thin. So we're having the stone reset."

"That's great." Jennifer was pleased that Leeanne was honoring Eddie's grandmother in that way.

"Well, with the baby and the body next door, we've been busy," Eddie said. "I dropped the ring off at the jewelry store, and we'll pick it up next week."

"Oh, good, you're coming back down," Jennifer said eagerly to Leeanne.

"No, I'm going to Skowhegan," said Eddie.

"Oh." Jennifer was a little disappointed.

105

"Of course, the baby and the murder are here," Leeanne said.

"Do you *want* to come down again?" Eddie asked.

Leeanne shrugged. "I'll talk to Mom. If she and Dad won't be too disappointed, I'd like to be where the action is."

They all laughed.

"Don't neglect your studies," Harvey said.

Leeanne met his gaze. "I won't. Promise."

"I think Mom would like to be down here, too," Jennifer said. "Maybe you could both come back. She was pretty impressed with her grandson."

"She's besotted. How could she not be?" Leeanne reached for Connor, and he was passed around again.

*****

At church that night, Connor was the star attraction. Harvey held him all through the service, refusing to give him up to the church ladies and teen-aged girls who offered to hold him.

Ruthann Bradley, Beth's sister-in-law, was one of the privileged few he surrendered his son to after the service ended. Jennifer told Ruthann to bring her two little ones over to the house soon.

"How's it going with Rick's job?" she asked.

Ruthann frowned. "Not so good." Rick drove a bulldozer for a private contractor, but the owner had been dealing with a severe medical problem and was thinking about selling his business. So far, his foreman was carrying on with the jobs already scheduled, but the owner was not lining up any new work.

"The construction season's just starting, but Rick's afraid he'll be out of work soon," Ruthann said.

Harvey and Rick had quite a discussion about it, and Harvey asked if the boss was ready to sell the business.

"Are you thinking what I'm thinking?" Jennifer asked.

Harvey shrugged. "I don't think I could just buy the business. The house took about half our stash. But there might be a way. . ."

"I think he's got a buyer, if he decides to go through with it," Rick said. "But if this guy buys him out, he'll probably absorb the equipment into the business he has now. I'm not sure he'd need all of the crew."

"Keep me posted," said Harvey.

Rick and Ruthann carried Jeff and Beth off to their house for dessert. Harvey and Jennifer packed up Connor, Leeanne, and Eddie, and went home.

Jennifer was exhausted, and Harvey put her back to bed. She curled up with Connor beside her.

"Half an hour," she heard Harvey say to Eddie. "We've got a huge amount of work to do tomorrow, and I expect you to be on time to run."

"Right, six o'clock," Eddie said. "Jeff should be here, too."

"Okay, well you two can say your goodbyes. Just tell me when you're leaving, so I can lock up."

Harvey came into the bedroom and sighed with contentment as he stretched out on the quilt beside Jennifer.

"Little pig," he said, as Connor gulped noisily. He touched the baby's hand, and Connor curled his fist around Harvey's finger. "This is what I've always wanted," Harvey said softly. "My own family in our own home. But I don't deserve any of it." He reached for the prayer list notebook and his Bible.

Jennifer was exhausted and a little apprehensive, but her joy outweighed her concern about the body found next door.

*****

Eddie sat down beside Leeanne on the couch and pulled her toward him. "*Viens, ma chérie.*"

She settled into his embrace, and he kissed her, savoring her scent and her warm lips. Leeanne slipped her hands up to the back of his neck and kissed him back. August. Four months, he thought. That's not so long.

His phone rang, and he pulled away from her, disgruntled. Leeanne was leaving in the morning, and he wanted to get in a few more kisses.

"Who calls you this late?" Leeanne asked as he eased the phone from his pocket.

"Nobody, unless a case is breaking." He looked at the screen and froze.

Chapter 11

"What is it?" Leeanne asked.

"It's—Can you excuse me a second?"

"Of course."

She moved away from him, and Eddie rose and walked out to the kitchen. He pressed the talk button. "Yeah?"

"Eddie?" Sarah's voice was unnaturally high.

"It's me. What's going on?"

"I need you."

"Something happen?" he asked warily.

"My sister—please, Eddie. I wouldn't ask you if it wasn't critical." Her panic was unmistakable.

"Okay. I'll be there. Your mom's house?"

"No, my father's."

He frowned. "I've never been there."

She rattled off an address. "Hurry."

"You there?"

She'd hung up.

Eddie strode back to the living room. "I'm sorry, *mignon*. I've got to go."

"Do you need Harvey?" Leeanne stood, her brown eyes troubled.

"No, it's—I can handle it. But tell him I'm leaving. Will you be here in the morning?"

"Yeah. I'll run with you guys if I can."

"Okay." He kissed her perfunctorily and hurried to the door, snagging his jacket on the way out.

It took him almost fifteen minutes to drive to Mr. Benoit's neighborhood and locate the house. Sarah's car was in the driveway. He parked at the curb and ran up to the door. As soon as he pushed the bell, Sarah flung the door open.

"What happened?" he asked.

"Nicole—in here." She grabbed his arm and dragged him into the house. Eddie didn't have time to look around, but he had an impression of a small, crowded living room, none too neat. Sarah propelled him down the short hallway and into a bedroom.

Sarah's sister lay curled on her bed. Slashes on her face trickled blood, and her shirt was dark with it. The stain soaked the chenille bedspread under her.

Eddie started toward Nicole, but shifted direction when he spotted a man's feet sticking out from behind the bed's footboard.

"Good night, Sarah! Did you call an ambulance?" He pulled out his phone.

"No. Eddie, she clobbered him, but good. I thought maybe we could drive him to the hospital."

"You're nuts!" He knelt by the sprawled body and put his fingers to the man's neck. A faint, thready pulse rewarded him, but blood was soaking into the carpet beneath his head.

Eddie stared up at Sarah in disbelief. "Did you want him to just bleed out? Sarah, you're a police officer. What is wrong with you?" He hit his speed dial for the com center. He could only see one good thing about the situation: the man bleeding all over the rug was not Sarah's father.

"No, don't—"

"Hi, Tammy. This is Detective Thibodeau. I need an ambulance—no, make that two—at this address. And no sirens."

Sarah gave up and strode to the bed, scowling. When Eddie finished the call, she was bending over her sister.

"Okay, honey, hang on. Eddie thinks we need an ambulance for you."

"No." Nicole's voice was weak but desperate.

Eddie said, "Get me some towels or something. Sarah, come on! You took the first aid refresher. Move it!"

Sarah stared at him for a moment and swallowed hard, then dashed out of the room. He noted a damp, bloody cloth on the nightstand. Apparently she had at least tried to tend Nicole's wounds.

110

She returned with an armful of ragged towels and face cloths. "That's the best I can do."

Eddie took them. He'd determined that the man's skull was fractured and didn't want to use much pressure, but he gently eased a towel under his head.

"How's your sister?"

"Not good."

"How bad is she hurt?"

Sarah hesitated. "He beat her up pretty bad."

"Those look like cuts and stab wounds."

"Yeah."

"Where's the knife?"

Sarah just looked at him.

Eddie swore. "Don't tell me you ditched it. Sarah, what are you thinking?"

"I don't know, I don't know. Nicole didn't want anyone to know. Eddie, she's pregnant. He wanted to—" She stopped and stared at him bleakly.

"He was trying to make her miscarry?"

Sarah nodded.

Eddie exhaled in exasperation and looked at the ceiling. "Last I knew, you and Nicole weren't speaking."

"Yeah, we're not. But. . . she's my sister, Eddie. She called me."

He got out his phone again.

"Who are you calling?" Sarah asked. "Harvey?"

"No. Jennifer just had her baby." The dispatcher spoke in his ear. "Hey, Tammy, it's Eddie again. I need some on-duty officers here. If you want to call the detective sergeant, that's okay, too."

"What have you got, Eddie?"

"It's a domestic, but it's messy, and one of our patrol officers' family is involved."

When he'd given a few more details, he signed off. Sarah was sitting on the edge of the bed, holding her sister's hand and sobbing. Nicole's eyes were closed, but she gripped Sarah's hand so tightly that her fingers were white.

"I'm going to get suspended, aren't I?" Sarah choked out.

"Maybe. Definitely, if it gets out that you tried to cover it up. Where's the knife?"

"I kicked it under the bed."

Eddie went to his knees and found it, amid boxes and dust kitties. He didn't touch it.

"Okay, I see it. Now, what did she hit him with?"

"A flashlight she had in her nightstand." Sarah stood slowly. "I hid it out back."

"Like you think our guys wouldn't find it?"

She sighed. "I dropped it over the fence into the next yard."

Eddie shook his head. "Brilliant."

"I thought I could get him out of the house and he wouldn't tell anyone."

"Sarah, he may die. Do you understand? Now, can you get that flashlight back in less than two minutes?"

"Maybe."

"Go." He thought he heard a siren approaching, despite his request. He hadn't told Tammy to relay the no-sirens request to the patrol officers.

Sarah took a deep breath and ran.

Two ambulances arrived with lights flashing. Eddie walked out to meet them and heard a faint siren approaching.

Jeff Wainthrop and Mark Johnson climbed out of the first ambulance with their gear. Liam O'Neill and a female EMT Eddie didn't know came from the second one.

"Hey," Eddie said. "We got two victims inside. A female about twenty-two years old. She was beaten and stabbed. She's Officer Benoit's sister. And she's pregnant. The male is older, maybe thirty, and he's got a severe head wound." He walked with them as he talked, leading them into the house and back to the bedroom.

Nicole opened her eyes. Terror flashed through them, and she struggled to sit up but sank back on the bloody pillow.

"Easy," the female EMT said, hurrying toward her. "I'm Sandy. Let me take a look at you."

"Her name's Nicole," Eddie said.

Jeff and Mark took over care for the unconscious man, and Liam assisted Sandy. Eddie stood back near the door. A moment later, Sarah came in behind him, carrying an item wrapped in a towel.

"That it?" Eddie asked, nodding toward her bundle.

"Yeah."

"Where did you pick it up?"

"Beside him."

Eddie frowned. "Okay, you moved it to make sure he wouldn't use it again, right?"

Sarah drew in a shaky breath. "Right."

He stooped and whispered. "Help me out here. Is it going to have dirt and crud all over it?"

"No. I wrapped it up before I tossed. I figured I'd get it later and get rid of it permanently, but I didn't want it on the premises in case. . ."

"Yeah, well I'll forget you just said that. You picked it up and wrapped it and set it aside to make sure he couldn't reach it while you helped Nicole. Right?" Eddie stared into Sarah's huge brown eyes. "Right?"

She nodded.

Eddie narrowed his gaze and bent close again. "It was Nicole who hit him, right?"

"Yes. She called me afterward."

"Okay." He took the bundle carefully. He could feel the long, heavy flashlight through the folds of the blue bath towel. Sarah knew better than to do something that foolish. But was he just as bad, encouraging her to bend the truth?

Mark was on his mic, relaying the male patient's vital signs to someone in the hospital ER when Bob Marshall and two uniformed officers walked in.

"Hey, Eddie, Sarah. What have we got?"

Eddie sighed. "Sarah's sister was attacked by her—what is he? Her boyfriend?"

"Was," Sarah said in a tight voice. "I don't think he will be after this."

"Why don't you come out into the other room and talk to me?" Bob said.

"There's a flashlight in that towel on the bureau," Eddie said, nodding toward Nicole's dresser. "That's what she hit him with. Sarah moved it because. . ." He couldn't say it.

"I was afraid he'd try to use it on me," she said. "His knife is under the bed. I kicked it away from his hand."

"Okay." Bob looked at one of the patrolmen. "Eric, you keep an eye on things. Don't move anything until I see it all. Come on out here, Sarah."

Eddie's phone vibrated, and he took it out. Leeanne had texted him. *R u ok?* He'd hoped she would be asleep by now. He walked slowly out into the living room.

"I called Eddie because—because I knew he'd come," Sarah was saying. "I panicked a little, I think. I mean, she's my sister. I just wanted to help her."

"Who called 911?" Bob asked.

She hesitated. "Eddie did."

Eddie nodded. No use lying about that, since the dispatcher would set the detective straight. He was glad Sarah had told the truth.

"What's the man's name?" Bob asked.

"Donnie something, I don't know."

"Does he live here?"

"No. My father does. It's his house. Nicole lives with our dad."

"Where's your father now?"

"I don't know." Tears streamed down Sarah's cheeks.

Eddie stepped over and handed her his clean handkerchief. "I'm going to make a phone call, but I'll be right outside. I'll be back in a couple of minutes."

She nodded, and Eddie went out. The house had a small front porch and he leaned against the outside wall for a moment, breathing slowly. When he felt clearheaded, he walked down the driveway and called Leeanne.

"Eddie?"

"Yeah, it's me."

"I'm sorry. I didn't want to bother you if—"

"It's okay. A friend needed some help, and I did what I had to."

"What was that?" Leeanne asked.

"I called the EMTs and. . .Hey, I'll come in the morning and tell you about it, okay? I need to stick around for a while here until the emergency personnel are done. I may have to take my friend to the hospital. Someone in her family's hurt."

"Okay," she said. "I love you, Eddie."

"I love you, too. Goodnight."

Jeff and Mark came out of the house with the man on a wheeled stretcher. Eddie walked over and fell in stride with Jeff.

"Think he'll pull though?"

"I dunno," Jeff said. "Somebody whacked him hard. I find it hard to believe the girl did it, especially in the shape she's in."

Eddie hadn't thought about that. Nicole was in serious condition too, and the man's wound was on the back of his head. He was suddenly very glad that he'd called Bob Marshall in and didn't have to lead the investigation himself.

He watched them load the ambulance. Jeff shut the doors.

"You running in the morning?" Jeff asked.

"Planning on it, unless I'm up all night. I'll probably take Sarah over to the hospital. Wait a sec, you're on duty. You can't run, can you?"

"I get off at six a.m. I might as well run before I sack out."

"Okay," I'll see you then. Eddie watched the ambulance pull out.

When he got into the house, Sandy and Liam were readying Nicole for transport. Sarah was sitting on the couch, still answering Bob's questions, but she looked about ready to throw something at him.

"I'm going to ask you again," Bob said, "who hit Donnie?"

"Nicole said she did. Check that flashlight for prints."

"I will."

Sarah held the detective's stare until Bob looked down at his notebook.

"And when you got here, he was laid out like that, on the floor?"

"That's right."

"Where was Nicole?"

"She let me in, but she could barely walk. He'd given her a good pounding, and she was doubled over. I got her to bed and did what I could for her until. . .until the ambulance got here."

Bob glanced at Eddie. "You beat the ambulance here."

"Yeah. I called them as soon as I knew what the situation was."

"Then what? It must have taken them at least five minutes to get out here."

"More like ten. I. . ." He ran a hand through his hair, trying to remember everything in sequence. "I checked the man for a pulse. He was breathing, but he didn't look good, and he was bleeding a lot. I had Sarah get me some towels, and I tried to help him while she tended to Nicole. That's about it." Eddie wished Harvey was there, but no way would he call his friend now. It was nearly midnight, and Harvey was on parental leave. He wouldn't spoil that.

"Can I go now?" Sarah asked. "I need to get to the hospital and make sure my sister will be okay."

"Sure," Bob said. "Are you on duty tomorrow?"

"Yes."

Bob sighed. "Call me before you go in."

"You think they'll put me on leave?" Sarah glared at him. "For helping my sister?"

"Sarah, a few things don't quite add up," Bob said gently. "They may want you to stand down until Nicole can give me her statement."

Sarah held the stare again, and this time she didn't win.

"All right, I'll call in. Now I'm going to the hospital."

"I'll drive you," Eddie said. He could tell Sarah was molten lava inside, ready to erupt. Not a good time for her to be driving.

116

Chapter 12

Eddie's alarm rang and he groped for it. The gray light coming in at the edge of the blind told him the sun was rising. He looked at the time. It was 5:45. He would already be late for the running date, with only about three hours of sleep under his belt.

Leeanne was standing in the driveway, talking to Jeff and Harvey when he got there. Great. He'd been careful not to give Leeanne any details, but Jeff had probably spilled everything to Harvey. And Leeanne. So now she knew it was Sarah whom he had rushed off to help last night.

He pulled in and shut off the motor.

"Hi," Harvey said as he got out of the truck.

"Hi." Eddie walked slowly toward them.

"Jeff was telling us about Sarah's sister."

"Yeah," Eddie said, shooting Leeanne a glance.

"Is she going to be okay?"

"I don't know. I left Sarah at the hospital finally. Figured I needed some sleep."

"You shouldn't have come to run," Jeff said.

"Well, *you're* here."

Jeff shrugged. "Yeah, but I got off duty a few minutes ago, so that's different."

Leeanne had said nothing, but she watched him with troubled eyes.

"So, do you know what happened to the guy?" Harvey said.

"Not for sure. Sarah thinks Nicole hit him, but I'm not quite married to that theory."

Harvey's eyebrows lowered. "You don't think Sarah did it?"

Eddie pulled in a breath and shook his head slowly. "I don't think she'd lie to me about that. But then, I never expected her to panic at a crime scene, either."

"How bad was it?" Harvey asked.

"She was pretty shook up when I got there. Her sister was barely conscious, and the guy on the floor was bleeding out. We didn't get much of a chance to talk before the EMTs got there."

"The word at the station when I left was, that guy's not going to make it," Jeff said.

Eddie sighed and let his shoulders slump. "I didn't know that. I did everything I could for him, which wasn't much, with that head wound."

"Could we pray?" Leeanne asked.

"I think that's a good idea," Harvey said.

They sat down in the breezeway and prayed for Sarah and Nicole. Leeanne slipped her hand into Eddie's and he gripped it hard.

"Who's investigating?" Harvey asked when they were through.

"Bob Marshall."

Harvey nodded. "Do you want me to go in this morning?"

"No," Eddie said. "You need to take your time off with Jennifer and Connor."

Harvey eyed him closely. "If you're sure you're okay."

"Me? I'm fine," Eddie said. "I'm not so sure about Sarah. She's supposed to go in this morning, too."

"She should ask for a personal day," Harvey said.

"Yeah, that's what I told her. Marshall told her last night to call him before she reports in. He might want her benched until they clean up this case."

"It wouldn't surprise me," Harvey said.

They set out to run, and Leeanne fell in beside him as they entered the park.

"You're quiet," Eddie said.

She shrugged. "I don't know what to think."

"Because I went to help Sarah?"

"Yeah."

"I'd have done the same for anyone."

"You called the ambulance."

"Yeah."

"Why didn't Sarah?"

Eddie jogged a few more steps before answering. "She wasn't thinking real clearly when I got there. But that's the first thing I did."

They ran on in silence, behind Jeff and Harvey. To Eddie's surprise, Leeanne kept up and didn't quit early. They were nearly at the end of their three-mile loop, and she was breathing hard but still looked fit, when Eddie's phone rang. He pulled it out and looked at the screen while he ran, but when he saw Bob Marshall's name on the screen, he slowed to a walk.

"Yeah?"

"Eddie, that you?"

"Yeah."

"It's Bob Marshall. You okay?"

"Yeah, just finishing my run," Eddie said. "What's up, Bob?"

"I just wanted to give you a heads-up."

"Yeah?" Eddie rubbed his eyes.

"We were still processing the scene when Mr. Benoit came home last night. He was very drunk."

"Oh, great."

"Yeah, well, we took him into custody. I was able to talk to Nicole Benoit at the hospital a few minutes ago. Between the two of them, I think we have most of the story now."

Eddie's stomach clenched. Sarah had sworn to him in his truck that she had not been the one to deck Donnie. If she'd lied to him. . .He waited for Bob to go on.

"It seems Mr. Benoit came home to find Nicole's boyfriend whaling on her."

"What? He was there? Sarah didn't say anything about her dad being there."

"Nicole didn't want her to know. She says her father whacked the boyfriend. Nicole screamed at him, and he dropped the flashlight and ran out."

"Sarah didn't know?"

"Nicole didn't tell her. She said her father and Sarah don't get along, and she didn't want Sarah to get him in trouble. Sarah was still at the hospital this morning. She waited in the hall while

I talked to her sister. I think Nicole was giving it to me straight. She was pretty cut up when we told her that her boyfriend died."

"After what he did to her?" Eddie shook his head.

"Yeah, well, I hate to say it, but I don't think it's the first time she's been beaten."

"Her father?"

"Maybe. The doctor told me she had bruises on bruises. But she's not talking about anything before last night."

"Okay."

Leeanne had gone on without him, and as Eddie walked up the sidewalk toward Harvey's house, the three of them went into the house.

"What do you want me to do?" he asked Bob.

"You're coming in this morning, right?"

"Yeah."

"Type up a statement and bring it to my office. I'll witness your signature. I told Sarah not to come in."

"Is she suspended?"

"No," Bob said. "She's wiped out, though. She insisted on staying with her sister, but she hadn't slept at all. Their mother got there just as I was leaving, and she had to deal with that, too."

"Sarah hadn't called her until then?"

"Guess not," Bob said. "I got the feeling there was bad blood between Nicole and the mom."

"Yeah, there is. Okay, Bob. I'll see you later. Thanks."

"No problem, Eddie. Just realize you'll have to testify. This could go to trial as a homicide."

Eddie stopped walking beside his pickup. "He was defending his daughter."

"Yeah. Well, we've still got a lot to process."

"So, they're charging Mr. Benoit?"

"Probably. I haven't talked to the D.A. yet. Maybe manslaughter. We'll see."

Eddie leaned against his truck for a minute before going inside. Questions flitted through his mind. Had Sarah really thought Nicole brained her boyfriend? Did Mr. Benoit have a lawyer? Would Sarah's tampering with the scene affect the investigation? He couldn't see any reason not to tell Harvey everything, but it was probably best to do that in private, not in front of Leeanne and Jeff.

*****

Harvey elected to stay home with Jennifer and Connor. After hearing the bare bones of Eddie's tale, Jennifer was surprised he didn't go to the police station. Her husband had spent fifteen minutes alone with Eddie in the study before they ate breakfast and Eddie drove off to get ready for work. Leeanne was subdued when she left for Farmington and her classes.

It was great to have Harvey around, but he fidgeted all day, calling his office at least a dozen times. After getting a lengthy briefing from Eddie around ten o'clock, he went next door to look at the basement again. The forensics team finished there before noon, and one of the officers, Paul Trudeau, came to the Larson house to report to Harvey.

"You sure you're done?" Harvey asked anxiously, "because the last thing I want to do is pour that concrete and wish I hadn't."

"Well," Trudeau said slowly, "if you're eager to do it, maybe you just want to pour a pad where the furnace is going, and leave the rest for later."

Harvey thought about that for a while after Trudeau had left. Then he went over to look at the basement again.

"I think he's right," he told Jennifer when he came back. "We can pour enough concrete for the furnace and leave the rest open for a while. Then if there's any question about the investigation, we can go back in there without breaking up an entire concrete floor."

"Is Eddie working on this case today, or Sarah's?" Jennifer asked.

"He and Tony are on this. He did have to spend some time with Detective Marshall this morning, but I think he's squared away on that for now. It's best if Legere's squad handles it."

"I wonder how Sarah's doing," Jennifer said.

"Keep praying for her." Harvey turned toward the bedroom. "I hear Connor. I'll get him."

Abby had lunch ready, and Harvey put Connor in his infant seat so he could sit up on the table and watch them eat.

"So when can they pour the concrete?" Jennifer asked.

"I'll call Rudy Thomas as soon as we're done eating," said Harvey. "We need to get the plumber in there to look things over, too."

They all digressed into baby talk then, trying to get Connor's attention. His eyes roamed the kitchen. He seemed to like the light fixture that hung down over the table, even though Jennifer turned it off so he wouldn't stare at the lights.

"We should hang a mobile or something from that," Abby said, reaching up to jostle it, making it sway slightly. Connor's eyes followed it.

"How long are you going to keep working?" Harvey asked.

"I'm not sure. Peter would be fine with me quitting, but I thought I might want to work for a while. Still, it would be nice to have the summer off with the boys."

Jennifer smiled at her sister's indecision. That was so typical of Abby. "Pray about it. I'm sure you'll make the right decision."

"At first I was thinking I'd work until the middle of May and then quit," Abby said. "I'd have more free time to prepare for the wedding. I just don't know."

"That would be great, if you don't need the money," Harvey said.

"Peter says I don't," Abby said doubtfully. "I have a decent savings account now, thanks to you guys putting me up for free all these months."

"It wasn't free," Jennifer said. "You've been my slave."

"Well, I might just ask for a leave of absence and go back to work in the fall." Abby smiled at her. "Or not."

"So you're not going to work for Peter after you get married?" Jennifer asked. Abby had mentioned the possibility before.

"I don't think so. Maybe later on. And if we decide to keep the boys home next fall—"

"You're going to teach them at home?" Harvey asked.

"I don't know. We're thinking about it."

"You should talk to Beth," Jennifer said. "She's not going to teach school anymore, but she plans to keep up her certification. And she wants to teach her own kids."

Abby nodded. "But I wouldn't have to be certified, would I?"

"No, anybody can teach their own kids," Harvey said. "Beth and Ruthann know all about it. Ruthann is starting to teach Clarissa her letters now."

"You're going to teach Connor, aren't you?" she asked.

"You bet she is," Harvey said emphatically.

Jennifer smiled at him. It was another part of his dream, and she'd decided she liked it.

"If Beth keeps her certification, she'll have fewer hassles with the state," she said. "She can offer support for other parents, too. She's already said she'll do that for us and Rick and Ruthann."

"Well, I'm not sure I'd be a good teacher," Abby said. "Peter says to just relax and have fun this summer and let Andy and Gary get used to me being the mom. They're really good, but I'm not sure they'd want to obey me all the time if I was their teacher. You know, the bad guy."

Jennifer laughed. "You wouldn't be the bad guy. If they're like most boys, they'd love you even more for giving them the chance not to go to school every day."

"Still," Abby said thoughtfully, "right now, they're never alone with me. Their father is always there, and Peter handles the discipline. When I'm home alone with them, I'll have to do that. It might change our relationship some."

"It might," Harvey agreed. "You and Peter need to talk a lot about that, and he needs to give you some practice in making decisions with the boys. Before they do something naughty, you need to have your mind made up how you'll handle it."

"Andy is so sweet," Abby mused, "but I'm sure Gary can be a handful. I really love him, but sometimes he's mischievous. I have to learn not to laugh at his antics, Peter said, or he'll just keep doing worse things. And he would miss his school friends, I'm sure."

Connor began to fuss, and Harvey stood up and took him out of his seat.

"Are you hungry, big guy?" He pinched the disposable diaper and said, "Oh, wet, huh?"

"I'll do it," Jennifer said.

"No, no, Daddy's going to do it," Harvey said, and went off with Connor.

Abby laughed. "Harvey's so funny. I've never seen a man so eager to change diapers."

"It's great," Jennifer said. "I don't think I've changed one since we've been home."

"That won't last," Abby predicted.

*****

Rudy Thomas and his concrete crew returned Tuesday morning. Harvey had offered to stay home again. Although Jennifer knew he loved being with her and Connor, she could tell he felt he should be at work.

"You go on," she said. "Chances are you'll be over here at least once to talk to Rudy, anyway."

"Okay, I guess you're right," Harvey said. "I need to check in with Mike about that attempted bank robbery and see if Legere's squad needs help."

"And have Bob Marshall bring you up to speed on Sarah's case?"

"Yeah." Harvey squeezed his lips together. "We should call it the Benoit case, not Sarah's case. As far as we know, she didn't do anything wrong."

"Except delay calling the ambulance until Eddie got there."

Harvey sighed. "Yeah. That's not like her. But this whole family dynamic of theirs is a little weird. I'm sure it was a very emotional time for her."

"It would be for anyone." Jennifer eased the baby from his arms. "Get dressed for work, Captain. I'll take care of the big guy today."

124

In addition to Harvey's concerns about Sarah's family and the skeleton next door, Mike had called him late Monday afternoon about the new case. It was the third attempted bank robbery in the city within two weeks, though only one had been successful. All took place at different banks, and Mike wasn't happy with the way Ron Legere's detectives had handled it. He wanted the Priority Unit to step in.

Nate and Jimmy had wrapped up their homicide, but Eddie and Tony were fully occupied by the skeleton case. Harvey told Jennifer that if he wanted to satisfy Mike with the Priority Unit's usual efficient response, he'd have to get into the robbery thing himself. Nate Miller would be the lead investigator, but Harvey would work closely with him, especially at the beginning.

Harvey's men were maturing and becoming more skilled at solving sensitive crimes, but all of them were young, and Harvey supervised them carefully, especially at the start of a new investigation. Nate was thorough and tended to approach his cases methodically. If he was lacking in one area, it was intuition. He always made the connections and drew the conclusions Harvey and Eddie would, but not quite as quickly. He was getting more proficient, though, and Harvey depended on him more and more for complex jobs, especially those involving computer crimes.

"Nate will need you today," Jennifer said. "Abby's here. We'll be fine."

He left reluctantly, promising to come home for lunch. Jennifer, Abby, and Connor spent a tranquil day. Janice came over for a few minutes, bringing one of her scrumptious pies, and Rudy came to the door once to see if Harvey was in.

"He'll be home for lunch, Rudy. Is anything wrong?" Jennifer asked.

"No, ma'am, I just thought I'd check to see if he, uh, wanted to look at the forms before we start pouring."

"Well, he gave you instructions yesterday," she ventured.

"Yes, ma'am, but the captain likes precision. I just thought he'd want to take a look if he was here."

"You may be right, but since he's not, just go ahead."

When Harvey came home at noon, she told him what Rudy had said, and he went right to number 135 and returned ten minutes later.

"How's Rudy's crew doing?" Jennifer asked, as he sat down at the table.

"Looking good over there," Harvey said with satisfaction. "I'm going to give Jeff and Beth a key, and they can start moving stuff in any time they want."

"Any word on Sarah?"

"Bob told me she's coming back to work tomorrow. She and her mother were moving Nicole home today—to their mother's house."

"Oh, that's a change."

"Yeah. Eddie can tell you more than I can, I'm sure."

He asked the blessing, and they began to eat. Abby jumped up in the middle of the meal to grab her phone and take a picture of Connor. She had made it her duty to take his picture every day. Jennifer spent long, languid hours nursing the baby and holding him afterward, while he slept peacefully in her arms. Jennifer's world seemed to be getting back to normal—the new normal, with Connor at its center.

*****

Eddie and Tony plugged away on the Carleton Fuller case all week, talking to the neighbors, the executor, the people at the nursing home, a Navy liaison, and the attorney who had drawn up Fuller's newer will. Meanwhile, Nate and Jimmy worked on the bank robbery case. They made swift progress under Harvey's guidance. Sometimes Eddie felt like he was wading through quicksand where the skeleton in the basement was concerned. Even so, he was glad he was working that case, not the bank heists.

Jeff had Friday and Saturday off that week, and he ran with Harvey and Eddie Friday morning, then ate breakfast with them at Harvey and Jennifer's house.

"If you don't mind, I'll take a load of stuff to the new house this morning," he said, slathering jam on his toast.

"Why should we mind?" Harvey asked. "We'll be thrilled when you're settled in there."

"Thanks. Beth wants to move books and china and stuff this weekend. When do you think the new furnace will be in?"

"I've asked them to bring it Monday. Rudy said the concrete should be ready by then."

"So, you think it will be up and running Monday night?"

"It should be. Do you guys want to move in Monday?" Harvey asked.

"No, I have to work Sunday through Tuesday. I'll have Wednesday and Thursday off next week. How about we move in on Wednesday?"

"Wonderful," Jennifer said.

Eddie sipped his coffee. "Let me know if you want me to bring my truck over after work."

"Thanks," Jeff said.

Harvey bounced Connor gently against his shoulder as he finished his toast and coffee. Jeff watched with tender eyes.

Jennifer started putting away the breakfast things, and Harvey said, "I've got to get ready for work. Here, Uncle Jeff, want to hold him?" and he passed Connor easily to Jeff.

When Harvey had left the room, Jennifer smiled at her brother. He held the baby as if he were a bottle of nitroglycerin. Connor began his rattly cry.

"Hold onto him, Jeff. Pull him right in against you, so he knows you mean business."

Jeff tried. Connor cried louder.

"You'd better take him," Jeff said helplessly.

"I think you'd better get some practice in." Jennifer wiped the table with the dishcloth.

Jeff boosted Connor up against his shoulder and held him there more firmly, bouncing a little, the way Harvey had. "You want a turn, Eddie?"

"No, you're doing good."

"How long does this go on?" Jeff asked.

Jennifer smiled. "Probably until I feed him."

"No, I mean, how many months?"

She laughed. "He's a pretty happy baby. They don't really cry much unless something's wrong, Jeff."

"Well, I hope Beth knows more about it than I do."

"Don't you remember when Randy was little?"

"Yeah, I stayed out of the house as much as I could," he said.

"It's different when it's your baby."

"I hope so, because I really want one. Beth is…well, we're hopeful."

"Really?" Jennifer looked at him to be sure she wasn't reading too much into his statement.

He nodded, blushing a little. "We think maybe…"

She walked over and put her arm around his shoulders. "You'll be a terrific dad." Tears came to her eyes, and she kissed his forehead. "I love you, Jeff. Now put your hand on the back of his head, like this. And Harvey will give you lessons anytime. He *loves* telling guys how to hold babies."

Eddie stood up. "Thanks for breakfast, Jennifer. I'd better get going, or the boss will beat me to the office."

He drove home and took a quick shower, thinking about all the people he had interviewed. Who else knew Carleton Fuller? Who saw him on a regular basis?

When he got to work, he passed Sarah in the foyer.

"Hey, how you doing?" He paused, and Sarah stopped walking too.

"I'm okay."

"Nicole still at your mom's place?"

Sarah's expression was almost a grimace, but she quickly hid it. "Yeah. She's doing better. She wants to go back to work Monday."

"That's pretty soon, isn't it?" Eddie asked. He wondered how long it took a woman to recover from a miscarriage. Physically, anyway. She would probably never get past it emotionally, not completely anyhow.

"She thinks she can, and her boss wants her to come back. Nicole didn't tell him everything—you know."

Eddie nodded. The part about her boyfriend was on the news, but she probably didn't want anyone to know about the baby.

"She's afraid she'll lose her job if she doesn't go back soon."

"That's rough."

"Yeah. Look, I gotta get moving."

"Okay. See ya."

She hurried toward the duty room, and Eddie headed for the stairway. He wondered about her father. He'd checked on the computer and seen that Mr. Benoit wasn't held over in jail. Maybe it was best not to get into it too deeply, but he did wonder if Nicole would eventually go back to stay with him again. Focus, he told himself. If only he didn't care what happened to Sarah's muddled family—or even what happened to Sarah.

"Hey, Shakespeare," Tony called with a grin as he entered the Priority Unit. Harvey and Nate were already at their desks, too. Tony got up and came over to Eddie's desk. "I've been roughing out a list of leads to check into today. You up for it?"

Eddie smiled. "That's my job." If anyone could help him focus on his work, it was Tony.

Chapter 13

Jeff's truck was at the new house at nine Saturday morning. Harvey went over to help unload boxes. Beth came to the Larsons' house to get Jennifer and Connor.

"Can I carry the little guy over?" she asked.

Jennifer grinned. "Sure. I'll bring my mop and bucket, and I've been saving some rags for you."

"Great. We've got liquid soap and cleanser." Beth carried Connor over to the new house in his infant seat, and Jennifer lugged the cleaning supplies. Jeff and Harvey were heading out to the truck.

"If you girls want to unload those boxes, we'll go for another load," Jeff said.

"Sure," Jennifer told him. Inside, she looked around the living room that was empty except for ten cartons. "What's in those?"

"Two of dishes and eight of books," Beth said.

"Okay. I'll wash down the kitchen cupboards first, and you dust the bookshelves. Then you can put the dishes where you'll want them."

The electricity was working, and the plumbing had passed inspection. Harvey had started a fire in their fireplace earlier, and the living room was quite warm.

"This is nice," Beth said happily, standing on a chair to dust the built-in bookshelves on one side of the fireplace. Jeff had brought two of their four straight chairs over the day before, with the sofa, his bike, and Beth's desk. On each side of the fieldstone fireplace stood three columns of shelves, each about two feet wide.

Jennifer looked around, imaging how the room would look with all Beth and Jeff's furniture in place. This reminded her strongly of the weekend friends had helped her and Harvey move into Mr. Bailey's house—their house now.

"I'm so excited that you're going to be here. We'll have to throw you a house warming."

Beth paused and wiggled her eyebrows. "That will happen next week, when they install the new furnace."

Jennifer laughed. "No, really. I think we'll do it. Invite all the church folks and your family and mine—"

"That's more people than we'll ever fit in this house," Beth said.

Jennifer tucked Connor's blanket securely around him in his seat. She took the bucket to the kitchen and ran water into it with some cleaner, then began scrubbing the cupboard shelves. When she had six cupboards clean, she left them open to dry and took the bucket to the living room.

"You shouldn't be carrying that," said Beth.

"It's not heavy. Besides, my brother was hinting that maybe you shouldn't be doing much lifting for a while, either." Jennifer looked up at her coyly, from under her lashes.

Beth tried to hold back a smile but couldn't. "I was going to tell you."

"You mean it's definite?" Jennifer barely kept from shrieking.

Beth nodded, and her smiled grew and grew. "As of this morning."

"Beth! Come down here, you—you—"

She climbed down, and Jennifer hugged her tight. "You can wear all my maternity clothes, and I'll save Connor's things for you."

Beth laughed. "Thank you. It's wonderful, isn't it? I don't think it's really hit us yet." She fumbled in her pocket for a tissue and wiped her eyes.

"God is so good." Jennifer pulled away grinning. "I remember the day I told Harvey I was pregnant. He rushed home carrying a teddy bear and said he was going to hire me a maid."

"I never heard about that."

"Well, it didn't happen. I suggested we get Abby to come stay with us. She was thrilled to transfer to the hospital down here. And it's been great."

"Yeah. That was a life-changing move for Abby," Beth said. "Come on, we'd better get some work done before the guys get back. Hand me those books, and I'll put them on the shelves."

"Oh yeah, the books. It took us days to move our libraries and arrange them the way we wanted." Jennifer pulled three books out of the first box. Definitely Beth's—education methods textbooks. "Want to hear a secret?"

"Sure. Can I tell Jeff?"

"Of course."

"What is it?"

"Mrs. Harder and Miss Hutchins, at 187, are thinking of selling their house."

Beth's eyebrows arched. "Isn't that the lady with the Wyeth sketch?"

"Right. The house that was supposed to get burglarized in November, but the idiots picked ours instead."

"They want to sell it?"

"Well, they're not positive yet," Jennifer said. "It was warm yesterday, and I put Connor in the stroller for the first time. Abby and I took him for a little stroll down the block. Mrs. Harder saw us out the window and ran out to see him. She begged us to go in for a cup of tea, so we did."

"And what happened?"

"She said she's never felt safe since last fall, even though she's got an alarm system and a little dog that yaps whenever anyone comes around."

"She said that?" Beth looked skeptical as she reached for the next handful of books.

"Well, not the yapping part. *I* said that. Anyhow, she told us her niece might move to Virginia, and if she does, Mrs. Harder said she doesn't want to stay there alone. She'll sell the house if her niece leaves."

"Wow. Did you tell Harvey?"

"Naturally."

"What did he say? Is he going to buy it?"

"Well, it's not actually up for sale yet." Jennifer handed her books so she could arrange them. "But he's definitely interested."

"For Eddie and Leeanne?"

"Uh-huh. Of course, we'd *really* like to see them in Bud and Janice's house, but Bud's not due to retire for a couple more years. And we don't really want them to move away, anyhow."

"Could you guys do that—buy another house right away?"

"Well, Harvey's planning to go talk to Mrs. Harder soon. If she's serious about it, he'll see what Eddie thinks. Eddie's got some money put away. He and Leeanne might be able to buy it themselves."

"That would be great."

Jennifer opened the second box. "Where do you want Jeff's airplane books?"

"Oh, let's put them down there." Beth nodded at a lower shelf.

Jennifer took the aviation books out a few at a time and stood them in the recess. Beth got down from her chair and looked through the boxes.

"Fiction, fiction, I want fiction," she muttered.

"Hey, this is weird." Jennifer pointed to the bookshelf. She had chosen one in the middle tier of shelves. Jeff's books stuck out almost flush with the front of it.

"What's weird?" Beth straightened and came toward her.

"The books you put in up there are back farther, and Jeff's stick out to the front of the shelf."

"A lot of them are big books," she said. "Maybe I should pull the little ones out, so they're all even. What do you think?"

Jennifer felt behind the books.

"I think this shelf is different, Beth." She checked the one above it, and the ones on either side. "Look, they're all about a foot deep, but this one isn't. It can't be more than six or eight inches."

Beth looked. "Huh. Maybe the chimney is behind it."

"That doesn't make sense. The one above it is deeper, and so are the ones on both sides."

The wood of the built-in shelves was stained dark, and it was hard to see the back wall.

"We need a flashlight," Jennifer declared.

"How about a lamp?" A small table lamp stuck from the top of one of the boxes of dishes, and Beth got it.

"There's an outlet." Jennifer pointed to the nearest one. The lamp's cord was only six feet long, and she couldn't bring it all the way to the shelf.

"Just hold it as close as you can," she told Beth. She took the books out, laying them on the shelf below, and peered into the recess. She caught a glimmer up high, just below the next higher shelf. She reached out and touched it. "There's something here, on the wall."

"What is it?"

"I don't know... a hook, maybe? No, it's a keyhole."

Beth's jaw dropped, and Jennifer thought her expression must mirror her own.

"A secret hiding place. Jennifer, a secret hiding place in our house! This is so exciting!"

Jennifer pushed on the board, but nothing happened. She tried to feel a crack or notch along the edges, but the board seemed to fit tightly.

Jennifer stepped back. "Take a look."

Beth set the lamp on the floor and came close. "Can't see a thing."

Jennifer picked up the lamp and held it as near as she could.

"I see it." Beth rapped sharply on the wood, and the sound echoed through the empty house. "It's hollow."

Connor stirred and fussed a little. Jennifer set down the lamp and went to rock his seat.

"How are we going to open it?" Beth asked.

"Harvey could probably pick the lock." Jennifer's faith in Harvey was boundless.

Beth turned to look at her. "What about that key?"

"What key?"

"In the lap desk."

"Of course," Jennifer said. "Do you think?"

A wild, hopeful look crossed Beth's face. "Where is it? Tell me, and I'll go get it."

"The lap desk is on the little wicker table in the sun room, under the Caron painting."

"I'll be right back." Beth raced for the door.

Jennifer went to the fireplace. Harvey had left several logs to one side, and she stirred the coals and put two sticks on the fire. Connor fussed again, and she took him out of the seat, wrapping the blanket snugly around him, and sat down on the edge of the raised hearth. The warmth of the fire felt good. She shielded Connor from its direct heat as he started to nurse.

The front door opened and she looked up quickly. Beth and Abby came in.

"Beth told me you found a secret drawer." Abby's gray eyes were wide. She was dressed in jeans and a sweatshirt, and she wore her hair in a long ponytail.

"Not a drawer exactly," Jennifer said. "A secret compartment, maybe."

Beth led her to the shelves, and Abby held up a flashlight.

"There it is," Beth said. "Hold the light steady, and I'll see if the key fits. Or do you want to, Jennifer? You found it, after all, and it's your house, and your key."

"No, it's *your* house," Jennifer said. "And, anyway, Connor's hungry. Go ahead and see if it fits."

"Harvey will be mad, if it does," said Abby.

"Why?" Beth asked.

"Because he missed it."

"Should we wait?" Beth looked questioningly from Jennifer to Abby.

The door opened again, and Jennifer pulled Connor's blanket up over the front of her blouse as Harvey and Jeff stepped inside.

"Hey, gorgeous." Harvey came toward her smiling. "Little pig eating again?"

"Harvey, wait 'til you hear," Abby shouted, and he turned expectantly toward her.

"What now? Not more bones, I hope."

136

"No, it's a secret compartment. Jennifer found it."

"What?" Jeff stepped to her side.

"Where?" Harvey asked.

Abby and Beth showed them the keyhole with the aid of Abby's flashlight.

Harvey said immediately, "I wonder if that key in the desk will fit it."

Jennifer smiled. Harvey *would* think of it.

Beth produced the key, which hung on a short loop of string, and dangled it under his nose. "We were just about to try it. You're the landlord. *Noblesse oblige.*" She put the key in his hand.

"I don't think that's what it means," he said, "but I'll take it."

"Hold on," Jennifer cried. "I want to see." She stood up with Connor on her shoulder, crowding close beside Abby so she could look into the shelf with them. "Okay."

"Ready?" Harvey asked with exaggerated anticipation.

"Ready," they all said.

He leaned in close.

"Is it going to go?" Jeff asked.

"Uh—not sure."

"If it doesn't, you can pick the lock," Jennifer said.

Metal clicked on metal. A creak was followed by a clack. Harvey said, "I think that did it."

He tried to pull the board out by pulling on the key, but the key just came away from the lock.

"Hmm." Harvey put both hands into the recess, and they all bumped heads, trying to watch what he was doing. He pushed along the edges of the board, as Jennifer had before they'd gotten the key. When he pressed the bottom edge, the board at the back of the shelf swung down toward them.

"What do you know?" Jeff said softly.

Abby pushed in closer with the flashlight. "What's in there?"

Harvey took a handkerchief from his pocket and unfolded it, then used it to carefully lift out two legal-size white envelopes. He handed them to Beth with the handkerchief around them and felt carefully inside the compartment with both hands.

"Guess that's it," he said.

They all stood there, staring at the envelopes in Beth's hands.

"Are you going to open them?" Abby asked.

"Let's go over to our house and sit down," Harvey said.

"Coffee break time," Jennifer agreed.

Harvey took Connor, and they all went across the lawns and into the Larson house. Connor fussed again, and Jennifer took him into the bedroom to change him, calling, "Wait until I come back!"

When she returned to the kitchen, they were sitting around the table with coffee mugs and muffins. A glass of milk waited for her.

"Let me hold my nephew," Abby said, and Jennifer handed over the baby.

She sat down beside Harvey. He had fetched a pair of sterile gloves, standard in his gear for police work, and held one envelope by the edges, between his hands. He squinted at the faded handwriting on the front. Nobody said anything.

"Last will and testament of Carleton G. Fuller," Harvey said at last.

"That can't be," Jennifer said. "Ralph Penninger was his executor, and they had the will. He said Mr. Fuller left his money to the hospital and the historical society, remember?"

Harvey nodded. "This is probably a copy."

"Or maybe this is an old will, and he wrote the other one later," Jeff said. "The envelope looks old."

"Should we call Mr. Penninger?" Jennifer asked.

Harvey's brow furrowed. "I'll think about it." He laid the envelope down and picked up the second one, again by the edges. The top was ragged, where it had been opened. "United States Navy." The words were printed in black in the upper left corner.

"The uniform," Jennifer said.

Beth laughed. "I was thinking the same thing."

Harvey nodded. "I guess we should call the authorities."

"But, honey, you *are* the authorities," Jennifer said.

He sat still for a moment, thinking, and they all waited. At last he said, "I'd better have Eddie here, at least. He's the investigating officer where the bones are concerned, and I don't want to be the only officer on the scene when this is opened."

"You think this has to do with the skeleton?" Jeff leaned in to look closer at the envelopes.

"Where *is* Eddie?" Beth asked.

"And where's Leeanne?" Jennifer added. Her younger sister had arrived at the house the evening before. "Is she sleeping in?"

"No," said Abby. "Eddie came to get her right after you and Beth went next door. They had left her engagement ring off at the jewelry store last week, and they were going to pick it up today."

"They might not be back for hours," Jennifer moaned.

Harvey took out his cell phone and punched Eddie's code. Jennifer prayed silently that he would answer.

"Eddie!" Harvey said, and they all breathed. "I may have some evidence for you here at the house. Can you come home soon?" He listened for a moment, and Jennifer imagined Eddie saying, "*Pour toi, mon ami? Mais oui!*"

Chapter 14

"Now what?" Jeff asked.

"How about we unload your truck while we wait for Eddie?" Harvey asked.

Jennifer felt a little let down, and she could tell from Beth, Jeff, and Abby's blank faces that they felt the same way, but it made sense.

Harvey wouldn't let Jennifer lug any more books or buckets. Jeff had brought Beth's rocking chair to the new house, and Harvey made Jennifer sit in it near the fireplace with Connor while Beth and Abby unpacked boxes and he and Jeff brought the rest of the things in from the truck. They put the dishes away in the kitchen, and Jeff took over the aviation books, placing them on a higher shelf.

When everything they'd brought was unloaded, Harvey examined the secret compartment minutely with a penlight, then closed it. He held the key out to Beth. "The chatelaine usually keeps the keys of the castle."

She laughed. "Why don't you put it back in the lap desk? If I put it somewhere over here in the middle of moving, we may never see it again."

Harvey pocketed the little key gravely and helped Jeff arrange the sofa and end tables to Beth's satisfaction.

Eddie's truck drove into Harvey's driveway. Jeff locked 135, and they all went next door.

First they had to show proper appreciation for Leeanne's ring. The diamond was smaller than Abby's, but of a respectable size, in a stylish gold setting. Leeanne was hugged and kissed, and Eddie had his back slapped by the men and was kissed by the women.

"It's the stone from my Mémé's ring," Eddie said. "We had it reset."

They all exclaimed over it again. It suited Leeanne somehow, as she displayed it demurely.

It was nearly lunchtime, and Abby recruited Beth to help her make sandwiches for everyone while Harvey explained the situation to Eddie and Leeanne and showed them the two envelopes.

"Amazing," said Leeanne. "I want to see the secret cubbyhole."

"I'll show it to you after lunch," Beth promised.

"So, should we open the envelopes, or enter them into evidence, or what?" asked Eddie.

"Well, we're not sure they *are* evidence yet," Harvey said. "I wonder if we should get a copy of Mr. Fuller's will. The one they went by when he died, I mean. Then there would be no question of whether this one matches it."

Eddie scratched his head. "I wish Pete was here."

Harvey snapped his fingers. "I'll call him." He smiled at Eddie and pulled out his phone.

Pete Bearse was a former colleague. He had worked with Harvey for eight years in the Priority Unit, taking law courses at night. He had quit the police force about the time Harvey married Jennifer, when he passed the bar exam. He had entered legal practice with a small Portland firm and was happy in his new profession.

"Pete's coming over," Harvey announced a couple of minutes later. He cautiously moved the envelopes to his desk in the study, and Beth and Abby began passing out paper plates for sandwiches and potato chips.

"I hope he gets here soon," Abby said, passing plates of carrot cake while Beth poured coffee. "Peter's coming to get me after lunch."

"Say, Peter ought to be in on this," Harvey said. "My other two brothers are here." Eddie and Jeff smiled benevolently. They didn't mind being building blocks in Harvey's new extended family.

"Maybe we should dust those envelopes for fingerprints," Eddie said.

"Won't Mr. Fuller's be on the one with the will?" asked Leeanne.

"One would think so," Harvey said, his brow wrinkled in thought. "But what about the other one? The corpse has some connection with the Navy, and the envelope is from the Navy."

Eddie got his fingerprint kit from his truck, and he and Harvey gleefully dusted the envelopes.

By the time Pete Bearse showed up, the living room was packed. Peter Hobart had come with Gary and Andy. Beth, Jeff, Eddie, Leeanne, Abby, and Harvey apprised the two Peters of the morning's events.

Jennifer had taken Connor to the bedroom for his lunch and tried to settle him for a nap. Every time she laid him in the cradle, he cried. Finally she gave it up and carried him out to the living room. Harvey provided Pete Bearse with latex gloves and held Connor contentedly while the lawyer examined the envelopes.

Pete Bearse hadn't changed since Jennifer had last seen him, unless he was a little balder. He was brusque, but friendly.

"All right," he said at length, "as I understand it, you bought the house, and the papers are signed."

"Yes," said Harvey. "We paid cash. The property is all ours now."

"Well, that includes the secret compartment and its contents, then," said Pete, "and anything else they left in the house, unless they wrote it in your contract otherwise."

"Nope. Nothing like that." Harvey always read the fine print.

"Then you can legally open those," Pete said. "You own them."

Harvey smiled. "Who wants to hold my son?" he asked magnanimously.

Half a dozen people reached for Connor. Leeanne won.

"Fine looking boy, Harv," Pete said.

"Thank you." Harvey took out his pocketknife and carefully slit the top edge of the first envelope. He gingerly pulled out a sheet of paper. "It's a will, all right. Pete?"

He passed the paper to Pete, who scanned it quickly.

"It's an autograph—that is, a handwritten will—dated … twenty-two years ago."

143

"That's ten years before he moved into that house," Harvey said.

Pete nodded. "Well, it says here he leaves everything to his wife, and if she predeceases him, to his nephew, Marcus Rutledge, son of his sister, the late Penelope Fuller Rutledge. Pretty simple will."

"But if he wrote another one later, it would supersede this one?" Harvey asked.

"Right."

Harvey nodded soberly. "Because we were told he left his estate mostly to charities. And his wife *did* predecease him. Is there anything in there about a bequest to the historical society or the cancer unit?"

Pete scanned the document. "Nope, nothing like that. Just the nephew."

"What about the witnesses?" Jennifer asked.

"Two witnesses." Pete scrutinized the paper. "Looks like Mabel Hart and John Graves." He handed the will back to Harvey.

"Guess we'd better get a copy of the other will," Harvey said. "If it postdates this one, there's no problem, right?"

"Unless you count the little matter of the corpse in the basement as a problem," Jeff said.

Harvey had to explain that to Pete. "And that brings us to this envelope that says U.S. Navy in the corner," he added. "Did I mention that we found parts of a naval uniform buried with the corpse?"

"Interesting," Pete said.

The envelope had been opened previously, and Harvey carefully separated the layers and took out the contents. He unfolded two sheets of paper.

"This is a promotion paper. Promoted to Ensign, Mr. Daniel B. Sanford." He sat looking at it for a moment, then passed it to Pete.

"Who's Sanford?" Pete asked.

"No idea." Harvey looked at the second sheet. "Discharge from the U.S. Navy. Ensign Daniel B. Sanford."

"When?" asked Eddie.

"Ten years ago." Harvey passed the paper to Pete, who held it up so that Eddie could see it without touching it.

"The wedding ring," Jennifer cried.

Harvey looked at her with immediate understanding. "Got to be." He leaned over and kissed her. "I told you, you should be in the unit."

"You'd have thought of it," she said.

He smiled.

"I've got my work cut out for me," Eddie said.

"Well, you can wait until Monday," Harvey told him. "It's been ten years. Another weekend won't hurt him any."

"You think the skeleton was this Daniel B. Sanford?" Abby asked.

Harvey shrugged. "I wouldn't be surprised. Eddie will find out."

Jennifer smiled at Harvey. He was restraining himself from going right to his computer in the study and getting to work. She had no doubt he could find the information faster than Eddie could, but he had made the decision to let Eddie handle this and be the one to track down Daniel B. Sanford's military file, among other things.

"Maybe this guy came to visit Mr. Fuller after he was discharged and died while he was there, and Mr. Fuller was scared to call the cops," said Leeanne.

"So he just buried him in the basement?" Jeff asked. "That's ridiculous."

Leeanne bristled. "Do you have a better explanation?"

"Yeah. Old man Fuller killed him for some reason and hid the body there. The perfect crime. Nobody knew a thing until after the murderer died a natural death," Jeff said.

"Well, *my* theory," said Abby, "is that somebody else killed the Navy guy and took the body in through Mr. Fuller's bulkhead door and buried him there, and Mr. Fuller never knew anything about it." Gary and Andy stared at her with round eyes.

Harvey laughed and turned to Jennifer. "How about you, gorgeous? You're the only Wainthrop who hasn't spun a tale yet."

Jennifer smiled. "I'll leave it to you and Eddie."

Harvey stroked her hair and let his hand rest on her shoulder.

"All right," he said, "next question, Pete. Should we enter these into evidence in the homicide case?"

"I think I would," he said, "at least until you've identified the remains and compared the wills. And, Eddie, you might want to check the documents for prints as well, not just the envelopes."

Harvey said, "Good idea. The prints on the envelopes might be different from the ones inside, if there are any."

Pete shrugged. "You can't always get them off paper, but give it a shot."

"The Navy ought to have Sanford's prints on file." Harvey dropped the envelopes and papers into a plastic bag and handed it to Eddie.

Harvey and Pete took off their gloves.

"Pete, will you have a cup of coffee?" Harvey asked.

"No, thanks," Pete said. "I'd better get home. But if you hit any snags, call me."

"Send me a bill," said Harvey.

Pete gestured dismissively. "It's on me. Great to see you again, and you, Jennifer." He nodded to her then stuck his hand out to Eddie. "Eddie! Sounds like you're doing a good job. Hang in there."

"Eddie just got engaged to my sister-in-law, there," Harvey said with a wave toward Leeanne.

"Hey, congratulations!" Pete eyed Leeanne and nodded again. "The old Priority Unit is changing, huh? All you old bachelors getting married."

Harvey walked with him toward the door, saying, "Yeah, we've got Nate Miller and Jimmy Cook in there now. You know them both, don't you? And Tony—"

"Tony 'Wonder Boy' Winfield?" Pete laughed.

They were all thoughtful when Harvey returned.

Abby said to her fiancé, "This isn't going to give the boys nightmares, is it?"

"I think it's awesome," said Gary, the nine-year-old.

"*I* think it's scary." Little Andy climbed onto his father's lap.

"Maybe we'll need a happy bedtime story tonight," Peter said.

Harvey looked at Eddie. "You contact the Navy first thing Monday, and check the fingerprints. See if they have Sanford's wife's name, too. That wedding ring is almost certainly Sanford's. Put Tony onto the wills. He can get a copy of the other one at the probate office. Check everything—signatures, witnesses, what have you. Maybe these witnesses on the old will are still living. And find out where Mr. Fuller lived back then, when he drafted the handwritten will."

"Well, I know where he lived before he moved here," Eddie said. "I found out yesterday that he moved here from Kittery."

"Good," said Harvey. "Just step in here and I'll help you firm up a list for Monday. Do you think you'll need more manpower?"

He and Eddie went into the study together.

Abby said to Andy and Gary, "Would you like to see the baby?"

Andy nodded, and Leeanne took Connor over close and held him at their eye level. Andy settled back on Peter's lap, studying Connor.

"Not so long ago, you were that size," Peter said to the six-year-old.

"How about me?" Gary asked.

Peter smiled. "No, you were never that small. Nine pounds, you were."

"How big is Connor?" Gary asked.

"Six pounds, twelve ounces, when he was born," said Abby.

Peter nodded. "Andy was seven pounds, two ounces. Not much bigger."

Gary looked at Abby. "Will we get a baby brother when you marry Daddy?"

Abby turned scarlet and looked at Peter helplessly. "Uh, well—"

Peter smiled serenely. "I told you, Gary. If God wants us to."

Abby sighed and slipped her hand through the crook of Peter's arm.

Gary looked critically at Connor. "Can I hold him?"

"If you are very, very careful," Peter said.

Gary sat down on the rug, and Leeanne lowered Connor gently into his arms, keeping one hand behind the baby's head.

"Isn't he something?" she asked, smiling.

"Yeah," Gary said soberly. He turned toward Leeanne, raising his arms a little, and she took Connor back.

"You look beat, Jennifer," Abby said. "You'd better have a nap. There's been a lot of excitement around here today."

"Well, Abigail," said Peter, "Do you still want to see Two Lights this afternoon?"

"I sure do," she replied.

She and Peter and the boys made a noisy exit, and Leeanne looked at Jennifer. "Abby's right—you should lie down while you have the chance. Connor's right on the verge of sleeping."

Jennifer had to admit she was tired, but she wasn't sure she could sleep. A dozen loose threads tangled in her mind. But Connor's eyes were droopy, and Leeanne was right. She needed to rest when she had the chance.

Leeanne was successful in laying Connor in his cradle without disturbing him, and Jennifer lay down on the big bed.

"Let me see your ring again," she said as Leeanne moved toward the doorway.

Leeanne came over and sat down on the bed.

Jennifer pulled her hand close. "It's really pretty."

"Thanks. We picked out the setting together. I love having Mémé Thibodeau's diamond, even if it's not big and flashy. So they did the resetting, which is what Mémé wanted. Her arthritis is so bad, she couldn't wear her ring anymore."

"What did Eddie's mother say about it?" Jennifer asked.

"Marie is fine with it. I'm just afraid Eddie's sisters will be jealous."

"Well, he's the only boy, and he and Mémé are very close," Jennifer said.

"I know. She's really special."

148

Jennifer squeezed Leeanne's hand. "You and Eddie will be happy."

"I can't believe we're getting married in August." Leeanne hugged Jennifer. "Thank you!"

"I didn't do anything," Jennifer said.

"You did everything. You found Harvey, and that started it all."

Jennifer laughed.

"It's true."

"No, honey, it's God's doing. He brought Harvey and me together, and Beth and Jeff, and Abby and Peter, and now you and Eddie. I thank him every day."

"Are you still praying for Mom and Dad?"

"Definitely. I was hoping we'd have a chance to talk to them last weekend, but I went to the hospital Friday night, and we never did get to talk about the Lord."

"I know. I kind of hesitate to say anything to Dad right now. I don't want him to get upset with me and Eddie."

Jennifer smiled and squeezed her hand. "Dad is very protective of his daughters. But when you're married, he'll trust Eddie to take care of you. You'll see."

"They never interfere with you and Harvey, do they?"

"No, never. In fact, Dad sometimes asks Harvey for advice." Jennifer liked that, and she was sure that it pleased Harvey, too.

"But Harvey is so much older than Eddie."

Jennifer smiled. "Not so old."

"I'm sorry. I didn't mean he's senile or anything. I just think Dad sees Eddie as a kid. He calls us 'kids.'"

"He'll always call his children kids. But he likes Eddie. And Eddie's right for you. I think he and Mom are beginning to see that."

"I can't imagine being with anyone else," Leeanne said.

"Eddie loves you very much."

Leeanne smiled. "I know. Isn't it great?"

*****

During supper that evening, Harvey took a call from Carl Turner.

"Sure," he said, and arched his eyebrows at Jennifer.

Not knowing what it was about, she shrugged.

"Come ahead," said Harvey. "We'll save you some dessert." When he'd signed off, and he said, "Carl wanted to know if they could come over for a little while. I think he's ready to talk."

"Great," Jennifer said. "We'll hold dessert. I hope they're bringing Julia."

"They are."

"Eddie and I will play a game with Julia," Leeanne offered. "Then you grownups can talk adult talk while we kids have fun."

Harvey looked at her, a bit bewildered, but Jennifer smiled. "Julia loves Masterpiece." She stood and began to clear the table.

When the Turners arrived, Julia was enthusiastic about the plan and having someone new to play with.

"Let's set it up in the sun room," Leeanne said. "I'll warn you, Eddie knows a lot about artists. Have you played this game before?"

Julia nodded solemnly. "I detest getting forgeries."

"Zen you must beware," said Eddie, putting on a sinister accent.

Jennifer set their dessert plates on a tray for Leeanne to serve when they were ready, and the others took theirs into the living room.

"Well," said Margaret, as she and Carl settled on the couch with their cake and coffee. "We've come to a decision."

"What kind of a decision?" Harvey asked warily.

"I checked with the zoning board yesterday," Carl said. "We can add an office to our house."

"An office?" Jennifer asked.

Harvey looked at Carl. "A medical office?"

"Yes. Margaret's office."

Jennifer pictured the spacious professional building Margaret and Carl shared, with a receptionist and a bookkeeper, two nurses, four exam rooms, a lab, and separate offices.

"You're going to have your office at home?" she asked Margaret.

"Yes. It's the middle ground you told me was there somewhere, Jennifer. I'm going to cut way back on my practice, but I'll still practice. I'll only take a few choice patients. Maybe a hundred."

"A hundred patients?"

"Well, they don't all come to you at once," Margaret said.

"Do we dare ask how many you have now?" Harvey asked.

"You don't want to know," said Carl. "We'll build an addition with a waiting room, an office, and an exam room. That's all she really needs."

"So, would you sell out your practice?" Jennifer asked.

"I don't think so." Margaret took a bite of her cake and frowned as she swallowed. "I'm still working on that. I'll keep practicing, but I think as my pregnant patients deliver, I'll steer them to other gynecologists. And some of them might want to stay with Carl. He's thinking of taking on a partner. Another family practitioner."

"Margaret will keep her hand in with a much smaller practice, and her patients will come to the house," Carl said. "She can be there for Julia."

"What do you think?" Margaret asked eagerly.

Jennifer frowned. "Well, it depends. Would I be one of those hundred privileged patients?"

Margaret smiled. "Of course. But I won't take any new patients."

"Oh, too bad. My sister-in-law Beth needs an obstetrician. I think you've met her."

"Sure, I know Beth. She's pregnant?"

"How come I didn't know this?" Harvey asked.

"I guess I didn't get a chance to tell you, with all the excitement today," Jennifer said.

"What kind of excitement?" Carl asked, so they had to tell them the latest news in the Mr. Bones mystery.

"How do you two get into all these situations?" Margaret asked.

Harvey shrugged. "Comes with the job."

151

"Sounds as if this one came with the house." Carl took a sip of his coffee.

"How's Julia doing? Still horse crazy?" Jennifer asked.

"No, actually, she's changed her mind," Carl replied. "She doesn't want a horse anymore."

"Really? That's odd."

"No, we gave her a choice," said Margaret. She looked at Carl, and he smiled.

"Margaret told her we'd build a little shed and get her a horse for Christmas," he said, "or build a new office for Mommy and get her a baby brother or sister."

Jennifer caught her breath. "Margaret?"

She nodded, smiling a watery smile. "Yes."

Carl grinned and slid his arm around her. "It's part of the deal. Julia picked the baby over the horse. What can I tell you?"

"Of course, we don't know if it will work out," Margaret said diffidently. "I'm past forty."

"You have patients who are over forty," Jennifer said.

"Well, yes, but I always have to tell them all those dire things—you know, how the risks are higher, and the chance of birth defects is greater."

"But those numbers are still very small," said Harvey.

"Yes."

"We had one perfect baby. We'll hope for another," Carl said.

"We'll pray for you," Jennifer told Margaret. "Every day, we'll pray for a healthy baby."

"I've thought some about praying and God," she said hesitantly. "Since I talked to you, Jennifer. But I don't know if it does any good."

"It will if you trust Christ," Harvey said. "He hears the prayers of those who trust him."

There was silence for a moment.

Carl said, "Could you just explain that to us, Harvey? Does everything you pray for come true?"

"Well, no, not always. I didn't mean that nothing bad would ever happen to people who trust Christ, or that prayer is guaranteed to give you the result you want. Christianity isn't about living a charmed life. It's forgiveness for every wrong thing you've ever done, or will do. It's eternal life, because God sent his Son to die for us and take our punishment."

Connor's cry came from the bedroom. Jennifer went to get him. When she returned, carrying the baby, Harvey was reading a verse she recognized from the book of Romans. Pastor Rowland had preached on it not long ago. Carl and Margaret both listened closely.

"The wages of sin is death," Harvey repeated. "That's what we should draw for wages—death. Because we've all sinned."

"Do you really believe that?" Margaret asked.

"Yes. And the next part, that the gift of God is eternal life."

Jennifer prayed silently as they talked.

"What do you think?" Carl asked Margaret.

She reached toward Jennifer and took Connor in her arms.

"I don't know," she said slowly, looking down at the baby. "I think—perhaps—you're right, Harvey. I just don't know."

Harvey sagged just a little. Jennifer wondered if he ought to press Carl, and if Margaret would follow her husband this time.

"I'm not very good at explaining things," Harvey said.

His humility touched Jennifer. Harvey was actually very good at explaining things, and patient, too. But at that moment he really believed he couldn't adequately express the gospel to his friends.

"It seems rather judgmental," Margaret mused. "Isn't it a fallacy to make generalizations about the entire world population?"

Harvey shook his head. "I'm not judging you, Margaret. Those are God's words, that all have sinned, not mine."

Jennifer clamped her teeth together. She wanted to say, "Margaret, do you think Harvey's too smart, too well-educated to believe this nonsense? Do you think only stupid people believe the Bible is true?" But she couldn't say that. And she certainly didn't want to get into a debate with two doctors. Carl and Margaret were not people who could be argued into heaven, of that she was sure. She had never felt so inadequate.

Chapter 15

Sunday, April 23

Harvey was restless Sunday afternoon. He did a little browsing on the computer but spent more time pacing and thinking.

"What is it?" Jennifer asked him at last. Leeanne had headed home, and Eddie had left. Peter and Abby were sitting in the living room, reading the Sunday paper with Gary and Andy. Jennifer sat on their bed, nursing Connor, and Harvey paced their bedroom.

"It's a lot of things, but ... Carl and Margaret mostly."

"You can't force them to believe."

"I know. I just wonder, with all these changes they're making, if they'll think they're okay now. They're doing things they hope will solve the problems in their family. But they still need the Lord."

"Yeah." Jennifer didn't know anything she could say to make him feel better.

Harvey sighed and stopped at the window. He stood looking out over the back yard, where a gentle rain fell on the grass and rose bushes. "Your folks, too. I know I shouldn't let it frustrate me, but I do."

"Do you want to drive up there?"

"Not today, and not without notice. I don't want them to feel ambushed."

Jennifer nodded. "I think Mom is very close to believing. I'm not so sure about Dad."

"And Travis," Harvey said.

"Yeah." Connor was done nursing, and she held him up to Harvey. When he took the baby, she rearranged her clothes and stood. "I worry about Trav, too, especially when he starts college in the fall."

"That could get messy. I hope your father's talked to him about drugs."

"Dad? You're joking, right?" As much as she loved her father, Jennifer didn't see him as one who gave preemptive advice on topics like drugs, alcohol, and sex.

"How about Jeff? Do you think Travis talks to his big brother?"

"Not much. When Jeff was living at home, I think he was too busy untangling his own problems."

"Don't tell me Jeff got into trouble at school." Harvey held Connor close, rubbing his back and eyeing Jennifer closely.

"He had his moments."

"Hmm."

At a knock on the door, Jennifer said, "Come in."

Abby peeked in. "Hey. Peter and boys are leaving."

"We'll come say goodbye," Jennifer said.

She went out to the entry, where Peter was helping Andy with his jacket zipper. "Come again soon, guys," she said.

"Thanks," Peter told her.

Gary met her gaze and said precisely, "Thank you for lunch, Mrs. Larson. It was delicious."

Jennifer smiled. Peter must have given instruction on what to say, because Gary hadn't been so painfully polite in the past.

"You're welcome, Gary. I hope you'll visit us again soon."

"'Bye! Thank you," Andy said, waving vigorously.

Harvey passed the baby to Abby and walked out to the driveway with them. Jennifer turned to Abby with a smile.

"Great kids you're getting."

"Thanks."

"So, only four more days of work for you." Their time with Abby was flying.

"Peter wants me to go over to his business Friday afternoon." Abby patted Connor's back as she spoke. "It's Gary's birthday. He'll take me with him to pick up the boys from school."

"What are you going to do?"

156

"We're going over to their house, and he and the boys will fix supper. He wants me to look the house over and make a list of what I think we need, and tell him if I want to redecorate anywhere."

"Wow. He and Harvey have a lot in common."

Abby laughed. "I feel kind of funny about it. I mean, they've lived there for years, and they must have things the way they want them."

"Not necessarily," Jennifer said. "Harvey never changed a thing after his wife left him, just out of apathy. Maybe Peter's been that way since his wife died. You've been to the house a few times. What do you think so far?"

"It's okay."

"Oh, come on, that's not very enthusiastic."

"Well, I've got to admit, the kitchen doesn't thrill me. Dark cupboards and green paint. Ugh."

"What would you like in there?"

"Maybe some nice, light wallpaper?"

"Tell Peter."

"Do you think I should?"

"Of course. He wants you to. He wants you to have a kitchen that will make you feel great when you're in there cooking for him and doing the dishes and all of that other neat stuff we do in the kitchen. And if you make it really attractive, he and the boys will want to spend time in there, too."

Abby chuckled. "Do you think he'd paint the cabinets?"

"I don't know. Men have this funny thing about painting wood."

"The stain is so dark, they're almost black."

"Ask him what he thinks." Jennifer walked toward the living room, and Abby followed.

"I don't want him to spend a lot."

"Why not? If he wants to do it for you, let him. That's another thing about men. If they have money, they like to use it to make their women happy."

"That seems so ... materialistic. And probably sexist."

Jennifer laughed and sat down on the couch. "Abby, listen to yourself. You're growing up. But I'll tell you something. Peter is a wonderful Christian man. He uses his money for the Lord, too. I don't think he's one who would let material things become most important in his life."

"Harvey's that way," Abby mused. "He's good at making money, but he uses it for other people."

"Uh-huh. He's not a spendthrift, but he likes using money to make things better. He likes a pleasant home, too."

"You guys have a beautiful home."

"Thanks," Jennifer said. "You will, too. Peter's house is nice. It's not as big as this one, but you can make it comfortable and cozy. It's been several years since a woman was there to make it special. I think Peter and the boys will be very happy if you feminize it a little. Just don't be too fussy, and use fabrics and things that are boy-proof."

"Thanks, Jenn." Connor gave a huge burp, and they both laughed. "Want me to put him in the cradle?"

"I'll take him."

Abby went upstairs, and Jennifer sat looking at Connor. "Hi, big guy. Are you happy now?" She heard the entry door open. "If you're not, you will be, 'cause Daddy's coming, and he'll want to play with you."

Sure enough, Harvey came to them like steel to a magnet. He cuddled in close to Jennifer on the couch and grinned at Connor.

"Hey, buddy. How you doin'?"

"You can take him," Jennifer said, "but don't toss him around. He's full."

"Would I do that? Maybe when he's older. Right now, we're just going to have a man-to-man talk." He eased Connor gently from her and settled him on his lap.

*****

Harvey laid Connor beside Jennifer in the morning.

"Don't get up. I'll eat breakfast with Eddie." He kissed her and Connor. "I might not get home for lunch today. We've got a lot to do on this Fuller-Sanborn case. On the other hand, I might, if we decide to revisit the crime scene."

"So, do you want me to pack you a lunch?"

"No, if I don't get home, I'll get something downtown."

Jennifer woke an hour later and called Beth, catching her as she was about to leave for school.

"I know you have to run, but I have more news," Jennifer said. "Margaret Turner says she'll take you as a patient, but you're like the last new patient she'll accept."

"Really? Great! I was hoping I could get her, or at least some female obstetrician."

"Well, she's cutting back on her practice. They're going to move her office home this summer, and they hope to have another baby."

"Hey, that's terrific. I know you guys have been praying hard for them."

"Well, they're not there yet, so keep praying," Jennifer said. "They seem to be really open to spiritual things right now, and they're making some progress in their marriage. But you'd better set up an appointment soon, and tell her receptionist you know she's not taking new patients, but she approved this personally."

"Will do. Is the furnace coming today?"

"That's the plan. Call me when you get home from school, and I'll give you an update."

The heating service truck arrived late that morning, and Abby went over to show the men exactly where not to step. Harvey had carefully cordoned off the side of the basement where the bones had been found and left strict orders that no one was to cross the line. The men had heard the story about the skeleton and looked a little apprehensive. By noon, the foreman was on the Larsons' doorstep, assuring Jennifer that everything was operational, and he had set the thermostat for sixty-five.

"You'll want to go over in an hour or two and check it. If there's any problem, give me a call." He put his business card and the bill in her hand.

"How much?" Abby asked when he had left.

"I think I'll let Harvey look at it." Jennifer pinned the bill, face down, to the little bulletin board beside the house phone.

Abby laughed. "It hurts you to spend money, doesn't it?"

"It's my upbringing. You know we always had to scrimp at home."

"Yes, but you don't have to do that now."

"I know. Harvey gives me shopping lessons sometimes. Remember the maternity clothes?" Harvey had sent her and Abby to the mall with their credit cards and demanded that Jennifer come back with a full wardrobe.

"Peter's even more generous, if possible," Abby said.

"Let him be. Like I said yesterday, you'll give him great pleasure if you spend a little of his money for new curtains in the living room, or new bedspreads for the boys. Something for your home together."

"I'm thinking about it," Abby said.

*****

Beth came after school with a carload of clothes, boots, pots and pans, and other small articles. She rang Jennifer's doorbell to let her know she was ready for some help.

"We ought to have a yard sale," she said. "I've thrown away a ton of stuff already, and we've only been married four months. How does it accumulate so fast?"

"I don't know," Jennifer said, "but wait and have your yard sale over here when it's warmer and you're settled. This is a better neighborhood."

Beth laughed. "You think we'd get higher prices over here?"

"Yup. And more customers. I'm serious. Maybe we can have one together this summer."

Beth checked their new house, and the temperature was fine, so Jennifer took Connor over and sat with him while Beth puttered, arranging the out-of-season clothing in one of the closets upstairs.

"I was going to move Jeff's hunting and reloading stuff over," she said, "but he doesn't want me to bring it until we're ready to sleep here. That's another thing about this neighborhood. More likely to be burglarized."

"You guys might want an alarm," Jennifer said.

Beth frowned. "Not that we'd have anything anyone would want to steal, except Jeff's guns."

They went downstairs, and she resumed arranging her kitchen cupboards and drawers. "I'm not cooking any more at the old house. Jeff's gone until Wednesday, anyway, so I figured I might as well eat up the leftovers and bring the kitchen utensils over. Tomorrow I'm going to move my pantry.

"Abby and I can help you," Jennifer said. "In fact, if you want, we could go over while you're at school and pack all the food in boxes and bring it over here. Then you can unpack it after."

"That's too much for you and Abby."

"Well, Abby would lug the boxes," Jennifer said.

Beth thought about it for a moment. "No, I think I'll ask my brother to help me tomorrow night."

"How's Rick doing? His job still holding out?"

"So far."

The front door opened, and Harvey and Eddie came in through the living room.

"Hey, Jenny! Hi, Beth," Harvey said.

"Is it five o'clock?" Jennifer asked, whipping her phone out. It was only four o'clock.

"No, we came to check on something."

"Good, because I haven't started supper yet."

"Beth, I hope you haven't dusted everything and scrubbed all the woodwork yet," Harvey said.

She eyed him cautiously. "Well, I've done some."

"How about in the master bedroom?" Eddie asked.

"No, I haven't done anything in there yet."

"Great." Eddie headed for the bedroom, carrying his fingerprint kit.

"What's going on?" Jennifer asked.

"The fingerprints on the documents." Harvey reached for Connor and took him from Jennifer. "We want a set of Mr.

161

Fuller's prints to check them against. I figured there'd be a lot of prints in this house now—all of ours, the real estate people, customers from the estate sale, the plumber … But there shouldn't be too many in the master bedroom. I don't think they let people in there during the sale. So Eddie's going to see if he can come up with a set."

"How about the nursing home?" Jennifer asked. "What happened to his effects from there?"

"Nobody seems to know," Harvey said. "Mr. Penninger has no clue. The staff at the home says Mr. Fuller's things were disposed of, but they have no record of how. Usually the family picks them up, but he had no family."

"What about that nephew? Marcus Whatever."

"Marcus Rutledge," said Harvey. "He never showed up."

"Did the lawyer try to find him?"

"I don't think there is a lawyer. Mr. Fuller wrote his own will, and Mr. Penninger filed in probate."

"Did he try to contact the nephew?" Beth asked.

"He says not. He didn't see any need for it, since Rutledge wasn't inheriting anything."

"Sounds funny to me," said Beth. "Wouldn't he be the next of kin?"

"As near as we can tell. Eddie's trying to construct a family tree for Carleton Fuller. There was a sister, Marcus's mother, but she's dead, and a brother who died in childhood. We're trying to find out if there are any cousins or other relatives."

"You could place an ad in the paper like Sherlock Holmes used to," Jennifer suggested. "You know, something like, 'Will any relatives of Carelton G. Fuller please contact the Portland Police Department. It will result in something to your advantage.' That ought to do it."

"But *would* it be advantageous to them?" Beth asked.

Harvey laughed. "You do know Sherlock Holmes wasn't real, don't you?"

"Of course. I was making a joke." Jennifer drummed her fingers on her chin. "Did Mr. Fuller have a police record?"

"Good thought gorgeous. You figure it out."

162

"I guess if he did, you wouldn't be looking for fingerprints here, would you?"

"Nope. We'd have them on file. Old Mr. F. seems to have been clean as a whistle. Eddie couldn't find anything on him."

"Was he in the Navy?" asked Beth.

"Nope. No military service. Too bad, since the Navy started fingerprinting all personnel over a hundred years ago."

"Haven't you found anything about the nephew?" Jennifer asked.

"Not yet. I've got Nate working on it as we speak."

"And what about Sanford, the man whose papers were in the secret hiding place?" Beth asked.

"We left Tony wading through the morass of Naval red tape. Should have a report soon."

Beth turned back to her sorting. "You guys have been busy."

Eddie came to the doorway. "Harv, this is weird."

"What is it?" Harvey moved toward him. Jennifer got up and followed him, and Beth was right behind her. "Don't touch anything," Harvey said over his shoulder as they entered the bedroom.

"Well, there are a few prints that I'm pretty sure are Jeff's. He and I were in here the other day. We'd better take prints from him and Beth and Abby and Jennifer, though, for comparison. But there are some I can't identify, too."

"People who packed up Mr. Fuller's things, probably," said Harvey.

"Should we fingerprint those real estate people?"

"Wouldn't hurt, just to make sure. What else?"

"Well, we should have done this before they took the furniture out, but we didn't know there was a body then," Eddie said with regret. "There are some prints on the woodwork and the window frame that match some of the envelope prints. And I got some from inside the closet door."

"So, those are Mr. Fuller's."

"If they are, Mr. Fuller was the last person to handle Sanford's Navy papers."

"Maybe he was," Harvey said. "He probably put them in the hiding place."

"But then, why aren't they the same as the ones on the old will?"

"The prints on the old will are different from the ones in the bedroom?"

"Right. The bedroom prints match the Navy envelope prints. Call them set A."

"What about the documents inside the Navy envelope?" Harvey asked.

"Set A."

"And the prints on the old will?"

"Set A and some from another person, call them B. And a few unidentifiable smudges."

Harvey was thoughtful. "Dust for prints in the upstairs bedrooms," he said. "Mr. Fuller lived alone here for a long time, but if anyone came for an extended visit—his nephew, for instance—they'd probably have slept upstairs."

Eddie took the fingerprint kit and headed for the stairs.

Chapter 16

Beth took the last few things from her boxes and put them in a cupboard. "That's it for today."

"Come on over to our house," Jennifer said. "You might as well eat with us."

Beth held the baby while Jennifer fixed supper. Harvey and Eddie came over about half an hour later, and it didn't take much persuasion to get Eddie to stay, too.

"I'll bring a device over tomorrow and get both your fingerprints," Eddie said as they ate stir-fry and rice. "Unless you want to come down to the police station in the morning."

"I can do that if it's easier for you," Jennifer said, and Beth nodded. "I could go on my way to school."

"Okay, thanks. Just tell the desk sergeant what you're there for, and that I sent you," Eddie said.

"No ink these days?" Beth asked.

"Nope. It's all electronic."

"Do you think they'd make a card with Connor's prints on it, for us to file?" Jennifer asked.

"Sure, if the little guy doesn't object," Eddie said. "We give out kits for parents. You have to do it the old-fashioned way, though."

"I can do it right here at home," Harvey said. "I've got everything we'd need except the official card."

"I've got some in my kit," Eddie said. "Once in a while I need to take prints and I don't have the machine handy." He shrugged. "Haven't done it for a year or two, though. Let me bring in my kit."

Harvey insisted on holding the baby during the process. Eddie inked Connor's tiny fingers and gently rolled them over the squares on the card. Connor didn't cry until Harvey started wiping his fingers clean.

"You and Winfield have got to get the real estate people's prints," Harvey told Eddie. "Try to get everyone who worked at the house. And try to find out what happened to Mr. Fuller's things from the nursing home. We need a set of prints that we know are his."

"How about from the things we bought at the sale?" Jennifer asked.

"Maybe," said Harvey. "Except at least ten people have handled the lap desk since then."

"I don't think anyone's touched my coffee can but me," Beth said. "Of course, the real estate agents had to touch it when they got ready for the sale. It had a price tag on it."

"Can you bring it to us?" Harvey asked.

"Sure."

"Don't touch it," Eddie said. "Pick it up with—no, wait. Is it next door? I'll just go over to your house with you and get it when you're ready, okay?"

"All right," said Beth.

Jennifer heard a faint beeping.

"I think your cell phone is ringing," she said. Harvey had taken off his sport coat and tossed it on the wicker settee in the sunroom before supper.

He got up and went in there and pulled the phone out of the pocket.

"Larson."

They all waited without speaking. It was always important when it was the cell phone. Only close family members and police officers had the number.

"Good work," he said. "Be sure to ask them for a set of prints on each subject. We've got some interesting developments on the prints from the house."

He came back to the table. "Winfield hit paydirt," he said. "Nate had found out where Marcus Rutledge went to high school and got a copy of his yearbook. It listed his future plans as a military career. He told Tony, and while he had the naval officer

166

on the line, Tony asked him to run Marcus Rutledge's name. Rutledge is in the Navy."

"He's on active duty?" Eddie asked.

"Yup. He's on the *USS Eisenhower* right now. Home ported in Norfolk, Virginia, but they're out on deployment in the Persian Gulf."

Eddie whistled. "How long has he been in the Navy?"

"Don't know. Tony's getting them to send us a report along with the Sanford file. Should have it when we get to the office in the morning."

*****

Tony Winfield rang the Larsons' doorbell the next morning as they were eating breakfast.

"Sorry to bother you, Captain, but this is important."

Harvey brought him into the kitchen, and Jennifer poured coffee for him. She saw Tony's curious glances. He must think they were an odd couple. Harvey was wearing his best suit, the one he had tailored in London, and Jennifer was barefoot, wearing a faded pair of jeans and Harvey's green Harvard T-shirt that hung nearly to her knees.

Tony opened his jacket and took out two sheets of paper.

"Don't know why I didn't catch this yesterday," he said. "I was so wrapped up in the Navy angle, I guess. It struck me first thing when I looked at it this morning." He spread the papers flat on the table and pointed to one. "This is a copy of the old will you found in the house."

Harvey nodded, and Tony pointed to the other sheet. "This is the last page of the new will the executor used."

Harvey looked closely at both, nodding.

"What?" Jennifer asked. She couldn't help it, the curiosity bubbled up so strongly inside her.

Harvey smiled. "Take a look, gorgeous. You'd have spotted it right off."

She looked at the two papers, not knowing what she was looking for. The witnesses were different for the two wills, and both were signed, "Carleton G. Fuller." But the formation of the capitals jumped out at her.

"The signatures don't match."

Harvey smiled. "That's my girl."

"But the old will was made twenty-two years ago, and the new one only three years ago," she said. "If he was ill when he made the second will, his handwriting might have changed."

Harvey turned to Tony. "Get hold of that handwriting expert we use. Paula can give you the number."

Tony nodded and gathered up the papers.

"If the second will is fraudulent, do we still own the house?" Jennifer asked.

Harvey hesitated. "Good question. Maybe I'd better call Pete again."

"Here's a thought," said Tony. "If the second will is fraudulent, why leave all the guy's money to charities? Why not leave it to a person, like, oh, I don't know, the murderer?"

"But Mr. Fuller wasn't murdered," Jennifer said. "He died in a nursing home. The guy in the basement was murdered."

Harvey had the look Eddie called "overdrive."

Tony eyed him curiously. Jennifer put her hand on his sleeve.

"Harvey?"

"Gorgeous, I'm going to give you a promotion." He pushed back his chair and stood up. "Where's my briefcase?"

His cell phone rang.

"Yeah, Mike? Okay, I'll get over there. Thanks." He stuffed the phone in his jacket pocket. "Gotta run. There's been another bank robbery. Mike's having the dispatcher call Jimmy and Nate, but I need to go. Is Connor asleep?"

"Yes," Jennifer said, walking with him and Tony toward the door.

"Well, give him a big kiss from Daddy." Harvey stopped long enough to kiss her soundly. "I'll call you."

"So long, Mrs. Larson," said Tony.

As they went to their vehicles, she heard Harvey say, "I'll call Eddie on my way to the bank. You guys have got to get right on this theory of Jennifer's."

Jennifer closed the door slowly, wondering what her theory was.

It came to her as she sat in the rocking chair about an hour later, feeding Connor. Abby was folding laundry in the utility room off the entry.

"Abby," she screamed. "Abby, come here!"

Abby tore into the living room. "What is it, Jennifer? A spider?"

"No. It's Mr. Bones. He's not the Navy guy. He's Mr. Fuller."

"Huh?" If ever Abby had a dumb blonde look, that was it.

"Sit." Jennifer pointed to the couch, still organizing her thoughts. "This morning I said something about Mr. Fuller not being the one that was murdered, and Harvey got the look. You know, *the* look."

"You mean, the Captain Larson in Action look?" Abby asked.

"Yes. And I think I just figured out what he figured out."

"Which is…?"

"Tony asked, if the second will was fraudulent, why wasn't the money left to the murderer. The skeleton was Mr. Fuller. This Navy guy at some point in the last twelve years came and murdered Mr. Fuller and buried him in the cellar, then assumed his identity."

"Jennifer." Abby shook her head. "How could anyone do that? People would know it wasn't him."

"He had no family. Just a nephew who's off on deployment most of the time. The nephew may not have seen him for years."

"But the neighbors would know," Abby persisted.

"Maybe," Jennifer thought hard about that. "I'm going to call Harvey."

*****

"We think alike, gorgeous," Harvey said.

"So, you're not upset that I called while you're working?"

"Am I ever upset when you call me?"

"No."

"I'm glad you did call," he said. "I gave Eddie the bare bones, no pun intended, of this theory so he can start working on it. I've got Nate and Jimmy chasing after the bank robber. We think we've got a positive ID this time, and they may be able to bring him in. I'm heading back to the station now and brainstorm with Eddie and Tony, but I'd like your thoughts."

"That's very flattering," Jennifer said. "I think Tony was really the one who saw it first."

"You're an ex officio member of the Priority Unit," Harvey said. "There are so many leads to follow, it's hard to know where to go first."

"Borrow some patrolmen from the day sergeant," she recommended. "If you've got the Navy reports, you should be able to track down Daniel Sanford or some of his relatives, and you might be able to contact Marcus Rutledge. And look for the people who witnessed the new will. But I think you should get some uniformed officers and send them over here. Canvas the neighborhood. Find out how long all the neighbors have lived here, and if they knew Mr. Fuller, and if they thought he'd changed at some point, or looked different suddenly—got glasses or a toupee or something. Hey!" She stopped as a new thought hit her.

"What, baby?"

"Ask Mr. Bailey."

"Of course!" Mr. Bailey had owned the Larsons' house for years. He and his wife Flossie must have known Mr. Fuller.

"It makes me wonder how well Ralph Penninger knew him, too," Jennifer said.

"And Bud and Janice," Harvey added.

"We could have a block party and have everyone give us their impressions of Mr. Fuller," Jennifer suggested, getting into the idea.

"No, I think we'll let the patrol officers handle it, gorgeous."

"Just a thought."

"Keep having thoughts. You've had several good ones today."

An hour later, a cab arrived at the house. The driver rang the doorbell.

"I have a delivery for Jennifer Larson," he told Abby.

Jennifer moved in behind her, with Connor on her shoulder. "I'm Mrs. Larson."

"Then this is for you, ma'am."

Abby opened the door, and the driver held out a bouquet of narcissus and tulips and an envelope.

Jennifer stared for a moment, then reached to take the envelope. "Thank you."

Abby carried the flowers into the kitchen and got the mayor's vase from the cupboard.

"They're beautiful," Jennifer said.

When Abby was done arranging the flowers, Jennifer handed her the baby and opened the envelope.

"To the most wonderful woman in the world. Meet me at Bleeker's for lunch? Harvey."

"Wow!" said Abby. "You'd better get dressed."

Jennifer looked down at her jeans and T-shirt, and the burp cloth over her shoulder. "You don't think I'd pass muster at Bleeker's?"

"Get moving!" Abby yelled. "I'll keep Connor."

*****

It was the most romantic lunch she'd had in a long time. Candles at midday, soft music, dim lighting, flowers on the table, and her husband. His eyes shone when she walked in behind the hostess. Abby had been right when she'd suggested the green silk dress Jennifer hadn't worn since the pre-maternity-clothes era.

Harvey stepped forward, took both her hands, and kissed her. Jennifer about melted.

"I adore you," he said softly.

She blushed a little, but it was so dark no one would be able to tell.

171

The hostess stood back and smiled as he held her chair for her. She handed them the menus. "Would you like a cocktail?"

"Pepsi for me and Poland Spring Water for the lady," Harvey said, his eyes not wavering from Jennifer's. He reached across the table and grasped her left hand. The hostess went away, and he said, "I missed you all morning."

"I think I needed this." Jennifer smiled into his blue, blue eyes.

"Good. I hoped it was the right thing."

They had seafood, which Jennifer rarely cooked at home, and made eyes at each other and talked softly about everything but Mr. Bones.

"Dessert?" their waitress asked.

"How about it, gorgeous?" Harvey asked. "Cheesecake?"

"No, I've been eating too much dessert lately. You go ahead."

"No, I'm stuffed." Harvey was a social sweet-eater. He usually passed on dessert, unless they were serving it to company.

The waitress left the bill, and he pulled out his wallet, wrote a generous tip on the slip, and closed the folder on his credit card. She whisked it away and had his card back in a couple of minutes.

"Let's get out of here," Harvey said.

He walked Jennifer to her van in the parking lot and turned her to face him, his hands on her shoulders.

"Let's do this again soon," he said.

"Anytime."

He kissed her passionately, right there in front of Bleeker's. People going into the restaurant stared, but Jennifer made herself not think about that.

He held her head against his shoulder afterward. "Don't worry about the people, gorgeous. We're just some nutty couple crazy in love."

"Harvey," called a male voice, and Jennifer whipped her head around.

"Well, John." Harvey turned around, keeping one arm around Jennifer, and extended his hand to a tall, gray-haired man

172

approaching with a shorter, fortyish fellow. John wore a trench coat, and the other man had on a police uniform that was different from Portland's.

"How you doing?" John asked heartily. "This is my deputy, Parker Dobson."

Harvey shook Parker's hand. "John, Parker, this is my wife, Jennifer. Jenny, this is John Hillman, the chief from Cape Elizabeth."

"Hello," Jennifer said as naturally as possible, which was difficult for her. Meeting new people was bad enough, but she felt like she and Harvey had been caught on Lover's Lane.

"Mrs. Larson," said John. Parker stared a little. He nodded quickly, then looked away when Jennifer looked at him.

"We've been to the chiefs' conference, and I was just talking to Mike Browning," John said.

"Oh, right, that's today," Harvey said. Portland was hosting a small conference for police chiefs and deputy chiefs in southern Maine.

"Didn't I hear that you folks have a new baby?" John asked jovially.

"Right," said Harvey. "Ten days old." He took his wallet out and showed the men a picture of Connor in the hospital.

"Nice baby," Parker said, and Jennifer tried not to smile. He sounded like a single man.

"Hey, great kid," John said. "But then, with parents like you two, he's gotta be good-looking, right?"

"Absolutely," said Harvey. "He's smart, too. Way ahead of the charts on eye contact and vocalizing."

John and Parker eyed him oddly.

Harvey laughed.

"Ha!" said John. "I get you."

Parker smiled faintly.

"Say, Harvey, Mike told me about this old corpse thing that happened in your house."

"Well, it's actually the house next to us. Jennifer and I bought it as an investment. We were having the furnace replaced, and the workmen discovered a skeleton in the basement."

"Man, that's something," John said. "We've got to get together and discuss it."

"Sure," said Harvey. "I've got to get back to the station now, though, and Jenny needs to get home." He had that right. Connor was probably screaming.

John and Parker went into the restaurant, and Harvey opened her car door for her.

"So much for being anonymous lovers in the parking lot," Jennifer said, getting in.

He bent down and looked into her eyes. "You aren't really ashamed to be seen kissing me, are you, gorgeous?"

"Ashamed? No, of course not. A little embarrassed, though."

"Why? I'm your husband."

"It's just ... you know, a private thing."

"Well, I'm sorry I embarrassed you."

Jennifer sat there for a moment, thinking about that. She came to a decision and got out of the van. "Don't be sorry. Kiss me again, handsome."

Chapter 17

Before he left the office that evening, Harvey printed out copies of Eddie and Tony's reports. He'd given it a lot of thought and decided to bring in a consultant on the case.

"You might as well read it, Jenny. You're right in the middle of this thing." Dinner wasn't quite ready, and they sat down in the kitchen. He handed her the folder across the little table.

"Really? I'm allowed?"

"I'd like to get your thoughts on the case."

"Wow." She smiled and opened the folder. For the next few minutes she didn't speak, but read intently. Harvey sipped his coffee and watched her, enjoying every second. He loved the way her eyebrows twitched when she read something especially interesting. At last she looked over at him.

"So Daniel Sanford's wife died."

"Yes, he was stationed in San Diego. She was killed in an auto accident. His pension checks since his discharge are directly deposited in a bank in … guess where?"

"Portland, Maine?"

"Close. Biddeford."

"His wife's name was Millicent," she said.

"Right. Millie, people called her."

"So it was his wedding ring."

"Had to be. The boys are looking for the marriage record. The Navy says Sanford enlisted in Boylston, Mass. Eddie's checking there for family information."

"And did they send you his fingerprints?"

Of course she would ask that. He smiled, thinking not for the first time that Jennifer would have made an ace detective.

"They did. Get this, gorgeous: Daniel Sanford's fingerprints, compliments of the U.S. Navy, match Eddie's Set A from the documents in the secret compartment."

Her eyes narrowed. "And the fingerprints from Beth and Jeff's bedroom?"

"That's right. It lends credence to your theory. The man who lived in that house for the last eight to twelve years was not Carleton G. Fuller. He was Daniel Sanford."

"Unbelievable," she said. "We lived right next to him."

"Only for a few months, and he was ill," said Harvey. "I only saw him a couple of times."

"I saw him once. He didn't look healthy then." She frowned. "I was out in the back yard, trying to prune the roses according to one of Flossie Bailey's books. I saw him over the fence. He had short, gray hair and a big nose, and a prominent forehead."

Harvey nodded. "Blue eyes, sunken cheeks. I remember him as about five feet, eleven inches, but slightly stooped. Thin—a hundred and fifty pounds. That description fits with his chart at the nursing home."

"Who called the ambulance when he was sick?" Jennifer asked.

"Ralph Penninger. He hadn't seen him for several days and went over to check on him."

"Did the boys find out how long Mr. Penninger lived there?"

"He and his wife bought the house at 133 seven years ago. They probably had more contact with Mr. Fuller than anyone else on the block, with the possible exception of Everett Bailey. I haven't talked to him yet. Thought maybe we'd ride down there and see him tomorrow."

"You and me?" she asked.

"Yes. Would you like to take a ride with me on business?" Mr. Bailey had moved in with his daughter Lucy, in Saco.

"I'd love to. Can we take Connor?"

"I think we have to," said Harvey. The baby couldn't be away from her for more than a couple of hours, and he wouldn't want to leave him that long when he could have him close by.

"So, is Ralph Penninger sure the Mr. Fuller he met when he moved in here was the same Mr. Fuller he sent to the hospital last fall?" she asked.

"He says there's no question. So does his wife, Loretta. Same man. They never had a doubt. When I hinted there might have been an identity switch, they were shocked."

"Of course. But the switch had to happen before they moved in. What about Bud and Janice? I saw Janice yesterday, but we weren't onto the switch then."

"Well, the officer who questioned them said they were adamant he was the same man who lived here when they moved in ten years ago."

"If they're right, Mr. Fuller was killed at least ten years ago," Jennifer said.

"Yeah. We're trying to locate his medical and dental records."

"Shouldn't be hard," she mused.

"It wasn't, for his recent records. His doctor is over on Franklin Street. But he only started going to Dr. Targay after he moved up here from Kittery."

"So he went to this Dr. Targay for twelve years?" she asked.

"Nine, actually. We haven't found evidence yet that he went to any doctor the first three years he lived here."

"Did Dr. Targay get his records from his old doctor?"

"They told Tony they'd sent a request. There was a note in his chart. But apparently they never got a response from the other doctor."

"But they had the doctor's name?"

"He's retired now. Tony's trying to find out if the records from his old practice in Kittery are still available."

Jennifer sighed. "So much legwork."

"That's the way most cases are," Harvey said. "You push paper and sweat over a computer and spend hours on the phone, until finally you get one little piece of information that ties everything together."

"What about Beth's coffee can?" she asked.

"Interesting thing. She hadn't opened it. The fingerprints on the outside were hers and Myrtle Holt's."

"So, did you open it?"

"The lid seems to be stuck. Maybe a little rusty. It's in my Explorer. I thought I'd ask Beth tomorrow if she minds if we proceed. It might damage the can or the lid if we pry it off, and I didn't want to do that without Beth's permission."

"Does it feel empty?"

"It's light, but there's something in it. Could be a few grains of coffee, but I don't think so."

"I'm burning enchiladas." Jennifer jumped up and went quickly to the stove. "Guess they're all right."

When they had assembled their meal and Harvey had prayed, she picked up Eddie's report again. Connor stirred in the bedroom, giving out a faint wail. Harvey had been listening for that signal. He brought him to the table and held him while he ate, burbling at him between bites.

"So, they haven't contacted the nephew yet," Jennifer said.

"No, Eddie spent a lot of time being shuffled from one official to the next, but he finally found out the *Eisenhower* is back in port. I told him to try again tomorrow."

Jennifer put the report down and took a bite of cheese and chicken, but her eyes were unfocused. Running over all the clues in her mind, Harvey figured.

"What's the connection between Fuller and Sanford? I mean, how did they know each other?"

"I wish I knew," Harvey said. "The only connection I can see, and it's a remote one, is that Sanford and Fuller's nephew were both in the Navy. But Sanford was thirty years older than Rutledge. Seems unlikely they'd be buddies. But Rutledge has been in the Navy fifteen years. We're trying to find out if he and Sanford were ever stationed in the same place."

Jennifer said, "Sanford was discharged ten years ago. That gives him and Marcus Rutledge five years of overlapping Navy time to connect."

"That's right. Tomorrow Eddie and Tony are going to hound the Navy about that." Connor began to fuss, and Harvey checked his diaper. "Guess I should have changed this guy." He stood up, and Jennifer followed him into the bedroom.

Harvey laid the baby on the changing table.

"Do you want me to do that?" she asked.

"Are you kidding? I've waited years for this." He unsnapped Connor's suit and carefully removed the disposable diaper.

"Harvey, I want to say something."

"What is it?" He reached for another diaper.

"Today was fantastic. At the restaurant, I mean. You make me feel really cherished. And, well, in the parking lot—"

He swung around to face her, keeping one hand on Connor's tummy. "I didn't mean to embarrass you."

"I know, and I've been thinking about that a lot."

"Sometimes I just need to hold on to you," he said, "but if you want me to quit kissing you—"

"Don't do that," she said in mock horror, and he laughed. "I was just going to say, it's okay. It means everything to me that you love me. So I hereby declare that you have permission to kiss me, anytime, anyplace."

He smiled and taped up the diaper, then walked toward her, holding Connor in the crook of his arm.

"How about here and now?"

*****

Eddie ate breakfast with the Larsons after he and Harvey ran on Wednesday, and they went over all the leads Eddie and Tony needed to check that day while Harvey and Jennifer drove to Saco. He also gave Eddie instructions to pass on to Nate, Jimmy, and the patrolmen who were helping with the Fuller case.

Abby came downstairs as Jennifer was putting Connor's jacket on him.

"Peter's taking half the day off, and we're going to help Beth and Jeff move," she announced.

"Great," said Harvey. "We should be home for lunch. We'll pick up pizza for the moving crew."

Eddie headed for the police station, and Harvey, Jennifer, and Connor loaded into Harvey's Explorer and headed south. Harvey had called Mr. Bailey, and he and his daughter were expecting them. It was a pleasant drive, and on the way they talked about Connor, the murder case, and Carl and Margaret.

"You feeling okay, gorgeous?" Harvey asked. He held her hand when he didn't need both his to drive.

"Pretty good," she said.

"You look great. Got your figure back, as they say."

She laughed. "I promise to gain more weight with the next baby."

He smiled. "Just don't be sick again."

"I'm taking Connor for a checkup Friday."

"Who's our pediatrician?" Harvey asked.

"Carl, unless you want someone else."

"No, I don't have a problem with that, unless you do."

"No." She squeezed his hand.

"When's your checkup?"

"A couple more weeks."

"Have you heard from Margaret?"

"No, haven't seen or heard from either of them since they came to the house."

"I should call Carl."

Jennifer nodded. "Invite them over again if it seems right."

Lucy Bainbridge and her father greeted them at her door with a smile.

"Come right in," Lucy said. "I was about to make tea. Will you join us?"

"Sounds good," Harvey said.

"Good to see you, Captain and Mrs. Larson," Everett Bailey said. "And look at the little fellow!"

Jennifer grinned. "Hello, Mr. Bailey. Thank you for letting us come."

Lucy made tea, accompanied by a plate of tiny tarts and fancy cookies. She gushed over Connor, and Jennifer let her hold him for a few minutes while the tea steeped. Lucy handed him back when she got up to pour. Harvey and Mr. Bailey discussed the flower beds.

"I've contacted Mr. Fournier, and he's going to come next week to look over the roses," Harvey said.

Mr. Bailey nodded. "He's excellent. If you want someone to work in the yard once or twice a week, he'll recommend someone good for you."

"Great." Harvey sipped his tea. "Well, Mr. Bailey, as I hinted on the phone, this is really an official visit, even though we're having a lot of fun."

Mr. Bailey smiled. "What is it, son? Something to do with Carleton Fuller, you said."

"Yes, sir. You knew he died a couple of months ago?"

"Yes, I read it in the paper. I thought at the time, what a waste. A lonely old man. When you don't have children, you don't have company and joy in your old age." He nodded toward Lucy. "My daughter and son-in-law have made me feel right at home here, and I'm so thankful. The Lord has really blessed me. The grandchildren come around often, and my two sons were up at Christmastime. Family is irreplaceable."

"I agree with you, sir," said Harvey. "One thing about Mr. Fuller not having been married was that no one seemed to know him really well. I'm wondering if you and Mrs. Bailey didn't know him longer than anyone else in the neighborhood."

Mr. Bailey pursed his lips. "We were there when he moved in."

"I was hoping you'd say that, sir. And you met him when he moved in, or shortly after?"

"We went over the day the moving van came. Flossie made cookies, and we took a plate. Didn't know he was single, of course. Thought there might be a family, or at least a wife."

"But he was all alone?"

"Yes."

"Did you visit back and forth?"

"Not much. But we'd see each other in the yard, or when we got the mail and the paper, you know. Flossie and I worked in the gardens a lot before she got sick, and I still puttered in the yard after that. I'd see Carleton in his yard. We always had a word."

Harvey nodded, then said seriously, "Now, Mr. Bailey, this is very important. I want you to think carefully, way back to a time

181

about ten years ago. Two years after Mr. Fuller moved in. Maybe a little more, or a little less."

Mr. Bailey cocked his head to one side.

"That when the murder took place?"

"Yes," said Harvey. "You've read about it?"

"Yes. I almost called you last week, but I figured you were busy."

"You can call me anytime, Mr. Bailey," Harvey said, with his irresistible smile. "What I want to ask you is this: was there a time when you noticed, or thought you noticed, a change in Mr. Fuller?"

Mr. Bailey sat quietly. Connor got his fist into his mouth, and he slurped a little. Lucy sipped her tea tranquilly.

"Well, now, it's funny you should mention it," Mr. Bailey said at last.

Jennifer held her breath. Harvey's face got that overdrive look. Waiting, thinking.

"There *was* a time. He'd had company." Mr. Bailey's eyes focused somewhere on the wall beyond Jennifer.

"His nephew?" Harvey asked softly.

"No, no, the nephew had been there before. At least once. I'd seen him go in and out a couple of times. I asked Carleton the next day who'd been there, and he said, 'That's my sister's boy.' Mark, I think he called him."

"Marcus Rutledge," said Harvey.

Mr. Bailey nodded. "Well, Carleton didn't have much company then, so I remarked on it. Then one night we saw a car in his driveway. I knew it wasn't his car. Carleton had an old Mercury. Flossie said she saw a man go in before supper. The car sat there all night. The next morning it was there early, but when we came back from church, it was gone."

"So, that was a Saturday night?" Harvey asked.

"Must have been. I remember we went to church the next morning."

"What kind of car was it?"

Mr. Bailey rubbed his forehead. "Maroon," he said at last. "Four-door. That's all I can tell you. Sorry, son."

182

"It's all right," said Harvey.

"You think Carleton killed somebody?" Mr. Bailey asked.

"We're trying to sort it out," Harvey said gently.

"Well, I didn't see the fellow. Flossie did, but I don't recall as she said what he looked like."

"Did she remark on his clothes?" Harvey asked.

"No, no, don't think so."

"Well, sir, after that, did you see Carleton Fuller?"

"Hmm. Don't think I did for a few days. I was going to ask him who the company was that stayed overnight. But I didn't see him, and I kind of forgot."

"When did you see him next?" Harvey asked.

He shook his head. "That was ten years ago, or eight, anyway."

"Yes, I know, Mr. Bailey. I'm sorry to have to press you like this, but you seem to be the only one in the neighborhood who remembers Carleton Fuller before that time."

"What are you getting at?" Mr. Bailey asked.

"Sounds like he thinks Mr. Fuller killed his company and hid the body," said Lucy.

"Well, maybe," Harvey said. "We just don't know what happened. I was wondering, sir, when you *did* see Carleton Fuller again, did he look the same?"

"Land!" said Lucy, "What do you mean, Mr. Larson?"

"Well, was his hair parted the same way, did he have more wrinkles, was his nose the same?"

"Hmm," said Mr. Bailey. "You know, I thought his nose looked funny. Maybe he had a cold or something. I don't know. But I saw him from a distance, I recall. He was driving out in his Mercury one day. Yes, I hadn't seen him for some time. Thought maybe he'd been away. But I saw him drive out, and I said to Flossie, 'Was that Carleton? He was wearing glasses.' Yes, I said that."

"He never wore glasses before?" Jennifer asked.

"Not that I recalled."

"So, he got driving glasses," Lucy said, watching Harvey carefully. Jennifer could feel an energy of excitement building up in her.

"Probably so," said Harvey. "Did you see him again soon?"

"No, not for a while. Flossie and I mentioned it several times. That summer he seemed to be gone a lot. Then he was back."

"You saw him again?"

"At first, we saw lights on in the house in the evening. Once in a while his car would go out, but he seemed to be keeping pretty close to home. Finally, Flossie took some soup over."

"Were you with her?"

"No, no. She told me she took the soup over, and he came to the door in his robe. She said he looked just awful. Said he'd been sick."

"Did he say what was wrong?"

"I don't know. He had arthritis, I knew that. Complained about it awfully in the winter, the first year he was there. Couldn't shovel his own walk that year."

"What about after that?" Harvey asked, so quietly, Jennifer could feel his tension.

"You know, he got better. I remember him raking leaves and shoveling a little later on. Usually he'd hire a boy to do those things, but he seemed to get around more than he did that first year or two. And I thought he could stand a little taller."

"Taller?" Harvey asked.

"Well, straighter, you know. Not so slouched."

"Mr. Bailey, are you sure he was the same man who lived next to you the first year?" Harvey said.

A moment of deadly quiet hovered, then Connor fussed.

"I'm sorry," Jennifer said to Lucy. "Is there a place where I could nurse the baby?"

Lucy took her into the kitchen and settled her there with a fresh cup of tea at her elbow.

"So, your husband thinks it was Mr. Fuller who was murdered?" Lucy asked.

"They don't know yet."

184

Lucy went eagerly back to the living room.

Chapter 18

When they left Lucy's house, Harvey had nothing conclusive, but in his notebook were the pertinent points of Mr. Bailey's account. Carleton Fuller had stayed out of sight for a while after his mysterious visitor had arrived. His appearance had changed superficially. His arthritis had gotten less severe, and he stood straighter.

"They didn't see him up close very often," Harvey said on the way home. "Flossie went into her wheelchair eight years ago. She probably never saw him up close after that. Only through the windows and across the yards. Everett called greetings to him and waved once in a while. A gray-haired man who'd gotten glasses."

"You'd think they'd have known, all the same."

"He may have taken steps so he'd look more like Mr. Fuller," Harvey said. "They were about the same age. Sanford was a few years younger."

"Daniel Sanford was in good health when the Navy discharged him," Jennifer said.

"Yes, and the man whose remains were found in the cellar had arthritis," said Harvey.

"Was there an autopsy on Mr. Fuller? The man who died in the nursing home, I mean?"

Harvey shook his head. "Nobody saw any need."

"Dental records?" she asked.

"Good thinking. Eddie's been looking for some older records. I think I told you he'd only found the recent ones." Harvey pulled into the parking lot of a pizza shop three blocks from home. "I asked Everett if he might possibly have anything with Mr. Fuller's handwriting on it, so we could compare it with the old will. He didn't."

"What happened to all the papers in the house?" Jennifer asked.

"Myrtle says they destroyed them."

"What? You're joking."

"No, they were to sell the contents of the house. Anything unsalable, they were to destroy. That included letters, old bank statements, anything like that."

"I don't understand."

"There was no family."

"The nephew."

"He wasn't mentioned in the will. There was nobody to take the personal papers like there usually is."

"There must be something with his handwriting on it," she said fiercely.

"Easy, Jenny. We'll figure this out."

He got out of the Explorer and went in to get the pizza. Jennifer unbuckled Connor and lifted him out of his seat and held him until Harvey came back, when Connor and the fragrant pizza were settled in the back seat together.

When they got home, Peter Hobart's car was parked behind Abby's in their driveway. Jeff's truck and Eddie's were in the driveway of 135.

Jeff came out and helped carry the pizza and drinks. Beth had paper plates, and they sat down in their new dining area and ate. Peter was wearing a gray sweatshirt and jeans. Jennifer was used to seeing him in suits, but the casual air looked good on him.

When Abby came to take Connor from her, Jennifer whispered, "Your guy's looking tough today."

Abby smiled and raised her eyebrows.

"How's it going?" Harvey asked.

"Great," Jeff replied. "We got the washer and dryer hooked up, and we've got just about all the stuff over here from the other house."

As they ate, Eddie told Harvey that the Navy's latest report indicated Marcus Rutledge's ship had docked two days earlier, and he was one of a hundred and fifty sailors given two weeks' leave. Rutledge had signed out, but no one had been able to tell Eddie where he had gone on his leave.

Harvey told them all what Mr. Bailey had said about Carleton Fuller.

"Man, it's gotta be true," Eddie said. "Somehow this Sanford guy knew Fuller didn't have any close friends or relatives and figured he could get away with it. He just laid low for a while, then gradually reappeared as Fuller, from a distance. If nobody saw him up close for a while, eventually they'd forget the details."

"Think so?" Beth asked.

"Well, a lot of the people on this street were elderly," Jennifer said. "Eyesight failing, and all that."

"Bud and Janice—" Abby began.

"They didn't live here then," said Harvey. "Neither did the Penningers. They all met Mr. Fuller after the switch was made. So they met Sanford, and thought he was Fuller. Never questioned it."

"Isn't there anyone else who would remember?" asked Beth.

"Well, Mr. Bailey's our best witness so far."

"Who lived on the other side, in the Penningers' house?" Jeff asked.

"Check on that, Eddie," Harvey said. "If the former owners are still living, we need to talk to them."

"The real Mr. Fuller bought this house," Jennifer said pensively.

"Yes. And Sanford came a couple of years later."

"Well, then, the real Mr. Fuller's signature must be on the deed to the house."

"Of course," said Harvey. "Gorgeous, I'm going to send you to the Academy for procedural training."

She smiled. It was an idle threat. They both knew she'd never leave home now that Connor was there.

"So, where's the deed?" Jeff asked.

"The registry of deeds, at the courthouse," Eddie said. "I'm on my way." He stood up, brushing crumbs from his clothes. "I'll compare the signature with the ones on the wills."

"You got it," said Harvey. "Call me as soon as you see it."

Peter stood up. "Thanks for letting me in on the sleuthing and the family moving bee," he said. "Don't know when I've had this much fun, but I'd better get back to business now."

"You going in those clothes?" Harvey asked.

"No, I'll stop at home and change," Peter said.

Abby passed Connor to Beth and walked with Peter to the door.

"So, Beth, can we open that coffee can now?" Harvey asked.

"You didn't open it?"

"No, I didn't want to scratch the paint without your permission."

"Let's do it," she said.

Harvey went to his garage to get the can. He returned with it, plus a screwdriver and small hammer. Abby followed him in.

"I think this will do it." Harvey held up the old, two-pound Chock Full O' Nuts can, black and yellow, with blue and red lettering. He placed it on the table, and Jennifer held it down. He put the blade of the screwdriver against the underside of the rim and tapped the end of the handle with the hammer. The lid popped off suddenly and flew off the table to the floor.

Harvey bent over the can and peered inside.

"Got tweezers, Beth?"

"Yes. Oh, where did I put them?" She gave Jennifer the baby and went into the bathroom, returning a minute or two later. "For a wonder, I found them." She handed them to Harvey.

He reached into the can with them and extracted three small pieces of paper.

"Looks like deposit tickets. Portland Savings Bank. A deposit of four hundred thirty-nine dollars, eleven years ago. Three hundred ninety-eight. Four hundred twelve."

"Is that bank still in business?" Beth asked.

"I think they merged with someone else a while back," Harvey said. "I can find out who on my computer at work. Then I'll go around and see the bank manager, and find out if Mr. Fuller had an account with them eleven years ago. The account number is the same on all three slips."

"Wouldn't the killer have destroyed evidence like that?" Beth asked.

"If he found it. Maybe he couldn't get the lid off, either."

*****

190

Harvey went home at suppertime elated. His afternoon's work had paid off. Jennifer was curled up on the couch with the baby, reading a novel, and something cooking smelled good.

"Hi." She stretched and let him take Connor. "I hope you don't mind—I got lazy and put a frozen meal in the oven."

"No problem." He bent down to kiss her. "I got some information this afternoon, sweetheart. Mr. Fuller had several accounts with the savings bank. A checking account and some investments. He bought municipal bonds and certificates of deposit through the bank. And guess what? They were all cashed out between six and ten years ago. A total of about six hundred thousand dollars."

"Not spectacular, but a respectable fortune," Jennifer said.

"Yup. And, you'll be interested to know, his signature on the deed to the house matches the signature on the older will."

"Hooray!"

"Yes, he wrote that will before he moved here."

"I'll ask again, do we still own the house?"

Harvey shrugged. "I tried to call Pete, but he was out. I left a message for him to call me as soon as he gets it. Eddie's got Mr. Fuller's dental records for the last ten years, and the Navy's sending Sanford's. Tony thinks he's located the retired doctor in Kittery. We may be able to get the old medical records from way back."

"What about a dentist from more than ten years ago?"

"Nothing so far."

"Maybe the Navy can help on that." Jennifer sighed. "I've been thinking about the wedding ring. Why did he bury it with Mr. Fuller?"

"It could identify him," Harvey said. "And Mr. Fuller was never married, so Sanford couldn't just wear it."

"Still, he kept the Navy papers," she reminded him. "He could have locked the ring in the cubbyhole with them.

"True. Maybe he didn't know about the cubbyhole when he killed him and was trying to destroy evidence of his identity in a hurry. Like the uniform jacket."

"Why didn't he get rid of his Navy papers in the course of ten years?" she asked.

"He probably needed them to open the bank account in Biddeford. He collected his Navy pension under his own name and would need proof that he was entitled to receive it, so he never totally destroyed his true identity. If he hadn't been so greedy…"

"If he hadn't been so greedy, he wouldn't have murdered Mr. Fuller." Jennifer said.

*****

When it was time to go to prayer meeting, Jennifer called and asked Jeff and Beth to ride with her and Harvey in her minivan. They planned to spend their first night at the new house, so they were next door, getting used to their new location. Jennifer was so happy, she couldn't stop grinning when her brother and his wife walked across the lawn to join them.

At church, everyone fussed over Connor again, and she realized she would have to get used to that until another baby was born into the congregation. She let Mrs. Rowland hold the baby for a few minutes, but Harvey claimed him for the duration of the Bible study.

On the way home, Jeff asked about the latest developments in the case. Harvey gave him and Beth an abbreviated version.

"I'd tell you more, but I can't jeopardize the case," he explained.

Beth said, "But, if the killer's dead …"

"We haven't proved that yet," Harvey said. "There are still a lot of unexplained things in this case. The investigation is still wide open. I'm sorry."

"It's okay," Jeff said. "Everyone at work asks me about it, though."

Beth gave an exaggerated shudder. "The other teachers can't believe we're actually going to sleep in that house."

"It's not like the body's still there," Jennifer said.

Harvey smiled at her. "Always practical, aren't you?"

Jennifer shrugged. "I can't see being squeamish about it now. But this case is so strange."

"How do you mean?" Beth asked from the back seat.

"Well, there may be no living perpetrator to prosecute, and so many civilians are involved. The family, I mean, and the neighbors."

"It's been hard to keep things confidential," Harvey said.

"Do you need to?" Beth asked. "I mean, the two principals are both dead. You said so yourself."

"Of course we can't keep it all hush-hush," Harvey said. "The basics have been on the news. I'd like to be able to announce that we've tied up all the loose ends, but we have a long way to go. For instance, we haven't proved conclusively that the man who died in the nursing home was Sanford."

"Isn't it obvious? His fingerprints were all over the house," Jennifer said.

"Well, I know, but, we need to put it all together and get the medical examiner's official opinion. And how did Sanford know Fuller? Sanford grew up in Massachusetts. Fuller lived in southern Maine. We haven't found any indication their paths crossed until Sanford visited Mr. Fuller ten years ago. *If* it was Sanford that Flossie Bailey saw from the window."

Jeff said, "Well, Beth and I won't blab anything if you say not to, but people *are* talking about it. Not the details, but the skeleton being found."

"I'm not worried about that," Harvey said. "It's your house now, and you can't help it if people ask you about it. But if you find any more evidence, let me know, of course. And if any reporters come around, send them to me."

They'd been home twenty minutes when Pete Bearse called.

"So, Pete," Harvey asked him, "if the older will, the one you saw, is genuine, and the newer one is fraudulent, where do Jennifer and I stand on the ownership of the house?"

He listened for a few minutes, then said, "Okay, it sounds as if I'd better give you a retainer and have you look into this. All right, if you say so. Drop by my office."

Mr. Fournier, the rose expert, came on Thursday afternoon and spent half an hour in the back yard.

"The roses look good," he told Jennifer. "If you want, I'll set up a feeding and pruning schedule and come back again in two weeks."

"I'd like that," Jennifer said. "We'd like to keep the flower beds in the condition Mrs. Bailey left them in."

He gave her the number of a horticulture student at the university, Penny Lancaster, who could work in the perennial beds and do general yard work.

"Thank you," Jennifer said. "I don't mind hard work, but I'm pretty ignorant about gardening, and with the baby and all, I think I need help with that."

She called Penny and arranged for her to come look at the gardens on the weekend. The student sounded upbeat and eager for the part time job. Jennifer looked forward to their first meeting.

Almost as soon as she hung up, Harvey called her from work.

"Hey, gorgeous, I finally got hold of Carl. He and Margaret are coming tonight."

"Great," Jennifer said. "We've prayed so hard for them all week."

"Yes, he said they've been really busy. He's had an architect draw plans for the addition, and Margaret keeps changing things. But he sounded happy about it."

"I'm glad, but let's keep praying," Jennifer said.

Abby's shift at work would be her last, as she had decided to take at least the summer off. With the wedding only five weeks away, she was full of energy and anticipation. She insisted on dusting and vacuuming the downstairs rooms.

"I'm not sick," Jennifer protested as Abby hauled the vacuum cleaner and cleaning caddy out of the entry closet.

"I know, but it's only a couple of weeks since you gave birth. You need to take it easy."

"Well, thanks. When you decide what to do for redecorating, I'll help you out."

"Deal." Abby headed into the hall bath with the caddy of cleaning supplies.

Jennifer made a batch of cookies, and when Abby left for work, she felt she had things under control. Connor was napping, the cookies were in Tupperware in the kitchen, and the house was presentable for company.

She sat down with her cross-stitch sampler. She'd been working on it for months. It was supposed to be Noah's ark, for Connor's room. So far she had Noah, Mrs. Noah, two crocodiles, two camels, an elephant and half a giraffe.

The doorbell rang, and she hopped up out of her chair. Jeff was standing in the breezeway.

"Hey, sis. Got any junk food?"

"Didn't Beth leave you anything to eat?"

"Well, she left me some bananas and a few cookies, but I ate those. She'll be home from school pretty soon, but I don't want to bother her. She'll be tired, and, you know, she's expecting, so I don't want her to feel like she has to cook."

"Jeffrey." Jennifer sighed. "If you really want to help Beth, why don't you go to the grocery store?"

"It's my day off."

"Exactly. So you're home. You can help Beth while she's working."

"I've been working all day, unpacking and cleaning the rugs."

"Okay, sit." Jennifer brought him a big blueberry muffin and a glass of milk. "Who does the grocery shopping at your house?"

"Beth."

"Well, that is one of the worst things a pregnant woman can do, especially one who's on her feet all day teaching. I think you need to start doing stuff like that for her."

He took a couple of bites, thinking about it.

"It's not like I'm lazy."

"I know you're not, but you might have to rethink the division of labor. How's Beth feeling?"

"Okay so far."

"No morning sickness?"

"No, she's the healthy type."

"So was I."

He took another bite of his muffin. "These are really good. Who made them?"

"Shop 'n Save."

"No kidding?"

"Nope. If you went over there and did the grocery shopping, you could buy some."

"Man, Jennifer, why are you so crabby?"

"Just tired, I guess. And Beth will be, when she gets home. You ought to fix dinner and give her a chance to take a nap."

"When am I supposed to see my wife?"

"I don't know. Didn't you say they were going to change your crazy schedule?"

"They're thinking about it. Four days on, three off, instead of three on, two off. I don't know if I like that. Four days in a row would be a lot."

"But wouldn't they allow you time to go home during the four days?" she asked.

"They're trying to work it out. What we guys really want is twelve-hour shifts instead of round the clock at the station."

"Well, I'm telling you, pregnancy is a wonderful time for a woman, but it's also very tiring."

"I tried to get a lot unpacked yesterday and today, so she won't do so much when I go back on duty tomorrow."

"That's good," Jennifer said. "Does she keep a running grocery list?"

"I'm not sure."

"Well, if you got her one of those magnetic pads, she could keep the list going, and when you have a day off again, like Monday, you could just grab the list and go to the store while she's at school."

"I'll do it," he said.

"Great."

"Got any more muffins?"

Harvey pushed buttons on his desk phone and sat back in his chair. "Hey, Arnie, how you doing?"

"Fine," Arnie Fowler said. "Maybe a little bored."

Harvey smiled. "Do you remember I asked you the day you came to the hospital about an old missing persons case?"

"Yeah, the kid. . .what was his name? Leonard?"

"Yeah, that's right. Jacob Leonard."

"So?" Arnie asked.

"I think it may be important."

"Okay. What do you want me to do?"

"I just read your report."

"If I remember right, I did all the standard stuff, Harv. Are you saying I missed something?"

"I don't know," Harvey said. "Probably not, but I wanted you to know we'll be talking to the parents again and putting out feelers on this guy. If he's alive, I want to meet him face to face."

"You think he's dead."

"If he's not, he's been awfully quiet for nine years."

"I hope you're wrong," Arnie said.

Harvey rubbed the back of his neck. "So do I."

Chapter 19

Carl and Margaret arrived a few minutes after seven, with Julia carrying a book about horses.

Margaret unrolled a large sheet of paper on the kitchen table. "I wanted to show you the plans for my new office."

She spread out the architect's drawing, and Harvey and Jennifer leaned in to study it.

"Really impressive, Margaret," said Harvey. "Waiting area, exam room, office, restroom. Looks like a big project."

"It will be worth it," Carl said. Margaret smiled at him, and he put his arm around her. "I can't wait to have Margaret at home again. Julia will have her mom with her all summer."

"I can't wait, either," said Julia.

"May she sit in the sunroom and read?" Margaret asked.

"Mom, I want to be where you are," Julia said.

"She can sit in on our conversation, if you don't mind," Harvey said.

"Oh, well, I wasn't sure." said Margaret.

Jennifer asked everyone what they wanted to drink, and they fixed their beverages and moved into the living room. Harvey carried the plate of cookies and set it on the coffee table. Jennifer was about to sit down when Connor cried in the bedroom and the doorbell rang. She looked at Harvey.

"Baby or door?" he asked.

"You get Connor, I'll get the door." Jennifer walked out to the entry and opened it. Beth and Jeff were waiting just outside.

"Do you have company?" Beth asked. "We can come another time."

"Come on in," Jennifer said. "The Turners are here. It'll be a good chance for you to say hi to Margaret and meet Carl."

She made the introductions and explained about Jeff and Beth moving into the house next door.

"Are you getting settled in?" Carl asked.

"Yes, we've finally got everything moved over from our old house," Beth said.

Margaret eyed her critically. "You must be exhausted."

"Well, I am kind of tired," Beth replied, "but Jeff is a real sweetheart. When I got home from school today, he made me take a nap, and he went to the Shop 'n Save for groceries."

Jennifer stared, wide-eyed, at her brother. He stared back innocently.

"You're coming to see me next week?" Margaret asked.

"Yes," Beth replied, blushing. "Thank you for agreeing to take me on."

"No problem. If construction goes as planned, you'll be coming to my new office at home by the first of July."

Harvey came out with Connor in the crook of his arm. "Here he is, all changed and ready for cuddling."

"Oh, may I?" Julia jumped up and went to Harvey's side.

"Sure." When Julia had seated herself, he placed the baby in her arms.

"Would you guys like something to drink?" Jennifer asked as Jeff reached for a cookie.

Beth said, "That's all right," at the same time Jeff said, "Sure, coffee's great."

Jennifer laughed.

"We shouldn't stay long," Beth said.

"Well, have a glass of milk and a cookie," Jennifer said.

With a little persuasion, she got them to stay another ten minutes. She noted that Harvey was the only one not eating cookies, and she had made them especially to replenish his carbohydrates.

"Don't you want one?" she asked.

"No, thanks. I think I'm a little sugared out. We had a cake party for one of the sergeants today, and I made the mistake of eating a piece."

"Okay." Jennifer frowned and glanced at Carl.

"Eat something not sweet later on," Carl suggested. "Crackers and cheese maybe?"

"Sure," Harvey said. "I'll make it my bedtime snack."

Jennifer was glad it was his doctor telling him what to eat, not her.

"We really ought to go." Beth stood to reinforce her words. "Margaret, Carl, nice to see you. You too, Julia."

Margaret was now holding Connor, and she smiled up at Beth. "I'll look forward to seeing you at the office, Beth."

Carl stood. "Great to meet more of Jennifer's family."

Jennifer walked with them to the door.

"Way to go, brother," she whispered when Jeff kissed her cheek. "Keep taking care of Beth. She's one in a million."

Jeff squeezed her. "Wake me up once in a while."

"You want some more coffee, Carl?" Harvey asked.

"Only if it's decaf," Carl said. "I have hospital rounds in the morning, so I want to sleep tonight. And Jennifer, aren't you bringing Connor in for his checkup tomorrow?"

"Yes, I am."

"He looks great," Carl said, gazing at the baby in his wife's arms. "We'll do all the routine stuff, though."

"Want me to meet you there?" Harvey asked.

Jennifer shrugged. "You don't need to. You guys must be busy."

"We are. Still playing tag with the Navy and trying to locate old neighbors and witnesses."

"Is that your Skeleton-Next-Door case?" Carl asked.

Jennifer smiled. "We call him Mr. Bones."

"I didn't know if I should mention it with your sister-in-law here," Carl said, "but I am curious about that."

"Thanks for your discretion," Jennifer said.

Harvey leaned back in his chair. "Beth's a little skittish about it, but I think they're getting over it. I mean, the remains were removed as soon as we found them. But we're talking about putting in an alarm system for them, just on principle."

"Not a bad idea," Margaret said. "With the increase in drug traffic, I guess there have been a lot more burglaries in town lately."

"Unfortunately, yes," Harvey said.

201

Jennifer had heard the dire reports on the news, and she knew Portland was no more immune to drug traffic than any other city, but it rarely touched her directly. The police force, however, was busier than ever with the effects.

Connor began to fuss, and Jennifer leaned toward Margaret. "I guess that's my cue."

She smiled and handed him over.

"Excuse me." Jennifer rose with the baby and hurried off into the bedroom to nurse him. She was glad no one had said she didn't need to leave the room. She wouldn't be comfortable with Carl's presence, even though he was a friend and a physician.

She heard their low, measured voices through the open doorway, but couldn't distinguish their words. She hoped the conversation would come around to important things. Silently, she prayed for Harvey, and for Carl and Margaret.

When she emerged a half hour later, she carried Connor to his father. Harvey looked up at her and smiled.

"Got his supper?"

"Yes, he's happy now. He might need a burp." Jennifer looked over at Julia, who held her book in her lap with a finger keeping her place. "Julia, I have some horse books in the other room. Would you like to see them?"

"Now, hold on," Carl said. "We're getting a baby, not a horse."

"I know," Julia said.

"Okay. Just wanted to remind you."

"So, it's official?" Jennifer arched her eyebrows at Margaret.

"Not yet, but that's the plan. It may take a while." Margaret shot a glance at Julia and shrugged.

Jennifer nodded. "Well, I think it's great. Come on, Julia. We have a bookcase in the sunroom that we let visiting kids browse." She took Julia in and showed her where she kept picture books, children's classics, and a row of nonfiction books for young people. Animal books and field guides took up most of one shelf. Some were books she had collected as a child, and others she had added more recently, with Peter's boys and Connor in mind.

A few minutes later, Harvey and the Turners came out of the living room.

"Thank you so much, Jennifer, Harvey." Margaret handed Connor over to Jennifer.

"Did you have a good visit?" she asked.

Margaret nodded. "We certainly have a lot to think about."

"Well, I'm not an expert," Harvey said, "but I'm happy to talk about this anytime. A year ago, Jenny and I were pretty much where you are. We didn't believe any of this. But we wondered. And we studied it. And we became convinced it's true."

"Thanks," Carl said. He reached for Connor's little hand. "So, I'm seeing the little guy tomorrow. He looks healthy."

"You can tell me officially at two o'clock," Jennifer said.

Julia sleepily put on her jacket, and Jennifer handed her a couple of books she had chosen.

"Are things ... going well?" Jennifer asked Margaret hesitantly.

"Well, they're better," Margaret said. "Carl says he's ready to visit your church."

"You, too, I hope." Jennifer hardly dared to think the whole family would come.

"Barring any untimely deliveries." Margaret bent to kiss Jennifer on the cheek. "Thanks again."

When they had left, Jennifer watched Harvey, waiting for him to speak.

"I don't know," he said softly, as they he had read the questions in her mind.

"They seem more open. Less skeptical."

"Carl might be close." Harvey shook his head. "I'm not so sure about Margaret."

"Maybe they just need to hear it one more time." Jennifer put her arms around him. "Not everybody is ready at the same time."

"But Carl...he can't make a move without Margaret," Harvey said. "I could see it."

"Then he's not ready. He needs to trust Christ on his own, not because Margaret does."

"Yeah."

"He's afraid he'll lose her if he does something she disapproves of too badly."

Jennifer pulled away so she could see Harvey's eyes. "She wouldn't leave him over this, would she?"

Harvey frowned. "I don't know."

*****

Abby slept late Friday morning, after her final shift at work. It was raining, and Jennifer spent the morning working on her computer programs and cuddling Connor.

"Want to go with me when I take Connor to his checkup?" she asked Abby when she finally came down for a late breakfast.

"No, Peter wants me to go over there early. We're going to drop by city hall first."

"City hall?"

Abby smiled over the edge of her coffee mug. "To file for the marriage license."

"Ooh, romantic stuff," Jennifer said.

"I'm starting to get a little nervous."

"What about, specifically? You're not having second thoughts?"

"No. I want to be Mrs. Hobart. I'm just a little on edge about being the second Mrs. Hobart, I suppose."

"Talk to him about it," Jennifer said.

"It's kind of hard to bring up the topic."

"Peter doesn't want to discuss Christine?"

"No, I mean it's hard for me. I don't like to think he'll be comparing me to her all the time."

"He won't."

"Gary does."

"What does he say?"

"Oh, things like, 'My mom used to do it this way.' 'My mom always made peanut butter cookies.' 'My mom used to sew clothes for me.' Things like that."

"Can you think of it as a blessing? That he remembers his mother, I mean."

204

Abby paused and looked at her coffee cup. "I'll try. It's hardly being the second Mrs. DeWinter. But Peter asked me if I wanted him to take down her pictures. I told him no."

"That's good, I think."

"Well, the boys need to know we're not pretending she didn't exist."

"Still, you ought to talk this all out with Peter, when the boys aren't around. Maybe the two of you can explain to Gary that you'll do different things with him, and he can still remember the special things she did. He probably doesn't really want you to do everything exactly the same way she did."

"You may be right. He might just be posting the news that he doesn't want to forget those things."

"Yeah. It is a big transition for the boys." Jennifer smiled. "I'm planning a house warming for Beth and Jeff a week from Saturday."

"I'll help."

"Thanks. Beth was hesitant at first, but she's warming up to the idea. It will be a chance for them to show off their new home to all their friends and colleagues at once."

Although it was still drizzling, it was warm that afternoon. The roses were putting out new leaves. Penny Lancaster came right after lunch, and Jennifer trudged with her around the front and back yards. The gardens weren't looking their best, but Penny was enthusiastic, and Jennifer engaged her to come back on Tuesday afternoons. She had no confidence at all in her own ability to keep the flowers happy.

She got Connor ready for his checkup and put a hooded sweater on him. In the garage, she buckled him into the built-in car seat in the van.

They sat for twenty minutes in Carl's waiting room. One mother had three children there. The baby was having his checkup, but she'd had to bring the three- and four-year-olds, one of whom had a rash he scratched continually. A little girl with a cast on her foot hounded her mother to read stories to her. Another woman had an obviously sick infant in her arms. The baby moaned, and his nose ran. Jennifer began to wonder whether she was really serving Connor's best interests by taking him to the doctor's office. She was relieved when the sickest child was called in to the exam area. Another fifteen minutes passed before the nurse called Connor's name.

"Well, Master Larson!" Carl grinned when he at last entered their cubicle.

"Your office is too busy, Carl," Jennifer said.

"I know," he said, as he washed his hands. "I'm getting a lot of peds patients lately. I think it will be good when Margaret moves her office home and I get a partner in here to help me out."

Margaret's waiting area was at the other end of the office suite, and was much quieter. Pregnant and menopausal women sat silently perusing magazines.

"Better start lining someone up," Jennifer said.

"Oh, I am. I've put the word out on a couple of online medical groups and messaged some of our old med school classmates." He checked Connor's eyes, ears, throat, and reflexes, and weighed and measured him.

"The little guy's gained almost a pound," he said. "Supplemental feedings?"

"Nope."

"Good going."

Jennifer smiled.

Carl lifted Connor off the scale and held him for an instant. "Are you and Harvey still praying for us?"

"Every day, Carl."

"Thanks. Would it be too presumptuous to ask God to give us a baby boy?"

She smiled. "I don't think so. I prayed hard for a son last summer and fall."

"Well, then ask for one in this model." He smiled down at Connor. "Margaret's a little apprehensive about being able to conceive at all," he added.

"Any indications of trouble?"

"No, it's early. But she is forty."

"Forty's not old." Jennifer felt she'd had this conversation too many times with Harvey. At least she had her ammunition lined up for Carl. "Lots of women over forty have healthy babies."

"I know."

"You need to reassure her constantly that she's not old, and that you love her." Jennifer had lots of experience there, and it always worked with Harvey.

Carl looked down at Connor and stroked his silky hair. "But if she doesn't conceive, I'm wondering if she'll be happy to stay home, or if she'll be all mad at me again for having her move her office."

"I thought it was her idea."

"We sort of worked it out together."

"Okay. Even if you don't have another child, Julia will benefit tremendously from this," Jennifer said with conviction.

"I think you're right. And Julia is so excited. She and Margaret have been picking out the decorations for the new office together. She feels really grown up. Yesterday she asked her mother when they could start decorating the nursery. Margaret told her they'd better wait until we know the baby's coming."

"It may take a while."

"Yes, I tried to explain that to Julia. I told her it will probably be a little late for Christmas, and we'll get her something else, too. Not a horse, though."

Jennifer was halfway home when her phone rang. She rummaged frantically in her purse with one hand, and finally pulled to the curb and found it on the fifth ring.

"Jennifer, it's Leeanne."

"Hi! Sorry to keep you waiting. I'm in the car."

"Sorry. I wanted to know if you can stand to have me come down again tonight?"

"Sure. I thought Eddie was going up there, though."

"He just called me and said his boss, who shall remain nameless, wants him to stick around this weekend. He said the case they're working on may break soon."

"Oh, terrific. Come on down. Your room is always ready."

"Does he mean the Fuller case, or am I allowed to ask?"

"It's the only case I know about that Eddie's working on right now."

"I'll be there for supper."

"Great." Jennifer glanced into the back seat. Connor was dozing in his car seat. She drove on home wondering what big break Eddie had found in the case.

Chapter 20

Jeff was on duty, and Jennifer called Beth as soon as she got home.

"Want to eat with us tonight? Leeanne's coming down."

"Sure. I just got home from school, and was wondering what I'd do tonight. I hate cooking for one."

"Well, you're eating for two, so you've got to make sure you get your nutrients. Why don't you take a nap and come over whenever you want?"

"Thanks, Jennifer."

Leeanne arrived at 4:30, while Jennifer was hurriedly peeling potatoes. Connor was screaming for a meal.

"My nephew is crying," Leeanne in a piteous tone as she walked through the door.

"Hi, honey. Can you pick him up? I just need two more potatoes, then I'll feed him."

Leeanne scooped him up out of the infant seat and kissed him. "How about I peel the potatoes and you feed him now?"

Jennifer took Connor gratefully and settled down to feed him. Leeanne took off her windbreaker and sat down with the paring knife in hand.

"How many people are you feeding tonight?" she asked in surprise, looking at the potatoes Jennifer had peeled.

"Well, you and Eddie and Beth, at least. I never know anymore."

"Abby and Peter?"

"No, it's Gary's birthday. They're having a party at Peter's house."

"Then I think we've got enough spuds," Leeanne said firmly. She rinsed them and put the pan on the stove. "Jeff's working?"

"Yes. I told Beth to take a nap, then come over."

"She doesn't have any trouble sleeping over there above the scene of the crime?"

"She doesn't seem to," Jennifer said. "But don't ask her, okay? Now that she's expecting, I don't want her getting a case of the jitters."

"I just think it's weird," Leeanne said. "I wonder how he killed him."

"Hit him over the head with something, I guess." Jennifer made a face at the thought.

*****

Eddie and Tony were working at their computers when Harvey strolled across the office.

"Did you guys get anything at all on the Leonard boy?" Harvey asked.

"Nothing," Eddie said. "We've checked everywhere."

"If he's alive, he's living under an assumed name," Tony said.

"It's possible." Harvey frowned. "I don't like that his story dead-ends at Carleton Fuller's house."

"Yes, especially since it was a few months after we think Sanford arrived there." Eddie pushed his chair back. "I've been thinking a lot about this, Harvey."

"Yeah?"

"Yeah." Eddie looked over at Tony. "Did you ever mow lawns for people, to make extra money?"

"No."

Eddie shrugged. "Figures." Tony probably never had a cash flow problem in his life. "I did."

"So?"

"So, imagine with me for a minute that you mow this guy's lawn every week in the summer. After a while, you get into a routine. You go to his back yard, you get the lawnmower out, you mow the lawn, you put the machine away, and then you go to the back door for your pay."

"Wouldn't the owner have to unlock the shed for you first?" Tony asked.

"Maybe. Or maybe he doesn't lock it. If he does, he'd probably give you a key after you've been doing it a while. Not to the house, just the shed."

"Okay." Tony frowned, as though he was thinking about it but failed to see the relevance.

"Jacob Leonard had mowed Mr. Fuller's lawn for two summers," Harvey said.

"Right." Eddie swiveled his chair to look at him. "And it was spring of the following year when he disappeared. Just as the mowing season was starting up again."

Harvey nodded.

Eddie leaned back in the chair and locked his hands behind his head, gazing at Tony. "So, one day, you go over and get the mower out. You're gassing it up, and this man comes storming out of the house. He says, 'What are you doing?' and you say, 'Mowing the lawn.' Then you take a good look at him, and you realize it's not the guy who lives there—the guy who always paid you every week. It's somebody else. So you say, 'Who are you?' And he gets this odd look in his eyes."

Enlightenment flashed in Tony's eyes. "Do I ask him where Mr. Fuller is?"

"You just might. Big mistake, if you do."

Tony let out a long, slow breath. "You think the impostor killed the kid who mowed his lawn."

"Possibility." Eddie sat forward and clicked on his computer. The screen saver disappeared. "The boy who mowed for Fuller ran away from home and never came back."

Tony nodded. "And it happened the day he was going over to ask about the mowing. I get you."

"Mr. Fuller claimed Jacob never went to his house that day," Harvey reminded them.

"He didn't waste time getting someone new to mow for him, and we talked to that guy," Tony said. "He was the one who witnessed the newer will several years later."

"But now we know that guy—Carter—only started the yard work after the real Mr. Fuller was dead."

Eddie nodded at him.

Tony smiled. "I gotta hand it to you, Shakespeare. Sounds like a plausible scenario to me."

"I should have had you guys look closer into that when Mrs. Leonard first came to see me," Harvey said. "Let's not make a mess of it now."

"What do we do?" Tony asked.

"I want you to check out the garden shed in the back yard. Pay special attention to the lawn mower and any other tools in there. And check for blood residue."

"Do the parents know you've reopened this?" Eddie asked.

"Not yet. I'll go see them if you find something. It could be a total rabbit trail. But Arnie made follow-up notations in the file for four years—until the Leonard boy would have been twenty-one. He didn't let the case go cold without a fight."

*****

Eddie followed Harvey home, and Beth emerged from 135 when they drove in. Leeanne and Eddie were kissing in the driveway again. Jennifer saw Janice peeking out her living room window. She waved, and Janice waved back.

Harvey turned to see who Jennifer was looking at, and he waved, too, then kissed Jennifer.

"How could all the neighbors *not* know what was going on here ten years ago?" Jennifer asked.

"Well, if Mr. Fuller had been kissing his wife in front of the house, they probably would have known every detail," he said. "But he was single, remember. Kept to himself."

"Yes, but still. People *do* notice things."

"Well, Eddie's tracked down the people who owned Ralph Penninger's house. Maybe we'll get some answers soon."

"How about the witnesses to the new will?"

"We've talked to them. It was the young man Fuller—or Sanford—hired to mow the lawn for the last nine years and a friend of Ralph's who was visiting that day. They don't know anything. We have something new to look into, though."

"Oh?"

"Tell you later," Harvey said. "Let me get out of this suit."

They went in and enjoyed a lively meal. Connor smiled and cooed. He was passed from lap to lap as they ate.

"No dessert tonight," Jennifer warned everyone. "Harvey and I are trying to watch our diet. Eat lots of meatloaf and veggies."

The doorbell rang.

"Thought I heard a car." Harvey got up and went to the entry.

He opened the door and said, "Well, hello! Good to see you."

Jennifer stood and carried Connor to the entry. Harvey moved over a little so she could see their visitor.

Greg Prescott stood in the breezeway, his uniform in perfect order except for a few water spots from raindrops. In his hand was bouquet of roses.

"Greg! Come right in," Jennifer said.

"You had the baby." He stared at Connor.

"Yes, two weeks ago. Please come in."

He followed them into the kitchen.

Eddie stood up. "Hey, Greg! What are you doing here?"

"I guess you know Eddie and Leeanne," said Harvey. "Have you met my sister-in-law, Beth?"

"Yes, we've met," Beth said. "Nice to see you, Greg."

Greg smiled politely, preoccupied. There was a pause, and he looked bleakly at Harvey.

"She isn't here, is she?"

"No," Harvey said quietly.

Greg drooped a little.

"Have you eaten?" Jennifer asked.

Greg looked at her blankly.

"Sit down," she said.

He shook his head. "I guess I'm too late."

Harvey put his hand on Greg's shoulder. "Step into the other room with me for a minute, Greg." He took Greg into the living room. Eddie, Leeanne, and Beth stared after them, then turned and looked at Jennifer. She sat down and held Connor up on her shoulder.

"Poor Greg," said Leeanne.

"He's such a nice guy," Beth added.

They finished eating quietly, and Beth and Jennifer cleared the table.

"Leeanne and I are going to catch a play at the university," Eddie said. "It's the Shakespeare festival."

"What are you seeing?" Beth asked.

"*Twelfth Night,*" said Leeanne. "If we go early, we're supposed to be able to get tickets at the door."

"Sounds like fun," Jennifer said.

"Do you and Harvey want to come?" Eddie asked.

Jennifer glanced toward the doorway. "We'd better stay here tonight. Besides, I don't think Connor would make it through a Shakespearean play yet."

"How about you, Beth?" Leeanne asked.

"Oh, you two don't want an extra person along on your date."

"We're beyond dating. We're engaged." Eddie sounded very content. "Come with us."

Beth smiled. "Are you serious?"

"*Mais, oui,*" said Eddie.

"Sure," said Leeanne.

Beth hesitated another two seconds. "I think I'd really like to."

"Great!" said Leeanne.

"Let me just call Jeff and tell him, so he won't be worried if he calls the house and I'm not there."

She got through to Jeff at the fire station, then pulled on her raincoat and ran next door for her purse.

"Think Greg's going to be okay?" Eddie asked Jennifer as they prepared to head out.

"I don't know. Pray for him."

When they had driven out in Eddie's truck, Jennifer fixed a plate of food and put it in the microwave. She started the dishwasher, picked up Connor, and walked slowly into the sunroom. At the living room doorway, she paused.

Greg was saying, "I brought this on myself, I know that. If I just hadn't been so stubborn! She would have married me, if I'd just been more patient."

Harvey glanced up and beckoned to Jennifer, so she walked in and sat beside him on the couch. He said, "Greg, I really believe Peter is the man God had lined up for Abby. I know that's hard for you to take, but that's the way it is."

Greg took a deep breath. "Well, Jennifer, I guess these are for you." He held the roses out to her.

She took them and tried to say thank you, but it stuck in her throat.

"Greg, I'm sorry," she managed.

He shook his head. "I knew I was wrong when I left. But I wanted things to go my way, on my terms. Now I've lost her."

"You lost her the day you made her choose," Harvey said gently.

"I've known all this time I still loved her. I just couldn't admit I was wrong."

"I fixed you a plate," Jennifer said softly.

Harvey stood. "Come have something to eat."

Greg looked at him, then at Jennifer and Connor. "I can't stay here. It's too—"

Jennifer thought he would say it was too painful, watching her and Harvey and the baby. He wasn't the first to envy the relationship and the home they had. Her resemblance to Abby must be difficult for him, too.

"They're not married yet," he ventured.

"No," Harvey said slowly. "I suppose if you want to see her, make your case—"

Greg hesitated. "I don't suppose that would help." He stood up. "Don't tell her I was here."

"Greg, I can't do that," Harvey said.

Greg bit his lip. "How could I have been so stupid?"

Jennifer thought he was going to cry.

"Greg, we've never stopped caring about you, or praying for you," Harvey said. "If there's anything I can do for you, please tell me. I mean that. But I won't keep this from Abby."

"Do you have a place to stay?" Jennifer asked.

He shrugged.

She looked at Harvey, knowing Greg couldn't stay in their home. "My brother will put you up, I'm sure."

"No, I'll head back to New York tonight."

"Greg, you can't just leave and not say anything to Abby," Jennifer said.

"He can't?" Harvey asked.

"Can he?" It seemed to Jennifer he ought to tell her how he felt.

"I don't want to distress her," Greg said. "Besides, that would be another blow to my pride, wouldn't it?" His tone was bitter. "Harvey, I guess you know I was engaged once. My fiancée broke it off at the last minute."

"You told me," he said.

"Well, that was my fault, too." He pulled a spotless handkerchief from his uniform pocket and wiped away the tears that had escaped the corners of his eyes. "I've struggled and struggled with pride for years. It took me three months this time. I finally told God on Wednesday I was tired of it. I was flying into New York last night. If there was a seat on a flight to Portland for me, I'd come up here and grovel."

"That's not what she wanted," Jennifer said, and he stared at her.

"Jenny's right," said Harvey. "She just wanted to be sure. She didn't want to make a mistake, and she needed time to know what God had in mind for her. I've got to believe that, even if you'd stayed, it would have turned out this way."

"Well, I'd better get going," Greg said tonelessly.

"We love you, Greg." Jennifer touched his sleeve. "You're our brother in Christ. We did hope for a while that you might be part of our earthly family, too, but God had another plan. That doesn't mean you have to cut yourself off completely."

"I can't ever come back here," he said.

"Don't say that," Harvey told him.

"I mean it. If you guys are ever in San Francisco, look me up. I'll always appreciate your friendship. But I can't come back here."

"Greg, don't be this way," Harvey said.

"I'm going to be alone the rest of my life."

Harvey winced. "I've been there, felt exactly that way before. Look, we know this isn't the time for it, but, Greg, if you just get down to brass tacks with the Lord on this pride thing, there's no reason why you shouldn't believe he's still got a wife out there for you."

"I'm thirty-five, Harvey."

"I was forty-one."

Greg stood for a moment in silence. "I hate San Francisco." He swallowed hard. "What's the baby's name?"

"Connor," said Harvey.

"Will you pray with me now, Harvey?"

Jennifer took Connor into the bedroom and nursed him, praying all the time. About five minutes later, she heard Greg leave, and Harvey came into the bedroom.

"I'm worried about him," she said.

"The Lord is holding on tight." Harvey sat down and put his arms around her. "I know right where he's at. It's awful to need someone to reach out to, and have nobody there. If he'll just rely on Christ now…"

"He seemed so strong in his faith last fall," she said.

"Yeah." Harvey eyed her thoughtfully. "I was going to tell you about the new leads in the case,"

"Yes, you were."

"Eddie and Tony will be over at 135 again tomorrow. Remember Mrs. Leonard? The woman who came and asked if the bones could be her son?"

"Yeah." Jennifer frowned. "I get the feeling you're going to tell me something bad."

"They'll just be looking for trace evidence, but I suppose I should warn Beth they'll be over there."

Jennifer pulled her long hair over her shoulder and sank back against the pillows. "I hope this will end soon."

"Me, too." Harvey held her close buried his face in her hair.

*****

Abby and Peter came in an hour later, and Gary and Andy were with them.

"So, ten years old!" Harvey said to Gary.

"Uh-huh," Gary said. "I got a model kit of a Sopwith Camel, and a microscope, and a soccer ball."

Abby and Peter were closing umbrellas in the entry, and Abby put them in the utility room.

"Pretty impressive haul," said Harvey.

"Do you like models, Captain Larson?"

"Yes, I do, but you'd better start calling me Uncle Harvey."

"Leeanne's here, but she and Eddie took Beth to a play," Jennifer told Abby.

"Great. We can go dress shopping tomorrow. Say, whose flowers?"

Her eye had fallen on the mayor's vase. Jennifer had removed the bouquet Harvey had sent her on Tuesday to a canning jar and placed Greg's roses in it.

"Don't tell me," Abby said quickly, "Eddie brought them to Leeanne."

"No," Jennifer said.

"Did Harvey send them to you with a box of doughnuts?"

Jennifer looked helplessly at Harvey.

"Abby, Greg was here," he said distinctly, but with a hint of compassion.

"Greg?" She stood with her hands on the back of a kitchen chair, staring at the roses, but not touching them. Jennifer could smell them from where she stood, six feet away. Abby breathed deeply a couple of times. "What did he want?"

"He ... wanted to apologize to you," Harvey said.

Abby turned slowly and looked at Peter. His brown eyes were cloudy, but he met hers unflinching.

Abby took a step toward him, and Peter met her in the middle of the kitchen and put his arms around her. He held her for a moment, then she turned to Harvey.

"Is he still around?"

"No, he was heading back to New York."

Tears streamed down Abby's cheeks.

Peter said quietly, "I'll take you to the airport."

"No," she said. "No, I think it's better this way." She wiped her cheek with the back of her hand, and Peter started fumbling for a handkerchief.

"You all right?" he asked.

"Yes." She took his handkerchief and asked Harvey, "What did you tell him?"

"That Peter was God's man for you. Did I say the wrong thing?"

"No."

Peter pulled her to him again and kissed her forehead.

"So, boys, come see the flight simulator on my computer," Harvey said. He took Andy and Gary into the study, and Jennifer went to the bedroom to check on Connor.

A few minutes later, Abby came in.

"Peter's gone," she said.

"Are you all right?"

"Yes. We're fine."

Jennifer smiled. Abby had taken the question in the plural, considering Peter's feelings intertwined with hers. "That's good. We'll keep Greg in prayer."

"I think God didn't want me here when he came," Abby said.

"It would have been difficult for you."

"How was he?"

"He was ... a lot of things. Contrite, mostly."

"Angry?"

"Maybe just a little. With himself, not with you. He's not blaming you."

Abby stood in silence for the space of two breaths.

Harvey knocked softly on the door. "Can I come in?"

"Sure," said Abby.

He walked to his side of the bed and sat down.

"Do you think Greg's all right?" Abby asked.

"I think so."

"Peter was beyond nice." She gave a little sniff.

"Peter's a great guy," Harvey said.

Abby began crying in earnest. Jennifer held Connor carefully with one hand and reached for the tissue box with the other. Connor stared up at her with wide eyes, so like Harvey's.

"Abby, are *you* okay?" Harvey asked.

"Yes. I'm sorry I'm weepy." She took the tissue box and pulled one out.

"That's all right." Harvey got up and came around the bed and put his hand on her shoulder. "Did you want to see him?"

"No. Really, I don't. I just wish he wasn't torn up about it. He really is a nice fellow. He doesn't deserve to be lonely and depressed."

"I'd say he'll get over it, but that's too trite," said Harvey. "If he trusts in God, he will, though. You know he will."

*****

Jennifer and Harvey were watching the late news in the bedroom, trying to get Connor down for the night, when Eddie's truck drove in and the front door opened. Rain was pounding on the roof of the addition where the bedroom was.

Connor stirred and began to scream. Harvey had just put him back in the cradle for the fourth time. Every time they settled him down, he woke up again and cried. They were starting to think they'd be up all night.

"Maybe we should just let him cry for a while," Jennifer said timidly, knowing Harvey hated to hear his son cry. It made him feel helpless, as though he, the daddy, had to do something, anything, to make the crying stop. Connor had just begun to cry tears, which made it even worse. Harvey couldn't stand it when he saw those tears on the chubby little cheeks.

"How do we know there's not something wrong?"

"Well, we don't use pins, so it's not that," she said. Harvey didn't think that was funny.

"Maybe he's sick," he said anxiously. "You'd better call Carl in the morning." He sat up on the edge of the bed, and she knew he was going to pick Connor up again.

He stopped where he was, his head turning toward the TV.

"What did he say?"

Jennifer reached for the remote and turned the sound up.

"—at the end of the runway at Portland International Airport," the local news anchor was saying.

"Get the baby," Harvey said.

Jennifer sighed and got out of bed, going around to the cradle. She picked Connor up and snuggled him against the shoulder of her pajama top.

"You naughty boy," she said tenderly. Connor stopped crying and breathed raggedly against her shoulder.

"There's a plane down at the airport," Harvey said, and her heart plummeted.

Chapter 21

Harvey pulled on his jeans and went to the doorway.

"Eddie, you out there?"

"Yeah, Harv, just heading out."

"No, don't leave. I want you to run out to the airport with me."

"The airport?" Eddie asked.

Jennifer pulled on her robe and followed Harvey into the kitchen. Eddie and Leeanne were coming in from the entry. Harvey switched the kitchen light on.

"There's a plane down. Didn't get off the runway fast enough on takeoff."

Jennifer grabbed for his arm. "Do you think it's Greg's plane?"

"Greg's flying tonight?" Eddie asked. "The wind is terrible."

"I thought we'd take a run out there," Harvey said. "It won't take long, and we'll sleep better if we know what's up."

"Okay, we'll take my truck," said Eddie.

"I'll get my shoes and we're out of here. Call the com center and see if they'll tell you anything." Harvey turned back to the bedroom.

Jennifer went quickly after him and laid Connor on the bed. He started crying again. She picked him up.

"Please don't let him scream all night." Harvey pulled on a sweatshirt.

"I won't."

He came to her and kissed her.

"Call me, Harvey, as soon as you know anything."

"I've got my cell phone."

"Should I wake Abby up?" she asked.

"No. We don't know he was on the plane. No sense worrying her."

He stopped in the entry for his jacket. Eddie went out ahead of him and started his truck and the blue flashing light on the dashboard. Harvey hung his badge around his neck outside the jacket, then turned around and kissed Connor softly, then kissed Jennifer hard. He held her against him for just a moment, then went past Leeanne and out to Eddie's truck.

Leeanne and Jennifer watched from the doorway until they could no longer see the blue aura of Eddie's light bouncing off the low clouds.

Leeanne turned to Jennifer, her eyes large and luminous. "What happened with Greg?"

"Nothing really. He said he was going back to New York. Abby took it on the chin, and Peter held her up."

"She saw him?"

"No. He left before they got back."

"Do you think it's his plane? The dispatcher couldn't tell Eddie much."

"I have no idea. You'd think they would have canceled flights in this weather. But the odds are that it wasn't his. I mean, it's over four hours since he left here. If planes are taking off, he would have gone as soon as he could."

Connor fussed a little.

"Is he hungry?" asked Leeanne.

"I don't think so. He's just fussy tonight."

"Let me hold him."

Jennifer gratefully passed the baby to her sister and made hot chocolate for the two of them. They carried it into the bedroom. Leeanne sat on Harvey's side with Connor in her arms, and Jennifer set her mug on the nightstand beside her and went around to her own side.

The local news was nearly over. A discouraging weather report was being aired. Then, in their last thirty seconds of air time, when the anchor usually said something witty to his female counterpart, they gave an update.

"More information on that plane crash at Portland International Airport," the anchor said, his face grave. "A commuter jet has gone off the end of the runway there. Firefighters and ambulances are on the scene. One source tells us the plane is burning at the end of the runway. Fourteen people were on board. It's not known yet if there were any casualties. We'll update you as more information becomes available."

Leeanne and Jennifer looked bleakly at each other.

"Let's pray," Leeanne said.

Jennifer left the television on with the sound low, but a late-night talk show came on. They prayed and talked and played with Connor, who was now wide awake.

"Maybe he just didn't want to go to bed," Leeanne said. "He's having fun now." She held him above her and waggled him a little, smiling and saying, "Hello, Connor. Hello, my favorite nephew!"

Connor spit curdled milk on her.

"Oh, yuck!" She sat up quickly. "Was that a nice thing to do to Aunt Leeanne?"

Jennifer took him while Leeanne headed for the bathroom to sponge her shirt.

The woman from the news appeared on the screen, and Jennifer grabbed the remote and punched the sound up.

"Leeanne, update!"

She came to the bathroom doorway.

"—fourteen people on board. Several have been taken away in ambulances. It's believed all fourteen survived, although the plane burned after the crash landing. Firefighters have extinguished the flames, and all passengers and the flight crew have been evacuated. I repeat, all fourteen people have been evacuated from the small jet that crashed on takeoff tonight at Portland International Jetport."

Location video came on of firefighters sending a spray of chemicals at the fuselage of a plane. Red and blue lights flashed in the background. The South Portland fire chief and a reporter holding a microphone appeared.

"The South Portland Fire Department worked with the airport crew on this emergency," the chief said. "We've practiced for just such a disaster, and everything has gone very well. There were several people with injuries, and they have all been taken to hospitals for treatment."

Her cell phone rang, and she grabbed it off the nightstand, lowering the volume on the TV at the same time.

"Gorgeous, it's me."

"What's happening?"

"It's not so bad," he said. "Fourteen people on the plane. A few were injured, most not seriously. Oh, and guess who I ran into in the airport."

"Not Greg?"

"Yes. He'd decided not to fly out because the wind was so bad. Only a few planes were going, anyway. He booked a room at the closest hotel. When he heard all the sirens, he came over to see if he could help."

"Thank God," Jennifer said.

"Yes. We should be home in twenty minutes."

*****

Harvey tried to sleep late Saturday morning, but he never could. Connor had given up before he got home and slept for six hours, a new record. When he started crying a little after seven, Harvey rolled over and tried to ignore him.

Jennifer got the baby and quickly changed his diaper, then tiptoed out to the living room where she sat with him in the rocking chair. Fifteen minutes later, she heard the shower running and knew Harvey was up anyway. She carried Connor to the kitchen and made a pot of coffee.

"Good morning," Abby said cheerfully, as she bounced into the kitchen. She had on plaid slacks and a navy knit top. "Did I hear somebody come in late last night?"

"Harvey and Eddie went out around eleven. They were gone for about an hour."

"Really? What happened?"

"A plane crashed at the airport."

"Our airport?" Abby turned toward her, fear in her eyes.

"Not Greg," Jennifer said quickly. "He didn't fly out last night. Harvey saw him."

Abby sighed. "Any survivors?"

226

"Yes, everyone on board. The plane was barely airborne when it crashed. It wasn't a bad smash-up, but it caught fire afterward."

Harvey came into the kitchen, his damp hair curling just above his collar in the back. "Good morning, ladies." He bent over and kissed Jennifer. "The boy slept through 'til seven?"

She smiled. "Yes, the boy did. Six hours. You ought to be in bed, though."

"Couldn't sleep any more. I'll give Eddie another hour, then we'll ride up to Auburn and see if we can find those old neighbors of Fuller's."

"The people who owned Ralph Penninger's house?"

"Yes, I'm going to call them before we leave."

"Take Connor and me," Jennifer said impulsively.

"Then we'd have to take Leeanne, too."

"Would that be so bad?"

Harvey considered. "Why not? A family outing."

"You won't be lonely, will you, Abby?" Jennifer asked.

"No, but when are we going to go shopping for bridesmaids' dresses?"

"This afternoon?"

"I suppose Peter and I should address the invitations," Abby said. "Do you mind if I ask him to bring Gary and Andy over here?"

"No, that's fine. It's wet out, though. Better have them bring some toys."

"Hey." Jennifer frowned at Harvey. "I thought you said Eddie and Tony would be working next door today."

"They're going to do that after we get back," Harvey said. "It's important for Eddie to get this interview."

The phone rang, and Jennifer answered it. Peter was on the other end.

"I just heard about the plane crash last night. Was anyone we know involved?"

"No, Peter, that was our concern as well. Harvey and Eddie went out to the airport, and everything's okay."

"Is Abigail up?"

"Yes, she's right here, awake and beautiful, trying to snatch the phone from me."

Jennifer passed her the receiver. She went to get Leeanne up, leaving Harvey dividing his attention between his oatmeal and his son.

*****

"These people owned 133 before Mr. and Mrs. Penninger?" Leeanne asked as Harvey drove up the turnpike in Jennifer's minivan.

"That's right, the brick house," said Eddie. "They bought it fifteen years ago, sold it to the Penningers eight years later. When Mr. Butler retired, they moved to Auburn to be near their kids."

"So they're pretty old," said Leeanne.

"Mr. Butler's seventy-three, and his wife's around seventy. They lived there when Mr. Fuller moved in, and for about five years after that."

Harvey caught Eddie's eye in the rearview mirror. "I'll let you handle the interview."

"Got it," said Eddie.

When they located the Butlers' house, Harvey and Eddie went to the door. Leeanne took Connor from the car seat and held him on her knees, cooing at him. After a minute, Harvey came out and approached Jennifer's window.

"Mrs. Butler says to come in. It's chilly, and she doesn't want you to sit out here with the baby."

Leeanne put Connor's hood up, and Jennifer shouldered the diaper bag. They scrambled between puddles to the door.

"Thank you, Mrs. Butler," Jennifer said as they shed their damp jackets.

"Now which one of you is Mrs. Larson?" She was a plump woman whose hair was still brown in the back, but iron gray in front.

"I am. This is my sister, Leeanne Wainthrop."

"Well, sit right down. Oh, what a sweet baby." She smiled and wagged her head at Connor. "I understand you live at 137 now."

"Yes, my husband and I bought the house from Everett Bailey last summer."

"He's a sweet man."

"Yes," Jennifer agreed. "He's gone to live with his daughter Lucy now, in Saco."

"Oh, yes, Lucy. I remember her. And Flossie passed on, of course."

"She's been gone over a year now."

"She was a good soul."

"Yes, I'm told she was a sweet lady, and very devout," Jennifer said. "She was ill for several years, though."

"She was in a wheelchair when we moved away. She had the most beautiful flower beds. Belonged to the garden club. She and I used to visit back and forth, before she got so sick."

"And what about the gentleman who lived between you, ma'am?" Eddie asked.

"Carleton Fuller?"

"Yes, ma'am."

"He wasn't very friendly," she said.

"Did he keep his house up?" Eddie asked.

"Well, yes, but not fancy. He wasn't much for flowers. Had bushes out front, and ivy over the porch, as I recall. He sort of let the flower beds go."

"He had a big back yard," said Mr. Butler. He was thin, with a little pot belly. His hair was snowy white, and he wore gold-rimmed glasses and had a neat, white mustache.

"Yes," said Harvey. "There's a nice lawn back there."

"He had one of the Carter boys on Martin Street come over and mow for him," Mrs. Butler said.

"That's right." Harvey nodded. "But before the Carter boy started doing that, he had a boy named Jacob Leonard. Do you remember him?"

Both the Butlers shook their heads. "I don't think so," Mr. Butler said.

"Was there a time when you didn't see Mr. Fuller for a while?" Eddie asked. "Maybe he went away, or was ill for several weeks, and you didn't see him at all?"

"Well, there might have been," Mr. Butler said vaguely.

"He usually went away every summer," Mrs. Butler said. "I think maybe he had a cottage, or a boat or something."

"Do you know where?" Eddie was writing in his notebook.

"Speculation," said Mr. Butler. "He never said anything about any cottage, Daisy."

"Well, he would be gone off and on for the whole summer most years," she said.

"And you lived beside him for five years," Eddie said.

"About."

"Now, just think about the first year he lived there," said Eddie. "What was his health, in general?"

"Oh, I don't know," Daisy said.

"He had rheumatism," said her husband.

"Arthritis, Thomas," said Daisy.

"Well, something like that. Complained awfully."

"Did he do yard work?" asked Eddie.

"Couldn't. He had that Carter boy come," said Thomas Butler.

"No, not then," said Daisy. "The first year he had the Haines boy, from number 145. Then the next summer he got the Carter boy."

"Why did he switch to the Carter boy?" asked Eddie.

"Heavens, I don't know. But Mrs. Haines said Carleton was rude to her son. I don't know the details."

"If anyone would know the details, you would," said Thomas.

Daisy glared at him.

"So, that summer he went away for a while," Eddie went on. "Did anyone mow the lawn for him while he was gone?"

"I don't recall," said Thomas.

"No, they most certainly did not," Daisy said emphatically. "The grass was quite long, and it looked just terrible. I said to Thomas, 'That Carleton Fuller is going to give our street a bad name. He ought to keep up his property.' I thought he was sick at first, or maybe dead in there. I sent Thomas over twice, to see if he was there."

"Was he?"

"No, Thomas said his car wasn't in the garage."

"I don't remember anything about that," said Thomas.

"Finally Flossie Bailey told me she'd seen him leave," said Daisy.

"But he came back?" Eddie asked.

"Yes, he came back."

"I don't recall any—" Thomas began, but Daisy cut him off.

"He came back in August," said Daisy. "I know because the cone flowers in the corner of our yard were blooming when I saw his car drive in. Clashed terribly."

Her husband scowled. "Flowers and cars don't clash."

"So he'd been away a long time?" Eddie asked.

"I'd say so," Daisy said. "Several weeks, anyway."

Eddie said, "I'd like you both to think back to when you first met Mr. Fuller. When he first moved in."

They nodded in unison.

"What did he look like?" Eddie asked.

"Gray hair, kind of stringy," said Daisy.

"No, he had short hair," said Thomas. "Always kept it short."

"That was later," Daisy insisted. "When he first came, it was longer. I think he didn't feel well that first winter. Didn't take care of himself, you know. When he went away that next summer, he came back looking a little more fit, and he'd cut his hair."

"Did he wear glasses?" asked Eddie.

"Oh, yes," Daisy said. "He didn't wear them all the time, but he had them."

"Did he have them when he first came, or did he get them later?" Eddie asked.

"I don't know," said Thomas.

Daisy thought for a moment. "Me either," she said at last.

"Did he wear them when he drove?" asked Eddie.

"Yes, he did," Daisy said positively.

"All right, I want to show you a picture," said Eddie. He took a folded piece of paper from his breast pocket and opened it. "Is this Carleton G. Fuller, the man who lived at 135 Van Cleeve Lane?"

He passed the paper to Thomas first.

"Hmm," said the gentleman. "It kind of looks like him."

Daisy got up and walked to her husband's chair and looked over his shoulder. "That's him when his hair was longer," she said.

"Are you sure?" Eddie asked.

"Well..." she faltered. "The nose doesn't look right, somehow."

"Do you recall Mr. Fuller ever having company?" Eddie asked, taking the paper back and folding it.

"Other than us and the Carter boy, you mean?" Thomas asked.

"Yes."

"Well, Everett Bailey might have gone over some."

He had a nephew in the service," said Daisy. "I think he visited once or twice."

"When?" asked Eddie.

"Oh, a long time ago."

"How long after Mr. Fuller moved in?"

"Let's see now," said Daisy.

"I don't remember any nephew," said Thomas.

Connor began to cry, and Leeanne stood up, carrying him to the window and joggling him a little.

"The nephew cleaned his gutters and raked his leaves while he was there one time," Daisy said. Must have been in the fall. That very first fall, I think, when Mr. Fuller was so stiff with the arthritis."

"Now, you said he was better afterward," Eddie said. "His arthritis got better?"

"Remission," Daisy said firmly. "He walked better the next summer, for sure. I still think he had a boat down at the harbor, or on one of the lakes."

"I'm going to show you another picture, and you tell me if it's Mr. Fuller." Eddie took a second sheet out and passed it to Thomas. Daisy leaned close.

"That's him," she said.

"Yes, I believe that's him," said Thomas. "I haven't seen him in seven years, but I'd say that's him."

"With the glasses," said Eddie.

"Yes."

"It's definitely him," said Daisy.

Eddie looked at Harvey, and Harvey shrugged a little.

"Well, thank you, Mr. and Mrs. Butler." Eddie stood up. "You've been very helpful." He put his notebook and the picture in his pocket and took out his wallet, extracting a business card.

"This is my phone number at the police station in Portland. If you think of anything more about Mr. Fuller, or his nephew, or other company he had, would you please call me?"

Thomas reached for the card, but Daisy snatched it from Eddie's hand. "We surely will."

"What's it for?" asked Thomas. "Is Carleton all right?"

"No, sir, he's dead," said Eddie.

Daisy blinked at him. "Why didn't you say so?"

Harvey said, "Mr. Penninger, who purchased your house, found that Mr. Fuller was ill last fall. He went into a nursing home, and he died last month."

"Land!" said Daisy.

Chapter 22

"What do you think?" Eddie asked when Harvey had started the engine.

"Where did you get the pictures?" Jennifer asked.

"Off his driver's license," said Harvey. "The first one was from twelve years ago, and the second one was when he renewed it six years ago."

"Can Jennifer and Leeanne see them?" Eddie asked.

"Sure," said Harvey.

Eddie handed them to Jennifer, and she unfolded them and smoothed them out. They were computer printouts.

"The DMV sent them to us," Eddie said.

"Well, everybody takes horrid pictures for their driver's license," Leeanne said, "but I'm not convinced those two pictures are of the same man."

Jennifer studied them critically. "Me either. The nose is different. The hair can be explained, and his eyes could have gotten worse so that he needed glasses, but what about the chin?"

"You're right," Leeanne said. "The chin is squarer on the newer picture. The older one has a much pointier chin."

"The eyes aren't even the same color, and his eyebrows arch differently," Jennifer said.

"Well, the color could be from the lighting or the printer," said Eddie. "They could both be categorized as blue eyes, which is what the license said. But I think you're right about the eyebrows. And, unless he started dying them, they went from mostly gray to mostly brown in six years."

"How did he get around the signature when he renewed the license?" Jennifer asked.

"Maybe he'd practiced forging Fuller's name by then, and the DMV clerk didn't notice a difference," Harvey said. "Or maybe the clerk just saw what he expected to see."

"You can renew your license at drug stores now," said Eddie. "They may have been in a hurry, and it just slipped by."

"Can you get a photo of Daniel Sanford?" Jennifer asked.

Eddie shrugged. "The Navy sent us one, but it's thirty years old. We've asked for a more recent one, and they're searching. But I'll tell you this. The best facial recognition software I can access says those are two different men."

Jennifer sat in silence for a minute. She looked over at Harvey. "So, do we own the house?"

Harvey's lips twitched. "Pete Bearse says if the new will is declared invalid, we'll have to settle with the nephew. So will Ralph Penninger, if he received compensation as executor. If the real Carleton Fuller didn't name him executor, he'll probably have to give the money back."

"Hmm. Another question." Jennifer eyed him pensively. "If Sanford cashed out Mr. Fuller's bonds and investments, what did he do with the money?"

"Just lived on it, I'd say," said Eddie.

"But he was getting his Navy pension, too. Didn't he collect as Daniel Sanford at the bank in Biddeford?" she asked.

"Yes." Harvey glanced at Eddie in his mirror. "Did you check on that?"

"Haven't had a chance to get over there."

"Check it Monday morning," Harvey said. "See if they have a positive ID on Sanford. Take the pictures with you."

"Will do."

Harvey glanced at Jennifer. "There were a lot of investments cashed out over time. More than one man would need to live on."

Leeanne said, "Maybe Daisy's right, and he bought a boat."

*****

When they got home, Abby met them at the door.

"Harvey, you'd better come right in and talk to Beth. Eddie, too."

"What's up?" Harvey could read the stress lines on Abby's face, unusual for the upbeat bride-to-be.

"I think Beth had better tell you," Abby said.

Gary and Andy were playing with a Lego set in the sun room. The adults went into the living room, where Peter was sitting on the sofa. The wedding invitations were spread out in piles on the coffee table, where he and Abby had been working on them.

Beth jumped up from the recliner.

"Harvey, I need to talk to you." Her face was pale.

"What is it, Beth?" He put his hand on her arm. "Sit down and tell me what's wrong."

Beth plunked down in her chair. "Someone's been in our house."

Jennifer shivered and held Connor close. Harvey glanced at her. Remembering the night their house had been robbed?

"When?" he asked.

"Last night, while I was at the play with Leeanne and Eddie."

"You're sure?" Harvey sat down in the rocking chair, drawing it close so that he and Beth were eye to eye.

"Yes, I'm sure. I didn't notice last night. It was so late, and I was tired. It was pouring rain when we came home, and I just ran inside and went right to bed. But this morning—" She broke off and looked around at them. "I was so scared." Her voice broke, and she started to cry. Leeanne brought the tissues. Jennifer passed Connor to Abby and sat on the arm of the recliner, her arm around Beth.

"What happened, honey?"

"I slept late," Beth said. "When I got up, the hiding place was open."

"The secret cubbyhole?"

"Yes."

Jennifer looked at Harvey.

He said, "You're sure you or Jeff didn't leave it open?"

"No. We gave you back the key, remember? I thought I might lose it. And it was definitely closed yesterday after school. I was putting more books in the shelves, but I didn't put any in that one. Jeff went to the fire station early yesterday morning and hasn't been home since."

"But it was open this morning?"

"Yes, and that's not all."

"What else?" Harvey asked.

"I called Jeff right away at the fire station. He told me to check in his sock drawer. He'd left a hundred dollars in there, from when he cashed his check. Five twenties."

"And?" Harvey asked.

"It's gone."

Harvey's heart sank. The others looked at each other helplessly.

"So, what did you do then?" Harvey asked.

"Jeff told me to come straight over here. I did. I didn't even stop to get my coat."

Beth wept, and Jennifer rubbed her shoulders, her gray eyes large.

Abby said quietly, "Jeff called right after Beth came. He told me he was afraid someone might be in the house, and he didn't want Beth to go back over."

"Could anyone have been in there this morning?" Eddie asked Beth.

"I don't know." Her dark eyes were wild. "I didn't go upstairs. I guess it's possible. And—I sure wasn't going to look in the basement."

Harvey nodded soberly. "Jeff's right. We'll go over and take a look. You stay here."

Peter stood up. "Should I come with you, Harvey? My first instinct was to go right over there and check for prowlers, but I thought if there was a burglary, I probably shouldn't touch anything. We knew you'd be back soon."

"You did the right thing, short of calling the police immediately," Harvey said.

"I thought of that," Abby said, "but Jeff wanted us to wait for you."

"How long has Beth been here?" Harvey asked.

"About an hour and a half. We've kind of been watching, but we haven't seen anybody poking around."

Harvey, Eddie, and Peter put on their coats. Harvey took Beth's house key and the key to the hiding place, and they went outside. They examined the driveway and the walk before going up the front steps of Beth's house.

Harvey looked closely at the keyhole and striker plate. "Someone had a key, I'd say."

"I'll check the back door," Eddie said.

Harvey kept Peter with him. "Just don't touch anything," he said.

Harvey went in through the living room to the kitchen and unlocked the back door from inside to let Eddie in.

"This one doesn't look tampered with, either," Eddie said.

"Let's take a look at the cubbyhole." On his way back to the living room, Harvey paused at the cellar door. It was closed, and the new deadbolt he'd had installed the previous week was in place so that no one could enter from the basement. He went into the next room and straight to the bookshelves. The hiding place was open, with the front board flopped down on the book shelf. Eddie was pulling on latex gloves, and Harvey stepped aside. "Just raise that board, would you?"

Eddie reached in and lifted the front piece with one finger and eased it into place, to hide the secret niche. Harvey took a small flashlight from his pocket and shined the beam on the small keyhole.

"Scratches. Someone's forced it open since the last time I looked at it."

"Yeah, but he probably knew it was here," Eddie said.

"Agreed. So the intruder had a key to one of the doors, but not to this. You'll want to dust this and the two doorknobs."

"Right."

"Just for drill, check the cellar door, too. And I'll take a walk around the neighborhood and see if anyone saw anything odd last night."

"We could call in one of the guys."

"Nah, then we'd be getting into overtime. I'll do it. People on this street are used to seeing me. But call Tony so you can get on the other part."

"What other part?" Peter asked.

"We've decided we need to check out the garden shed. I guess I'd better tell Beth about that."

"You could just wait until Jeff is here," Eddie said.

Harvey's eyebrows met as he frowned. "Tell me the second you find anything."

"Right."

*****

Beth was breathing rapidly. "Do you think someone could have been in there last night when I came home?"

"Oh, I doubt it," Jennifer said, but the idea made her flesh crawl.

"You didn't notice the cubbyhole when you went home?" Leeanne asked timidly.

"No."

"Have you eaten anything?" Jennifer asked Beth. It was nearly one o'clock.

"She wouldn't eat," Abby said. "Peter and the boys and I had sandwiches. She did drink a cup of tea, but that's it. And no breakfast."

"All right, Mrs. Wainthrop," Jennifer said sternly, "you are expecting a baby, who happens to be my nephew or niece. If you're going to stay in my house another minute, you're going to eat something. Come with me."

Beth stood up shakily, and Jennifer put her arm around her and took her to the kitchen. Leeanne and Abby followed, Abby bringing Connor.

"How are you guys doing?" Abby asked the boys as they went through the sunroom. "Need some cookies now?"

"Yes," cried Andy.

"Okay," said Gary.

Jennifer got the cookies out, and Leeanne poured milk for Beth, Gary, and Andy. Abby put Connor gently into Beth's arms, and her expression softened immediately.

"Would you hold this little guy while I get you a sandwich?" Abby asked.

"Of course." Beth held Connor's head up to her cheek.

The phone rang, and Jennifer grabbed it. "Hey, Jeff."

"Is Beth all right?" Jeff asked.

"She's okay," Jennifer said. "Harvey and Eddie, and Peter are at your house looking for evidence."

"Do they know anything yet?"

"Not yet."

"Okay, let me talk to Beth."

She stretched the cord to Beth at the table.

"Hi, honey," Beth said mournfully. "I'm okay. They're feeding me. I'm not. Really, I'm okay. Do you want Harvey to call you when he comes back? All right ... I love you, too."

She handed the receiver back to Jennifer.

The women chatted to cover their nervousness as they waited for the men to come back. Jennifer steered the conversation toward Abby's wedding plans and the open house for Beth and Jeff. After Leeanne had changed Connor's diaper, Jennifer sat down to feed him in the living room, and Beth sat with her. Abby and Leeanne set Gary and Andy up with games on the computers in the study. Leeanne came into the living room, but Abby stayed with the boys.

At last they heard the front door open and the men's voices as they wiped their feet and took off their coats. Jennifer passed Connor and the burp rag to Leeanne, and quickly straightened her clothes.

Harvey went straight to Beth. He sat down on the coffee table, facing her, and took her hands in his.

"Beth, there was a man in the house last night. As near as we can tell, there was only one. He left fingerprints on the hiding place and the dresser, and Eddie's going right to the police station and run them on the computer there."

Beth nodded, her brown eyes large and fearful.

"Did he go upstairs?"

"I think so. There was a little mud on the stairs and in the hallway up there. Eddie didn't find any fingerprints upstairs, but he didn't dust the entire house."

"You couldn't," she said.

"Well, you don't have much furniture up there," Harvey said. "I don't think he stayed up there long."

"Not—all night?" she asked.

"I don't think so. But, I'm going to tell you straight, okay?"

"Yes."

"He went in the cellar."

Beth closed her eyes.

"He smoked a cigarette down there," Harvey said.

"The smoke. I smelled it last night," she said in a tight voice.

"You did?"

"I wasn't thinking. I was so tired. When I went in the house, after Eddie and Leeanne and I came back here, there was a faint smoky smell, but I thought it was from the fireplace, because of the rain. You know how smells seem stronger when it rains?"

"In the little house we used to rent, the living room rug held an odor," Jennifer said. "When it rained we'd smell it. Remember?"

"Yes," said Beth. "I thought it was that. The fireplace, or the rug." She took hold of Harvey's lapels. "Was he there then, Harvey? Was he in the house then?"

"I don't know. But if you smelled the smoke, we know he was in there before you went home. He didn't go in while you were sleeping."

She nodded, and Jennifer thought she might collapse any minute.

Harvey said, "I want you to stay here with us until Jeff comes home. I'm going to get a locksmith to come and change all the locks today."

"It will cost you a fortune on the weekend," she said.

"That doesn't matter. We need to protect our family and our property."

"You think he had a key?" she asked.

"We couldn't find any sign of forced entry."

"The basement?"

"The bulkhead has a padlock on it, and there are only two small windows. Neither one has signs of recent tampering. They're both muddy on the outside and dusty on the inside, and they don't open easily."

Beth nodded again.

Harvey went on, "We checked every door and window. You did lock up before you went to the play?"

"Yes. Everything was locked, anyway. I only opened the front door."

"Did you lock the front door when you came over here for supper?" Harvey asked.

"Yes, I'm sure I did. I had to unlock it when I went back for my purse. It was while Greg was here, remember?"

"I remember," said Eddie.

"I locked it again when I came out. I'm positive. I've been a little uneasy because of the burglary you guys had last fall. Jeff said he'd get an alarm, but we hadn't done it yet."

"I'll get you an alarm," Harvey said. "You don't have to worry about that, or pay for it. I'll have one installed Monday. Beth, I'm sorry. This shouldn't have happened. If I'd thought—" He broke off, shaking his head.

"You couldn't predict it," she said.

"Maybe I could have."

Jennifer said to Leeanne, "Will you check the guest room upstairs, and see if it has everything Beth will need? There should be new toothbrushes in the linen closet, and I'll send up a clean nightgown."

"I can go get my things, if one of the guys will go with me," Beth said.

"No, I don't want you to go over today," Harvey said. "Eddie might want to do a little more work over there. Just stay here with us, all right?"

"All right."

"I'm so sorry," Harvey said.

Beth wiped away a tear. "Jeff wants you to call him."

"Sure." Harvey went into the bedroom and closed the door.

Peter said quietly, "Well, Jennifer, I guess I'd better round the boys up and head for home."

"You don't need to," she said.

"You folks could use some quiet, I think. Perhaps I'll take Abigail with us, if she's willing. We could finish the invitations

243

over there, and we'll go to Pastor Rowland for our counseling session later."

Jennifer nodded, and he went into the study where Abby and the boys were playing computer games.

Jennifer convinced Beth to lie down, but she wanted someone to stay with her. Leeanne offered to sit in her room and read, and Beth went up the stairs with her.

"I know I'm being a sissy," Beth said as they went.

"No such thing," Leeanne said.

Eddie left for the police station, and suddenly Jennifer was alone. Connor drowsed in her arms, and she took him into the bedroom. Harvey was still talking to Jeff on the phone.

"He might have been," Harvey said. "One of the neighbors saw a car parked a little ways up the street last night. She wasn't sure what time it left, but it could have been your uninvited guest. I'm sorry Jeff. I feel as if we didn't do all we should have for Beth. Maybe I shouldn't have let you move in before this investigation was finished, but it seemed pretty conclusive. We just had to find the evidence. I was sure the man impersonating Fuller was the murderer, and he's been dead for more than a month."

He paused, listening.

"We will. I asked her not to go over until you're home, but I suppose she'll want her clothes for church tomorrow. If she insists, I'll go over with her in the morning. All right, if you can."

Jennifer laid Connor cautiously in the cradle. He sighed and slept on. She covered him with a blanket.

Harvey stood beside her, looking at the baby. "Thank you, Jenny," he said softly.

She looked up at him.

"He's everything I've always wanted in a son, and more."

"He's a gift from God," she said.

"Yes." He turned her toward him and hugged her. "Jeff's going to try to get off for an hour or two this evening and come over to check in on Beth."

"I think that would be good. Leeanne is putting her to bed upstairs for a nap. Peter and Abby are gone, with the boys, and Eddie went to the station."

"Well, he's getting his overtime this week." Harvey sighed. "I told Jeff my concerns about the boy who mowed the lawn. He said to do whatever we need to in the garden shed. He hasn't put any tools in there yet. But he also asked me not to mention that angle to Beth."

"I don't see any reason to get into that with her," Jennifer said. "It's only indirectly related."

"Yeah. But I'd better call the locksmith."

When he had arranged for a man to come later that day, at an exorbitant price, Jennifer asked him, "Who saw the car last night?"

"Janice. It wasn't directly in front of 135, but she noticed it. Not many people park at the curb on this street, unless a driveway is full."

"You didn't mention that to Beth."

"No. And it may have nothing to do with the intruder. Janice didn't know what time the car left. I asked a couple of other neighbors, but nobody else remembered seeing it."

"You think this break-in has to do with the homicide?" Jennifer asked.

"I don't know. But if the person who was in the house last night had a key ... well, I don't know what to think. Yet."

He sat down on the bed and pulled her down beside him.

"Who would have a key to that house?" Jennifer asked.

"We do, Beth and Jeff, maybe Ralph Penninger."

"How about the boy who did yard work for Mr. Fuller, or Sanford, or whoever he was?"

"I doubt he'd give him a key," Harvey said, "especially if he had something to hide."

"Well, how about the real estate company? Did they give us all the keys?"

"Good question."

"And all the workmen who've been through there in the last couple of weeks," Jennifer said. "Did you give any of them keys?"

"No. The furnace man, the plumber, and the concrete crew all came here to get the keys, didn't they?" he asked.

"I think so."

"And they all returned them?"

"I think so. But isn't it possible they could have had a duplicate made before bringing ours back?"

"Yeah, it's possible, but whoever was in there knew about the hiding place. That seems to eliminate the workmen."

"Unless one of them had a connection to the house that you don't know about."

Harvey sat deep in thought. After a minute, he said, "Who would you give a key to?"

"For next door?"

"No, for our house."

"Oh. Relatives, neighbors. How many people do have our keys?"

He started to list them. "Abby, Leeanne, Eddie—"

"You gave Eddie a key?" she asked.

"Yes, when we went to your folks' for the weekend. I told him to keep it. And Bud and Janice have one."

"We have one of theirs," Jennifer said. "But they wouldn't use it unless they had a very good reason."

"Right. Anyone else?" he asked.

"Jeff and Beth have one."

"Of course."

"I think that's it."

"Relatives and very close friends," he said. "So who did Mr. Fuller—or Mr. Sanford alias Fuller—give his keys to?"

"As far as we know, he didn't have any close friends," Jennifer said slowly. "And he probably didn't trust many people."

"Right. The Baileys and the Butlers certainly weren't on those terms with him. Apparently he had no pets or plants to be cared for while he went away in the summer. I'll ask Mr. Penninger if he has a key. That leaves relatives."

"Does he have any relatives, other than the nephew?"

"Eddie and Tony did a search. They didn't find any other living relatives."

"But the nephew only visited him once in ten years."

"That's not necessarily true," Harvey said. "The Baileys knew of one visit. Mrs. Butler also knew about the nephew. She said he came once or twice, and there might have been more visits she missed."

"Do you think the nephew had a key?"

"It's possible."

"Harvey, are you saying Mr. Fuller's nephew was in the house last night?"

"I'm not saying anything. We'll see what we learn from the fingerprints."

Jennifer thought for a moment. "If no one notified Marcus Rutledge of his uncle's death, he could have come here expecting to see him alive. No one answered the doorbell last night, so he let himself in. Instead of his uncle's possessions, he found strange furniture. In the bedroom, a woman's clothes were hanging in the closet. He went upstairs, and the bedroom he used to sleep in when he visited was empty. He checked the cellar and found ... what?"

"A new furnace, and crime scene tape around a recently dug up portion of the dirt floor," Harvey said.

"Yes." Jennifer met his gaze. "A spot he might have reason to be wary of."

"The cigarette butt was inside the crime scene tape," Harvey said. "Footprints, too."

"So, he looked at the grave site. What kind of shoes?" she asked. "Sneakers?"

"No. Leather soles. Size eleven."

"You picked up the butt, of course."

"Of course." He smiled at her. "You know, gorgeous, we spend more time detecting than cuddling lately. Something's out of kilter here."

He drew her toward him, and she went willingly into his arms.

Chapter 23

Harvey was next door, supervising the locksmith, when Jeff came. He parked in his own driveway and went to talk to Harvey. Jennifer went upstairs and woke Beth. Leeanne was in her room, at work on the computer.

Jennifer put her hand on Beth's shoulder. "Beth, Jeff is home."

Beth opened her eyes. "He's here?"

"He's outside, talking to Harvey. They're having new locks put on your house."

Beth sat up. "I must have slept. What time is it?"

"Four-thirty. Do you feel all right?"

"I think so. Just a little groggy."

The rain had stopped, and the lowering sun cast feeble rays on the top of the Parkers' tallest maple tree.

"Maybe I should go over now and get a few things, if Jeff's there," Beth said.

"I'll go with you."

Beth put on her shoes, and Jennifer told Leeanne they were going. Leeanne promised to keep her ears tuned for Connor's cries.

"Your shoes will be soaked," Jennifer said as she and Beth walked over the lawns.

"We should pave a path from your front door to mine." Beth chuckled, and Jennifer was glad to hear her laugh.

The locksmith moved aside and opened the door wide for them. Harvey and Jeff were standing in the living room near the bookshelves, looking at the hiding place.

"Beth!" Jeff moved quickly toward her and wrapped his arms around her. The look on his face was one of grief, and his hand trembled as he put it to her hair and held her close. His blond head came down against her dark one, and they stood, not speaking, for several seconds. Harvey came to Jennifer and put an arm around her.

249

"I thought I'd get a few things to take to Jennifer's," Beth said at last.

"Come on, I'll go with you." Jeff took her into the bedroom.

Harvey looked down at Jennifer. "I don't like to think that he could have been here when she came in last night."

Jennifer nodded. "He may have waited in the cellar until she went to sleep, then come up and gone out."

"Thank God he didn't harm her." Harvey's arms tightened around her.

"Just as likely he'd already left when she got home," she said. "Beth says the smoke smell was faint. If he was smoking when she came in, the air would have been thick. Beth isn't around people who smoke much. She'd have realized it was more than a damp house odor."

"We were home while they were at the play," Harvey said. "No cars came into their driveway all evening."

"Would we have noticed?" Jennifer looked into his eyes. "We were in the living room with Greg for a while, then we watched the news. Connor cried so much last night, we might not have heard anything."

"If there had been a car in the driveway over here or at the curb when Abby and Peter came home, Abby would have noticed," Harvey said.

"Yes, probably she would. And there was no vehicle there when Eddie and Leeanne came home and brought Beth."

"He probably came while they were at the play, like Beth said, and left before they returned," Harvey concluded.

Beth and Jeff came back into the room. Beth was carrying her toothbrush and had a dress and a few other articles of clothing over her arm. Jeff carried her purse and shoes.

"Did you check your purse now?" Harvey asked.

Beth turned a shade paler, and took the pocketbook from Jeff and opened it.

"My cash and credit cards are here."

"Good," Harvey said. "I didn't mean to scare you. Let's go over to our house."

250

He spoke to the locksmith on the way out, and they went to their kitchen.

"Can you stay to supper, Jeff?" Jennifer asked.

"Yes, I can stay the night, unless my pager goes off."

"Great," said Harvey.

"How come?" Beth asked, leaning against him.

"I told my captain what happened, and he told me I could. If they really need me, he'll page me. But when the shift changes at six in the morning, they'll be short one man anyway, so I have to be back."

"We can stay at our house," Beth said. "I won't be scared, if you're there."

"No, if I got paged in the middle of the night you'd have to wake up Harvey and Jennifer and come over here. Let's just sleep in their guest room tonight."

"Pretend it's the Hilton," Jennifer said. "We'll give you the big towels and the coffee maker in your room."

Jeff laughed. "You don't need to do that. It will be great just to sleep where there aren't four guys snoring at different pitches."

When they went out, Tony Winfield's Mustang was parked in the Larsons' driveway, right behind Eddie's pickup.

"My guys are checking your shed," Harvey said.

Jeff slowed his steps. "For what?"

"Anything they can find."

"Because of the break-in?"

"No, I was going to have them take a look in there anyway."

Jeff eyed him for a moment. "Okay, Harvey. Do whatever you think is best."

*****

Leeanne was setting the table for supper when Harvey heard Tony and Eddie talking outside. He went to the door and opened it just as Tony was about to punch the bell.

"Hey, Captain. We're done over there."

Harvey stepped outside and closed the door. "Find anything?"

"Yeah," Eddie said. "There's a spot on the floor that's probably blood. We took samples, and Tony's going to drop them at the lab. Could be from an accident."

"There's spatter, too," Tony said. "Not much, but a couple of spots on the wall. You can't see it with the naked eye."

Harvey nodded. "I wish that lawnmower was in there, but I checked. They sold it the day of the estate sale."

"You think the kid's buried in the yard?" Tony asked.

Harvey let out long, slow breath. "I wish I knew. It seems unlikely he'd bury him out in the open, with other neighbors so close. What kind of a floor does that shed have?"

"Wood. The whole shed's pre-fab," Eddie said.

"Can we move it? It's not on a slab?"

"No, I think we could move it, but we might just be able to lift out the flooring."

"Do it. If it wrecks the material, I'll fix it after."

"Okay," Eddie said. "When? I was planning to run the fingerprints I collected today in the house first thing in the morning."

"Maybe I'll see if we can put a CSI team on it. Let me talk to the chief."

"I'll head out then," Tony said.

"Yeah. Thanks for coming, Tony," Harvey said. "Don't forget to log your hours."

He managed to put the case out of his mind during supper and spent a pleasant evening with the family and Eddie. At eight o'clock, Jennifer sent Beth and Jeff upstairs, so Jeff could sleep as long as possible. She and Harvey spent an hour reading the Bible and praying through their lengthy list.

Connor woke at two-thirty, and Jennifer took him into the bed for his feeding. A half hour later, Harvey woke again when he heard quiet footsteps on the stairs. He sat up and groped for his pants.

"What's going on?" Jennifer asked sleepily.

"I think Jeff is up. Go back to sleep, Jenny."

He went out of the bedroom. The dim light over the kitchen sink was on, and he found Jeff there.

"Hey. They called me for a fire."

"Want something to eat?"

"I'd better get going. Just checking to see if there was any coffee left."

Harvey got him a mug. Jeff poured what coffee was left in the pot into it and stuck it in the microwave for a minute. Harvey opened a container and put a muffin in Jeff's hand.

"I'll put the coffee in a travel mug for you, if you want."

"Thanks." Jeff took a bite of the muffin.

Less than two minutes later, Harvey was resetting the burglar alarm while Jeff drove out. He went back to the bedroom, switching lights off on the way, and undressed in the dark.

"What time is it?" Jennifer asked.

"Quarter to four. They called him for a fire."

"At least he got some comfort time with Beth."

"Yes, I think it was the best thing for her." Harvey rolled back into bed and was asleep almost instantly.

*****

Before Sunday school started, Eddie dropped onto the pew beside Harvey. "The fingerprints from Beth's house aren't in our system."

"Check with the Navy tomorrow," Harvey said. "We need Rutledge's prints."

"I'm all over it," said Eddie. "Where's Leeanne?"

"Went to the singles class."

"Catch you later." Eddie headed for the hallway.

Abby leaned toward Jennifer. "We never did get to the mall yesterday. We need to settle on the dresses for you and Leeanne! She's going home today."

"Let's just order that one from the catalog," Jennifer said. "The one Mom liked."

"Do you think it's formal enough?"

"I don't know. How formal is the wedding?"

"Evening wedding. Tuxedoes." Abby frowned and lifted her shoulders.

"Will we wear gloves?" Jennifer asked.

"No, that's medieval."

Peter came in smiling and sat beside Abby, his arm across the back of the seat.

"Peter's really progressing," Harvey observed.

Jim Rider, the quarter's teacher, stood to open the class, and they gave him their attention.

*****

"I can go home now," Beth said, when they had eaten lunch. Mike and Sharon Browning and Eddie had joined the Larsons, too. Abby had disappeared with the Hobarts.

"Better stay here until morning," Harvey said. "Jeff will be here shortly after six, to run with Eddie and me, then he'll want to collapse in his own bed. You can go home then."

"I'll go over with you this afternoon if you want to get anything," Jennifer said.

"Would you mind if I got a peek?" Mike asked. "I've been curious ever since Harvey told me about the basement."

"Feel free," said Beth. "I haven't seen the basement yet, and I'm not sure I ever want to."

Jennifer met Harvey's troubled gaze. Would Beth ever be comfortable in the house after all that had happened? Every time Jennifer wakened in the night, her heart pounded until she identified the sound that had roused her. Beth might be nervous about the cellar as long as she lived there.

They all walked over together. Beth laid out the clothes she wanted to wear to school the next day and checked the refrigerator to see if anything needed to be used up or thrown out. Mike, Eddie, and Harvey had a tour of the cellar, then Harvey unlocked the cubbyhole and showed Mike where the papers had been found.

"Hit this Navy connection hard tomorrow," Mike advised.

Eddie nodded. "That's my strategy."

"I hope our prowler is foiled, now that the locks are changed," Harvey said. "Tomorrow I'm calling the security company that did our house and have them set up a similar system here for Beth and Jeff."

"Does the alarm ring at the police station?" Beth asked.

"No, it rings at the security company office. If it goes off, they call the house to see if everything's okay. If no one answers, or if you tell them something's wrong, they call the police."

"Could they set it up so it rings at your house, too?" Beth asked.

"Maybe. Would that make you feel secure?"

"It might. I mean, when Jeff's at work. You're so close."

"I'll ask them tomorrow," Harvey said.

The women went back to 137, and Harvey took Mike around to the shed in the back yard. Eddie pointed out the places where he and Tony had found trace evidence of old bloodstains.

"Yeah, okay," Mike said. "I'll set it up first thing in the morning if you want. I think it would be easier for them to move this shed than tear out the floor and replace it."

"If you think that's best," Harvey said.

Mike glanced around the little building, scowling. "Yeah. With it empty, it shouldn't be too heavy. I'll see what they need for equipment."

*****

Margaret and Carl Turner, with Julia, came into the church just before the evening service began.

"Hello! Welcome." Jennifer kissed Margaret on the cheek.

"We planned to come this morning, but I had a delivery," Margaret said. "Mrs. Baker wouldn't wait."

Carl and Harvey shook hands.

"How are you feeling?" Margaret whispered to Jennifer.

"Pretty good."

"Where's the baby?"

"Leeanne's got him, behind us."

Margaret looked back to where Leeanne and Eddie were sitting. Leeanne was cuddling Connor, her last chance before leaving for Skowhegan again.

"He's such a doll," Margaret said. "I want one just like him."

"We're praying about that request," Jennifer told her, and Margaret nodded sagely.

"Mommy, may I sit with Leeanne and Eddie?" Julia asked. Margaret smiled. "All right."

Julia wriggled out past Carl and into the next row. Leeanne grinned at her and let her take the happy baby into her arms.

When the songs, testimonies, and prayer had finished, Pastor Rowland began to speak about God's desire for them all to live in obedience to him. Jennifer scribbled notes in the margin of her Bible, wishing she had her notebook along. The pastor's meekness struck her freshly as he counseled each of them to obey God, without lifting up himself as an example. The model he gave was Christ, and Jennifer felt she fell very short in that discipline.

As they sat, she felt Margaret's tension growing. Jennifer glanced at her. She was gripping Carl's hand, but her eyes stayed on Pastor Rowland. Jennifer prayed silently for her.

Harvey nudged her slightly and pushed his notebook toward her. Beside his neat outline of the sermon were the words, "Pray for Carl."

It reminded Jennifer of his words a few days earlier, that Carl couldn't move without Margaret. If Margaret could yield her self-worth to Christ, Carl would follow with relief and gratitude. But for Carl it would be unthinkable to break new spiritual ground without his wife. It would be a new rift for him, a broader gap than the one caused by her professional pride and his desire for more children.

When the message had ended, Pastor Rowland had the congregation stand and offered an invitation to those who wanted prayer. It wasn't something he did every week, but occasionally he felt led of God to do so. Harvey held Jennifer's hand tightly, and she could almost feel his prayers radiating. They sang a hymn softly, and a woman stepped into the aisle farther down and walked to the front.

Suddenly Carl took his hand from Margaret's and stepped into the side aisle. Margaret stood trembling beside her. Jennifer kept up her prayer, wondering if she should speak to her. Walking to the front of the church would be an act of humility for Margaret, and humility was something she avoided at all cost.

256

Perhaps she would consider dealing with God in private, but not in front of the entire congregation, several of whom were her patients.

Jennifer glanced at Harvey, but his eyes were closed.

"Margaret," she whispered.

"I should go," Margaret said, but she stood there unmoving.

Jennifer wasn't sure if she meant she should follow Carl, or that she should leave. "Would you like me to go with you?" she whispered.

Margaret shook her head. Her eyes were brimful of tears, and she blinked furiously. She's angry, Jennifer thought, but with Carl, for going, or with herself for staying? Or perhaps because Carl went without her.

Then Julia walked past them in the aisle. Margaret gasped. Her eyes followed her daughter, as she walked to the front and Carl embraced her. The pastor spoke to them both. Margaret sank to the pew.

Jennifer sat down beside her and put her arm around her shoulders. "Margaret, dear Margaret."

The music ended.

Pastor Rowland asked Jim Rider to close the service in prayer, and he stayed with Carl and Julia. Mary Rowland spoke with the woman who had gone down first.

"I'm too late," Margaret whispered.

"No, you're not," Jennifer said. "God will meet you anytime."

Margaret stood up, shaking, and edged toward the end of the pew. At last, as Jim Rider prayed, she stepped out hesitantly, then more quickly walked down the long side aisle. She crumpled against Carl, and he put his arm around her, with Julia on his other side. Jennifer closed her eyes. During the prayer, the pastor had taken the family through a side door.

Harvey reached for Jennifer, and they stood hugging and crying in the pew. All around them, people were moving, gathering their things.

"Let's sit," Harvey said, they sat down together. He bowed his head. "Lord, please help Carl and Margaret now, and Julia,

257

too, to surrender everything to you," he prayed, close to Jennifer's ear.

"Amen," she said.

Leeanne and Eddie came in beside them and sat. Connor was still awake and happy. Harvey reached for him and took him into his arms, and a look of joy and peace settled over him.

"We have so much to be thankful for," he said.

They continued to sit as the church slowly emptied. Peter and Abby came over, and Abby kissed Jennifer and Harvey.

"You planted the seed," she said.

Peter took her with him and the boys. "I'll have her home before midnight," he promised.

"I'm not worried," Harvey said.

Beth came to the end of the pew with Rick and Ruthann. Rick held Ethan, who had recently taken his first steps. Clarissa held Beth's hand.

"Ethan is getting so big," Jennifer said with a grin.

"He'll be a year old on Tuesday," Ruthann told her. "Harvey, Beth told us she's staying with you tonight. Pretty scary, what happened this weekend."

"Yes," Harvey agreed. "We've had the locks changed, and I'm putting in a security system for them."

"Beth seems to think the prowler's connected somehow to the bones you took out of the cellar," Rick said.

"Well, we don't know. It's pretty bizarre, no matter how you look at it."

Beth said, "Well, in spite of the prowlers, skeletons, and secret panels, Jeff and I are having that house warming Saturday, and you're invited."

"That sounds like a big project," Ruthann said.

"Jennifer's planned it, and we decided we want to entertain all the people we love in our new home," Beth said. "Mom and Dad are coming from Freeport. I'm inviting Jeff's parents, too. All the extended family on both sides, and our church friends, the teachers I work with, and the guys from the fire department and their wives. We'll have open house from two to four, and we're not going to let this cloak and dagger stuff spoil it."

"Good for you," said Rick.

Jennifer wondered how Harvey felt about that many people tramping through a crime scene, but he smiled at Beth.

"Let your sisters-in-law do the work," he said.

"I will. I'm making cookies and punch for refreshments, but Jennifer and Abby are doing most of it."

"I'm making meatballs and finger sandwiches," Jennifer said. "Is the unpacking under control?"

Beth scrunched up her face. "Maybe after school tomorrow you could help me make a list of what I need to do."

"I'll bring some fudge when we come," Ruthann said.

Rick nudged her. "Well, Ruthie, come on, we need to get these hooligans to bed."

"What's the word on your job, Rick?" Harvey asked.

"I'm still working, so it could be worse."

"If you hear you're getting laid off, tell me. If I hear of any openings, I'll let you know."

"Thanks."

"Maybe Peter would have something," Leeanne said.

"Maybe." Harvey looked at Rick. "Did you go to college?"

"Just two years. Kind of wish I'd finished now."

Ruthann didn't say anything. She had had a year of Bible school, and had left to marry Rick.

Beth walked with them to the doorway, then came back to Jennifer and Harvey.

"Are you going to wait for Carl and Margaret?" Eddie asked.

"Thought I would," said Harvey.

Leeanne turned and looked at the clock on the back wall. "I really need to get going."

Harvey stood up, Connor in his arms. "Give us a hug."

Leeanne kissed him, then the baby. She hugged Jennifer tight.

"Are you coming back down next weekend?" Jennifer asked.

"Couldn't miss Beth and Jeff's house warming."

Jennifer smiled. "Tell Mom and Dad their room will be waiting."

"No, I want them to stay at our house," said Beth. "That is, if your mom will stay at Chez Murder, and if we can get a bed into the guest room by then."

"All right, but send us your overflow guests," Jennifer said. "If you need extra linens or anything like that, tell us."

"No doubt Travis and Randy will want to stay at Beth and Jeff's house," Eddie said.

Leeanne nodded. "Yes, but they can sleep on the floor."

"They'd probably rather sleep in the cellar," said Eddie.

"Nix on that," Harvey said, rolling his eyes.

"Viens, ma chérie." Eddie slipped his arm around Leeanne as they walked toward the double door.

"Be at my house at 6:15, Ed," Harvey called after him. "Jeff will run and pray with us, then we're going to crack this case."

Eddie waved and called, *"A bientôt."*

Beth gave Harvey a wan smile. "Think we'll ever know what really happened?"

"I sincerely hope so. And then we'll pour the rest of the concrete and finish off that basement into a rec room you'll be happy to show your guests."

The side door opened, and Pastor Rowland and the Turners came into the auditorium.

Harvey stood. Carl walked toward him, smiling, and held out his hand.

"Thank you, Harvey," Carl said.

Margaret went straight to Jennifer and put her arms around her. They didn't speak. After a moment, Julia tugged at her mother's arm.

"Mommy, I want to hug Jennifer, too."

Jennifer gave her a squeeze. "Julia, I'm so happy."

"We love Jesus now," Julia said.

Carl cleared his throat. "We're going to have a few sessions with the pastor. I can't tell you two how much you've helped us."

"Harvey," Margaret began, turning to him, "I want to apologize for all the times I put you down for being religious."

Harvey shrugged. "I didn't take offense, Margaret."

"I know. You wouldn't. I understand now."

Carl said, "We'll be back Wednesday night. I may call you before then, Harv."

"Call me anytime. I mean that."

They all went out to the parking lot, and Beth rode home with Jennifer and Harvey.

"This is almost like when we were roomies," Jennifer said when they sat in the sunroom eating popcorn.

"Yes, but I'd make Harvey leave if it got this late on a Sunday night," Beth said.

Harvey smiled. "But you always let me kiss Jennifer in the kitchen first."

Chapter 24

Harvey came home for lunch on Monday, and Beth and Jeff came over for an update on "their" case. Beth was taking an extended lunch hour from school. Eddie came in with Harvey, and Jennifer threw an extra plate on the table.

"Good news, neighbors," Harvey said. "I'll let Eddie give you the lowdown. It will be good practice for the press conference he's going to hold in a couple of hours."

Harvey asked the blessing, and they all began to make Italian sandwiches, passing cheese, ham, salami, pickles, green peppers, and black olives.

"So, what did you find out, Eddie?" Jeff asked. He had run with Eddie and Harvey early, then slept most of the morning.

"Well, the Navy finally sent us Sanford's dental records and a twelve-year-old photo. He was definitely the man who lived in your house for the last ten years or so. I took their dental records to 'Mr. Fuller's' dentist here in Portland, and it's a match, all right. The Navy photo is of the man on the renewed driver's license, too, and the people at the bank in Biddeford identified him as Daniel Sanford, who's been collecting the Navy pension every month."

Harvey said, "I think our evidence that Sanford was impersonating Fuller is conclusive enough to stand up in court now. I called Pete Bearse, and he's meeting with Ralph Penninger. They'll probably file a motion in the district court to have the will reconsidered."

"Will there be a trial?" Beth asked.

"No, a judge will probably examine both wills and the evidence we've collected that says Carleton Fuller died about ten years ago. The judge will rule on which of the wills is valid. Pete will prepare the brief."

"Are you guys going to have to pay big bucks for this?" Jeff asked uneasily.

"Well, we're hoping the court costs will come out of the estate," Harvey said. "Unfortunately, the estate is about several hundred grand smaller than it should be. Sanford cashed out all of Fuller's investments and, as far as we can tell, spent the money. The house was just about all that was left."

"What about the nephew?" Jennifer asked.

"We're trying to locate him, for several reasons."

"He inherits, if the old will is valid," said Abby.

"Right, but ... " Harvey hesitated, flicking a glance at Beth, then picked up his milk glass and took a sip.

"What?" Beth asked.

Harvey looked across the table at Eddie. "It's your case, Ed."

Eddie swallowed the bite he was chewing. "Rutledge, the nephew, is the guy that broke into your house Saturday."

"You're sure?" Jeff asked.

"Yup. The Navy sent us his prints. They said if he's involved in a crime, they'll send M.P.s to take him back to Norfolk."

"Was it a crime, if he had a key and didn't know his uncle was dead?" Abby asked.

"He stole Jeff's money," Eddie said. "His fingerprints were on the dresser."

"So, where is he?" Beth asked.

Harvey shook his head. "We wish we knew."

Eddie said, "He's due back on the base by midnight Sunday. We may just have to wait and see if he goes back there. If he does, the Navy will hold him."

Beth frowned. "Will they send him back here?"

"Not for stealing a hundred dollars," Eddie said. "But if we tie him to something more serious..."

"Like a murder?" Jeff asked.

"Yes. If that happened, we'd ask for extradition."

"So, how much of this are you giving to the press?" Beth asked.

"Well, we don't want to scare him off," Harvey said. "We won't mention Marcus Rutledge. But Eddie will tell them we've established that the body found in the basement was Carleton G. Fuller's, and the man who died in the nursing home a month ago was Daniel Sanford, who apparently assumed Fuller's identity, lived in his house, and claimed his financial resources over the last ten years."

"Not that he killed Mr. Fuller?" Jennifer asked.

"Well, we haven't proved that," Harvey said.

"But you've proved the bones were Mr. Fuller's?"

"I finally found his old dentist in Kittery," said Eddie. "He drove up this morning with Carleton Fuller's dental records and spent an hour in our lab with two techs and the skull and teeth from the basement. He says they're Mr. Fuller's teeth. The older fillings are unmistakable."

Beth shivered. "Poor Mr. Fuller."

"It's strange," Jennifer said. "I feel as if we knew him, but we never did. He was killed years ago."

"Is it worth the trouble to prove Sanford murdered him?" Jeff asked. "That one dead man killed the other, I mean?"

"Well, if he didn't do it, that would be worth proving," said Eddie. "It would mean someone else did it."

Beth's lower lip trembled. The thought of Marcus Rutledge entering her house three nights before was enough to shake anyone.

Jeff pulled her close to him. "This whole thing makes me mad. What's the next step?"

Eddie paused with his sandwich in midair. "We're still trying to establish that Sanford knew Fuller, or that he knew his nephew. So far, the only link we've found is that Sanford's and Rutledge's ships took part in an exercise together thirteen years ago. They were deployed in the Mediterranean at the same time and had shore leave in Marseilles about the same time. It's possible they could have met then, but we're not sure they did." He took a big bite of his Italian sandwich.

"Do you think this Rutledge is hanging around here?" Jeff asked, his eyes hard.

"We don't know," Harvey said. "If he came to collect on the estate, he ought to step forward. It's possible he came expecting to see his uncle, but if so, he ought to have come openly and asked you why you were living in the house and what happened to Mr. Fuller."

Eddie swallowed. "Off the record, we suspect he came to rendezvous with Sanford, maybe get some money from him. If that's the way it was, he got a surprise and is lying low to see what's up."

Abby said, "If he reads the paper tomorrow, he'll know some of it."

"Yeah," Eddie said. "We can't help that. Maybe it will help flush him out. Especially if he doesn't know we've connected him to all of this."

"Ryan didn't find out about the break-in?" Abby asked.

"Eddie logged it Saturday night," Harvey said. "Either he hasn't checked the police log since, or he hasn't made the connection. I'm sure if he realized the break-in occurred at the house where the skeleton was found, he'd have been haunting my office this morning for another front-page story."

"What about the garden shed?" Jeff asked.

"I checked in with the officer in charge over there. They say there's no grave beneath the shed."

"Well, that's a relief." Jeff picked up his sandwich. "Isn't it?"

"Yes," Harvey said. "The lab is going to great lengths to see if they can tell who the blood belonged to, but it's been compromised through what I'm guessing were cleaning efforts."

"You're not going to dig up the whole yard, are you?" Beth asked.

"I don't think so. They're using a drone to take aerial shots, and they've got other equipment that might give some hints if there *is* a grave over there."

"A drone?" Jeff said, frowning.

"Aerial photos can show up ground that was disturbed, even a long time ago," Eddie said. The vegetation looks different, and there might be small differences in the elevation."

"Huh." Jeff took another bite of his Italian.

"So, Eddie," Jennifer said, trying to sound cheerful, "we'll see you on the news tonight."

266

"Yeah, I guess I'd better get back to the station and change into my suit before the press conference."

Abby grinned at him. "I'll tape it for Leeanne. Knock 'em dead, friend."

*****

The wedding plans kept Abby and Jennifer engrossed that afternoon. While Connor napped, Jennifer laid out the pages for the wedding program on her computer. Abby spent a long time on the phone with Angela Williams, the church's social committee chairman, discussing the refreshments and decorations. Abby and Angela agreed to meet at the church the next day to go over the details.

Janice came over for tea, and they brainstormed on flowers. Janice offered to give Abby any of hers that bloomed at the right time. Sharon Browning had said the same on Sunday, and Jennifer thought that, with what her own yard would provide, they'd have plenty for the reception bouquets. Janice had the knack of arranging flowers, and Abby was very pleased with her suggestions.

"I'll make all the men's boutonnieres for you, if you want," Janice said. "We can use lily of the valley, or little white rosebuds if Jennifer's rose bushes cooperate."

"Penny tells me there should be plenty," Jennifer said.

"That would be wonderful." Abby's wedding planner was slowly filling up, and she had checked off many items on the endless lists.

Hammering in the back yard drew Jennifer to the patio door. On his side of the fence, Jeff had two sawhorses, some lumber, and a Skill saw out there, with his open toolbox sitting nearby.

She went outside and called to him. "What are you doing, Jeff?"

"Putting a gate in the fence. Harvey said it's okay, and he'll have your gardener plan some kind of camouflage flora around it."

Jennifer stepped out and walked across the back yard. "Yeah, he asked Mr. Fournier to sketch something. We thought about

267

one of those evergreen mazes, but we decided it would take too long to get to the gate if we were in a hurry. Maybe a walkway under a trellis with roses trained over it, or something like that."

She told Abby and Janice, and they wanted to see the new gate. Jennifer put Connor in the corduroy front carrier that had been Margaret's baby gift, and they all went out to view Jeff's handiwork.

Beth, just home from school, drove into her driveway and came into the back yard. "Come on over, ladies, and have a cup of tea," she said.

"We just had one, but we'd love to visit for a minute," Jennifer said.

They stepped through the gap Jeff had opened in the board fence and went in through the back door, into Beth's kitchen.

"Oh, this is so attractive," Janice said.

"Have you ever been in the house?" Beth asked.

"No, but I've wondered what it was like inside. I've looked across at it for seven years."

"You need the tour," Beth said.

Jennifer sat down in her rocking chair. "I think Connor's ready for a snack."

Abby went with Beth and Janice. As they came downstairs from viewing the still-empty guest rooms, Janice said, "Of course you can have it. I've been telling Bud it's just in the way down cellar. We were going to have a yard sale this summer, but I'm sick of tripping over it. Send Jeff across the street and I'll show him where it is."

"Janice is giving me a double bed for the blue room," Beth told Jennifer, her eyes glowing.

"It's in pieces in the family room downstairs," Janice said. "We had it in the spare room for ages, but then we put the computer in there. I finally had Bud take the bed down so we'd have more space."

"If you really don't want it anymore, that would be super," Beth said.

Janice hugged her. "We're so thrilled to have you and Jeffrey on the block. Mr. Fuller wasn't the cheeriest neighbor, you know."

"So I've heard." Beth looked at her watch. "Eddie's press conference is probably over."

"Janice," Jennifer said, "you might as well know that Eddie's held a press conference this afternoon. He'll be mentioning Mr. Fuller on the news tonight."

"Really? I'm intrigued."

"I guess we'll let you hear it from Eddie on TV," Jennifer said.

"All right, Bud and I will be glued to the set."

The front doorbell rang, and Beth walked over and opened it.

"Hello, my name is Ryan Toothaker. I'm with the *Press Herald*—"

"I know who you are," Beth said.

"I was wondering if I could ask you a few questions about the house, Mrs. Wainthrop."

Beth turned to Jennifer with a helpless look. "Do I have to talk to this man?"

Jennifer stepped forward. "Hello, Ryan."

His eyes widened. "Oh, Mrs. Larson. I didn't realize you were here."

"Beth Wainthrop is married to my brother," Jennifer said. "She'd prefer not to discuss the house's history just now."

"I just came from a press conference at the police station," Ryan said.

"We know."

Ryan smiled with chagrin. "I thought maybe I could get the new owner's thoughts on living in a house where such an unusual crime took place—a man impersonating his victim for ten years."

"They haven't proven that Sanford killed Fuller," Jennifer said. "Anyway, I don't think the Wainthrops want to discuss it."

"We don't," Beth said emphatically.

On the sidewalk, a photographer was setting up to take pictures of the house.

Leeanne's last day of classes for the semester was on Thursday, and she and her mother arrived at supper time. Her dad would drive down on Friday with Randy and Travis, when they got home from school.

Marilyn came with one suitcase and a dress bag, but Leeanne was staying for good, or rather, until the middle of August, and she brought a carload. Harvey and Eddie carried her things upstairs, and then Jennifer and Leeanne took their mother to Beth and Jeff's house.

Jeff was at the fire station, but Beth welcomed Marilyn eagerly and took her through the house. Abby and Jennifer had urged Beth to stay at the Larsons' house Wednesday night, but she had insisted she would be fine. However, she sounded delighted at the prospect of having Marilyn in residence for a few days.

"You must be thrilled to be moved," Marilyn said, looking around at the living room in the new house.

"We are," Beth assured her. "It's so much nicer than the rental."

Already, Beth had managed to make the cottage feel cozy. Her needlework was everywhere, on bright cushions and wall hangings. Nobody mentioned the murder, and Beth didn't offer to show off the basement or the garden shed that was now back in position. The alarm system was in place, with a buzzer that would ring in the Larsons' kitchen and at the security company's office. Beth and Jeff had toughened themselves to keep reporters at bay.

Upstairs in the larger of the two small guest rooms, Jeff had helped Beth wallpaper in cream and blue and set up the Parkers' castoff bed. Beth had hung lacy curtains. One of her samplers and her framed baby picture and Jeff's hung on the walls. Harvey had given them a dresser from their own guest room, over Jeff's protest.

"It doesn't look right at our house," Harvey said. He told Jennifer in private to pick out whatever she wanted to replace it.

270

Jennifer and Abby had baked all week for the open house, and Beth had pitched in, too. They would probably have lots of food left over, as several friends from church had promised to bring dishes as well.

After supper, all the women gathered at Jennifer's, and she and Leeanne tried on their bridesmaids' dresses. Their mother coaxed Abby to put on her wedding dress, too, they all stood around and cried. Harvey and Eddie went outside to play basketball at the hoop on the front of the garage, escaping the feminine ambiance.

They came back in about nine o'clock, after the women had changed back into their casual clothes. The two men were tired and sweaty. Harvey broke out the Gatorade. Jennifer offered to make a pot of tea.

"I think Beth and I should head on over to her house," Marilyn said. "Beth has to work tomorrow, and you know mothers-to-be need their rest."

"I'll walk over with you," Harvey said. "I just want to make sure you're comfortable with setting the alarm, Beth."

"Thanks." Beth gathered her things, and the three of them went out the patio door to walk across through the gate in the backyard fence.

"Where's Peter tonight?" Eddie asked Abby.

"There was a parent night at Gary and Andy's school."

"Why didn't you go with him?" asked Eddie.

"We don't have to see each other every night."

"Why not?" Eddie asked, tipping up his Gatorade bottle.

Abby made a face at him. "Because we're mature. We'll be together every day soon. Meanwhile, we decided to let Peter handle the school event on his own. He thought I'd like to have an evening with my mother and sisters."

Harvey came in and closed the patio door. He held out his arms to Jennifer, and she went to him, to be wrapped in his secure embrace.

"How can you hug him when he's all sweaty?" Abby asked, wrinkling her nose.

"I thought you were mature," Eddie said. "What's a little sweat between people who love each other? Right, precious?" He pulled Leeanne to him and kissed her.

"You guys are disgusting," said Abby.

Leeanne laughed. "I haven't seen this guy for four days," she said. "I'll take him anyway I can get him."

"What's your excuse?" Abby said to Jennifer. Her older sister smiled, knowing Abby was only half in earnest.

"Does she need an excuse to hug me?" Harvey asked in mock consternation.

Eddie grinned at her. "Do you think Peter never sweats, Gabby Sis?"

Abby seemed to actually consider the question, and Harvey and Eddie started laughing.

"We've got to get Peter over here to play basketball tomorrow night," Harvey said.

"I don't know, Abby might break the engagement if she saw Peter with his hair messed up," said Eddie.

Abby pulled her shoulders back with dignity. "I'm going to bed. Good night, O sweaty men and the women who love them." She held her head high as she left the room.

"I'm dying for a shower," said Harvey, "but I didn't want to admit it while Abby was disdaining us."

"Doesn't Abby know Peter works out at that gym over by his business just about every morning?" Eddie asked.

"I think she knows. She just hasn't seen him at seven in the morning, when he's dripping sweat," Harvey replied.

"Boy, is she in for a rude awakening in about a month. Peter's in great shape. Does she think he stays that way selling cars?"

Harvey rinsed his Gatorade bottle and tossed it in the recycling bin. "I'm gonna hit the shower."

"Go ahead," Jennifer said. "Connor has plans for me." The baby had been fussing a little, and she knew he was ready to eat and settle down for five or six hours' sleep.

"Did you talk to Carl?" Harvey asked anxiously.

"Yes. He said to let him cry for a while. Otherwise, he'll never go to bed without fussing."

"No kidding," Harvey said.

"Nope. Carl and Margaret both said, as long as we know he's fed and dry, to let him cry it out a few times, and he'll go to bed fine after that."

"Are you putting him to bed now?" Leeanne asked. "Let me squeeze him first." She took the baby and held him in her arms.

Connor squirmed let out a threatening, "Eh-eh-eh."

Eddie stood close behind Leeanne and watched, smiling, over her shoulder.

"Cutest baby I ever saw," he said.

"So, you think babies are worthwhile after all, Eddie?" Jennifer asked with a big smile.

"I never said they weren't," he protested.

"True, but there were days when I thought you'd just as soon never see a pregnant woman again."

"Well, you know." He shrugged. "You and Lisa, *enceinte* at the same time."

Jennifer smiled. "How is your sister?"

"Okay. She's got another three weeks to go. She was so jealous when she heard you went early." He smiled. "They say it's different when it's your own."

"It will be," Jennifer promised him.

Eddie looked down at Connor. "I still say he's a cute kid."

Leeanne laughed and turned her face to kiss him.

"I suppose I ought to go home and de-sweatify myself," Eddie said.

"Already?" Leeanne wailed. "I've hardly seen you."

"You have tomorrow off?" he asked.

"Yes, I start at the paper Monday."

"Well, if you can stand it, I'll stay a while. If you and Harvey don't mind," he said deferentially to Jennifer.

"Just give me Connor and mind your p's and q's."

"What does that mean?" Eddie asked Leeanne as she left them.

Chapter 25

Jennifer woke Friday morning to the sound of men's voices in the kitchen. It was nearly seven, and the smell of fresh coffee beckoned to her.

She dressed quickly and went to the kitchen. Harvey, Eddie, and Peter were eating breakfast in their running clothes.

"Hi, Peter," Jennifer said. "What's the occasion?"

"These guys dragged me out to run this morning so they could put one over on Abigail," he said. "I'm not sure I should be part of this little swindle."

"Swindle?" Eddie's eyebrows shot up. "She doesn't believe you ever sweat, Peter. I think if she's going to marry you in a month, she should see the real you."

"Yes, it's more like a moment of truth," said Harvey. "Would you run up and tell Abby that Peter's here, sweetheart?"

"You guys." Jennifer shook her head, but she went up the stairs and knocked on
Abby's door. The response was a moan from within.

"Abby, your fiancé is here," Jennifer said brightly.

"Huh?"

"Peter's here, honey. He wants to see you."

Her door opened and she stood there in her pajamas, staring in disbelief. "Peter's here *now*?"

"That's correct."

"There's nothing wrong, is there?"

"I don't think so."

"What does he want?"

"Uh, I think he'll tell you when you go down there."

"Tell him I'll be there in a minute," Abby said.

Jennifer went back to the kitchen. "Abby will be right down. Are you sure you want to do this?"

"Why not?" asked Harvey. "Abby needs a dose of reality."

"You've got a mean streak. I never would have believed it." Peter was looking doubtful.

275

Eddie said, "Two people don't really know each other well enough to get married if they've never seen each other at seven in the morning. Don't you think so, Peter?"

"Well…"

•His gray T-shirt was half soaked with sweat. Jennifer had certainly never seen him so informal.

"Come on," Eddie said. "If you marry Abby without her knowing what you do every morning, she could die of heart failure the morning of June fourth."

"Oh, I don't think I'll go to the gym the day after the wedding," Peter said.

"Maybe this is a little sadistic," Harvey said.

"Having second thoughts?" Jennifer asked.

"It should be between the two of them."

"No, she was making fun of us last night," Eddie said.

"Well, yeah, but we don't want to make her cry or anything," said Harvey.

"What on earth are you guys talking about?" Abby asked from the doorway. She looked wide awake, and very pretty in black slacks and a plaid sweater. Her blonde hair hung loose over her shoulders.

"About what you'll say when you see Peter all sweaty," Eddie said. "He is human, after all, you see."

Abby looked at Peter and laughed.

Peter's mouth opened, then closed, then he started laughing, too. He stood up and went toward her.

"The guys are under the impression that you think I never exercise," he explained.

"Idiots," she said. "You went running with them?"

"Yes. I hope that doesn't alienate you, because I really like my future brothers-in-law."

"You should do this with us all the time," Eddie said. "Jeff comes when he's not working. Monday, Wednesday, and Friday we run and eat breakfast together and pray."

Peter shrugged. "Sounds great, but I have to get the boys ready for school. In fact, if I don't leave right now, they'll be late. I told Gary I'd be gone when he got up, but to go ahead and eat cereal and make sure Andy was up. But I don't like to leave them alone. I really need to go home and get changed and take them to school."

"Hey," said Eddie, "after you get married, Abby will be there. Then you can come run with us."

"What's your opinion, Abigail?" Peter asked, looking at her anxiously.

"It's cheaper than going to the gym," she said. "Of course, I know you like to lift weights, and you would be exercising different muscle groups, but—"

"So you *did* know." Eddie's disappointment was comical.

"Of course I knew! You think I'd marry a man I don't know? He drops the boys off at school, then goes to the gym before he goes to work." She rolled her eyes and turned to Jennifer. "How did they think he got those muscles?"

Harvey and Peter laughed, and Eddie looked disconcerted.

"I'm sorry, Abigail, I've really got to get out of here," Peter said softly. "Please don't take this personally."

She smiled. Leaning forward carefully, she kissed him without touching the rest of him. "It's nice to see you. Take a shower."

"Meet me for lunch," he whispered. Only Jennifer was close enough to hear. Abby nodded slightly, and he said, "I'll call you."

When he was out the door, Harvey said, "Well, Ed, I guess our little stunt backfired."

Eddie reached for the box of Wheaties. "I don't know. At least we know she knows what he looks like and smells like after a workout, and she didn't throw the ring at him."

Harvey smiled. "I think we'd better get moving, too."

Abby serenely poured herself a cup of coffee. "Why didn't you take Leeanne with you? She likes to run."

"Maybe next time," Eddie said.

"It was a guy thing today," Jennifer told her, and Abby nodded sagely.

She looked at Eddie. "Maybe you should take up weight lifting on Tuesdays and Thursdays." She took her coffee mug and walked out of the room.

*****

Peter called Abby an hour later, and she laughed a lot during their conversation.

"I'm meeting Peter downtown for lunch," she told Jennifer and Leeanne, her eyes gleaming.

"Maybe we could meet Harvey and Eddie," Leeanne said.

"Well, we need to keep Mom entertained today while Beth's at school," Jennifer reminded her.

Marilyn came over from Beth's house about half past nine, and they spent the morning in Leeanne's room. Marilyn, Abby, and Jennifer took turns holding Connor and helping Leeanne unpack her luggage and boxes, until it was time for Abby to leave for her lunch date.

Harvey and Eddie came at noon, and Eddie told the story of Peter's running with them that morning.

"She actually kissed him when he was sweaty?" Leeanne asked in glee. "After what she said last night, I never would have thought so. Wish I'd seen it."

"No hugging," Eddie noted. "She kissed him at arm's length."

Leeanne laughed, and Marilyn shook her head.

"What is it with you young people? In the old days, when we didn't have showers, what do you think people did? If your man came home sweaty, so what?"

"Oh, right, Mom, and you were sweaty, too, from chopping all that wood and making candles all day," Leeanne laughed. "You aren't *that* old."

"I never knew Abby was that fastidious," Jennifer mused. "She used to make mud pies with the best of us."

"I think it was nursing school that did it," Marilyn said. "She's always washing her hands."

"So, what's the scoop on Mr. Bones?" Leeanne asked. "Anything new?"

Harvey frowned. "The judge is going to rule on the wills Monday."

"What do we do if he says we don't own the house?" Jennifer asked.

"First of all, it's a she. Judge Boyer. If she says the old will is valid, we have to try harder than ever to find Marcus Rutledge."

"I was really hoping he'd surface," Eddie said. "We've checked hotels and airlines, the usual, but no luck. He should show up in Norfolk Sunday, though."

Harvey's cell phone rang, and he pulled it from his pocket. "Yeah, Tony?" He listened, and everyone else stayed quiet until he spoke again.

"I'll be in soon. Print out everything you've got. We may need to take a ride."

"What is it?" Eddie asked when he put the phone down.

"Tony's been working on the loose ends, including Sanford's financial records."

"Yeah, I told him to. And?"

Harvey smiled. "There's no boat, but guess who invested in real estate several years ago. I'm talking, within a year after the switch was made."

"No kidding."

"Nope." Harvey stood. "Let's get going."

"You didn't finish your lunch," Jennifer protested.

"Sorry." Harvey kissed her. Eddie gulped down the last of his milk and pushed his chair back.

"*A ce soir, ma belle. Merci,* Jennifer." He followed Harvey out the door.

*****

The Wainthrop women went to a party store that afternoon and ordered paper plates, napkins, balloons, and confetti for the wedding. Jennifer also bought flowered cake plates and napkins for the house warming. They stopped at the church to look over the available vases and candelabra for the wedding. When they got home, Beth was home from school, and they went into Open House Preparation Mode.

Abby and Leeanne went over Beth's already spotless house with dust cloths and the vacuum cleaner. Marilyn helped Beth assemble the centerpiece and a fruit bowl, and Jennifer cut vegetables for a platter while Connor sat watching.

Beth stood frowning, with the refrigerator door open. "I don't think I have enough room in my fridge for everything."

"We can take some things over to our house for tonight," Jennifer said. "Are you using your Crockpot?"

"I don't think so."

"May I use it? I want to make two kinds of meatballs."

"Sure." Beth opened a cabinet and took out the pot. "I wanted to make those tiny cream puffs tonight. I'll fill them in the morning." She laid out the dishes she planned to use the next day. "I need more serving dishes."

"How many? You can borrow anything you want," Jennifer assured her.

"Well, a couple of cake plates and a big bowl or two, at least. I bought Styrofoam cups for coffee. Is that tacky?"

"No," said Marilyn, "when you're expecting this many people, it's practical."

Jennifer passed Connor to her mom for a burp and began folding the fancy paper napkins into triangles. "Want me to bring the dishes over now?"

"Maybe," Beth said. "It might help me see if I need anything else."

"I'll help you," said Marilyn.

"Abby, can you help us, please?" Jennifer asked. "I want to take Beth's Crockpot over, and we're bringing back some dishes for her."

"Sure thing." Abby pulled on her Irish knit sweater.

"I'll carry this little bundle," Marilyn said, wrapping Connor's afghan around him.

"Just leave him here," Beth said. "He'll be fine."

"I think he needs a dry diaper, and Jennifer doesn't seem to have made it over here with one."

Jennifer frowned. "You're right. I'd just changed him when we came over. Thought he'd last a while. I'll have to start leaving a package of disposables over here."

She picked up the Crockpot and went out the back door with Abby and her mother. The sun and a light wind had done their work. The lawn was dry, and bright new grass was forming a carpet over the backyard. They went through the gate into her yard. Penny had been to the house on Tuesday and cleaned a lot of dead leaves and stalks from the flower beds. Daffodil and hyacinth shoots were poking up with a promising air.

Jennifer unlocked the patio door and took Connor to the bedroom for a change. When they returned to the kitchen, Marilyn and Abby had located the serving dishes Beth wanted.

"Maybe she'd like that candy dish, too." Jennifer handed the baby to her mother and reached high in the cupboard for it.

"Harvey's home," Abby announced.

"Is it that late?" Jennifer threw a glance at the clock. "I don't even have the table set."

"I can do it," said Marilyn. "You and Abby take the dishes to Beth. Leave Connor here."

Jennifer pulled a pan of lasagna from the refrigerator and stuck it in the oven, then went to the front door. Harvey was just coming in.

"Howdy." He set his briefcase on the floor and took her in his arms and kissed her. "Eddie's coming in a few minutes."

"Okay, but supper's not quite ready. We've been working over at Beth's for the party. Abby and I are going to take a few dishes over to her, and we'll be right back."

"Need some help?" he asked.

"No, why don't you get changed. Supper in thirty minutes."

"Great." He kissed her ear and let her go. Abby had the glass bowls in her arms. Jennifer picked up the plates and a large tray, and they went to the sunroom and out the patio door.

"This is going to be so neat when you have the landscaping done," Abby said as they went through Jeff's gate. "Harvey will have so much fun building the swing set."

"It will probably end up more like a playground," Jennifer said. "You know Harvey. Nothing but the best for Connor. I'm sure there will be lots of things Gary and Andy will enjoy. He's talking about a little castle for a playhouse, with a working drawbridge."

Abby went up the two steps to Beth's back door, juggling the bowls and turning the doorknob. Jennifer waited, and Abby tried again.

"That's funny. The door's locked. You didn't lock it when we went out, did you?"

"No. We were coming right back, so I left it unlocked."

Abby leaned toward the glass panel and looked inside, raising her hand to knock so Beth would open the door for them. Her hand froze in midair.

"Jennifer!"

"What?"

"Beth's not in the kitchen."

"So? Knock loud. She'll hear us."

"The refrigerator door is wide open."

A cold wave of fear hit Jennifer. "Let me see."

Abby stepped down, and Jennifer mounted the steps.

In the kitchen, the napkins lay in piles on the table, some folded, some not folded. The light beamed out from inside the refrigerator, its door pulled wide against the cabinets on the other side. She could see beyond into the living room. The lights were on, and the rocking chair and part of the coffee table and sofa were visible.

"Can you see Beth or Leeanne?" Abby asked in a stage whisper.

"No."

A shadow moved in the depths of the scene, and Jennifer made out a person standing back to her, inside the living room door.

"I see someone."

"Who, Beth?"

"No, I think it's a man."

He had on a navy blue shirt or jacket, and jeans. His hair was dark and short.

"Should we knock?" Abby asked.

He turned just a bit more. In his right hand he held a pistol.

"Get down!" Jennifer dropped quickly below the glass, and Abby crouched with her on the steps.

"He's got a gun."

Abby stared at her, eyes wide and questioning.

"We've got to get Harvey," Jennifer said.

"Did you see Beth or Leeanne?" Abby's eyes were frantic.

"No. Just the man."

"Let's go."

They clutched the dishes to themselves and ran, bent over, to the gate. Abby fumbled to unlatch it, and they went through. Jennifer didn't stop to fasten it. At the patio door, she gasped, "Knock. I don't have my keys out." The patio door couldn't be opened from outside without the key.

Abby set down her dishes and pounded on the glass. Her mother came into the sunroom, an expectant look on her face.

"Forget your key?" she asked. "Well, Abby, you didn't—"

"Where's Harvey?" Jennifer asked, too loud.

"He said he was going to take a shower."

Jennifer thrust the plates and tray into her hands and ran to the bedroom. The bathroom door was shut, but light came from under it and she heard the shower running. She barged in.

"Harvey, there's a man with a gun in Beth's house!"

The water stopped and he stuck his head out around the end of the curtain.

"What did you say?"

"There's a man with a gun in Beth's house. The back door was locked when Abby and I went over, and I saw a man with a gun. Harvey, Beth and Leeanne are in there!"

He grabbed a towel. His clean clothes were laid out for him.

"What should I do?" Jennifer asked as he began to dress rapidly.

"Call Eddie on my cell phone. Star-five. Get him over here, and have him call Nate and Tony."

She ran out to his nightstand and snatched up his phone.

"Eddie! It's Jennifer. Get over here right away! We've got a 10-32 at Beth's house." She had the somewhat outmoded police code down cold from her work in the records department the previous summer, and she was sure Eddie would understand.

"Is Harvey there?"

"Yes. He told me to call you, and to have you get Nate and Tony."

Harvey emerged from the bathroom in his jeans, T-shirt, and sneakers. He caught his .45 off the dresser on his way to the door.

"I'm on my way. ETA two minutes," Eddie said.

In the sunroom, Marilyn said, "Harvey—" then the patio door closed.

Jennifer stuck Harvey's phone in her pocket. Connor fussed in his cradle. She picked him up and went into the sunroom, clutching him tightly.

"What's happening?" her mother demanded. "Abby said there was a man over there, and the door was locked."

"That's right."

Abby raised her eyebrows significantly at Jennifer behind their mother's back. So, she hadn't told their mom about the gun.

Jennifer opened the glass door quietly and stepped out onto the flagstoned patio. Across the fence, Harvey was at the side of the back steps next door, peering cautiously through the glass in the door. He ducked down below the window level and crept beyond the steps, along the back of the house. He disappeared around the far end of the cottage, and Jennifer waited for him to reappear. It seemed forever.

Abby opened the door a crack.

"What's going on?"

"Harvey looked in the back door, then went around the back of the house."

Jennifer went inside and walked through the kitchen to the entry. Abby followed. They went into the breezeway, and Jennifer stepped down onto the walk, looking past the garage, along the front of Beth and Jeff's house. She couldn't see past the entry that jutted out onto the lawn. A flagged path led from it to the driveway.

Jennifer walked carefully along the front of her garage and stood near the end, out of sight of most of Beth's windows, rubbing Connor's back without thinking about it and waiting for Harvey.

"There's Eddie," Abby said, directly behind her, and she jumped.

His truck came down the street quickly, but with no lights or siren. Jennifer waved, and he pulled into the Larsons' driveway.

She and Abby ran to the driver's door as he jumped out.

"What's up?"

"There's a man with a gun in Beth's house," Jennifer said. "I saw him through the back door window. Harvey went around behind their house. I think he's trying to see in the windows and find out where he is."

"Everybody okay?" Eddie asked, reaching under his open denim shirt and drawing his pistol from his shoulder holster.

"We don't know."

He looked at her sharply. "Beth's inside?"

"Beth and ... "

"Eddie, Leeanne's in there," Abby cried.

His lips tightened. "Get in the house."

"There's Harvey," Jennifer said as her husband appeared at the corner of Beth's house and came quickly toward them.

"Jenny, go inside," was the first thing Harvey said.

"I was worried about you."

"Take Connor inside," he said sternly.

She turned away, feeling a little sick.

"Call Jeff," he added, as an afterthought.

She swung around to face him. "Is Beth all right?"

"He's got them both in the bedroom. I'm not sure what he wants."

Jennifer's lungs squeezed tight, and she could barely inhale. Marilyn stood in the doorway, and Jennifer handed Connor over to her.

"I've got to call Jeff." She took her own phone from her pocket.

"Did Harvey speak to that man? Who is he?" her mother asked.

"Mom, let's take Connor in the house," Abby said. She went past Jennifer and took her mother and the baby in and closed the door.

Jennifer hit Jeff's number, but he didn't answer. She had to think for a moment to remember the non-emergency number at the fire station.

"Is Jeffrey Wainthrop in, please? This is his sister, Jennifer Larson. We have a family emergency."

She waited. Harvey was talking to Eddie as Eddie took a Kevlar vest from his truck. Harvey gestured toward Beth's house, and Eddie fastened the vest and moved from behind his pickup to the end of the garage, watching the other house.

Harvey walked toward her. "You got Jeff on the line?"

"They're getting him." She pulled his phone out and handed it to him.

"Thanks. It wouldn't be a bad idea to have them send an ambulance over. Tell them to stand by down the block. No sirens. You got it?"

She nodded.

"Then call 911. Tell Charlie Doran we want backup, and patrolmen to control traffic. When the rest of my men get here, brief them and tell them Eddie and I are going to try to get in."

She nodded again.

He sighed. "Come here, gorgeous. Don't look so scared."

"You don't have your vest." She tried not to cry as he crushed her against his chest for a second.

"Tony's bringing it, so send him around back as soon as he's here. God is in control, Jenny."

He kissed her quickly, then turned away. She stood on the path, between the breezeway and the driveway.

"Jennifer?" Jeff said in her ear.

"Jeff, you've got to come home, and bring the ambulance, or have someone else bring it."

"Is somebody hurt?"

"No, I don't think so, but, Jeff, that man is in the house again."

"The prowler?"

"I think so. A man with a gun, anyway."

She saw Harvey take a key from his key ring and give it to Eddie, then he went into Jeff and Beth's back yard, and Eddie approached the entry. "Harvey and Eddie are going in after him. Jeff, Leeanne and Beth are inside."

"Beth is—what are you saying?"

"Hostages, maybe. We don't know why he's here, but he's holding them in your house."

"Oh, my—"

"Just get over here, Jeff. Harvey says park the ambulance down the block, and don't use the siren."

He hung up.

Jennifer punched 911.

"Portland emergency."

"Charlie! It's Jennifer Larson."

"Mrs. Larson, I'm tracking the Priority men now on your street."

"Yes, my husband told me to ask you for more backup. He needs traffic control, too."

Nate Miller's car was approaching. He signaled and almost turned in at 135, but she waved and motioned him into her driveway.

"Miller's here now, Charlie. Looks like Cook's with him, and Winfield's Mustang's right behind him."

"Copy that," said Charlie, "we're in contact with Winfield."

"I'm hanging up," Jennifer said. "Send more men."

Nate and Jimmy got out of Nate's car, looking at the house next door.

"Harvey's gone around back, and Eddie just went into the front entry there," she said. "Harvey needs his body armor."

"Tony!" Nate turned and motioned to Tony. Tony got out of his car and came quickly to them. He had his vest on and another in his hand. "Take the captain's vest into the back yard.

He went around back." Nate turned to Jennifer. "How many people in the house?"

"My sister Leeanne and my sister-in-law, Beth. And the gunman. Harvey said he's got them in the bedroom, which would be on the far corner."

"Jimmy, go around there in case he goes out a window," Nate said. "I'll follow Eddie in the front door."

"What if he comes out the garage?" Jennifer asked. The garage door was down, but still.

A commotion arose down the street, and Jeff came jogging down the sidewalk.

"That's my brother," Jennifer told Nate. "It's his house, and his wife inside."

Nate went quickly to meet Jeff. "Stay out here with your sister, sir. We'll handle this." He headed for the front door, and Jeff stood bleakly watching him, his fists clenched.

"Jeff," Jennifer called.

He looked at her.

"Come over here, where you're not such a good target."

He walked toward her, watching his house all the time. "What happened?"

"Nothing that I know of. I think Eddie might be inside. I'm not sure. I haven't heard any shots."

"Well, that's something, I suppose," he said grimly.

Harvey came out the gate in the fence from Jeff's back yard, and Jeff strode quickly to meet him. Harvey put his hand on Jeff's shoulder and drew him back into the shadow of the Larsons' garage.

"Everything's quiet right now," Harvey said.

"Is Beth okay?"

"Yes, I think so. But he knows we're out here, and he won't come out."

"He's holding Beth and Leeanne hostage?"

Harvey nodded reluctantly.

"Oh, man!"

"Take it easy, Jeff." Harvey raised his phone and pushed a couple of buttons. "Mike! Harvey. I need a negotiator ASAP. Can you come to my house?"

Sirens sounded in the distance, the volume rapidly increasing. Jennifer put her arms around Jeff. Tears ran down her cheeks.

Chapter 26

Two patrol cars turned onto the street and approached, sirens blaring and lights flashing. Abby and Marilyn came into the breezeway, and across the street Bud and Janice came out of their house and stared over at them.

Harvey walked to the curb and began giving orders to the four uniformed officers that had arrived. He assigned two to approach the house and sent the other two into the street to reroute traffic around the block and tell the neighbors to stay out of sight.

"I don't want to lose any civilians," he told Sarah Benoit. Sarah trotted across and spoke to Bud and Janice.

"Jennifer," her mother called, "what's happening?"

She squeezed Jeff's arm and left him at the edge of the garage and went to Marilyn and Abby.

"The man won't come out," she said. "Beth and Leeanne are okay, but he won't let them go."

"What does he want?" Abby asked.

"We don't know yet. Mike is coming to negotiate."

"Is there anything we can do?" Marilyn asked.

"Pray and make coffee?"

"The lasagna's done."

"Take it out," Jennifer said. "Abby, call Pastor Rowland. Where's Connor?"

"I put him in the seat." Marilyn glanced toward the kitchen. "I can see him from here. He's fine."

Within ten minutes, at least a dozen police officers were deployed around the little stone house. Harvey appeared now and then, giving orders or talking into his cell phone or a patrolman's radio. Jennifer's fear grew with each minute, until she felt ill. Her silent prayers were disjointed and panicky.

Peter Hobart came running down the sidewalk and up the driveway.

"What happened?" he asked.

"Did Abby call you?"

"No, we had a date. They wouldn't let me drive down here. When I told them my fiancée was your sister, they told me to walk on down. Where's Abigail?"

"She's fine," Jennifer said. "It's Leeanne who's not. Leeanne and Beth."

"What is it?"

"A man with a gun. He's got them in Beth and Jeff's house."

"Oh, Jeff, I'm so sorry!" Peter clapped Jeff on the shoulder. "I'm sure you've been praying…"

"I could use someone to pray with me," Jeff said.

Jennifer had prayed silently, screaming to God, the whole time, but she hadn't offered her brother the comfort of hearing her pray. She thanked God for sending Peter. They stood together by the garage and bowed their heads.

Mike's Lincoln pulled into Jeff's driveway, and Harvey joined him there. Mike had on a bulletproof vest. Jeff left his post and walked briskly across to stand beside Mike's car. Peter and Jennifer followed him, but hung back a few yards. Jennifer was sure Harvey wouldn't want her in the middle of things, but she couldn't repress her anxiety for Leeanne and Beth.

"You want to use the speaker?" Harvey said.

"How about I try to call him?" Mike took out his phone.

"Use mine. The number's programmed," Harvey said. He took his phone out and punched the code for Beth's phone.

Mike put Harvey's phone to his ear and waited.

"Hello, this is Chief Browning. What do you want?"

They all held their breath.

"My name's Mike Browning," Mike said distinctly. "I'm the Portland chief of police. What's your name? John? All right, Mr. Smith." Mike rolled his eyes at Harvey. "Mr. Smith, there must be a reason you're doing what you're doing. Care to tell me about it?"

There was a pause. "Your money? What money is that, Mr. Smith?"

Jeff's eyes were hard as he listened.

"Is there a landline in there?" Mike whispered.

Jeff shook his head.

Harvey motioned to one of the patrolmen, Ray Oliver. He came quickly toward Mike and Harvey.

"So, you're saying somebody around here owes you money, Mr. Smith?" Mike said.

"Where is he now?" Harvey asked Ray.

"He's in the bedroom using somebody's cell phone."

"Mrs. Wainthrop's," Harvey said. "Chief Browning's talking to him," said Harvey. "Could you see the women?"

"Yes. Mrs. Wainthrop's sitting on the bed, and the other girl is on the floor across the room, sitting with her back to the wall. He's tied their hands with belts or something."

"What's the weapon?"

"We think it's a nine-millimeter."

"And where's Eddie Thibodeau?"

"Not sure. He's definitely inside. Nate Miller's in the entry with a radio. He said Eddie got in."

"The alarm didn't go off?" Jeff asked.

"I think Beth had it turned off because they were running back and forth between our house and yours this afternoon," Harvey said.

"I left your back door unlocked," Jennifer sobbed. "I'm sorry, Jeff."

"Jenny, you shouldn't be over here," Harvey said. He turned to Ray. "You got any extra vests?"

"One, anyway," the man said.

"Can you get it for my brother-in-law, here?" Harvey said. He looked at Peter and said firmly, "Peter, I'd like you to take Jennifer to my house and see that she stays there. Sit on her if you have to."

"Harvey, my sister's in there," Jennifer said.

"Yes, and I don't want to endanger sundry other members of her family while we try to get her out." He wasn't angry, but she could see that her being there was distracting him from the job at hand. Even so, she lingered.

Mike said, "Harvey, here's the deal. This guy, alias John Smith, says somebody who was living here owes him a hundred grand. He came to collect, and the guy wasn't here. He's keeping Leeanne and Beth until he gets his money."

"Who did he say owed him the money?" Harvey asked.

"Just the guy who lived here."

"Did you tell him he's dead?"

"Not yet."

The patrolman came back with the bulletproof vest and helped Jeff put it on.

Peter murmured, "Perhaps we'd better go to your house, Jennifer."

They were about to step away from Mike's car when a chair crashed through Jeff's living room window onto the lawn. A man was silhouetted briefly, framed in jagged glass.

He screamed, "You'd better listen!"

Mike put the phone to his ear. "Mr. Smith? Mr. Smith, it's Browning. I'm listening."

He had stepped away from the window. An officer used the entry wall as cover, and another hugged the far corner of the house. They trained their weapons on the broken window.

"Mr. Smith?" Mike said into the phone, then to himself, "Come on, pick it up!" He straightened. "Mr. Smith, stay with me. Perhaps we can get the money for you. Can you give me the name of the man who owed you the money? I see ... Hold on." Mike turned to Harvey. "His uncle, Carleton Fuller."

Harvey nodded. "It's Rutledge. Should I talk to him?"

Mike handed Harvey the phone.

Harvey said, "Hello. This is Captain Larson, and I knew your uncle. If you're Marcus Rutledge, we've been trying to contact you and tell you that Mr. Fuller is dead, and his estate belongs to you. If you want to claim his estate, just come on out here. I'll set up a meeting for you with the executor."

Jeff was staring toward the house, and sweat beaded on his forehead.

"No, Mr. Rutledge, we'd just like to talk to you peacefully about this. You don't need to stave up the house or hold those two women. Just step on out here into the yard, and we'll talk.

Throw the gun out first and step out with your hands above your head."

Everyone watched the front door.

Harvey sighed and held the mute button.

"He says he's not coming out."

Mike scowled. "Ask him why not."

"Why won't you come out, Mr. Rutledge? I told you, we've been looking for the heir to this estate. Marcus Rutledge was the only living relative we knew about, and the only person mentioned in Mr. Fuller's will. You said your uncle lived here, so I figured you must be Rutledge. I'm not playing games with you."

"Tell him to let the ladies go," Mike said.

"Look, if you don't want to come out, at least let the women leave," Harvey said persuasively. "It's not doing you any good to keep them in there. One of them's expecting, did you know that, Mr. Rutledge? She ought to come out and see her doctor. Her husband's waiting out here. Just let her go now."

Jeff stared at Harvey, his eyebrows raised in question.

"He says he'll think about it," Harvey said.

Suddenly Rutledge appeared at the broken window again, but this time he was holding Leeanne in front of him, the gun pointing out toward the onlookers. Leeanne's face was pale. Jennifer's heart lurched, and she renewed her silent prayers.

"You get me a hundred grand in cash and guarantee I drive away without being followed, and I'll come out," he yelled.

Mike reached inside his car and turned on the loudspeaker. "Let the lady go," he said on the speaker.

"Oh, no. You bring the money. Half an hour, that's what you've got."

"You've got to let the women go first."

"I'm making the rules," Rutledge yelled. "Bring it, or I send this pretty little thing out the window and use her for target practice."

Mike leaned on the roof of his car. "All right, we've got to appease him." Over the speaker he said, "Well, Rutledge, the bank's closed, and that would take us a while."

"Thirty minutes," Rutledge countered.

Mike turned the speaker off. Rutledge and Leeanne disappeared from the window frame.

Jeff said, "What now? You're not really going to try to get the money?"

"Of course not," Mike grunted.

The sun was setting beyond the back yards, far past the houses on the next street. Another patrolman, Joe Clifford, came running through the gate from the backyard.

"Captain, he's left Mrs. Wainthrop alone in the bedroom, and we think we can take her out the window."

"All right," said Harvey. "Be quick, and be quiet. Can she help?"

"No, sir, he tied her hands and feet. They're going to put an officer in to lift her out."

Harvey turned around. "Jeff, Jenny, go to our house and go out through the patio door and wait. But stay on our side of the fence. No matter what."

Jeff was already running across the driveway. Harvey squeezed Jennifer's arm.

"Go, baby."

Peter and Jennifer followed Jeff.

"Jennifer," Marilyn cried as Jennifer barreled into the kitchen.

"Not now, Mom."

Abby threw herself into Peter's arms. He stood, holding her. Jennifer tore after Jeff, through the sun room and out into the back yard. He was already at the gate he had built, his hands on the latch, waiting.

Jennifer went and stood beside him. Two officers flanked the back door of the cottage, and two more were posted farther along the back wall, beneath windows. Another was at the side of the garage, on the near side of the house. No one moved.

"They're going to lift her out the bedroom window on the other end of the house," Jennifer hazarded.

"Why couldn't they take her out of that window?" Jeff muttered. The bedroom had two windows, one on the back of the house and one on the north end. Jennifer could only see the one on the back.

Inside the house behind them, Connor was crying.

"You'd better go in," Jeff said.

"I want to stay with you. I want to help you."

"There's nothing you can do but pray," he said. "Go feed Connor, and pray."

"All right."

She went slowly in at the patio door. Marilyn was pacing in the kitchen, holding Connor. "Shh, shh," she said over and over.

"Here, Mom."

Marilyn turned and put the baby in her arms.

"Is Leeanne all right?" she asked.

"I think so. She's scared, of course."

"And Beth?"

"They think they can get Beth out."

"That's what Peter said."

"They'll bring her across the back yard if they get her."

Her mother went out and stood beside Jeff, with her arm across his back.

Jennifer stood at the glass door where she could see out. After a minute, she dragged a wicker chair to where she could at least see Jeff and her mom. She sat down with Connor.

Outside, men yelled and several patrolmen ran across the lawns. She leaned forward, trying to see more. Jeff opened the gate and ran through it, and a moment later came back with Beth, his arm around her. Marilyn ran ahead and opened the glass door.

Jeff sank onto the settee and pulled Beth down into his arms. Two officers and Marilyn came in behind them.

"Are you all right, Mrs. Wainthrop?" Patrolman Joe Clifford asked, crouching before Beth.

"I—I think so. Leeanne—"

A popping noise sounded outside, and Jennifer stiffened.

"What was that?" Marilyn asked.

Nobody said anything. Beth's eyes were huge. Abby and Peter came from the living room, holding hands.

"Was that gunfire?" Abby asked. "Beth!"

"Praise God," said Peter.

Abby hugged Beth, but Beth stayed seated with Jeff. He pulled Beth close to his heart, stroking her hair.

"Everybody stay in the house," said Joe. He and the other officer went quickly out the door and headed for the fence.

Jennifer kissed Connor and put him back in her mother's hands. He started screaming immediately, but she ran through the kitchen and out onto the driveway. A dozen men had converged on the front of the house, at the entry and under the broken window. They were all talking at once, but she couldn't make out anything.

At last Mike and Harvey came out the front door of Jeff's house.

Mike held his hands up. "All right, all right, coming through. Get the ambulance down here."

Jennifer held her breath.

Eddie came out then, carrying Leeanne, and Nate Miller behind them. Leeanne was conscious, Jennifer could tell, because her hands were clasped tightly around Eddie's neck.

The ambulance met them at the end of the driveway. Jennifer ran down there as Eddie laid Leeanne tenderly on the stretcher and the EMTs took her pulse and blood pressure.

"Eddie, is she all right?"

"I think so. He choked her a little when he had her at the window, and he slapped her. I want a doctor to look her over. I'm going with her."

"Is Jeff's wife okay?" one of the EMT's asked, and Jennifer recognized Mark Johnson.

"Yes, she's shook up, but otherwise all right," she said. "Do you need Jeff?"

"No, we're fine. Tell him to stay here. He doesn't need to come back to the station tonight."

It seemed to take them forever to get Leeanne into the ambulance. Jennifer was able to get close and give her a hug.

"I'm okay, Jennifer," Leeanne said hoarsely. "Tell Mom and Daddy I'm okay."

"I will."

"And tell Harvey that man killed his uncle."

"He told you?" Eddie asked, incredulous.

"He said if they didn't bring him the money he'd whack me over the head the way he did his uncle."

"Did Beth hear that?"

"I don't know, but when he was tying us up he was complaining about that other man stealing his money. He said he and Sanford buried his uncle in the basement, and Sanford was supposed to give him half the money. He said he wasn't leaving without it."

Eddie climbed in with her, and the ambulance left.

When Jennifer turned to go back to the house, Harvey was right behind her.

"Come here, gorgeous." He hugged her tight. "You're hard to keep down."

"I'm sorry. I had to see if she was all right."

"I know."

"Rutledge threatened her, and he told her he'd kill her like he did his uncle," Jennifer said through tears.

"He won't be hurting anyone else."

She squeezed him. "Connor's starving."

"Let's go in."

"Who's mopping up?" she asked.

"Nate can handle it from here. I told him to report to me in half an hour."

Harvey kept his arm around her, and they walked up the driveway. When they were nearly to the breezeway, Jennifer's father drove in. He, Randy, and Travis jumped out of the car.

"What's going on?" Travis yelled.

"What happened?" asked George.

Randy stood by the car, watching the policemen, still thick on Jeff and Beth's lawn.

"They made us stop at the end of the street and wait. We've been out there twenty minutes," George said.

"Had a little excitement tonight," Harvey told him. "Come on in, and I'll tell everybody at once."

Jennifer took Connor into the bedroom to feed him while her mother and Abby set the table. They sat down to lasagna, and Harvey told how Eddie had waited inside the house, hoping for a chance to disarm Rutledge.

"He had sneaked across to the kitchen," he told his rapt audience. "When Rutledge left the bedroom and threw the chair through the window, Eddie hid behind the open refrigerator door. Rutledge kept Leeanne with him. Eddie couldn't see a way to take him down without endangering Leeanne."

By the time Rutledge had demanded the money, Nate was in position in the entry and had the front door open enough that he and Eddie could see each other. Eddie had signaled him to wait.

Rutledge discovered Beth's rescue through the bedroom window after the officers lifted her to safety, and he had fired several bullets out the bedroom window. The officers had fired back when Rutledge's head appeared at the window for a second, and Leeanne had dropped to the floor. Eddie and Nate had rushed into the bedroom and shot the man several times at point blank range.

"So, I guess you won't be staying at our house tonight, Dad," Jeff said.

George shook his head. "I should think not."

"You'll stay here in the guest room," Jennifer said. "Beth and Jeff can sleep in Leeanne's room, and she can bunk with Abby. Randy and Travis can sleep on the floor down here."

"The boys could go home with me," Peter said. "Gary and Andy would love it."

Harvey got up and went to the entry and looked out.

"The M.E.'s here," he said when he returned to the table.

"Probably a real mess over there," said George.

Jeff hadn't let go of Beth since she'd come out of their house, and neither of them was eating. "I want you to see Dr. Turner," he said.

"All right," Beth said. "And if you folks won't think I'm rude, I think I'd like to lie down now."

Jennifer went with her and Jeff up the stairs. Jennifer was going to strip Leeanne's bed for them, but Beth wobbled on the stairs, and she figured it was better for Beth to lie down immediately.

"Take the guest room," Jennifer said. "It's all made up. I'll change Leeanne's bed later for Mom and Daddy."

"Thank you, Jennifer," Beth whispered.

"Do you want me to call Margaret?"

Jeff said, "Please do. Will she come here?"

"I think so, especially when I tell her what happened."

She went into Abby's room and made the call. Margaret agreed to come immediately. Harvey was waiting at the bottom of the stairs, holding Connor, when Jennifer went down.

"Is Beth really all right?" he asked.

"I don't know. She looks awful. I think it's a good idea to have her checked over. I thought Connor was in bed."

"I just wanted to hold him," said Harvey. Connor slept peacefully in his arms.

Marilyn brought Nate into the living room.

"Harvey, the press is clamoring for something official. Can you come?" Nate asked.

"It's Eddie's case, but he's gone to the hospital." Harvey sighed.

"I don't have all the details," Nate said. "I suppose Winfield could—"

"Oh, the press would love that," said Harvey. "I can just see it: Anthony Winfield, nephew of the governor and PPD spokesman. I'll come. How's it going out there?"

"They took the body to Augusta. The bedroom's a real mess. The living room's not too bad. Most of the glass went outside. You need to cover the window."

"I'd better call a cleanup crew," Harvey said. "Jenny, make sure Beth knows her open house is postponed."

"I think she figured that out. I'll call Mary Rowland, and she can send it around the phone chain."

Harvey went with Nate toward the doorway.

"Wait," Jennifer called. "You're not taking Connor with you, are you?"

He smiled. "Guess I'd better leave the boy here." He gently shifted him into her arms.

The enormity of it hit her. "Harvey, I had him over there. If Mom hadn't brought him along to change his diaper, he'd have been in there with Beth and Leeanne."

Harvey's eyes clouded, and he touched Connor's cheek, then looked at Jennifer. "Don't agonize over it, Jenny. God works these things out in His own way. Just be glad."

Chapter 27

When they learned Harvey was going to give a press conference, the family scrambled for sweatshirts and shoes. The Wainthrops and Hobarts went out with Jennifer and stood in the driveway. Harvey gathered the reporters a few yards away, in Jeff's driveway. Ryan Toothaker practically salivated, his pen and notebook poised. Leeanne had lost out on another hot story. Three television camera crews set up their microphones and lights.

Harvey took out his pocket notebook and held it up in the twilight.

"All right, I'm only going to do this once." He looked around at the reporters. "You all know me, I guess. I'm Captain Harvey Larson, but this isn't really my case. Detective Edouard Thibodeau's been the investigating officer all along, and he'd be standing here right now, except his fiancée was injured here tonight, and he's gone to the hospital with her."

Jennifer turned Connor, so he could see his father. He wouldn't remember, and in some ways she was glad, but she would be able to tell him later, "When you were three weeks old, you were at your father's press conference on the Fuller case."

"I'll run through the basics of this case," Harvey said. "You go to the police station tomorrow at 3 p.m., and Detective Thibodeau will give you any additional information he sees fit to give you. By the way, that's T-H-I- ..."

They all chuckled as Harvey painstakingly spelled Eddie's name for them.

"This house was bought twelve years ago by a man named Carleton Fuller. Mr. Fuller had a nephew, Marcus Rutledge, who was in the Navy. We're not sure how it came about, but Rutledge met up with another sailor, Daniel Sanford. Sanford was near retirement age, and we believe he and Rutledge cooked up a scheme to get hold of Fuller's money. About ten years ago, Rutledge either brought or sent Sanford here to his uncle's house.

One of them killed Mr. Fuller and buried him in the cellar. The skeleton that was discovered here April thirteenth was Mr. Fuller's."

The reporters scribbled furiously.

"Meanwhile," Harvey said, "Sanford assumed Fuller's identity. His appearance was similar enough to Fuller's that, by keeping his distance from his neighbors for a while, he was able to live in Fuller's house and live on his investments. One way or another, he passed himself off as Fuller for ten years. Then he died a natural death, last month. The executor sold the house. My wife and I live next door, and we decided to buy this house as a rental for my wife's brother, Jeff Wainthrop. That's W-A- ..."

Jennifer smiled and shifted Connor to her other arm.

"When we went to put a new furnace in a few weeks ago, the workmen discovered the real Mr. Fuller's remains. We think Rutledge and Sanford had an arrangement whereby they would share Fuller's money. But nobody notified Rutledge of Sanford's, alias Fuller's, death. Rutledge's ship was on deployment. When he got into port and got two weeks leave, he came to Maine to collect some cash from Sanford. The only trouble was, Sanford wasn't here. Strangers were living in his uncle's house. Rutledge went into the house last Friday, when no one was home, using a key he'd obtained years ago. He stole some money and left. Today he came back."

Harvey paused and looked over toward his family.

His voice broke a little when he said, "Two members of my family were in the house this time. My wife's sister, Leeanne Wainthrop, and her brother's wife, Beth Wainthrop, were in the kitchen when Rutledge went in through the back door. He held them at gun point for about an hour and tied their hands. Later he tied Mrs. Wainthrop's feet as well, leaving her in the bedroom and taking her sister-in-law into the living room with him. He broke the window there and threatened to harm Leeanne Wainthrop if we didn't bring him a hundred thousand dollars in cash and give him a ticket out.

"Our officers were able to get Beth Wainthrop out through the bedroom window. A gun battle ensued, during which

304

Rutledge was killed. Miss Wainthrop—that is, Leeanne, was slightly injured during the time she was a captive. She was transported to Maine Medical by ambulance. The investigating officer, Detective Thibodeau, is her fiancé, and he rode with her. I think that's about it."

The reporters surged forward with questions. Harvey took a few, then held up his hands.

"People, I'm tired. I'd like to go home now and sit with my family and thank God they're all alive. You come to the station at three o'clock tomorrow and ask for Detective Thibodeau."

He walked over and took Connor, put his other arm around Jennifer, and walked with them steadily to the house without looking back. Jennifer heard Nate Miller say, "No, no, that's it. Let the captain alone."

"Harvey," George said when they were safely back in the kitchen, "Peter and I could take some plastic over and cover that window."

"Thank you, George, I think that would be good," Harvey said.

"Should we ask Jeff?"

"No, don't bother him," Harvey said.

Abby went to the garage with her father and Peter to look for the roll of plastic Harvey thought he had there.

Harvey sank wearily onto the couch, still holding Connor close.

"Should I have the boys bring their things in?" Marilyn asked.

Jennifer said, "Yes. They can get the sleeping bags out of the closet in the nursery. All the camping gear is up there." She put her arms around Harvey's neck and leaned on his shoulder. His head came down softly against hers.

When the boys came through with their luggage, Marilyn came with them.

"Dr. Turner is here, Jennifer."

She stood and went to meet Margaret.

"Are you okay?" Margaret eyed her anxiously.

"Yes. Everyone's fine."

"Where's Beth?"

"She's upstairs in the guest room. Thanks for coming."

Jennifer took her up and knocked softly on the door. Jeff opened it, and she left Margaret and went back down to Harvey.

*****

When Margaret came down fifteen minutes later, Jennifer stood up.

"Everything okay?"

Margaret sighed and sat down in the recliner facing them. "She's had a major shock."

"I feel so bad," Jennifer said. "I'm not sure she'll want to live in that house now."

"Well, time will help for sure, but I think she should stay here for a few days, if that's all right with you."

"Of course," Harvey said.

"Keep her quiet. I'd like her right in bed for twenty-four hours. Can Jeff be with her?"

"They told him to stay tonight, and he starts two days off in the morning, anyway," Jennifer said.

"Good." Margaret's lips tightened. "I'd rather have her in the hospital, but that would mean moving her. Just keep a close eye on things. Is Abby here? Maybe she could check Beth every couple of hours."

"Yes, she's next door helping cover the broken window," Jennifer said. "She'll be here."

"All right. And I told Jeff, if there's any bleeding at all, call me."

"Margaret," Jennifer said, suddenly afraid, "you don't think she might lose the baby?"

"She's strong," Margaret said. "We'll hope for the best."

"We're all praying."

Margaret smiled. "We'll pray, too. Is Leeanne all right?"

"We think so. Haven't heard officially," said Harvey.

"Would you like me to call the hospital?"

"Thank you," Jennifer said. "That would ease all our minds."

306

Margaret called and reported that Leeanne was doing fine, and Eddie would bring her home.

Peter renewed his bid to take Randy and Travis home with him. They were agreeable, and in the end they went with Peter, taking the sleeping bags.

Marilyn and Jennifer went upstairs to change Leeanne's bed.

"Leeanne can have my bed, and I'll sleep on the couch," Abby said. "She's probably not feeling so great right now."

When Eddie brought Leeanne home, they all crowded around, wanting to see for themselves that she was all right.

"She's not supposed to talk a lot tonight," Eddie said. "Bruised larynx."

Abby brought her a cup of peppermint tea, and Eddie hovered over her.

"Think I can get a statement from Beth tonight, Harv?" he asked.

"Better wait until tomorrow," Harvey said. "But I think this case can really be closed now."

"Yes," Eddie agreed. "From what Leeanne tells me, Rutledge and Sanford were both there when Fuller was murdered, but it sounds as if Rutledge actually did the deed."

"Sanford threw his ring and uniform in the grave when they buried him," Harvey said.

"I guess so. Rutledge had talked him into staying here in his uncle's place."

When her mother offered to put Leeanne to bed and Leeanne didn't protest, Eddie went home. Jennifer sat with Harvey on the sofa, her head on his shoulder. Connor slept against his father's chest, oblivious to the turmoil around him.

"Let's pray for Leeanne and Beth," Jennifer said.

Harvey's voice held a weariness she hadn't heard for a long time as he petitioned God.

"Did you eat enough?" Jennifer asked anxiously when their prayers were finished.

"I think so. I just need to unwind."

There was kindling in the woodbox, and Jennifer went to the fireplace and began to build the foundation of a fire. Harvey came over after a minute and laughed.

"Gorgeous, you do some things very well, but making a fire ain't one of 'em."

He held Connor out to her and took over at the fireplace. Harvey was a one-match man. Jennifer laid Connor on the couch and went to the bedroom for a quilt and pillows. When she came back, a comforting blaze crackled on the hearth, and Harvey was once again holding the baby. She spread out the quilt, and he lay down with Connor on his chest. Jennifer sat beside them, watching the fire.

Jeff came down quietly after half an hour. He pulled the recliner as close to the fire as Harvey's feet would allow.

"How's Beth?" Jennifer asked.

"She's sleeping right now. Jennifer, I'm scared."

"I know." She reached for his hand. "We've been praying. Did you see Leeanne?"

"Yes. I'm glad she's all right."

Harvey stirred and opened his eyes. "Hey, Jeff," he said quietly, patting Connor's back.

"I told Beth we'll postpone the open house," Jeff said. "I'd better call the fire station and the church and Beth's principal and have the word passed around."

"Maybe you should ask the principal to get a sub for Beth for next week," Jennifer said.

"I don't want her to go back to work."

"Well, if Margaret says she shouldn't, they should put her on sick leave."

"Margaret said she'd come see her again tomorrow." Jeff ran his hand through his unruly hair. "I just wish I could do something."

"You are," Jennifer said. "Just stay here with her and reassure her."

"She hasn't had any bleeding," he said.

Harvey looked up at Jeff. "Stay here with her tomorrow. We'll do anything we can to fix things up next door. I'll get someone out here with new glass for the window, and I'll have somebody take care of the bedroom. Jeff, if Beth doesn't want to go back there, we'll understand."

"She was terrified," he said. "Ever since they found the bones, I think she's been scared to be there alone."

"With you gone nights so much, it may be better to just cut your losses and move out," Harvey said.

"We gave up the other house."

"I know. We'll make sure you have something, brother. And you can stay here until we find something."

"What about the house, though?" Jeff asked. "Can you rent it to someone else?"

"I think so. I don't think Eddie would mind living there. I'm not sure about Leeanne. If they don't want to, we'll just advertise."

"We may not even own the house," Jennifer reminded them.

"Right," Harvey said. "It gets more and more complicated. Judge Boyer has her work cut out for her now."

Jeff called his captain, and Jennifer called the pastor and Beth's principal. Harvey roused himself and put Connor in the cradle.

"I meant to tell you something else." He stepped back from the cradle and turned toward Jennifer.

"The property Daniel Sanford bought is an old farmhouse with about thirty acres in Lisbon. Nobody's lived there since before he bought it."

"I wonder why he didn't rent it out or resell it," Jennifer said.

"Excellent question. We've got a State Police team set to search the property tomorrow. If they find anything suspicious, my squad will go up there."

"Okay. Thanks for telling me."

Jeff joined them in the sunroom, and they all went into the kitchen. Marilyn and Abby were puttering around, laying out dishes for breakfast. George sat at the table, eating pie and drinking coffee.

"I'll bet you're hungry now, Jeffrey," his mother said.

"Kinda."

Marilyn fixed him a plate of leftover lasagna and offered Harvey a piece of pie, but he went for an English muffin and a glass of milk instead.

George said, "Eddie certainly is showing devotion. Was it all right for him to leave the scene like that, Harvey?"

"In this case, yes. I was there, and he left Nate in charge of the investigation. If it had been Jenny, I certainly would have gone."

"How's Beth doing?" Abby asked.

"All right, I think, but maybe you should check on her," Jennifer said.

Jeff and Abby went quietly up the stairs.

"Abby and I froze some of the food you girls prepared," Marilyn said.

"Good. They want to reschedule the open house. I think Jeff wants to wait and see what Margaret says about Beth tomorrow before they set a new date, though."

"Should we go over and see about the food at Beth's?" Marilyn asked.

"I'll go with you," Harvey said.

He and George both went over with them. While Marilyn and Jennifer tidied up the kitchen and decided what to do about the food, the men went into the bedroom to inspect the damage there.

"It could be worse," Harvey said. "I should have called a cleaning crew right away. Still, if they can get in there in the morning..."

It was just after nine, and he decided to try to call someone.

Jennifer and her mom packed away the food that could be frozen, and they carried the rest over to the other house.

"Good thing we hadn't made the sandwiches yet," Jennifer said, closing the door on her overloaded refrigerator.

She went into the bedroom. Harvey was sitting on the bed, talking on the phone. Jennifer looked down at their baby and marveled again at his perfection.

"Well, there are some blood spatters on the wallpaper and the rug," Harvey said. Maybe some on the bed linens. I don't think it's all that bad, but if you can't get the rug completely clean, I'll have it replaced."

When he had hung up, he said, "They'll come at eight in the morning. I told them we'll let them in to clean, and they'll have us inspect when they're finished."

"I think Connor's down for his long stretch," Jennifer said.

"Then we'd better sack out, too, while we have the chance."

They went out and said goodnight to her parents.

"Mom, Dad, I'm so glad you were here tonight," Jennifer said.

They both kissed her, then Marilyn kissed Harvey, and George clapped him on the shoulder.

"Didn't know my daughters were in for such goings on when they moved to the city," he said gruffly. "I know it's not your fault, Harvey."

"If it's anyone's fault, it's mine," Jennifer said. She couldn't fight back the tears. "We have such a perfect baby. If Jeff and Beth lose theirs—"

"Jenny, Jenny." Harvey put his arm around her. "You've got to quit thinking that way. We run outside for a few minutes all the time and leave the door unlocked. This is not your doing."

When her parents had gone upstairs, he took her into the bedroom and held her for a long time.

Chapter 28
Saturday, May 6

In the morning, Margaret came to see Beth and gave her opinion that things would be fine. However, Beth should have another day of bed rest, at least, and take it easy for a while. Jeff asked if she ought to take some time off from work, and Margaret thought that would be a good idea, so Jeff called the principal and asked him to arrange a substitute for a week.

Harvey's glazier and cleaning crew were on the scene early, and by noon number 135 looked as peaceful as ever. Harvey went around removing the crime scene tape. Eddie's Dodge pickup pulled in, and Eddie conferred with Harvey in the driveway for five minutes, then they came inside.

Leeanne was feeling better and protested when the family tried to fuss over her.

"Don't baby me," she said.

"He hit you," her mother objected.

"I'm going to be fine. I'm a little sore, but I'm going to start my job Monday. Period."

"Maybe you should call your editor and see if he'd like a first-person account of your ordeal for the Sunday paper," Harvey suggested.

"Did you have to say that, Harv?" Eddie asked. "I've been trying to tell her she needs to take it easy."

"Well, it would give her something to think about," he replied.

When Jennifer went up to see Beth later, Leeanne was typing away at the keyboard in her room. Jennifer peeked in the doorway. Eddie was sitting backward on a chair, morosely watching her work.

Fifteen minutes later, Jennifer passed her door again. Leeanne was alone in her room, still typing. Jennifer found Harvey and Eddie downstairs in the study.

Harvey turned to her as she entered the room. "I've had a call from the nursing home administrator. They found Mr. Fuller's effects."

"Where?" Jennifer asked.

"In a box in a closet. He says there's not much, but there are a couple of letters and some personal things. Eddie and I are going over and collect the box."

Marilyn helped Jennifer fix lunch for a crowd, and Peter brought the four boys over.

"I think it's warm enough to eat on the patio," Jennifer said.

Her mother fixed an attractive tray for Beth, and Jeff and took it upstairs. Everyone else ate at the picnic table. Harvey and Eddie came home just as they were about to have dessert. They heaped their plates and joined the rest outside.

"Sanford, alias Fuller, had a letter from Rutledge while he was at the nursing home," Harvey told them. "It came to Van Cleeve Lane and was forwarded to him at the home."

"What did it say?" Jennifer asked eagerly.

"Rutledge was mad," Eddie said. "He wanted to know why Sanford hadn't sent any money for a while. Said if he didn't get his share, he was going to turn Sanford in for something that apparently happened several years ago."

"Some other crime?" Abby asked.

"Yup," Eddie said. "We'll give a copy to the Navy. We can't really tell from the letter, but it sounds as if Sanford was involved in something before he was discharged, and Rutledge knew about it."

"What if it was the boy who mowed lawns?" Jennifer asked. "He could blackmail him for that."

"Maybe," Eddie said, "but I got the impression it was something earlier. Maybe Rutledge had used that as leverage to get Sanford up here in the first place. We'll probably never know all the details."

"But they weren't bosom buddies," Harvey said.

"I think they had a deal to split all the money, but Sanford reneged," Eddie said. "Rutledge didn't come up here often, but Sanford was supposed to send him half every time he cashed out one of Fuller's investments. But he held out on him. I don't think he'd sent Rutledge any money for a long time, and Rutledge came to settle up."

"Sanford must have bought the land in Lisbon with his take from one of the first cash-outs." Harvey shook his head. "Why do you suppose he made a new will in Fuller's name?"

"I dunno," said Eddie. "If they had a falling out, maybe he just wanted to get one back on Rutledge. One final way to get at him. The house was all that was left. It should have gone to Rutledge, but this way, Sanford kept him from getting it."

"He must have thought it was pretty funny, leaving what was left to charity," Harvey said. "There was no way Rutledge could claim it. If he denounced Sanford, he'd be tied to the murder."

"Yeah, I'm guessing they had a fight somewhere along the way," Eddie said.

"We made a copy of the letter, and Pete Bearse is sending it to Judge Boyer today," Harvey said.

"Did you find out where Sanford spent his summers?" Jennifer asked.

"Not at his Lisbon property. There's no furniture in the house. I really have no idea, but I think he did meet Rutledge at least a couple of times and pass him some money," Eddie said.

Leeanne frowned. "Rutledge was ranting about the money last night, how Sanford had stiffed him."

"I think he was cashing the bonds out faster than Rutledge wanted him to," Eddie said. "Rutledge probably expected Sanford to actually live on his Navy pension. They could take their time liquidating the bonds and CD's, so no one would get suspicious. But Sanford stepped up the timetable and kept most of the cash."

"I wonder if he spent it all or has it stashed somewhere," Harvey said. "There may be a bank account, or other property we don't know about yet."

"Maybe Daisy was right, and he's got a sailboat somewhere," Jennifer said.

Harvey looked at Eddie. "We need to make a search for a boat or more real estate in either Fuller's or Sanford's name."

"We're doing that. That's how Tony found out about the farm." Eddie wrote himself a note anyway in his regulation notebook.

"Can I put that in my story for the paper?" Leeanne asked. "I mean, the part about the letter in his stuff at the nursing home, and them fighting over the money?"

"Sure," said Harvey. "Just let me proofread your story before you send it, and I'll make sure you've got all the facts straight. I know that's not the usual way, but we're in a hurry, right?"

"Yeah, and I'm not officially an employee yet."

Leeanne spent another hour at the keyboard, and Eddie went out on the driveway to shoot basketball with Harvey and Jeff. Peter looked wistful, but he didn't have a change of clothes along, and he and Abby were headed for a counseling session with the pastor later.

Jennifer took Connor up to the guest room and spent some time with Beth, revising the plans for the house warming.

"Are you sure you want to stay there?" Jennifer asked. "Beth, if it's too difficult for you, we'll understand."

Beth smiled wanly. "No, I think it will be okay, now that this case is closed. But you can be sure I'll keep the alarm on all the time, and I want another lock on the bulkhead door."

"No problem," Jennifer said. "Harvey is serious about finishing the basement. You can have a nice family room down there, and it will look totally different."

"I think it would be nice for Jeff to have a workshop," Beth said. "He can do his reloading and stuff down there. I don't know as I want to spend a lot of time in the cellar."

"Whatever you want."

"Right now what I want is to get out of bed," Beth said.

"Margaret says you ought to stay put until tomorrow."

"I know, and she won't let me go to church. Abby is going to teach my Sunday School class for me. But I'm going to get up and eat lunch with everybody tomorrow."

"You'll be the guest of honor," Jennifer said. "If you're feeling really well, tomorrow afternoon we'll go through my maternity clothes. You can take what you want to use, and I'll pack the rest away for next time." Beth reached for Connor, and Jennifer gave him to her.

"I can't believe we're going to have one of these."

Jennifer smiled. "It's going to be great, Beth."

Leeanne came in from her bedroom.

"Story all done?" Jennifer asked.

"Yes. I sent it by e-mail, and I just spoke to the editor. He says it looks great, and it will be on the front page tomorrow. My first-person account as a hostage is the main story, and they'll run a shorter sidebar with the information Harvey and Eddie gave me on the case."

Jennifer gave her a hug. "That's terrific. Mr. Russell must be happy to be getting you as an intern."

"I'm not sure," Leeanne mused. "It might be like when Harvey got Tony Winfield. His famous relatives were a bit of an encumbrance."

"Do you think it will make it harder for you, having relatives and friends in the police department?" Beth asked.

"Oh, not really, but some of the reporters with years of seniority might have their noses out of joint. Ryan Toothaker was really mad when Harvey gave me the story on the Hawkins case in January. He's been writing about this Fuller case since they found the skeleton. He may feel I'm stealing his thunder this weekend."

"Ryan will survive," Jennifer said. "He had page one this morning."

"Well, it's a real advantage to me to know the Priority captain so well, and to be on a friendly basis with the chief of police." Leeanne shrugged. "But maybe they'll make me do drudge work all summer. You know, obituaries and upcoming

317

events, that kind of thing. Maybe they'll purposely keep me away from the police station."

"If they do, just take what they hand you and make the best of it," Beth counseled.

Leeanne nodded. "I've been praying about it. I want to have a good attitude, and be a testimony for the Lord in the office, no matter what my job is." She looked at Beth speculatively. "I don't know if you want to talk about it or not—"

"I think I do." Beth held Connor close. "When he took you into the living room, I was terrified. I was so scared he would really hurt you, Leeanne!"

"Yeah, I was scared, too," Leeanne said. "I was praying all the time, and the adrenaline was really pumping. When he took me back in the bedroom and you were gone, I didn't realize what had happened at first. I was petrified because I was alone with him then. But then I realized you'd got out, and I was so happy. I didn't care what happened to me then." Tears flowed down Leeanne's cheeks. "Beth, I'm so glad you and the baby are all right."

Jennifer squeezed Leeanne's hand. "You must have been scared when he started shooting out the window."

"It didn't really sink in until the cops started shooting back. I just dropped to the floor and tried to make myself small. Then Eddie and Nate came in ..." her voice trailed off.

"Eddie was terrific," Jennifer said. "He was in the house a long time, but he couldn't get the drop on Rutledge."

"I know," Leeanne said. "I'm really, really thankful we all got out of that one."

*****

Leeanne's article was the subject of much talk at church the next day. She took compliments with modesty, surprised by the magnitude of the public's reaction. She fielded telephone calls much of the afternoon.

"CBS is sending a camera crew here from Boston," she said incredulously. "Can you believe this? They want to interview me. Me. Not Eddie or Harvey or Jeff and Beth. Me."

"When?" Jennifer asked.

"Tomorrow afternoon. I told them I'm starting work at the *Press Herald* tomorrow, and they said they'll set it up with Mr. Russell. This whole thing is incredible."

"Maybe they'll offer you a job on *60 Minutes*," Harvey teased.

"*Tiens!*" Eddie glared at him. "Would you quit saying things like that, Harv? Next thing you know, she'll be postponing the wedding and going off to New York or someplace."

"No way," said Leeanne. "I am going to be Madame Thibodeau on August twelfth, and nothing is going to get in the way of that."

Eddie seemed somewhat mollified.

"Besides," Leeanne added, "I don't want to be a broadcast journalist. I get too nervous just interviewing people for articles. I told them I get terrible stage fright, but they still want to interview me. Maybe I can learn something from watching a pro do an interview with a nervous subject."

George, Marilyn, Randy, and Travis left after lunch, promising to come back whenever Jeff and Beth rescheduled the party. Beth had come down for lunch, and she sat with Jeff in the lawn swing afterward, enjoying the warm sun. They decided to move back next door that night, and Jeff would go to the fire station early in the morning for his next shift.

"Beth, I'd be happy to stay at your house with you while Jeff's on duty," Abby said.

"You don't need to," Beth replied graciously, but Jeff seized the offer.

"Hey, I think that would be great." He turned to Beth. "Honey, she came down here to help Jennifer when she needed it, and now you're the one who's going through a rough time. Let her come."

"Let's think about it," Beth faltered.

"If you want me to, I'd be happy to stay over there," Abby said. "Leeanne's here now, and we'll all be so close, we can help each other."

"Maybe that would be good," Beth said. "I feel so helpless. I shouldn't be afraid. I know the Lord is with me. I just keep seeing that man holding the gun at Leeanne's ear." Beth was near tears, and Jeff put his arms around her.

"Honey, it's okay. But it's okay to let your family help you, too."

Eddie came out through the patio door.

"Where's Leeanne?" Jennifer asked.

"On the phone again. Mayor Weymouth is telling her what a credit she is to the city. She just moved here Thursday, for crying out loud!"

"Eddie, Leeanne's young, and she's excited," Harvey said. "Cut her a little slack."

"You must be proud of her," Beth said.

Eddie shrugged. "Well, natch."

"So, just chill out a little," Harvey said. "This is her time in the limelight. It will pass, just like it did for you with the Sobbin' Women to-do."

Eddie sighed and sat down at the picnic table. "I'll just be glad when she's my girl again, not the city's."

*****

Harvey and Eddie ran Monday morning, then ate breakfast at the Larson house. Leeanne changed her clothes twice before she was satisfied. She wanted to look like a reporter, not a newbie intern.

"My first day on a new job, and a TV interview this afternoon," she said fretfully, as she sat down beside Eddie at the table.

"You'll be great," Harvey said.

"Want me to drive you to work?" Eddie asked.

"I don't know. What if I need my car?"

She decided to drive herself to work, and Eddie sat with his arm around her, as though he dreaded the moment she would leave. It was as bad as when she had come weekends and then headed north again.

"It's only eight hours," she reminded him.

"Nine counting lunch," Eddie replied.

"Now, remember, we're going to the courthouse this morning," Harvey said. "The judge is supposed to rule on the wills at ten o'clock. I doubt if you'll need to contact me your first day, Leeanne, but if by any chance you do, I won't be at the police station from ten to eleven or so."

"Call me if you can meet me for lunch," Eddie told her.

"Okay. Can I call you, Harvey, if I need a pep talk?"

"Sure. Any time except the hour or so I'm in court. Use my cell phone number."

Eddie finally left to get changed for work, and Leeanne drove off, nervous but determined, toward the newspaper office.

*****

So many family members were interested in the Fuller case that Harvey contacted Pete Bearse about it and then called Jennifer.

"Pete says to bring the whole family to court if we want."

"Well, Peter Hobart's interested in sitting in," Jennifer said. "Beth and Abby will come with me."

"Fine," Harvey said. "Eddie will go in his official capacity. It's too bad Leeanne can't be there."

"Maybe she could, if you asked John Russell. It's another part of an ongoing story, and she's been a big part of it. He might let her do another article today."

"I think I'll give him a call," Harvey said.

When Jennifer, Abby, and Beth got to the courthouse, Harvey and Eddie were waiting on the steps. Harvey came to the minivan and took Connor out.

"John's sending Leeanne and Ryan both over, and a photographer," Harvey said.

"Not another media circus," Jennifer wailed.

"I hope not. I don't think the TV stations are onto this angle. It's an exclusive for the *Press Herald*. I had to agree to Ryan to let him save face. Leeanne is supposed to watch and learn."

"So Ryan's writing the story?" Abby asked. "That's not fair. Leeanne's a great writer, and it's her family."

"But it's supposed to be an unbiased news story, so maybe it's better this way," Jennifer said.

"I don't know as I like her working with Ryan," Eddie said fretfully.

321

"Relax, Eddie, he's married," Harvey said.

Peter Hobart pulled into the parking lot in a demo car and joined them as they entered the courthouse. They were directed to a hearing room and sat down to wait.

"Judge Boyer should be with you in about five minutes," the clerk said.

Harvey called Jeff at the fire station and asked if he could come over.

A couple of minutes later, Leeanne walked in with Ryan Toothaker at her side. A long-haired photographer followed them, with a camera bag slung over his shoulder. Eddie went to meet Leeanne and kissed her, then held a chair out for her.

"Thanks for calling us, Captain Larson," Ryan said. "Your sister-in-law never said a word about this."

Leeanne blushed. "I wasn't sure I was supposed to."

"If there's news out there, you can't sit on it," Ryan said.

Jeff came in, and Connor began his rounds of the aunts and uncles. The women began discussing new plans for the housewarming, contingent on the judge's ruling.

Pete Bearse arrived, and he shook hands with Harvey. The men immediately launched into a discussion of the Fuller case. Ryan and Leeanne took notes, but Harvey was being careful of what he said.

A middle-aged woman came to the door. She was pretty, with dark blonde hair that waved over her shoulders and a softly constructed pink suit with a gray blouse. Jennifer thought she was a clerk who would tell them the judge would be delayed, but Harvey jumped up and said, "Good morning, your honor," and she realized it was Judge Boyer.

"My, this is quite a gathering," she said. "I see the press is represented."

"Is that a problem, your honor?" Harvey asked.

"No, I guess not, if you and Mrs. Larson have no objection. I'll just ask the photographer not to take any pictures in the courtroom, please."

The photographer sighed and went out into the hallway.

Harvey made introductions, and the judge looked just a little overwhelmed.

"I've reviewed the documents and the brief that were presented to me in this case," she said formally, opening a black folder. "Is there anything you would like to add at this time?"

Pete said, "Your honor, were you able to view the letter I sent over on Saturday?"

"Yes, Mr. Bearse, and I found it very interesting. It appears that Mr. Rutledge and Mr. Sanford conspired to murder Carleton Fuller and steal his estate. We have two wills, one written by Mr. Fuller more than twenty years ago, and one written by one of the conspirators three years ago. It is my judgment that the newer will is fraudulent, and therefore, the original will, written by Mr. Fuller, is to be enforced."

Harvey sighed deeply. Connor, who was with Jeff just then, began to burble happily at his uncle.

Pete said, "Your honor, the question is, who owns the house that the Larsons bought in good faith?"

"Well, all of Mr. Fuller's property should rightfully have gone to his nephew when he died. But I'm informed that Marcus Rutledge admitted last Friday that he killed his uncle." She looked expectantly at Harvey.

Harvey nodded and gestured toward Leeanne. "My sister-in-law, Leeanne Wainthrop, witnessed Rutledge's statement to that effect, a few minutes before his death."

"Did you give the police a sworn statement after the shooting incident?" Judge Boyer asked Leeanne.

"Yes, ma'am." Leeanne's voice shook a little.

"I have a copy of her statement and the police report from the incident here, your honor," said Eddie. "Also Beth Wainthrop's statement, saying Rutledge claimed Sanford helped him bury Mr. Fuller." He held out several sheets of paper, and Judge Boyer took them.

"Perhaps I should recess to look at these," she said. "However, there is no question that the older of the two wills is to be recognized as valid."

She scanned the reports, and appeared to slow down and read one section carefully. She looked up and said to Pete, "Mr. Bearse, I suggest you file a petition in probate, on behalf of your clients. A hearing might be needed to make it official, but it seems to me that the estate will go to the next of kin after Marcus Rutledge. Since he admitted to killing the testator, this state will not allow him to inherit the estate."

"The police department has been looking for any other living relatives of Carleton Fuller for some weeks now, your honor, but they haven't found any," said Pete.

"Hmm. I suppose this thing will drag on for months while some law clerk covers the same ground the police department has." She turned to Harvey. "Captain Larson, was it your unit that researched this man's family?"

"Yes, your honor. Not me personally, but the Priority Unit."

"Hmm, yes. Well, you see, I happen to know that the Priority Unit is the best there is. If you didn't find any kin, no one else will, either. Of course, you might be construed to benefit from Fuller's lack of relatives, and we don't want a scandal involving city employees." Her brow furrowed. She sat still for a few seconds, then said, "Give me a notarized statement telling who conducted the research and handled the investigation, and I will accept it."

"Yes, ma'am. I'll have it in your hands this afternoon," Harvey said. "I was on the edge of the investigation, you understand. It happened in a house I had bought, right next door to my residence. I couldn't very well stay out of it altogether."

"I understand," Judge Boyer said.

Pete cleared his throat and said, "Your honor, my office also did some searching for Rutledge, who could not at first be found, and any other relatives of Carleton Fuller. We also came up empty-handed."

"Send me a detailed report of the sources you checked." The judge looked at Eddie. "Detective Thibodeau, perhaps you will handle the statement I asked for from the police department, so that Captain Larson doesn't have to handle it?"

"I'd be glad to, your honor," said Eddie.

"Good. Now, these are the people who live in the house?" the judge asked, looking down the table toward Jeff and Beth. Beth was now holding Connor.

"Yes, ma'am," said Harvey. "My wife's brother, Jeffrey Wainthrop, and his wife, Beth."

She smiled. "The family resemblance is very strong. All right, you have my judgment. The old will is valid, but Rutledge cannot inherit. I will examine the reports to see if I feel the search for other relatives was complete. If so, the state will take charge of whatever was left of Fuller's property."

Pete said, "We believe all his investments were taken by Rutledge and Sanford, your honor, and all that was left when Sanford died was the house and its contents and another piece of property outside the city. The contents of the house were sold, and part of the proceeds was paid out for his burial expenses. There was a residue of nine hundred thirty-four dollars, which is being held in escrow. The house was sold to the Larsons. That money is also being held."

"It wasn't distributed under the fraudulent will?" the judge asked.

"No. The Realtor got its percentage, but the rest was to have been paid out to Maine Medical Center and the local Chapter of the Humane Society. However, the skeleton was discovered in Fuller's house before the payments were made, so the rest of the money from the sale of the house was held pending the outcome of the investigation."

"Very good. Was the executor paid?"

"Not yet. He was to have been paid at the same time the charities were paid."

"All right," Judge Boyer said, "I'll see those reports on the Fuller family later." She shifted in her chair, as if to rise. Beth passed Connor to Abby.

"Your honor," Harvey said humbly, "may I ask you a straightforward question?"

"Of course, Captain."

"My wife and I bought the house from the estate. Does this change that? Does the state own the house now, or do we?"

She opened the black folder and frowned at what was in it. "Captain, I will file a formal motion within forty-eight hours on that matter, but I will tell you that I am leaning toward saying the house is yours. You paid a fair price in good faith, and the state of Maine would only lose money by reversing that. It would involve more court costs, at the least. My recommendation will be to let the sale of the house stand. The money from the sale will revert to the state if no heirs are found."

"Would it matter if Rutledge had a will?" asked Harvey.

"No. Because of his crime, he forfeited all rights to the estate. His heirs cannot inherit what he cannot inherit."

"Thank you, ma'am."

She smiled at Harvey. "That's a beautiful baby, Captain."

*****

Jennifer had forgotten about the photographer. When they went through the courthouse door into bright sunlight on the steps, he loomed before them and snapped a picture of her and Harvey, who was, of course, carrying his son.

"This family can't stop making news," Peter Hobart said.

"Are you sure you want to join it?" Jennifer asked.

"I'll take my chances."

Harvey buckled Connor into his car seat.

"Beth, what's the word on Rick's job?" he asked.

"I forgot to tell you. His boss is selling out, and the new owner wants Rick to stay on."

"Great," Harvey said with satisfaction.

Harvey's phone rang, and he pulled it out. After frowning at the screen, he put it to his ear. "Yeah, Mike? Is that right? Okay, I'll let my guys get some lunch, and we'll head up there."

"Lisbon?" Jennifer asked.

"Yeah." Harvey looked over at Eddie. "There's an old hand-dug well on the property, and the forensic team has found something. Call Tony, will you? We can all go up there in my vehicle. They're setting up their equipment, but they won't remove anything until we get there."

Jennifer sighed. "I hoped we'd have a peaceful summer."

"This won't take long to close out," Harvey said. "We should know within a couple of days whether or not it's the Leonard boy. Maybe even today."

"I'll hold you to that. We've got a housewarming and two weddings coming right up. That's all the excitement I want for a while."

She went home and spent the afternoon with Connor and working on her computer programs. She made a lot of progress, but the house was entirely too quiet. As soon as Beth came home from school, she bundled up the baby and went next door.

"It looks like they cleaned up everything," she observed when Beth let her in the front door.

"Yeah, it's not bad. It's still a little creepy, but I try not to think about it."

"I don't mean to sound trite, but God is with you," Jennifer said.

Beth gave her a serene smile. "I know. He was with Leeanne and me on Saturday, too. I knew that whatever happened, we were in God's hands. But I was still petrified. Especially when I started hearing noises—like the glass breaking."

Jennifer put her arms around her. "It's going to be okay now."

"I know." Beth pulled backed and swiped a hand across her eyes. "I'm glad you and Harvey are next door."

Leeanne came home before Harvey did, exhausted but excited over her first day on the job.

"Ryan wrote up the story about the will, and he even asked me for some clarification. He's not such a bad guy. And man, is he fast at pounding out a story."

Harvey was late coming home, and Jennifer was glad she'd made stew in the slow cooker.

"I dropped Eddie and Tony at the police station," he told Leeanne. "They have a lot of paperwork to do."

Leeanne frowned. "I thought the state police were handling it."

"They're doing the recovery, but I'm pretty sure this is tied to our case. If the M.E. can identify the body, and if it is the Leonard boy, then we'll take over from there."

"Wow." Leeanne let out a big breath. "Do you really think he killed that poor kid when he came to mow his lawn?"

"Off the record?" Harvey asked.

She smiled. "Yeah. For now."

"In that case, yes, I do."

Later in the evening, when he and Jennifer were alone in the bedroom with Connor, she watched him as she brushed out her long hair.

"Was there any evidence that made you think it was Jacob Leonard in that well?"

Harvey sighed and sank down on the edge of the bed. "Yeah. It's a young male, for one thing, and the M.E. estimates the body's been there more than five years but less than twelve. And..."

She waited. After a moment he turned to gaze at her, and his blue eyes were filled with sadness. "There were bits of clothing and a pair of eyeglasses. A few coins, none newer than the year he disappeared. And a house key."

"A house key?"

"Yes. Eddie will go with a state police detective to see the Leonards tomorrow. They still live in the same house. If it's their key and their son's glasses, we can draw conclusions, even before we get the final autopsy report."

"It makes me sad." Jennifer laid her brush on the nightstand.

"Me, too. Come here, gorgeous."

She turned out the lamp and snuggled close to him.

"Mrs. Harder called me at the office," Harvey said softly. "She's ready to put her house on the market. I told her that Eddie and I will go over and look at it tomorrow after work. I suppose you and Leeanne will go along?"

"I'd love to, and I'm sure Leeanne will want to see the place. You don't think there are any unsolved crimes associated with that house, do you?" Jennifer asked anxiously.

"Well, I did ask her if there are any secret hiding places in the house." Harvey kissed her, and Jennifer clung to him.

"What did she say?"

He chuckled. "She said her father was a very creative man."

THE END

Dear Reader,

Thank you for choosing *The House Next Door*. This is Book 5 in the Maine Justice Series, which features the men of the Priority Unit and their families. These characters care about justice, love, and faith, and I hope you enjoyed their adventure. Group discussion questions are just a few pages away.

This series is dear to my heart. I hope that if you enjoyed it you will tell other readers and perhaps post a review on Amazon, Barnes & Noble, Goodreads, or other venues of your choice.

The series will continue in *The Labor Day Challenge*, where the Priority Unit competes against another city and gets a surprise. For a sneak peek at Book 6, turn the page. Investigate the murder with them while they try to honor a fallen officer.

Sincerely,

Susan Page Davis

About the author: Susan Page Davis is the author of more than seventy published novels. She's a two-time winner of the Inspirational Readers' Choice Award and the Will Rogers Medallion, and also a winner of the Carol Award and a finalist in the WILLA Literary Awards. A Maine native, she now lives in Kentucky with her husband Jim, two of their six children, and two cats, sweet Sora and naughty Arthur. Visit her website at: www.susanpagedavis.com, where you can see all her books, sign up for her occasional newsletter, and read a short story on her romance page.

Find Susan at:
Website: www.susanpagedavis.com
Twitter: @SusanPageDavis
Facebook: https://www.facebook.com/susanpagedavisauthor
Sign up for Susan's occasional newsletter at
https://madmimi.com/signups/118177/join

Excerpt from *The Labor Day Challenge*

"Hey, it's a real body," Eddie said as they entered the room. "Male Caucasian, age thirty, five-foot-ten, a hundred and seventy-five pounds."

The 'victim' lay face down on the blue and brown oriental rug in front of the comptroller's desk.

"Cool," Tony said, heading for the desk. "I thought they were going to use a dummy."

"All right, spread out, and be extra careful, guys," Harvey said, after a cursory glance at the body. "Eddie, you deal with the corpse. The rest of you check everything for prints. They may have brought in objects from outside, like those books in the shelves. Be quick, and try not to get in each other's way."

Eddie walked over to the 'corpse' and looked down. The man was wearing a gray pinstriped suit, and blood oozed from beneath his chest, soaking the rug and pooling on the oak floor beside it.

"That fake blood is pretty convincing." He bent over the man. "Hey, Joey."

Harvey glanced sharply toward him. "It's Joey Bolduc?"

"Yeah, I guess they got a dummy after all," Eddie deadpanned.

Jimmy Cook snickered, opening his fingerprint kit by the window.

Harvey spotted a spanking new copy of Stephen King's latest novel on the top shelf and reached for it with his clean handkerchief.

"Hey, Joey, how'd you pull this detail?" Tony called.

Bolduc lay still.

"Well, he's not breaking character," Nate said. "Gotta give him credit for that."

Eddie's expression changed as he studied Bolduc's body. He reached down suddenly and touched the man's neck, above the collar.

"Harvey." His voice rose, and Harvey froze, his hand in midair as he stretched for the book.

He glanced toward Eddie, then went quickly across the room and knelt beside Joey Bolduc.

"Harvey, he's not breathing."

Nate, Jimmy, and Tony, swung toward them.

"You're kidding," said Jimmy.

"They used a real body, a real *dead* body?" Tony quavered.

"No pulse," Harvey confirmed.

Nate swore.

"*Ne jure pas,*" Eddie said gently.

"I was talking to him this morning. He was helping them set up," Tony protested.

"They killed him? This doesn't make sense." Jimmy's eyes were round and his breathing shallow.

"Idiot," said Harvey. "They didn't kill him for the game."

Jimmy ducked his head, flushing. "I didn't mean that."

Harvey stood up, rubbing the back of his neck. "Sorry, Jim. This is a shock. Call the M.E., Eddie. And don't touch anything, guys. This is for real." He took out his cell phone and punched two buttons. Eddie pulled his phone from his jacket pocket and went into the hallway.

"Mike?" Harvey said into his phone. The other three men stood listening. "Our unit's in the comptroller's office for the game, you know? Yeah, but, Mike, it isn't a game. Joey Bolduc's been murdered. Can you get over here?"

*****

"All right, you know what to do," Harvey told his men as he pocketed the cell phone. "Let's secure the scene and get to work."

Eddie came back from the hallway. "Dr. McIntyre's on the way, and Hogan's coming down from Augusta."

"The chief M.E.?" Harvey was surprised.

"He wants to make sure everything is by the book, I guess. McIntyre sounded quite irritated."

"He always sounds that way," said Harvey. "Call for a photographer."

"Got it."

Harvey stood for several moments staring at Bolduc's body, taking in every visible detail. A gunshot wound to the chest? Surely someone in the building would have heard the report. Although the city offices were closed for the holiday, dozens of people had helped organize the challenge.

Two members of the judging team appeared in the doorway just as Nate Miller stretched the yellow "police line" tape across it.

"You fellows are taking this seriously," said Myron Stickle.

"Can't come in here, sir." Nate fastened the tape across the doorway in front of him.

"We have to verify your discoveries, or you don't get points," said Bert Fontaine, South Portland's fire chief.

Harvey went to the doorway. "The game's over, Bert. We have a real crime to solve. We'll forfeit to Bangor on the game, I guess."

"What are you talking about?" Startled, Fontaine peered past him into the office.

"That's not the dummy." Stickle strained forward, stretching the yellow tape.

"A real body was lying on the rug when we got here," Harvey said. "I've sent for Chief Browning and the medical examiner."

"Why, I—" Stickle took a handkerchief from his pocket and patted his forehead with it. "This is highly irregular."

"Who is it?" Fontaine asked.

Harvey hesitated. "We'll have to notify the next of kin first, sir, but it's a city employee."

Mike stepped off the elevator down the hall and walked quickly toward him.

"Excuse me, gentlemen," he said when he reached the judges. "We'll brief the mayor as soon as possible. You might want to wait down in her office."

Harvey unfastened the yellow tape and lifted it for Mike. As he reached to put it back in place, he stopped with his hand on the doorjamb.

"Eddie, here's your bullet hole. Looks like it hit the doorjamb edgewise."

Mike stepped back into the hallway and examined the woodwork from the other side. "Must be still in there."

Eddie came to look.

"Mark that. We'll have to cut it out," Harvey said.

"Okay."

Harvey locked eyes with him. "This is your party. I'll be here every step of the way. If you need someone to run errands or get coffee, I'm your man."

Eddie snorted. "I can think of better ways to put you to use."

"Well, just a suggestion: I think you'd better interview the setup crew ASAP. Find out if Joey ate lunch with anyone. He called us at the office about 11:45. That was the last we heard from him. Someone must have seen him after that."

"Emily Rood was working with him." Eddie carefully examined the hole in the woodwork. "Too bad we'll have to remove a piece of this."

"Yeah. Talk to Emily first if you can."

The photographer arrived, and Harvey stood back for a moment to watch. Eddie went into action, snapping orders at his men and the photographer.

Mike nodded at Harvey. "He does all right, doesn't he? Too bad you can't read his handwriting. I'll go run interference with the mayor." When he passed Eddie, he said, "I'll hold the press off for a while, but plan to give them something within a couple of hours."

Ron Legere, the detective sergeant, arrived at the doorway. "Hey, Harvey, you want my crew to come help you?"

"It's not that big a room, Ron," Harvey said. "We've got more people in here already than I like to have, but we can use your men to do background work."

Legere nodded. "Festival committee, family, active cases, collars recently released."

"You got it," Harvey said. "And Detective Thibodeau would like an immediate interview with Detective Rood."

"I'll send her over." Legere peered over Harvey's shoulder. "Can I see him? You understand, Harvey. I'm his supervisor."

"Of course. Come on in."

Ron strode across the room and crouched beside the body. He let out a deep sigh. "Man. This is just wrong." He stood up.

"Can you locate Joey's family and break the news to them?" Harvey asked. "The M.E. will be here any second, and I'm afraid the ID is going to leak out before we can tell his family. Joey was married, wasn't he?"

"The operative word being *was*," Legere replied. "Divorced last spring. His parents live in Deering. They may be here today, but I didn't hear him say so. There's a brother, too."

"Where's his ex?"

"Not sure. I'll find out. What about the girlfriend?"

Harvey raised his eyebrows.

"You know," Legere insisted. "Patrol officer Higgins."

"Sarah Benoit's new partner?"

"Yeah."

"Were she and Joey close?"

"She's been seeing him for a couple of months, I think. She's on traffic duty today."

"Best call her in and break the news. You don't want her hearing it elsewhere. There are probably rumors already."

"Sure. Report to you, Harvey?" Legere asked.

"No, this is Eddie's case. He discovered the body."

Legere nodded. "I'll put every man on it."

The medical examiner arrived, and Harvey knelt beside him, watching closely as Dr. McIntyre made his initial examination.

"Gunshot wound to the heart at close range," McIntyre muttered. "Bullet passed through, and out to the left of the spine."

"It's in the woodwork over there." Harvey pointed toward the doorway, and McIntyre squinted at the splintered wood. "I figure the shooter was standing behind the desk."

"Pretty straightforward, but we won't take him until Dr. Hogan gets here." McIntyre lifted Bolduc's right hand and scrutinized it, then let it fall. "Temperature ... let's see..." He scrawled notes on a clipboard. "I suppose you want the clothes and effects."

"Yes, sir," said Harvey. "Can you estimate time of death?"

"You in charge, Captain?"

"Actually, Detective Thibodeau is. Direct reports to him." Eddie was closing his cell phone. Harvey called him over.

"Well, it can't have been much more than an hour," Dr. McIntyre said. "Two at the most."

Harvey left Eddie with the doctor while he checked with the other men on their progress.

"There are a million fingerprints in this room," Nate complained. He was still dusting woodwork, while Jimmy searched for matches on the portable computer.

"Whose, so far?" Harvey asked.

"The comptroller's, his secretary's, the mayor's. We've got a list of the people on the setup committee, but we'll have to get their prints for comparison."

"Jimmy, you handle that," Harvey directed.

"Then there's Governor Johnson's prints, and Joan Benoit Samuelson's," Nate went on.

"For the game," Harvey said. "I suspect you'll find Stephen King's on one of those books up there."

"I got it," Jimmy Cook called from across the room, looking up from the computer. "I think we've got Steve's and Tabitha's both. And have you ever heard of Ian Crocker? He showed up in the computer."

"Olympic swimmer," Harvey said. "I'd rule him out. That one's for the game, too."

"There's a slew of unidentified prints," Nate concluded.

"We need a list of employees, janitors, anyone who was in here regularly, in addition to the outsiders who came in for the game." Harvey ticked them off on his fingers. "Did any of the Bangor team come up here?"

"No, they're all down in the city clerk's office. They were kept secluded before that, just like us."

"Anybody tell them about this?" Harvey asked.

"They're probably still down there feeling a dummy's pulse," Jimmy said.

Nate stood up. "This is going to take a lot of time, Harvey."

He nodded. "I've put Eddie in charge, but I'll be right here with you. If you need someone to help run prints, I'm available."

"Does Martha Stewart live in Maine?" Jimmy called.

"She's got a summer home in Bar Harbor," Tony said. He was on his knees near the body, picking up hairs from the rug with tweezers. "Uncle Bill and Aunt Laura went to brunch with her. I hear she's death on trespassers. Should we put out a warrant?"

"Ha, ha," Harvey said. "I'd say you've found all the celebrity prints. Let's get on with it."

"Say, Captain." Tony stood up.

"What, Winfield?" Tony's brain worked in odd but wonderful ways, and Harvey always listened when he had an inspiration.

"Well, I was just wondering ..." Tony looked at the body thoughtfully.

"You were wondering," Harvey prompted.

Tony looked at him then, a grin spreading over his boyish freckled face. "Where's the real dummy?"

Eddie and Dr. McIntyre looked up, and Harvey knew everyone in the room was pondering the question.

Harvey said, "It's your call, Eddie."

Eddie returned his gaze and stood up slowly. "Okay, Jimmy, you and Nate stay on the fingerprints. Tony, I want you to get a couple of patrolmen and start a search for the dummy. I'll be surprised if it's not in the building." He turned to Harvey. "Could you help me, Harv? Just go over the body with me and make sure I don't miss anything?"

"Sure."

Dr. McIntyre got stiffly to his feet. "Well, gentlemen, I'm stepping downstairs. I'll be back up when Dr. Hogan arrives." He ambled toward the doorway, raised the yellow tape, and ducked under it.

Eddie swallowed. "This one's getting to me, Harv."

"It's because you know him."

Eddie nodded. There were beads of sweat on his forehead, although it wasn't hot in the room.

"You okay?" Harvey asked.

"I think so."

"Take your jacket off."

Eddie peeled off his sport coat. "Have they dusted this chair yet?"

"Here, lay it on my briefcase."

Eddie draped his jacket over the briefcase. "As far as I can tell, Joey was just carrying his usual gear. His gun is in his holster. He didn't draw it. So, he didn't realize he was in danger, right? I mean, he'd have reached for his weapon if he knew he was going to be shot at."

Harvey nodded. "He didn't stand a chance."

"The way he fell," Eddie mused. "Splat on his face. His arms weren't spread out."

They pondered every nuance for the next few minutes. At last Harvey stood up. "I think you've analyzed everything."

"Captain?" Tony was at the door.

Harvey smiled. "Tell Detective Thibodeau."

"Oh, right. Sorry, Eddie."

"'S'okay," Eddie said.

"We've got the dummy. He's sitting on a toilet in one of the stalls in the men's room down the hall."

"That's creative." Eddie reached for his jacket. "Did you dust for prints?"

"Not yet. We probably won't get any prints, except for the setup crew."

"Don't assume that." Eddie followed Tony into the hallway. A knot of people filled the end of the hall, kept back by a uniformed officer.

"Your public awaits you." Tony nodded toward the group, and Eddie glanced at them.

"I guess they want a press conference."

"You wanna see the real dummy first?"

Eddie sighed. "Tony, it's a dummy. You don't have to say *real* dummy. I mean, it's not like Joey is a *fake* dummy."

"But why did they bother to move him?" Tony asked, heading for the men's room.

"If they left him in the office, anyone looking in there would see two bodies. This way, they just saw Joey and assumed it was the dummy. It bought them time."

End of Excerpt

Discussion questions for *The House Next Door*
for Book Clubs and other groups

1.   Harvey can't wait to be a father. He's into all things baby.
     What sort of dad do you think he will make? Do you have
     any parenting advice for him?

2.   Harvey and Jennifer are excited about the house next
     door as a possible new home for Jeff and Beth. Jeff is not
     so excited, since he thinks it's out of his price range.
     Should Harvey butt out and let them find their own
     housing? Do you think he meddles too much in his
     family's lives?

3.   Carl and Margaret both seem to be holding back
     spiritually because of a little thing called pride. Harvey
     and Jennifer are young Christians, and Jennifer is slightly
     intimidated by the pair of doctors. How might she better
     relate to Margaret? Are you uncomfortable witnessing to
     your friends?

4.   Jennifer is a bit blasé about the corpse next door. Is it
     because she's a cop's wife, or is she just preoccupied with
     her pregnancy?

5.   When Jennifer goes into labor, she gets a little irritable,
     but Harvey takes it in stride. Have you ever barked at a
     loved one and had to apologize? Do you receive criticism
     as graciously as Harvey?

6.   Jennifer isn't always good at doing what Harvey wants.
     When a prowler comes to Beth's house, he tells Jennifer
     several times to go home. How is her presence
     endangering other people?

7.   Abby is concerned about her role as a stepmother. What
     advice would you give her?

8. Leeanne still hovers between wanting to please her parents and wanting her independence. Does Eddie help or hinder her? Are they really ready for marriage?

9. Beth is afraid to stay alone in the new house. Would you sleep in a house where you knew someone had been murdered? How about a house where you knew someone had broken in recently?

10. The neighbors, past and present, play an important role in the solution of this case. How well do you know your neighbors? Would you check on them if you didn't see or hear from them for a while? How long before you'd go check?

Made in the USA
Coppell, TX
17 September 2020